TAKING A CHANCE ON LOVE

Joan Jonker

BCA

LONDON NEW YORK SYDNEY TORONTO

This edition published 2001
By BCA
By arrangement with Headline Book Publishing
A division of Hodder Headline

CN 5498

Typeset by Avon Dataset Ltd, Bidford-on-Avon, Warks

Printed and bound in Germany by
GGP Media, Pössneck

To old friends from my teenage years. I knew them then as
Tommy Seymour, Nita Williams, Doreen Halliday,
Letty Kennedy and Wendy Teague.

True friendship lasts forever.

Dear Readers

This book is written with you in mind. From your letters, I have come to know what you enjoy and what makes you laugh and cry, and in this book, I have tried to give you these in equal measure. I think I have succeeded.

Happy reading.

You take care now.

Love Joan

Chapter One

'Mam, can I go out for a bit, to see Joan? Just for a quarter of an hour before me dad comes in?'

'Mrs Flynn won't want yer being in the way while she's seeing to the dinner, sunshine.' Elizabeth Porter shook the white tablecloth she was holding before laying it over the table and running a hand over it to smooth out the creases. 'Whatever it is yer want to talk about, it can't be that important it won't wait until we've all had our dinners.'

'I won't be in Mrs Flynn's way, Mam, 'cos I won't go in.' Ginny Porter was fourteen years of age and the spitting image of her attractive mother: fair hair, blue eyes, a set of white, even teeth and a slim figure. 'Me and Joan can talk outside.'

'It's freezing out there, yer'd be turned to blocks of ice in five minutes.'

'Ah, go on, Mam, yer didn't stop our Joey from going out.' Ginny knew her mother would see how unfair it was to treat her differently from her brother. After all, she was thirteen months older and leaving school in two weeks. 'As soon as I see me dad walking up the street I'll come in.'

Elizabeth, or Beth to her friends and neighbours, tutted. 'Oh, all right, but get the knives and forks out of the drawer for me first. And when yer see yer dad, give our Joey a shout and tell him to come in pronto.'

A few minutes later, Ginny was sounding the knocker on the house next door. She was hoping to see Joan's face, but it was Mrs Flynn who opened the door. 'Can Joan come out for a few minutes, Mrs Flynn, just until the dinner's ready?' Ginny asked.

'It's bleedin' freezing out there, girl, come on in.' Dot Flynn held the door wide. 'Hurry up, I'm letting a draught in.'

Ginny shook her head. 'Me mam said I hadn't got to get under yer feet, so could Joan come out, just for ten minutes?'

'Oh, suit yerself, girl, it's too bleedin' cold to stand here arguing the fat. I'll send our Joan out to yer.' Dot was grinning as she shook her head. 'The sooner you two leave school and get yerselves a job, the better.'

Ginny chuckled. 'We've already spent our first two weeks wages, Mrs Flynn. High heels and proper stockings, those are our first priority.'

'I would have thought yer first priority would be getting yerselves a ruddy job! Yer have to work for money, yer know, girl, it doesn't grow on trees, worse luck.' Mrs Flynn turned her head and shouted in a voice loud enough to wake the dead, 'Joan, yer mate's here! Get yerself well wrapped up 'cos it's bitter outside.'

'Why didn't yer come in?' Joan asked when she appeared struggling into her coat. 'Me mam doesn't mind, yer know that.'

'I know she doesn't, but it's not fair to have me hanging around when she's busy. Anyway, it's only for ten minutes, until me dad gets home from work.'

The two girls leaned back against the wall of the two-up-two-down terraced house, their arms crossed over their chests and their hands tucked into their armpits for warmth. 'Have yer thought any more about what Miss Jackson said today?' Ginny asked. 'You know, about what sort of work we'd like to do?'

'I mentioned it to me mam, and she said Vernon's is a good place to work. The only trouble is, yer have to work every Saturday night and I don't know whether I fancy that or not.'

'Yeah, I'd thought of that,' Ginny said, bringing out a hand to rub her nose which was beginning to feel like a piece of ice. 'The thing is, Joan, we won't be able to pick and choose, we might have to take what comes along. A case of like it or lump it.'

Joan had a high-pitched giggle, and it could be heard now in the silent street. 'This is what me mam said.' To do herself justice and really get into the part, the girl folded her arms and hitched up an imaginary bosom. ' "Just listen to me, my girl, and get it into that thick head of yours that not many people like their jobs, but they have to work to live. No one can live on bleedin' fresh air and water, unless they're a ruddy fish. Mind you, sometimes when ye're sitting with yer mouth open, yer remind me of a fish." ' The impersonation was so good, Ginny was doubled up and her laughter encouraged Joan to carry on. ' "One of them fish what sit in the window of Harry Barlow's fish shop. Flat out on a cold slab with its eyes and mouth wide open. Not a friend in the world and nothing to cover its modesty, poor bugger." '

'She's a scream is your mam,' Ginny said. 'I'm sure if we took her with us when we go for an interview she'd talk us into a job.'

'Yeah, I can see how funny she is now. But I couldn't when I was younger and getting a clip around the ear for giving her cheek. Ye're dead right about her coming to the interview with us, though. They'd give us a job just to shut her up.'

Ginny saw her dad passing the gas lamp at the corner of the street and moved away from the wall. 'I'd better get in, me dad's on his way. And we haven't really got any further, have we? D'yer want to come to ours tonight and we can have a good natter?'

Joan's mind went to the fire that was roaring up their chimney, and the thought of leaving that to come out into the cold didn't appeal, even though it was only next door. 'No, you come to ours and I'll show yer the scarf I'm knitting.'

Ginny had already taken to her heels and shouted back, 'Okay, see yer later.' She carried on running past her own front door towards the father she idolised. Clinging to his arm, she smiled up at him. 'Hi-ya, Dad.'

'Hello, pet!' Andy Porter was a really handsome man. Tall and well-built, he had raven black hair, deep brown eyes, strong white teeth and a marked cleft in his chin. 'You should be at home in front of the fire in this weather.'

'I know! I've only been out five minutes and me feet are like blocks of ice.'

Andy turned his head when he heard running footsteps behind them. It was Joey, his thirteen-year-old son, and he was moving at such speed his father had no trouble guessing he was going to take a flying leap on to his back. 'Move away, Ginny, before yer brother sends yer flying.'

Joey paced himself perfectly. He took a running jump, wrapped his arms around his dad's neck and hung on like grim death until he felt his legs being supported from behind. 'Hi-ya, Dad, how was work?'

'I can't tell yer right now, son, 'cos I'm being strangled.'

'Get down, yer big soft ha'porth,' Ginny said. 'Ye're too big now to be wanting a piggy-back. Besides which, me dad's been working all day, he's probably tired.'

'I'm only thirty-seven, pet, not an old man yet.' His white teeth flashing, Andy turned his head to say to the grinning boy, 'I just hope yer grow out of it by the time ye're twenty-one.'

'I'll be as big as you then, Dad, so I can give *you* a piggy-back.'

As they reached their house, the front door was opened and light streamed into the dark street. 'Come on, hurry up.' Beth shivered with the cold they brought in with them. 'Take yer coats off and warm yerselves by the fire while I put the dinners out.'

The children elbowed each other out of the way to be first to hang up their coat, thus allowing them to nab the best speck by the hearth. But after hanging his own coat up, Andy walked through to the kitchen. His wife was spooning mashed potato on to the four plates set out on the draining board. She smiled when he slipped his arms around her waist and kissed her neck. 'I'd rather warm meself on you than the fire,' he said. 'Yer give out more heat and send a warm glow right down me whole body.'

'Go on, yer daft nit, the dinner will be stiff if I leave it out here much longer.' But Beth's heartbeat raced as it always did when the man she adored touched her. She'd fallen in love with him when she was sixteen and her feelings had grown deeper with each passing year. 'Go and have a warm while I carry these plates through.'

'What are we having to eat, Mam? I'm starving.' Joey sniffed up and then grinned. 'It's me favourite – sausage and mash. Yummy, yummy, watch out tummy.'

Beth, carrying two plates in each hand, put one down in front of each chair. 'Anyone listening to you would think yer never got a decent meal. We might not get many luxuries but at least we've never gone hungry, which is more than a lot of people can say.'

Andy picked up his knife and fork and cut into one of his two sausages before glancing down the table at his wife. 'If it ever came to the push, where we had to live on dripping sandwiches, we'd still be lucky 'cos we can feast our eyes on the prettiest mother in the whole neighbourhood.'

Ginny stopped chewing. 'Ah, that was a lovely thing to say, Dad, it sounded dead romantic.'

Joey pulled a face. 'Yer mean it sounded dead soppy.'

'Wait until yer get yerself a girlfriend, son,' Andy said, 'then yer won't think it's dead soppy to say nice things to her.'

The boy spluttered. 'Me! Get a girlfriend! I'm not ever going to have no girlfriend 'cos they never stop talking and they're dead bossy.'

'Thanks very much, son,' Beth said, hiding a smile. 'I didn't realise I talked non-stop and was dead bossy.'

'Oh, I didn't mean you, Mam! I'd have you for me girlfriend, any day. Only me dad got there before me.'

Andy chuckled. 'If I hadn't, son, you wouldn't be sitting here now eating yer favourite meal of sausage and mash. Yer could have ended up with a bad-tempered mother who looked like a witch, with a long hooked nose, hairs growing out of her chin and a broomstick standing under the stairs which she used to fly on every night when she went to meet other witches. She'd lock yer in yer bedroom when yer gave cheek

4

and, on top of all that, she couldn't cook for love nor money.'

'Huh! I wouldn't stay if I had a mam like that, I'd run away from home.' Then Joey's brow furrowed as he tried to figure out how he came to have such a lovely mother instead of a witch on a broomstick. 'How could I have . . .'

Beth could see the possibility of her son asking some awkward questions and she cut him short. 'Can we have less talking, please, and get on with our dinner?'

'I'm not talking, Mam, and I've nearly finished mine,' Ginny said. 'Will it be all right if I go to Joan's after? Miss Jackson asked us today what sort of work we'd like to do when we leave, and we want to be able to tell her tomorrow instead of standing there looking stupid. That's if we can make up our minds, like, 'cos although we'd like to work together, we might have different ideas.'

'Yer might have to take what's on offer, pet,' Andy said. 'But if yer did have a choice, what would yer like to do?'

'I keep changing me mind, Dad! But I think I'd rather work in a shop than a factory. Still, like yer said, we might have to take whatever's going.'

'It would be nice if you and Joan did get taken on at the same place, love,' Beth said, ''cos yer've been mates all yer lives. But I don't think it's a good enough reason for taking on a job yer don't really fancy. After all, living next door, yer'd be seeing Joan every night, so it's not as though it would affect yer friendship.'

'Yer mam's right, pet, you go for whatever yer think is best for you, and Joan can do the same. And I think it might be best, anyway, not to be in each other's pockets all the time. At least yer'd have plenty to talk about when yer did get together.'

'Yeah, there is that to it.' Ginny placed her knife and fork neatly in the centre of the empty plate. 'I'll take this out, Mam, and put the kettle on to wash the dishes. Or would yer rather I made a pot of tea, first?'

Andy gave a quick reply. 'Oh, tea first, pet, if yer don't mind. I haven't had a decent cuppa all day. I don't know what they put in the pot at work, but it certainly doesn't taste like tea.'

'Tea it is, then.' Ginny stood up and smiled at her mother. 'You stay where yer are, Mam, I'll see to it.'

Joey, who favoured his father in looks, gave a broad wink. 'I bet she won't be saying that when she starts work. She'll expect to be waited on hand and foot.'

'Hey, watch it, you,' Ginny said from the kitchen door. 'Any cheek

5

out of you and yer can forget about the comic I promised to buy yer every week.'

But Joey knew his sister wouldn't let him down, so he winked again. 'See what I mean? She's throwing her weight around already!'

Ginny filled the kettle and put it on the stove before returning to the living room. 'I won't be throwing me weight around, brother dear, but the comic does come with certain strings attached.'

Her brother's eyes narrowed. 'Oh, aye? I knew there'd be a catch in it, that it was too good to be true. What's the strings ye're talking about?'

'Well, I used to run to the corner shop for our mam when she ran out of anything, so you'll be able to do that for her. And ye're big and ugly enough to fill the coal scuttle before yer go to school in the mornings as well.'

'Blimey! All that for a penny comic? Oh, I'll have to give it some careful consideration before I agree to those terms.'

'If I were in your shoes, I wouldn't spend too much time in considering, son,' Beth said, her face serious as though the subject was one of importance. 'With the penny pocket-money I give yer, that means yer'd have tuppence in yer pocket every Saturday. Enough to go to a matinee at the pictures, or even buy two comics.'

Joey didn't intend to spend too much time in consideration, but it wouldn't do to give in too easily or his sister would be adding more chores for him to do. After all, as he'd said, girls were bossy beggars. Mind you, he didn't need the enticement of a penny to do jobs for his mam, he'd do them anyway 'cos he loved her. Still, as he'd heard his grandma saying, 'If yer look after the pennies, the pounds will look after themselves.' So if there was a penny going spare, he may as well be the one to look after it. 'Okay, Ginny, ye're on.'

Her face deadpan, Ginny said, 'Oh, I almost forgot. I'd like yer to clean me shoes every night for me, too.'

His eyes bulged, his jaw dropped, and the look of utter horror on the boy's face was enough to send his parents and sister into fits of laughter. When he'd recovered enough to speak, he said through gritted teeth, 'Yer know what you can do, don't yer? Yer can go and take a running jump.'

'Oh, son, if only yer could have seen yer face.' Beth wiped away a tear of laughter. 'It was a picture no artist could paint.'

'We're going to have trouble with her,' Joey grunted, jerking his head towards his sister. 'If she thinks I'm going to be her slave for a penny, she's got another think coming. If she wants a slave, she should look in a second-hand shop for an old lamp, like what Aladdin had. If she gave it a good rub a genie would appear and he'd be her slave and give her three wishes.'

Ginny was shaking with laughter. 'I don't want yer to be me slave, Joey! I'm not that big-headed. I'll be quite happy for yer to be me dogsbody.'

The boy's brown eyes were twinkling with mischief and he was having a struggle to keep his face straight. 'Mam, d'yer know what Mrs Flynn next door shouts when she's chasing the kids away from her front door? I know I'll get a smack if I say it, so would you do it for me? Just pretend ye're Mrs Flynn and tell our Ginny what to do.'

'I will not! I know I've told you to sod off when yer've been getting under me feet and I've been in a bit of a paddy, but it's not ladylike and I don't think I should be saying it to Ginny on behalf of a thirteen-year-old boy. So no, I will not tell yer sister to sod off.'

Joey gave a cheeky grin. 'Thanks, Mam, that should do it.'

The two children were very close, and would stick together through thick and thin. All the kids in the street knew that if they picked on one of the Porter kids, they'd have the other one to reckon with. They shared many of their parents' characteristics, one being a fine sense of humour. This came into play now as Ginny said, 'Ay, Mam, where's the nearest second-hand shop from here? I'd be better off with a genie who wouldn't answer me back and wouldn't be moaning all the time. And I'd probably get an old lamp for a couple of coppers.'

'There's a second-hand shop on Rice Lane, sunshine,' Beth said. 'I'll have a look in there next time I'm passing.'

Andy was sitting shaking his head. 'I don't know who's the daftest, ye're all crazy.'

'Ay, Dad, if yer think we're crazy, yer should come with me tonight to the Flynns' for half-an-hour. There's never a dull moment in there with Mrs Flynn, she's an absolute scream. And Mr Flynn and David are the same – they're all crazy. Going in there is as good as going to the pictures to see Laurel and Hardy. They never stop laughing and talking and it's hard to get a word in edgeways.' Ginny heard the piercing whistle of the kettle and jumped from her chair. 'I'll make the tea while Joey clears the table.'

Her brother heaved a sigh. 'See, I told yer, all girls are bossy.' He got to his feet and began to collect the empty plates. Then he had a thought and called through to the kitchen, 'If they never stop talking, and yer can't get a word in edgeways, how are you and Joan ever going to tell each other where yer'd like to work?'

'Easy-peasy,' Ginny called back. 'We let them get on with it while we sit on the stairs for some privacy. Yer see, Joey, where there's a will, there's a way.'

Dot Flynn was tall and thin, with mousy-coloured hair and hazel eyes. She was an active woman, always on the go, and she kept her house like a new pin. Although she talked a lot, and her language was sometimes very colourful, she had a heart as big as a week. She would never turn anyone away if they were in need. Like all their neighbours, the Flynns didn't have much money, but Dot would never see anyone without a loaf in the house, or a penny for the gas meter. They were a bit better off financially now their fifteen-year-old son, David, was working, even though he earned very little as an apprentice, and Dot was happy with her lot in life, so happy and content that she was seldom seen without a smile on her face. When she opened the door to Ginny that night, she was beaming.

'You again, is it, girl? I'm beginning to get confused into thinking I've got two daughters.'

Ginny grinned as she stepped into the tiny hall. 'Me mam's just asked me why I don't bring me bed down.'

'Trying to get rid of yer, is she? Well, tell her there's no room at the inn, we're fully booked.' Dot closed the door and pushed the girl into the living room. 'Joan's down the yard, but she won't be long 'cos it's freezing in that lavvy.'

'Oh, blimey, look who's here.' David's long legs were stretched out in front of the fire. He was tall for his age, and a nice-looking lad with his father's sandy hair and blue eyes. He had a happy, open face, the only flaw on it the few pimples dotted on his chin and cheeks. They were the bane of his life, a real embarrassment, and he found little consolation in his mother telling him that all lads his age suffered from them, and they'd disappear as he got older. 'I suppose you and our Joan are going to talk the socks off each other for a few hours and we'll get no peace.'

'That's no way to talk to a visitor.' Dot pushed at his legs. 'Get those long things out of the way and let someone else see the fire.'

The man of the house, Bill, lowered his paper. 'Hello, love, come and get a warm and take no notice of the queer feller. Put his ignorance down to his age.'

David sat up straight. 'Ay, I'm not ignorant!'

Ginny stood near the fire rubbing her hands. 'No, I wouldn't say yer were ignorant, David! It's just that yer've got no manners.'

8

When Joan came in her nose was bright red and her teeth were chattering. 'I wish we had an inside lavvy, Mam, like some people do. Two of the girls in our class have got a proper bathroom in their houses.'

'Good for them, girl! And one of these days, yer never know, we might have a house with a bathroom, too! But until then, light of my life, yer'll just have to make do with an outside lavvy and a tin bath. That's all me and yer dad have ever known and it hasn't done us no harm. We might have had frozen backsides a few times, but nothing more serious. Besides, while ye're sitting on the throne out there, ye're exposed to the elements with the door falling to pieces and ye're getting plenty of fresh air. That's more than yer posh friends at school get. I bet they haven't got rosy cheeks – on their faces or their backsides.'

'Oh, Mam, d'yer have to be so rude?' Joan raised her eyes to the ceiling. 'Honest, I'd be ashamed to take yer anywhere.'

'Ah, what a shame, I've upset yer! Silly me, I keep forgetting yer have a very sensitive and delicate nature. So I'll rephrase what I've just said for your benefit.' Her arms wrapped around her thin waist, Dot struck a pose. 'I do hope your posterior didn't suffer from the icy winds that are inclined to blow under the door of our outside lavatory. We could, of course, repair the door, but I'm inclined to be against that idea because I believe it has its advantages. You see, if it was comfortable out there, my husband would slip down the yard when no one was looking, with the *Echo* tucked under his arm, and he'd sit there for hours on end, reading it from cover to cover, while we'd be running around with our legs crossed.'

Joan exchanged looks with Ginny and they both burst out laughing. But the loudest laugh came from Bill because his wife had him spot on. He enjoyed the quietness of the lavvy to read the paper in peace, and had made a habit of it. Mind you, he didn't sit for hours, but why worry about a small detail when people were having a laugh at his expense? His wife was able to make a joke out of anything and he admired her for that. He remembered the first time he'd taken her out on a date and thought now what a pleasure it still was to be in her company. Attractive, warm and funny, it was a combination he couldn't resist and they'd married the following year.

'I hope the whole street haven't been told about the *Echo*, the lavvy and me? Or is that why Mrs Stevenson from number three always has a grin on her face when she sees me?'

Dot chuckled. 'Bill, ye're the talk of Irwin's, the butcher's, the baker's

9

and the candlestick maker's. Not to mention every wash-house from here to the Pier Head.'

Thinking, wrongly as it happened, that Mr Flynn might be feeling embarrassed, Ginny came to his aid. 'My dad reads the *Echo* in the lavvy, too! But only when the weather's warm, like, not if it's freezing cold.'

'I knew your dad was a man after me own heart, we seem to share a lot in common. In fact, right now I bet he's wishing the same thing as me – that we were going to the pub for a pint.'

'You crafty bugger, Bill Flynn!' Dot wagged one finger. 'Yer got that in very nicely, didn't yer?'

'Yer wouldn't begrudge yer hard-working husband a pint, now would yer? It's not as though I'm out every night drinking until the pubs close. One pint never did no one any harm.'

'Well, if you're going out, I'm going out. You go to the pub with Andy and I'll sit with Beth to pass an hour away.'

David groaned. 'Ye're not both going out and leaving me with these two, are yer? I'll not only be bored stiff, I'll have an earache into the bargain 'cos they natter non-stop. I wouldn't mind if it was anything interesting, but it's just rubbish.'

'It won't be rubbish tonight, 'cos we're going to discuss what we want to do when we leave school.' Joan pulled tongues at her brother. 'Just because ye're fifteen doesn't mean ye're all grown up, yer know. Even though ye're a year older than me and Ginny, it doesn't mean to say ye're more intelligent. I bet we could both knock spots off yer.'

'Ginny might, but you certainly couldn't, ye're as thick as two short planks. Me dad asked if yer'd like him to get an application form for yer from Dunlop's, but yer dithered and couldn't make up yer mind. And yer'd stand a good chance of being accepted with me and me dad working there.'

'Ooh, that would be good, Joan,' Ginny said. 'They're bound to look more sympathetically at an application from an employee's relative.'

'Yeah, but what about you? I thought the idea was that we'd try and get a job together. That's what we said.'

'I know what we said, Joan, but it mightn't be possible. Me dad said tonight we might have to take what's on offer.'

'And yer dad was right,' Dot said. 'There's thousands of people out of work in Liverpool, mostly men with families to keep. Times are hard, and the men that have got a job are lucky. And you're lucky, too, 'cos employers are more likely to take school-leavers on because they don't have to pay them much in wages.'

'You're telling me,' David said. 'I get paid in buttons, even though I work as hard as the older men do.'

'Yer've got a job, son, so stop moaning.' Bill pushed himself up from the couch. 'I'll swill me face and then give Andy a knock.'

'I'll nip next door and let him know, so he can start getting ready.' As Dot was slipping her arms into her coat, she looked at Ginny. 'Yer know, girl, Bill could get you an application form for Dunlop's, if yer want. Not that it means yer'd definitely get a job, but it's worth a try.'

'Thanks, Mrs Flynn, but I'll see what teacher has to say tomorrow. Yer see, I quite like the idea of working in a shop if it's possible. I don't know if there'll be any vacancies, not with so many of us leaving school and looking for a job, but I'd like to see what Miss Jackson has to say first.'

'If that's what yer fancy, girl, then you go all out for it. But it's only three weeks to Christmas now, so yer better start putting the feelers out. As yer say, there'll be hundreds of kids looking for work and I doubt if there's that many jobs going. Have a talk with yer teacher tomorrow and see if she has any ideas.' Dot had her hand on the door handle when she turned to look at her son. 'You behave yerself, David, and don't be giving the girls a dog's life. Bury yer head in a book or something, and leave them to it. I'm only next door if anyone needs me for anything.'

Bill came through from the kitchen with a towel in his hand. 'Are you still here?'

'I'm going, I'm going, I'm going! Ta-ra!'

Chapter Two

There was surprise on Beth's face when she opened the door. 'I didn't expect to see you, I thought yer'd be curled up in front of the fire.'

'I would have been if my feller hadn't decided he felt like a pint.' Dot brushed past and went into the living room. She ruffled Joey's hair while smiling at Andy. 'Bill will be knocking any minute to see if yer feel like going down to the pub with him.'

Andy beamed as he quickly vacated his chair. 'I never say no to a pint, Dot, so I'd better give meself a swill before he comes.' On his way to the kitchen he added, 'I'm not getting changed, though, he'll have to take me as I am.'

'Bill's not getting changed either, so yer'll be in good company. And anyway, nobody goes to the pub dressed up, they'd get laughed at.'

Beth shook her head. 'I think they want their bumps feeling, going out on a night like this. They'll be frozen before they get there, then they'll stand in a draughty pub drinking cold beer. They're crazy!'

Andy put his head around the kitchen door. 'Yer don't begrudge me a pint, do yer, love? I mean, if yer don't want me to go, I won't.'

'Oh, aye, and be the worst in the world! No, if you're daft enough to leave a nice roaring fire, then far be it from me to stop yer.' There was a tenderness in Beth's eyes which belied her words. She would never begrudge her husband anything. 'Just remember Christmas isn't far off and yer'll need money to buy presents, so don't go mad. No whisky, just two pints of beer and that's yer lot.'

'Whisky! When have I ever bought a glass of whisky? I'm not partial to it, so I wouldn't buy it even if I was loaded. I much prefer a glass of bitter.'

When the knock came, Andy backed into the kitchen. 'I'll just run the comb through me hair, then I'm ready. So there's no need for you to leave yer warm spot, I'll open the door to Bill and grab me coat off the peg at the same time.'

But old habits die hard, and Beth followed him to the door. 'I'll keep the fire going for yer and have the kettle on the boil.'

When she heard the front door close, Dot sighed and shook her head. 'I suppose yer know that with you spoiling Andy, my feller thinks he should get the same treatment? Ye're making all the women in the street suffer 'cos ye're too soft with him.'

Beth used all her strength to push the heavy couch nearer to the fire. 'I don't know how yer have the nerve to say that, Dot Flynn! No man is more spoiled than your Bill! At least I don't have Andy's slippers warming by the fire when he comes in, and I don't put two spoonsful of sugar in his tea and even stir it for him.'

Joey's head was moving from side to side as he kept up with their talk. He loved it when his Auntie Dot from next door came in, she was so funny. She wasn't his real auntie of course, like Auntie Flo from next door the other side wasn't his real auntie, but they were as good as.

'Ye gods and little fishes! Warming my feller's slippers and stirring his tea isn't spoiling him, girl! It's not like I wait on him hand and foot.'

Beth waved to one end of the couch. 'Sit yerself down there and get comfortable. And shut up about your feller, 'cos we all know yer check him every morning before he goes to work, to make sure his ears are clean and he hasn't got a tidemark.'

The springs in the couch twanged when Dot plonked herself down. And when she began to shake with laughter, they twanged even louder. 'Ay, we often have a laugh about tidemarks. Bill says he's got one ear sticks out more than the other because his mam used to pull at it when she was dragging him back to the kitchen sink every morning to get a proper wash. I tell him it's that one ear sticking out what stops him from being more handsome than your feller.' She noticed Joey sitting quietly with his head bent over the open book on his knee, which he obviously wasn't reading. 'How are you, lad? Are yer fed up listening to what Ginny's going to do when she leaves school and gets a job? I know I'm fed up with our Joan. She thinks she's going to break eggs with a big stick on her first week's wages. It's all a novelty to her and I've had a bet with meself that it'll be two weeks before the bubble bursts and she realises yer have to work for yer money.'

There came a frantic rapping on the window and both women jumped. 'In the name of God, who can this be?' Dot pushed herself up. 'They'll get a piece of my mind, frightening us like that. I nearly jumped out of me skin.'

The words were no sooner out of her mouth than they heard the front door being opened, and Andy came in, followed closely by Bill. Both men looked agitated and Dot moved to stand next to Beth. 'What's happened?'

'It might be nothing, love, but we thought we'd be on the safe side and tell yer.' Andy looked to Bill for a nod of confirmation. 'We were near the pub when we saw old Mrs Bailey walking on the opposite side of the street. She looked a bit strange, and she had no coat on, only a cardigan. Anyway, me and Bill went after her to ask if she was all right, 'cos no one in their right mind would go out on a night like this without a coat. We caught up with her and asked where she was off to, but she seemed to look right through us as if we weren't there.' He looked to his mate. 'Isn't that right, Bill?'

'Yeah, she definitely looked as though she was walking in her sleep. We tried asking where she was going, but she just brushed us aside as though she'd never seen us before in her life! Then she carried on walking and turned into County Road. There's no shops open at this time of night, so the Lord knows where she was headed.'

'One thing's for certain, she'll catch pneumonia if she's out long 'cos it's freezing and she was only wearing a dress and cardi.' Andy looked at Beth and spread his hands. 'There was nothing we could do, love, we'd have frightened the life out of her if we'd laid hands on her and tried to get her home.'

'Did yer try telling her who yer were?' Beth asked. 'Heaven knows, she's known yer long enough.'

'We tried a few times, but as I said, she looked right through us.' Andy ran his fingers through his thick mop of black hair. 'She had a strange look on her face as though she was in another world. Anyway, me and Bill thought we should tell yer in case she goes missing, or gets lost.'

Beth and Dot exchanged glances, then nodded. 'We'll put our coats on and see if we can find her.' Beth handed her neighbour's coat over before reaching for her own. 'Did yer say she turned right into County Road?'

'That's the last we saw of her,' Bill said. 'We would have followed her, but yer can imagine what people would think if they saw two men manhandling an elderly woman. We'd have been lynched.'

'Come on, Dot, let's go after her before she gets too far away.' Beth bent down to look into her son's face. 'Joey, you stay here and read yer book, we'll be back as soon as we can.'

'What about me and Bill?' Andy asked. 'Shall we come with yer?'

'No, me and Dot are better on our own. It might be an idea to knock next door for Flo then we can search each side of the road.'

'That's a good idea,' Dot said. 'And what about Lizzie, over the road? She knows Hannah Bailey very well, and we could pair off then.'

15

Beth took her purse from a glass bowl on the sideboard. 'I've got me key, Joey, so don't answer the door to anyone without first asking who it is.' She gave each of the men a gentle push. 'You two go and have yer pint. We know where yer are if we need yer.'

Once outside Dot said, 'I'll nip across for Lizzie while you give Flo a knock. The sooner we start the better.'

Within five minutes, there were four women standing beneath the street lamp. Flo Henderson, who was Beth's other next-door neighbour, was a small woman in height, but large in figure. She was eighteen stone the last time she stood on a weighing machine, and she swore she'd never do it again because the machine was a ruddy liar. She had dark hair, brown eyes, a round happy face and a fantastic sense of humour. The last woman to join the group was Lizzie O'Leary who lived facing Beth's house. She'd come over from Ireland with her husband, Paddy, nearly fifteen years ago, but she still had the Irish lilt to her voice. 'How long is it since yer husband saw Hannah, me darlin'?'

'It can't be more than twenty minutes 'cos we haven't wasted any time. Me and Dot thought we could pair off and walk both sides of County Road. Mind you, Andy said Hannah didn't seem to know where she was, so she could be wandering aimlessly, not knowing one road from another. She may have turned down one of the side streets for all we know. Still, we'll have to keep our eyes peeled and hope for the best.'

'I'll come with you, queen,' Flo said, 'and Lizzie can pair off with Dot.'

'Then let's make a start.' Dot linked arms with Lizzie. 'We'll check shop doorways and entries as well.'

'We mustn't lose sight of each other, though,' Beth warned. 'Otherwise we won't know what's going on. If anyone does find her, give a shout to let us all know.'

The women paired off to cover both sides of the road, checking doorways and entries, but there was no sign of their elderly neighbour. As they neared Spellow Lane, Beth began to lose hope. Five main roads ran from the junction there, making their search impossible.

'I don't think we're ever going to find her, it's like looking for a needle in a haystack. Once we get to Spellow Lane we've had it 'cos there aren't enough of us to cover all the roads. I think we should turn back and notify the police.'

'Ye're probably right, queen, because we could walk the streets all night and never find her. The police are our best bet.'

Beth nodded as though coming to a firm decision. 'Once we get to

Spellow, I'll call the others over and see what they say. But we can't hang around or Hannah will freeze to death if she's out much longer with just a cardi on. The police would find her a damn sight quicker than we will.'

Flo pulled her friend closer for warmth. 'It's a worry, isn't it, queen? I can't think what came over Hannah to do such a thing, she's usually very sensible.'

'From what Andy said, she didn't seem to know what she was doing. And that's the worrying part of it, 'cos if she's confused, she could walk for miles and end up in a place that's not familiar to her.' Beth halted her friend at the edge of the pavement and waited for a tram to trundle by before shouting across the wide road, 'Dot, will you and Lizzie come over so we can discuss what we should do next?'

The two women listened to what Beth had to say about going to the police. They agreed it would be the sensible thing to do, but the Irish woman asked if they shouldn't cover the area they were in first. 'There's so many places she could be around here, me darlings – a tram terminus around that corner where she could be sheltering, and there's Burton's shop doorways and pubs on every corner. Sure, it'll not take us five minutes, and it's meself that'll feel better knowing we've at least looked everywhere possible. It would be terrible if we gave up and she was only yards away from us.'

'Okay, you and Dot try the terminus while me and Flo have a look in shop and pub doorways. We'll cover the next block and meet yer back here in ten minutes. If any of yer want to go home then, 'cos it is bitter, I don't mind going to the police station on me own. I can hop on a tram here and it's only about eight stops.'

There were loud protests. 'I came out with yer, girl,' Dot said, 'and I'm sticking with yer until we find Hannah. I'd rather be out here freezing than sitting in front of a fire and worrying meself to death.'

'And I ain't leaving yer, either.' Flo's sharp nod set her layers of chins in motion. 'We'll stick together.'

Lizzie agreed. 'Sure, I'd never forgive meself if anything happened to the poor woman, she's a friend of mine.'

Beth gave a sigh of relief. She'd never been in a police station in her life and didn't fancy going into one now on her own. 'Okay, girls, we'll stay together. One for all and all for one, eh? But we'll do what Lizzie suggested first, then meet back here in five to ten minutes.'

Dot cupped Lizzie's elbow and turned her head each way to make sure the road was clear. 'Hang on, girl, wait until this tram passes.' Then, when the coast was clear, they made haste to the pavement opposite. 'Let's try the tram terminus first.'

The wind whipping their cheeks was bitter, and the women clung together for warmth. There weren't many people about and the terminus appeared at first sight to be empty. 'She's not here,' Dot said, 'let's turn around and try Burton's doorways.'

Lizzie gripped her arm. 'Just a minute, me darlin', there's someone standing against the wall. They're in the shadow, so they are, but whoever it is has a head of white hair like Hannah's.' As they drew nearer to the figure, she took her arm from Dot's and hurried forward. 'Praise be to God, I think we've found her.'

As Dot followed, her heart was racing fifteen to the dozen. When she saw Lizzie holding her arms wide she knew she was extending them to the old lady they were all so fond of, and felt weak with relief. But as she came closer, she saw Lizzie's arms were being pushed away. Oh, it was Hannah, all right, thank God, but a Hannah who was acting strangely.

'It's Lizzie O'Leary, me darlin', and, sure, yer know me well enough to know I wish yer no harm. Come to me and I'll put me coat around yer to warm yer up.' But there was no recognition in Hannah's faded eyes, only fear. The more Lizzie coaxed, the more agitated the old lady became. Her whole body was shivering from cold and her lips were blue, but she still had the strength to resist Lizzie's pleading.

'Lizzie, I'm going to get Beth and Flo. It's obvious Hannah doesn't know us and we're making her more afraid. But something has to be done quickly because she must be frozen through to the marrow.'

'I know that, me darlin', and it's very concerned I am. Sure, I was only speaking to the dear woman this afternoon, so I was, and she was perfectly all right then. Something drastic must have happened since to have affected her mind like this. I'll stay with her while you fetch the other two. Perhaps between us we can fix her up with a coat and take her home. In her own surroundings she may come around.'

Dot Flynn did everything quickly, that was her nature. Whether it was making the beds, washing the dishes or ironing, she moved with speed. But she'd never moved as fast as she did when she ran in the direction Beth and Flo had taken. Her feet didn't seem to touch the ground and her breath hung in the cold winter air.

The road was so deserted and quiet that running footsteps shattered the silence and caused Flo to turn her head. She swung herself around, taking Beth with her. 'It's Dot, they must have found Hannah.'

Dot just nodded in reply and then she bent and put her hands on her knees while she fought for breath. After a few seconds she straightened up and croaked, 'Me chest is sore from running so fast, but we've found her. She was by the tram terminus as Lizzie said she might be. We'd better get back to them because Hannah's blue with the cold. You two can run on, if yer like, I haven't got the breath left.'

'No, we'll walk with yer,' Beth said. 'How is Hannah, does she know yer?'

Dot shook her head. 'No sign of recognition at all. She wouldn't let us near her! Lizzie wanted to put her coat around her, but Hannah just pushed her away. I don't know what's happened to cause it, but it must be serious. She obviously needs help.'

'She might be better when she's in her own house, in familiar surroundings.' Beth quickened her pace. 'Surely between the four of us we can get her home?'

'Yeah, we'll manage that, queen, even if we have to carry her between us,' Flo said. 'But I don't think she should go to her own house until we know if it's safe to leave her on her own. Better if she comes to one of ours and we can see for ourselves how bad things are with her. I doubt if yer'd get a doctor to come out this time of night anyway so someone will have to keep an eye on her.'

'We'll worry about that later,' Beth said. 'The first thing is to get her out of the cold and into a warm house. I've got me purse with me, so we'll take a tram home.'

'That's if she'll let us help her, we can't make her.' Dot sighed. 'Wait until yer see her and yer'll know what I'm talking about.'

When they reached the terminus, it was to see Lizzie standing against the wall with Hannah. Tears came to Beth's eyes when she saw the state of the elderly woman. 'Oh, sunshine, ye're blue with the cold.' She slipped her coat off and held it out. 'Come on, let me put this around yer.'

The fight seemed to have gone out of Hannah, and she allowed the other women to put the coat over her shoulders. But she obviously didn't recognise them. Her eyes were darting everywhere like a frightened animal caught in a trap and looking for a means of escape.

Flo undid the buttons on her coat and slipped one arm out. Then, holding the coat wide, she said to Beth, 'We'll share this, queen. At least it'll keep some of the cold out and anything is better than nothing.'

Lizzie had managed to get Hannah's arms into the sleeves of Beth's coat. She fastened the buttons and turned the collar up for protection against the wind. 'There yer are, me darlin', isn't that better? And when we get yer home, a nice cup of hot tea will do yer the world of good.'

Hannah put up no resistance as she was led around the corner to where the number twenty-two tram would stop to take them home. She didn't say one word and her eyes stared straight ahead as though she was sleep-walking. This worried her neighbours, but by an exchange of glances it was silently agreed to leave things be until they got home. If they upset her now there was no telling what she would do.

When the tram came, Beth and Flo stood back until the other three women were aboard. Then Flo slipped out of her coat altogether and pushed Beth on to the platform. 'We'd look bleedin' soft trying to get on with one coat between us, queen, so you go ahead. I don't feel the cold as much as you, anyway, me fat keeps me warm.'

The conductor came down the stairs just as Flo was trying to lift her leg high enough to climb on board. 'Why do they make these bleedin' steps so high, the stupid buggers? Do they think everyone's six foot tall?'

'What's the matter, Flo? Legless again, are yer?' There wasn't a conductor or driver on this route who didn't know her. She stood out not only because she was small and fat, but because she always had a smile and a joke for everyone. 'That'll teach yer to have one too many milk stouts.'

'Ha-ha, very funny, I'm sure.' Flo grinned up into his face. 'Give us yer hand, Charlie, or I'll be here all bleedin' night.'

After he'd pulled her on to the platform, Charlie eyed her up and down. 'Where's yer coat? Don't tell me yer came out without one on a night like this?'

Flo clamped her lips together and wagged her head from side to side. 'Silly me! I've only gone and left the blasted thing in the pub.'

The driver, tired of waiting for the bell to tell him to move on, took it upon himself to set the tram in motion. 'We haven't got all night, Charlie, we'll be late getting back to Fazakerley.'

'Hang on a minute, Bob, this lady has left her coat in a pub, she'll want to go back for it.'

'She can get off the next stop and walk back.' It was a cold job driving a tram in this weather, and Bob's hands and feet were freezing. The sooner they got to the terminus, the sooner he'd get a cup of hot tea and a warm by the stove. 'It's not far to walk, and as she's just told her friend, she's got plenty of fat on her to keep her warm.'

Flo bristled. 'Oh, I'm fat, am I? I've a good mind to give yer a black eye for that, clever bugger! And what would yer wife think if yer went home with a shiner? She'd think yer'd got fresh with someone else's wife and the husband belted yer one.'

The conductor was leaning against the stairs that went up to the top deck, grinning. 'If he got fresh with you, Flo, would your feller belt him one?'

'Nah, I wouldn't wait for my feller, I'd do it meself. He's only the size of sixpennyworth of copper, I could knock him out with one hand tied behind me back.'

Bob, who was six feet two and well-built, was chuckling at the thought of being floored by a woman who came no higher than his chest. Someone would have to lift her up to reach him! 'The next stop's coming up, Flo, d'yer want to get off and go back for yer coat?'

'No, I won't bother, lad, it's not worth it. I bought the coat second-hand from Paddy's Market about fifteen years ago so I've had me money's worth out of it. Besides, I wouldn't recognise the blinking thing 'cos it's changed colour about six times since I bought it.'

The conductor held on to the bar as they neared the tram stop, and looked out to see if there were any passengers waiting to board. 'All clear, Bob, yer can carry on.' Then he narrowed his eyes and gazed down at Flo. 'Yer've been pulling me leg, haven't yer?'

'Of course I have, soft lad! Yer'd fall for the ruddy cat, you would. Still, it helped pass five minutes away, didn't it?'

As she moved from the platform into the aisle, the conductor said, 'Yer may as well buy yer tickets now, save me a journey down the tram.'

Flo's body began to shake with laughter. 'Ooh, aren't I the silly one, lad? D'yer know what I've gone and done? Only left me purse in the pocket of the coat what I left in the pub! But don't look so down-in-the-mouth, me mate's got the money. She's the pretty one with the fair hair. If yer ask her nicely, she'll pay yer for our tickets and we'll settle up with her when we get home.'

Her neighbours had been watching and listening with smiles on their faces. You could rely on Flo to brighten up the proceedings no matter where you were. The only one who didn't appreciate the exchange was Hannah. She was sitting by a window looking out, but her fixed stare told her friends she wasn't seeing or hearing anything. At least they had the consolation of knowing she was safe and out of the cold for now. Perhaps when they got home they might get more response from her. If not then a doctor would have to be called because they were out of their depth. They couldn't deal with something they knew nothing about.

Beth and Dot linked arms with Hannah as they walked up the street. She hadn't put up any resistance to getting off the tram, but by neither word nor deed had she shown any interest in them. It was as if everything had been wiped from her mind. She didn't even glance at the house which had been her home for over forty years.

21

'We'll take her in my house,' Beth said, 'because there's only Joey there and it'll be quieter than anywhere else.' After opening the front door, she went in first to warn her son to be quiet and not ask any questions.

Hannah had been in this room hundreds of times over the years, but now she stood like a stranger in an unfamiliar house. There was no emotion on her face or in her eyes. 'Let me take yer coat off, me darlin',' Lizzie said, 'and you sit here by the nice warm fire.'

'I'll put the kettle on for a cuppa.' Beth was really concerned and at a loss as to what to do. They couldn't just put her in her own house and leave her to it, not the state she was in. And who could say she wouldn't take to the streets again in the middle of the night?

Dot came into the kitchen. 'I've just been thinking, girl, that we couldn't take her home if we wanted to, 'cos she hasn't got her key on her.'

'Me head's splitting thinking about it. I don't know what we're going to do, sunshine, I haven't got a clue.' Beth poured boiling water into the brown teapot. 'We'll try and get a hot cup of tea down her first, to warm her through, then we'll put our thinking caps on.'

Dot carried the cup and saucer, taking great care not to spill any because they all knew how fussy Hannah was. You always got a china cup in her house, even if it was an odd one bought from TJ's out of their oddment bin. 'It's not china, girl, but it's clean and there's no cracks in it.' Dot was lifting the cup from the saucer, thinking she'd hold it to Hannah's lips, but to her surprise the old woman stretched out her hand and took both cup and saucer from her. Without a word of thanks, she raised the cup to her mouth and began to drink, leaving the onlookers baffled.

Flo was the first one out to the kitchen followed by Lizzie and Dot. 'I've never known nothing like it in me life, queen, she's got me beat. She's sitting there drinking the tea as calm as yer like! Yer'd think she was in Reece's cafe sitting with a lot of strangers! And she might as well be, 'cos she doesn't know us from Adam!'

Lizzie was leaning back against the sink with her arms folded. 'I remember when I was in me teens back in Ireland, there was an old lady lived in a little cottage not far from us, and she was the same as Hannah is now. But it didn't happen overnight with her, sure, it happened slowly, over a good many years. She was a lovely old soul, so she was, and everyone was kind to her.'

'Hannah's case is different,' Beth said. 'I don't think it's anything to do with her age, it's happened too quickly. And anyway, even in their

22

dotage, old people don't stop talking like she has. There's got to be something brought it on, a shock perhaps, but how are we going to find out if she won't tell us?'

'I think we'd better go back in to her,' Flo said. 'Let's just talk and act natural and see if it has any effect. If it doesn't, the only thing left is to get a doctor out to her.' Her hands on her hips, she jerked her head. 'Come on, let's hear a few jokes and some laughter. That might just do the trick.'

One by one the women trooped out, to see Hannah sitting with the empty cup in her lap and her eyes staring into space. 'Oh, have yer finished yer tea, girl?' Dot asked, adding a note of laughter to her voice. 'We haven't even been offered one yet, which shows what a lousy host Mrs Porter is.' She raised her brows to Beth. 'I like two sugars in my tea, please, and I think Hannah would like another cup.'

Joey watched with curiosity in his eyes. All the women were talking and laughing now, even though no one had said anything funny, but Mrs Bailey wasn't joining in, she just sat there drinking her tea and not saying a word. Then there came a single rap on the window and his mam jumped to her feet. 'That's our Ginny's knock, I'll let her in.'

Beth's intention was to have a quick word with her daughter, but Ginny brushed past without giving her a chance. 'Ooh, we've got a houseful! Is it a party or can anyone come?' The girl was smiling happily when she noticed Hannah. 'Hello, Mrs Bailey, I hope they're not getting yer drunk?'

All eyes were on the old lady, and as the women were to tell their husbands later it was as if a light had suddenly been turned on in Hannah's head. She glanced around, confused at first, then she smiled at the young girl who called in every day to see if she wanted any messages. 'Hello, sweetheart, isn't it too cold and dark for you to be out?'

Chapter Three

After a short, stunned silence, everyone began talking at once. Not to Hannah, or about her, but about anything else under the sun to give them time to consider what to do. Glances were exchanged between the four neighbours, and shoulders were shrugged as if to ask, 'What now?' Should they tell her they'd found her wandering the streets in a daze, or wait to see if she mentioned it of her own accord?

Hannah listened to the chattering and smiled when she thought it was expected. But secretly she was confused. She didn't know why she was here, couldn't for the life of her remember even walking up the street. There was something niggling in her head but she couldn't bring it to mind. Except perhaps for a gut feeling that it was something bad or unpleasant. Yet what would it have to do with her being here, in the Porters' house, with the other neighbours? Was it someone's birthday? No, it couldn't be, there were no cakes and no birthday cards taking pride of place on the sideboard. And there were no husbands here. She closed her eyes, wishing her mind would clear so she would know what was happening to her. Please God, she prayed softly, don't let me be losing the run of my senses.

Beth had been watching Hannah closely and could see the woman was confused and ill at ease. 'Are yer all right, sunshine? Yer look worried to death.'

'To tell the truth, Beth, I was just thinking I must be getting very forgetful in me old age. I mean, yer must have invited me, but I can't remember what for.'

The chattering stopped and every face turned to Beth. They could see she was undecided as to how much to tell Hannah, and held their breath as they waited. This would need plenty of tact so as not to upset the old lady.

'Don't yer remember, sunshine? Yer weren't feeling very well so I brought yer here so yer'd have some company and I could keep me eye on yer.' Beth's hand swept round to indicate her neighbours who were leaning forward in their seats. 'And, of course, when this lot knew, they came in to keep us company.'

'D'yer know, I can't remember.' Hannah rubbed the heel of her hand over her eyes, as though trying to clear them. 'Yer wouldn't think I'd forget not being well, would yer? And I don't even recall yer bringing me up here!'

'I know why that is, queen,' Flo said. 'Yer had a bit of a temperature, and that muddles yer up in yer mind. It's happened to me when I've had a bad cold and I haven't known whether I was coming or going. But it doesn't last long, and yer'll soon be as right as rain.'

'Of course yer will, me darlin', so don't be worrying about it. We're all here to look after yer, so we are.'

But Beth wasn't happy about this. It was all very well everyone telling the woman she was going to be all right, but they didn't really know she would be. 'Joey, I think it's time for yer to go to bed, yer dad will be in soon. So poppy off, there's a good boy.'

Any other night the lad would have protested, but he'd seen and heard enough in the last hour to know things weren't what they appeared to be and was sensible enough not to argue. 'Okay, Mam, I'm feeling tired anyway.'

Beth gave him a kiss and patted his bottom as he began to climb the stairs. 'I'll tell yer all about it in the morning, son. Goodnight and God bless.'

Ginny couldn't make head nor tail of what was going on. Their three neighbours were always in and out of each other's houses, but unless they'd been having a party, she'd never known them all to be here at the same time. And although Mrs Bailey wasn't as bright or talkative as she usually was, she didn't seem to be sick. 'How are yer feeling now, Mrs Bailey, have yer still got a temperature?'

Before Hannah could answer, Beth said, 'I think she's better than she was. And she'll be even better after another cup of tea. So be an angel and give me a hand, will yer, sunshine?'

'We'll all have one too, if yer don't mind.' Flo was never backward in coming forward. 'Me throat's as dry as a bone.'

'I'm going to run short of milk for the breakfast,' Beth told her. 'So I'll have to scrounge some off yer.'

Lizzie, who had a husband and four children to cater for, was the first to offer. 'Sure, if it's milk ye're short of, me darlin', I can spare a pint.'

'As long as yer don't leave yerself short, I'll be grateful. I can pay yer back when the milkman comes in the morning.'

'Ah, there's no need for that, not at all, at all. Isn't it meself what's drinking yer out of house and home.'

26

Beth chuckled. 'Two cups of tea are hardly drinking me out of house and home, Lizzie. But I'll be glad if yer can spare me a pint.'

'I can let yer have a cupful, queen,' Flo said, not wanting to be thought mean. 'And I wouldn't want it back off yer.'

It was Dot's turn to chuckle. 'She'd have a job to give it yer back if it had been used.'

'Oh, ye're there, are yer?' Flo's chins did a little dance. 'Yer hate to be left out, that's your trouble. It's a wonder yer haven't gone one better and offered to bring a ruddy cow!'

For the first time Hannah laughed, and it was like a tonic to all of them because they knew a laugh is as good as a dose of medicine any day. Over the years, when they were down in the dumps because they were skint and worried about where the next meal was coming from, they'd always shared what little money and food they had. And they'd always managed to chase the blues away with a good laugh.

In the kitchen, Beth turned on the tap so her words couldn't be heard in the living room. Very briefly, she went over the events of the evening with Ginny. She ended by saying, 'I don't know what to do, sunshine, 'cos I don't like the idea of her being alone in that house of hers. If anything happened I'd never forgive meself.'

'Well, let her stay here tonight. I'll sleep on the couch and she can have my bed.'

'Are yer sure, sunshine?'

Ginny nodded. 'I don't mind, Mam, honest. I love Mrs Bailey, she's a smashing woman.'

Beth slapped an open palm to her forehead. 'She'll need a nightdress and slippers but she hasn't got a key with her for us to go and get them! When we found her she didn't have a handbag or anything.'

'Perhaps the back door's been left on the latch, yer never know,' Ginny said, hopefully. 'Shall I ask her?'

'No, I'll do it, sunshine, all casual like. I don't want to upset her if I can help it. So if you'll see to the tea, I'll ask her if she'd like to stay the night, and try to work the conversation around to how we can get into her house.' Beth turned back at the door. 'Be as quick as yer can with the tea 'cos I'd like me mates to be gone by the time yer dad gets in.'

Ginny huffed, 'There's not much chance of that, Mam, they hate to miss anything.'

'I'm going to tell them yer said that!'

Her daughter grinned. 'They can't argue 'cos they know it's the truth! They're the best neighbours anyone could have, and if they are nosy, it's in the nicest possible way.'

27

Beth returned to the living room with a smile on her face. Taking a seat next to Hannah, she said, 'Our Ginny is pestering me to ask yer to stay the night here, save going home to an empty house. She said yer can have her bed.'

'Oh, that's nice of her, sweetheart, but I couldn't do that! Chase a girl out of her own bed? No, that wouldn't be fair when I've got a perfectly good bed at home.'

Ginny came through from the kitchen carrying two cups of tea. 'Ah, go on, Mrs Bailey, I want yer to stay. I can sleep on the couch, dead easy, and yer could have yer breakfast with us. Go on, please, 'cos we've never had visitors stopping overnight.'

Flo added her weight. 'Ye're daft if yer refuse, Hannah, I know I wouldn't if I was asked. Your fire will have well gone out by now, so yer'd be going home to a freezing house.'

She frowned. 'I'm sure I banked me fire up before I came out, and I haven't been here that long, surely?'

'Yer've been here quite a few hours, sunshine, but what difference does that make to yer sleeping here tonight?' Beth asked. 'I can go down and put the guard in front of the fire and pick yer nightdress and slippers up.'

Dot also tried egging her on. 'If I had the chance of being waited on hand and foot, I'd jump at it. The trouble is, I never get asked.'

'Yer know why, don't yer?' Flo nodded her head knowingly. 'Because yer talk so much, no one would get any sleep.'

'Flo Henderson, you're a fine one to say I talk too much when you could talk the hind legs off a donkey.' Dot pretended to be really put out. 'I feel so insulted, I'm cut to the quick.'

The diversion was giving Hannah time to think. For some reason she couldn't fathom, she didn't want to go back to her own house. And that worried her, 'cos she loved the little house she kept like a palace. It held memories of her beloved husband who had died just days before he was due to retire from work at sixty-five. She still saw him in every room, still talked to him every day as she was dusting and polishing. And there were memories of their only child, John, dashing in from playing footie with his socks hanging down over his shoes, his knees filthy and his face as black as the hobs of hell.

Just then a sharp pain stabbed through Hannah's head. It was so severe, it caused her to cry out and press her hands to her temples. It only lasted seconds, and when it had gone her head was clear and slowly her memory was returning. 'Oh, dear God, he's dead!' She rocked back and forth, her anguished sobs filling the room and frightening those around her.

'What is it, sunshine?' Beth put an arm across the old lady's shoulders and pulled her close. 'Yer said he was dead, who did yer mean?'

'Our John.' Her wail sent cold shivers down the spines of those listening. 'He's dead and I'll never see him again.' Hannah's only son was married with two grown-up children. Five years ago, when there was no work to be had in Liverpool, he'd taken his family to live in Birmingham where he was able to find a job. She'd only seen him a few times since, because they couldn't afford the train fare, but he never failed to write to her every week. This week's letter had been written by his wife, Claire.

'Oh, come here, sunshine.' Beth pressed the white head to her bosom and rocked her like a baby. 'Yer've got all yer friends around yer, ready to help in any way they can. So when yer feel up to it, tell us what happened.'

Lizzie felt in her pocket for a hankie and passed it to Beth. 'Give her this, me darlin', it is clean, I haven't used it.'

When the sobbing subsided, Hannah wiped away her tears and blew her nose. 'I get a letter every week from our John, as yer know. Well, today, I was ready to go to the shops when the postman came along with the midday delivery. When I saw the Birmingham postmark I knew it was from John and put it on the sideboard to read when I got back.' There was a catch in her voice and she stopped for a while to compose herself. 'But it wasn't from John, it was from his wife. Claire had written to say he'd died of a massive heart attack on Monday. Sudden, she said. He suffered the attack at six o'clock, not long after he got in from work. The ambulance came quick, but John was dead by the time they got him to the hospital.'

It was all too much for the old lady and she broke down, again her sobs pulling at the heartstrings of her friends. 'I'm sorry.' She turned her tear-stained face to Beth. 'It's just that I can't take it in that I'll never see him again.'

'Listen, sunshine, you cry all yer want, 'cos we're all crying with yer. Why didn't yer come to one of us as soon as yer'd read the letter, instead of going through all that pain on yer own?'

'Well, yer see, I didn't read the letter when I got back from the shops. I kept looking at it on the sideboard, dying to open it, but like a child promising herself a treat, I decided to leave it until after tea, when I could pull the chair near the fire and read me son's letter in peace. He always wrote three pages, full of how his job was going and what the kids were up to. And there was always something for me to laugh at, 'cos if yer remember, our John was always laughing and playing tricks on people.'

'I remember him well,' Dot said, sadness and disbelief in her voice. 'He was a good bloke, always the gentleman.'

'What else did it say in the letter, me darlin'?' Lizzie asked. 'Did his wife give yer any more details?'

'I didn't read it all, I couldn't, me head was whirling. I remember now, I just threw it on the floor and ran out of the house as I was, no coat or anything. I was out of me mind, didn't know what I was doing. It's still hazy, but I can recall passing neighbours who asked me what I was doing out without a coat, but I didn't even look at them, I just kept walking. Your Andy and Bill tried to get me to go home, but the way me head was, I didn't even know who they were.'

'They came and told us, sunshine, and they were so concerned, we got together and set off to find yer.'

'I'm sorry to have caused yer so much bother, I wouldn't have done if I'd been thinking straight. But it was such a shock . . .' Sobs cut Hannah's words off. Then, tears streaming down her face, she said, 'I mean, yer don't expect yer son to die before yer, do yer? It just doesn't seem fair.'

Beth glanced at the clock. Andy would be in any minute, and the chances were that Bill would come with him to find out what had happened. She didn't think Hannah was up to going all through it again, it was too painful. 'Ye're staying here tonight, sunshine, so I don't want any argument out of yer. One of the ladies will come with me to get yer nightie and slippers, and yer coat, and then I can make yer nice and comfortable. But the thing is, yer've no keys on yer, so how do we get into yer house?'

Hannah frowned as she pushed her hands into the deep pockets of her cardigan. 'I have a habit of sticking the key in me pocket. Ah,' she held it aloft, 'thank God! That's saved a lot of trouble.'

Beth took the key. 'Come on, ladies, let's get going! Ginny can keep Hannah company for ten minutes.'

Flo's mouth gaped. 'What the hell d'yer need all of us for? There's no point in four of us traipsing down the ruddy street and back again.'

'Yer'll only be traipsing back as far as yer own houses, sunshine, that's the point. Andy will be in soon and he won't be expecting a houseful! Besides, Hannah's had enough company for one night, her head must be spinning.'

'Well, I like that!' Flo lumbered to her feet. 'Some mate you are, telling us all to sod off.'

'Stop yer moaning, Flo,' Dot said. 'Ye're not the only one being told to sling their hook, so save yer tears 'cos yer won't get no sympathy.'

'Who asked you to put yer oar in?' Flo muttered as she buttoned her coat. 'Ye're always butting in where ye're not wanted.'

'Come on.' Beth herded them out, then turned at the door. 'I won't be long, Hannah. If yer want a drink, Ginny will make one.'

When the door closed, Ginny went to sit beside their visitor. 'They're hilarious, aren't they? Anyone would think they meant it when they argue, but they don't. They're good mates.'

'I know that, sweetheart, they're the salt of the earth. And what they've done for me tonight proves it. There's not many folk would go out on a night like this to look for a neighbour who's gone missing.'

'I'd go looking for yer, Mrs Bailey.' Ginny put her arm across Hannah's shoulders. ''Cos I think ye're a little love.'

Outside, Lizzie said, 'You go on ahead while I nip across the road for the milk I promised yer. I'll be right behind yer, so I will.'

And she was right behind them when Beth put the key in Hannah's door. 'We're lucky the gas hasn't run out and the light's on. At least we can see what we're doing.'

'There's the letter on the floor.' Flo made a dive for it and waved it in the air. 'She's lucky it missed going in the fire.'

Beth quickly plucked it from her hand. 'I think Hannah should be the first one to read that, sunshine. After all, it is addressed to her.'

But Flo wasn't convinced. 'I think we should read it first, queen, so we'll know what to do. It's probably giving all the details of the funeral and everything, and she's bound to be upset. We could break it to her gently, like, and then she won't take it so bad.'

Dot shook her head. 'Beth's right, we shouldn't read a private letter. Hannah will tell us what she wants us to know when she's feeling more like herself.'

'If she can get a good night's sleep first, then the poor soul might be more up to it. News like that would be a shock to anyone, never mind a woman of her age and John being all she had in the world.' Lizzie put the milk on the table and took a miniature bottle of brandy out of her pocket. 'I always keep one of these in the house in case it's needed. If yer could give it to Hannah in a cup of tea before she goes to bed, me darlin', it'll help her to sleep.'

'Thanks, Lizzie, that's a godsend. I'll make sure she gets it down

31

her.' Beth placed the tiny bottle on the table next to the milk. 'Now, I wonder where we'll find her nightdress and slippers?'

'The slippers are here, by the side of her chair,' Flo grunted as she bent down to pick them up. 'Knowing Hannah, her nightdress will probably be folded up neatly on her bed. But I ain't walking up those bleedin' stairs 'cos they kill me.'

'Will you come up with me, Dot?' Beth asked. 'I don't like rooting in someone else's house, it doesn't seem right. But she's got to have a nightdress, so needs must when the devil drives. And a clean pair of knickers if we can find them, in case she's not in a fit state to come back here tomorrow.'

They found the nightdress folded under a pillow on the bed, and the first drawer they opened contained knickers, vests and brassieres. 'My God,' Dot said, 'this drawer puts mine to shame. Everything is so neat and tidy while mine are a mess.'

'Ye're not on yer own, sunshine, 'cos my drawers don't bear inspection. I put everything away neatly, but by the time the kids have rummaged through them, everything is topsy-turvy and the clothes are creased to blazes.'

As they walked down the badly lit staircase, Dot chuckled. 'I remember me ma shouting at me for not keeping things tidy. She used to call me all the lazy articles going 'cos I was too idle to look after me own clothes. God rest her soul, but if she's looking down on me now I bet she's saying I'm getting what I deserve.'

Flo was waiting at the bottom of the stairs with her hands on her hips. 'Ye're not half bleedin' slow! Yer've been gone that long, I was beginning to think yer'd hopped into bed.'

'We got what we wanted anyway so stop yer moaning.' Beth reached for Hannah's coat which was hanging on a hook near the front door. 'I think that's everything, isn't it?'

'The house was wide open to the world, me darlin', so it was. Anyone could have come in the back way 'cos the poor soul had run out without locking the door. But everywhere is safe now, and I've put the guard in front of the fire 'cos there still some life in it and it's better to be sure than sorry.'

'That's it, then! You're the tallest, Lizzie, so would yer be an angel and reach up to put the light out?'

When the room was plunged into darkness, Beth said, 'I'll open the front door and we'll be able to see by the light from the street lamp. I should have thought of that before I asked yer to put the light out, Lizzie, but I've got a head like a ruddy sieve.'

The light from the street lamp didn't come fast enough to help Flo, though, and she walked straight into the living room door. She didn't hurt herself because her layers of fat kept her safe, but she wasn't going to tell that to the others until she'd received the amount of sympathy she thought she was entitled to. 'Oh, my God, I've knocked all me front teeth out! Which silly bugger deliberately left the door open for me to walk into?' When the fuss she was expecting didn't come, she wailed, 'Ooh, I'm in agony. Someone run for a doctor quick, 'cos I think me nose is busted, me eye is hanging out and I've lost all me front teeth.' With a chubby hand covering her face, she staggered to the front door to find her friends standing on the pavement looking up at her. 'A fine lot of mates you turned out to be, I must say. I could be dead for all you care.'

Beth pretended to be hurt by Flo's words. 'Ah, that's not nice now, sunshine, is it? Not when we've been standing here finding solutions to all yer problems. Dot is going to bandage yer nose up, Lizzie is going to put yer eye back in its socket, and I'm going to come down first thing in the morning to find yer missing teeth.'

Flo stared down at them for a few seconds then she began to shake with laughter. Her mountainous bosom and tummy went up and down while her chins did a quickstep. Her laughter lifted the pall of sadness which had enveloped them all for the last few hours. When she could speak, she croaked, 'Ay, queen, that was good, that was. I couldn't have done better meself in that short time. Mind you, while your brain was working, my eye crawled back into its socket 'cos it was frightened of missing anything, and me nose pulled itself back into shape. And, yer'll be glad to know, me teeth are safe in me pocket, all present and accounted for.'

'What about yer cauliflower ear?' Lizzie asked. 'Has that gone back into shape?'

'Cauliflower ear! How the hell could I get a cauliflower ear when I walked face forward into the bleedin' door?'

'I only hope Hannah's door is in as good shape as you are, girl,' Dot said, deadpan. 'I've got a feeling that in a collision with you, it was bound to come out the loser.'

'Oh, very funny, I'm sure, Mrs Clever Clogs. Perhaps . . .' Flo's words trailed off and her mouth opened in fright when she was pulled unceremoniously from the top step. Her little legs kicking the air, she landed on the pavement in front of her friends. 'In the name of God, queen, what did yer do that for? I could have broken me flaming neck!'

'I had to do something to shut yer up, sunshine, otherwise we'd be here all night. As yer well know, I enjoy a laugh as well as the next one, but there's a time and a place for everything. And while the place is right, the time isn't, 'cos I've left our Ginny sitting with Hannah.' Beth closed the front door and pressed it to make sure it was securely shut. 'Now I don't want any of yer to think I'm keeping Hannah all to meself and leaving you out, but I'd say she's gone through enough today and we should let her settle down a bit.'

'I agree with yer, me darlin', I do that, right enough,' Lizzie said. 'As long as yer know we're there if yer want us. I'm sure Flo and Dot will say the same, that yer can knock for us any time, night or day.'

'All yer've got to do is bang on the wall, girl, and I'll be there like a shot.' Dot linked Beth's arm and they began to walk up the street, followed closely by Flo and Lizzie. 'Even if it's the middle of the night, I won't mind.'

'If I don't hear from yer before, queen, I'll call to yours at ten o'clock to see how Hannah is and if yer want anything from the shops.' Flo was very curious about the contents of the letter and didn't like the idea of having to wait until tomorrow to find out. But she'd have to tread carefully or her mates would jump down her throat. So she tried to make her voice sound casual when she asked, 'Are yer going to give her the letter when yer get in?'

'I don't know, sunshine, I'll see how she is then. I'm going to play it by ear. If she asks about it, I won't lie, I'll give it to her. If she doesn't mention it, I'll hang on until the morning. With a bit of luck, and Lizzie's brandy, she'll have a decent night's sleep and be better able to cope.'

'So we've all got to wait until tomorrow to find out what's going on?' Flo wasn't best pleased about this. 'I still think we should read what's in it. I'm sure Hannah wouldn't mind in the least.'

'Flo, yer can be a nosy cow sometimes,' Dot said. 'What difference does it make to us what happens? It's Hannah's business. We'll give her all the help we can, but we can't take over from her.'

'Nosy cow? I've a good mind to clock you one, Dot Flynn. Talk about the pot calling the kettle black! Anyone in this street will tell yer I keep to meself and don't meddle in other folk's business. I'm the leastest nosy person in the neighbourhood.'

'Ye're also the most ignorant.' Dot knew that if she took offence Flo was capable of knocking her out for the count. But she had one advantage over her little fat friend – she could run faster. 'There's no such word as leastest.'

'Oh, isn't there now, smart arse? Well, it's of little significance to me whether there is or not.' When Flo saw Dot's mouth gape, she grinned. 'It's all right, queen, I don't know what that means meself, and I couldn't spell it to save me life.'

At that point they all came to a halt outside Flo's house and Beth didn't want to stand around talking because she'd been out too long as it was. 'I'll have to be getting in, Hannah will wonder what we're doing in her house. But I'll see yer all in the morning. And thanks for helping me out, I wouldn't have attempted it on me own. In fact Hannah would still be lost if it weren't for you. So it's a pat on the back all round for the faithful four, and I'll bid yer goodnight and God bless.'

When Beth closed the door behind her, she stood in the tiny hallway and listened. First she heard Andy's quiet voice, and then Hannah's. She couldn't make out what they said, but there were no tears or sobs which was a good sign. So after patting her pocket to make sure the letter was still there, she took off her coat and hung it with Hannah's on one of the hooks behind the door. Then she walked into the warmth of the living room.

'Did yer think I'd left home, Hannah?' Beth was pleased to see Ginny sitting next to the old lady on the couch with their arms linked. 'I'm going to put the blame on Flo because she'd keep yer talking until the cows come home. Besides which, she has the broadest shoulders to put the blame on.'

Her husband smiled. 'Only a coward puts the blame on someone else.'

'That's me, sunshine, a coward through and through. Anyway, I've got yer nightdress and slippers, Hannah, plus a change of undies. And Lizzie gave me this bottle of brandy for yer, with strict instructions that yer drink it in a cup of tea before yer go to bed. It should help yer get a good night's sleep.'

'That was kind of her. Yer've all been so good, I don't know what would have become of me if yer hadn't come looking for me. I've put yer to a lot of trouble.'

'It was no trouble at all, sunshine. That's what friends are for! And you'd have done the same for any one of us.' Beth carried the pair of slippers over to the couch. 'Put these on, sunshine, and yer'll be more comfortable. I'll put the kettle on for a pot of tea, and light the oven to warm up the shelf so it can go in the bed to take the chill off it.'

'Ye're spoiling me, sweetheart, I won't want to go home at this rate.'

'Well, then, yer can stay with us,' Ginny told her, 'for as long as yer like.'

35

Beth watched Hannah putting her slippers on, and thought the old lady seemed a lot more at ease now. It would be an act of cruelty to give her the letter and bring back all the sadness and heartache. Far better to let her have a good night's sleep, please God, and then help her through the ordeal tomorrow. After Andy had left for work, and the children were off to school, the house would be quiet and peaceful. That would be the best time, if there was a best time, to talk about the tragic news the letter had brought.

'Andy, would yer be an angel and put the kettle on for us, please? And put a light to the oven for me.' Beth sent him a message with her eyes. 'And stay out there for a few minutes so a certain lady can put her nightdress on in front of the fire.'

Hannah shook her head. 'Yer can't send a man out of his own room for me! I'll get undressed upstairs.'

Andy jumped to his feet. On his way to the kitchen, he bent down to look into Hannah's eyes. 'No, you won't, Mrs Woman, yer'll let me wife make yer nice and comfy. Then, with a tot of brandy inside yer, up to yer nice warm bed and yer'll sleep like a baby.'

Chapter Four

Beth stood in the middle of the living room. The only sound she could hear was the ticking of the clock. She'd got up at six o'clock to clean the grate out and light a fire in case Hannah couldn't sleep in a strange bed and got up early. But Andy had left for work at half-seven, the children had gone to school at half-eight, it was nine o'clock now and there was still no sound from the bedroom upstairs. She'd been growing concerned when it got to eight o'clock so she'd crept upstairs and opened the bedroom door a fraction. At the sound of Hannah's gentle snoring, she'd breathed a sigh of relief.

There was a tap on the window and Flo's face could be seen peering through the net curtains. Beth couldn't keep a grin back because she knew her neighbour's curiosity was the reason for this early visit. But she was going to be disappointed because there was no news to give. And she wasn't going to be asked in, not while Hannah was still in bed.

'What are yer doing here at this time? I'm not asking yer in, sunshine, because Hannah is still in bed and I don't want to wake her up. The longer she sleeps, the better.'

'Did yer give her the letter, queen? And if yer did, how did she take it?'

'I haven't given it to her yet, I didn't have the heart. By the time I got in last night, she seemed to have calmed down, talking to Andy and Ginny, so I thought it best to leave well alone. When she gets up, I'll give her some breakfast, then give it to her. And as soon as I think she's fit for visitors, I'll give yer a knock on the wall.' She saw the disappointment on Flo's chubby face and felt a bit mean, but right now Hannah was the person to worry about. 'I know ye're concerned about her, sunshine, but I really believe it would be best to take things slowly. And I know yer'll understand and agree.'

'It's a case of having to, queen, if ye're not going to let me in. But I'll be listening for yer knock, so don't forget.'

'I promise.' Beth put her fingers to her lips and blew a kiss. 'I'll see yer later.'

After closing the front door, she stood in the hall and her eyes went to the pocket of her coat. She could see the letter and couldn't help wondering if there was anything in it, apart from what Hannah had told them, to cause her more heartache. Acting on impulse, she plucked the letter from the pocket and carried it through to the living room. There was still no sound from overhead, no creaking bed springs or floorboards, so she pulled out a chair from the table and sat down. The three pages were crumpled, so she laid them flat and ran the side of her hand over each page to straighten it. She noticed there were stains on the top page where the ink had run, and knew right away that the smudges were made by falling tears. A great sadness came over her as she thought of the heartache and suffering of the woman writing to say she'd lost the man she loved, and the children had lost their dad. Beth could imagine how she would feel it anything happened to Andy, and wished she could throw the letter in the fire and pretend it had all been a bad dream. She couldn't do that, of course, because unfortunately it wasn't.

Beth sighed as she fingered the pages. Claire had probably written to tell her mother-in-law of the funeral arrangements, and it was important that Hannah knew these details as soon as possible so she could reply immediately. But wouldn't it be better for her to hear it by word of mouth, rather than from pages smudged with the tears of a heartbroken woman? Surely Hannah would understand and appreciate Beth wasn't being nosy, merely trying to lessen the pain as best she could?

Knowing she didn't have much time to worry about the rights and wrongs of what she had in mind, Beth began to read. She had just finished the last line on the third page when she heard movement above. She quickly folded the letter and put it behind the clock on the mantelpiece before walking to the foot of the stairs.

'Are yer ready to come down now, sunshine?' she called. 'Or would yer like yer breakfast in bed?'

'I'll just put me dress on, sweetheart, then I'll be down.'

'Okay, I'll put the kettle on and make us some toast. But don't stay up there too long, sunshine, or yer'll freeze to death. Yer'd be better bringing yer dress down and putting it on in front of a nice roaring fire. There's no one here but me, and yer've got nothing that I haven't got so don't be modest.'

'I think I'll do that. I've got me cardi on over me underskirt, so I'm decent enough, as long as you don't mind.'

'Yer can't look any worse than I look first thing in the morning, sunshine! And I'll let yer into a secret as long as yer don't tell – I've seen Flo in a state of undress and, believe me, that is a sight to behold. But does she care? Does she heckerslike!' Beth was looking up the stairs when Hannah appeared on the tiny landing. 'D'yer know what she told me when I said she should cover herself up? Apart from telling me to sod off, I mean. She said God didn't give her that magnificent body to hide it away, and if I didn't like it, I could bleedin'well lump it!' When Hannah reached the bottom stair, Beth smiled and asked, 'Did yer sleep all right, sunshine?'

'Like a top, sweetheart. I don't even remember me head hitting the pillow, I must have dropped right off. It will have been the brandy.'

'That's good, yer'll feel more up to the day ahead if ye're not tired.' Beth led her to the couch and took the dress from over her arm. 'I'll draw the curtains over while yer get dressed, so yer've no need to worry about being seen. While ye're doing that, I'll see to some breakfast.'

'If it's not too much bother, Beth, I'd like to have a bit of a swill, to wake meself up proper.'

'Hang on a minute then, and I'll pour some water out of the kettle into a bowl for yer. And while ye're getting washed I'll put some toast under the grill for us. I haven't had any breakfast yet, I was waiting for you. I thought we could have a chat while we're eating, before the gang decide to put in an appearance.'

Hannah looked more like her old self after she'd had a wash, donned her dress and borrowed a comb off Beth to tidy her hair. 'Thanks very much, sweetheart, I feel more like a human being now.'

Beth waited until they'd eaten their toast and were on their second cup of tea before bringing up the subject that was weighing heavy on her mind. 'Hannah, I've got a confession to make, and I hope yer won't be mad at me. I thought long and hard before doing it, but in the end I decided, as a friend, I'd be doing more good than harm.'

'I know yer'd never do anything to harm me, sweetheart, so take that frown off yer pretty face and tell me what it is yer've done?'

'Well, I brought the letter up that yer got from Claire, sunshine, and after the kids had gone to school, and I was sitting on me own waiting for yer to wake up, I read it. Not out of curiosity, but I thought if I explained to yer what was in it, it wouldn't be so hard as yer reading it yerself. I hope I did the right thing?'

Hannah placed her cup carefully in the saucer before answering. 'I'm glad yer did, because I was dreading the thought of even touching those pages. I'd much rather hear it from you.'

'I hope ye're ready for it, sunshine, but it really has to be done now. Yer see, Claire will be waiting for an answer, and I think yer should get a letter in the post today. I'll write it for yer, if yer like, as long as yer tell me what to say.'

'I wouldn't know what to say, I only read the first page. But I'd be grateful if yer can help me find the right words to say how heartbroken I am for her and the children.'

Beth lowered her head so she wouldn't see the hurt that must surely come to the eyes now focused on her. 'Well, Claire said the funeral is on Monday, but she's not expecting yer to attend, what with the long, tiring journey and the train fare to Birmingham.'

That was the worst part over, and when Beth lifted her head she went on talking quickly so the older woman wouldn't have time to dwell on what she'd said. 'I thought perhaps we could send a postal order in the letter, to pay for a wreath from you and the neighbours. I know the others would want to show their respect, and a wreath would make up for yer not being there in person.' When Hannah didn't answer, Beth carried on. 'I know yer'd like to be there, sunshine, but it's too long a journey for yer. And it's not as though yer'll never see Claire or yer grandchildren again, 'cos they've asked if they can come up.'

There was emotion now on Hannah's face. 'Did Claire say that? Oh, that would be marvellous! I haven't seen her or me grandchildren for five years.'

'Actually, sunshine, Claire said they would like to come back to live in Liverpool. They never really settled down there because they lived in a street where the neighbours kept themselves to themselves and they haven't made any real friends. The children really want to come back to Liverpool.'

Beth took a sip of her tea before asking, 'Ye're not upset with me telling yer these things, are yer, sunshine?'

'To tell yer the truth, sweetheart, when I knew our John was dead, I was praying that God would take me too, 'cos I felt I had nothing to live for. And it'll take me a long time to get over it. But knowing that his wife and my grandchildren are coming back into me life, well, that has certainly heartened me, 'cos they are part of my son.'

'There's more to come, sunshine, and I think it's best if yer hear the lot in one go. Claire asks in the letter if they could stay with you until they find a place of their own? They won't have a lot of money by the time they've settled everything down there, but the children will be able to find jobs and Claire said she'd go to work so they'd soon be on their feet.'

Hannah was nodding her head slowly as pictures flashed through her mind of the two children. 'John used to tell me all about them in his

40

letters. He was so proud of them. Bobby, me grandson, he's sixteen and been working as an apprentice gas fitter. And the girl, Amelia, she's fifteen and works in a factory.'

'It would be nice for yer to have them stay with yer for a while, wouldn't it? They'd be good company for yer, and yer could get to know yer grandchildren.'

'It would be lovely, sweetheart, but where would they all sleep? There's only the back bedroom and I couldn't expect the lad and girl to sleep in the same room. They're at the age where they'd be embarrassed.'

'Don't forget that I've got a boy and a girl, Hannah,' Beth said, 'and we manage all right. And what about Lizzie and her tribe? She's got four children and they don't seem to have any problem. They're packed in pretty tight, like, but it hasn't done them any harm and they all get on like a house on fire.'

'Yes, I know, but like you, most of the people in the street have made the back bedroom into two rooms, while mine's the same as it was when the house was built.'

'It would be no problem dividing the room, sunshine, yer only need some sheets of hardboard and . . .' The loud rap on the knocker had Beth pushing her chair back. 'I bet yer any money that's Flo! I'll break her neck for her.'

On her way to the door, Beth happened to glance at the window and, sure enough, there was her neighbour, both hands on her eyebrows, peering in. 'She's a nosy so-and-so. She wouldn't be the least bit embarrassed if the pair of us were naked. We would be, but not the queer one.'

There was a frown on Beth's face when she opened the door, but behind the frown there was a smile lurking. 'I told yer I'd give yer a knock when we were ready for yer! Ye're an impatient article, Flo Henderson, couldn't yer have waited a bit longer?'

'I haven't got all bleedin' day to sit on me backside, queen, just waiting until yer decide to give me a knock.' Flo folded her arms under her mountainous bosom and stood firm. With mutiny written on her face, she said, 'And don't tell me I can't come in again, 'cos if yer do I'll just walk through yer.' With a sharp nod of the head, she added, 'So there!'

'D'yer know what, Flo Henderson? When yer were a little girl and one of yer mates wouldn't let yer play with her ball, I bet yer used to cry, stamp yer feet and say yer were going to fetch yer dad out to her.'

Never one to be beaten, Flo managed to put a surprised expression on her chubby face. 'How did yer know that, queen?'

Beth threw up her arms. 'I can't win, so I don't know why I bother. Yer can come in, but only after yer've given Lizzie and Dot a knock. I don't want anyone complaining that they've been left out.'

When Flo crossed the cobbled street, her body seemed to bounce like a rubber ball. For all the weight she carried, she was very light on her feet. Of course that was only when she was asked to do something she wanted to do. If she didn't want to, then she played the wounded soldier and nothing would budge her.

'We've got visitors coming, sunshine,' Beth said when she went back into the living room. 'Yer don't mind, do yer? It's just that me mates are concerned for yer and I couldn't leave them out.'

'I'll be glad to see them, to thank them for what they did last night. Yer find out who yer real friends are when ye're in trouble, don't yer, sweetheart?'

'Yer can say that again, sunshine! I soon found out who me friends were when times were hard. And I wouldn't swap them for all the tea in China.' Beth giggled. 'I wouldn't tell them that, though, or they'd get big-headed.'

Flo was first in, and she struck a pose. With one hand cupping her chin, she gazed around the room. 'I didn't know yer'd decorated, queen, yer didn't say.'

Beth looked puzzled. 'What are yer on about? We haven't decorated.'

Flo gave Hannah a sly wink before saying, 'Oh, yer do surprise me. Mind you, it's so long since yer let me into this room, I'd forgotten what yer wallpaper was like.'

'Ye're a cheeky article, you are.' Beth's face was stern as she wagged a finger, but in her heart she felt like kissing her neighbour's chubby face because Hannah was laughing aloud. 'I'm going to tell your husband he should put his foot down with yer.'

Flo's tummy shook. Her husband, Dennis, was the most quiet, passive man imaginable. He'd never been known to raise his voice to his wife or their two daughters. 'He tried to put his foot down with me once, not long after we got married. Didn't do him no good, though.' Her eyes twinkled with mischief. 'Haven't yer ever noticed he limps a bit? It's his left foot he has trouble with, especially in the winter. I was aiming for his right but lost me balance a bit and went way off target.'

'May God forgive you, Flo Henderson, for some of the things yer say about Dennis. Yer don't know ye're born, having him for a husband.'

'I'll do a swap with yer, if yer like, queen, my feller for yours. And

42

I wouldn't diddle yer either. I know I'd be getting the best of the bargain so I'll give yer ten bob cash in yer hand to make up for my feller not being as good-looking as yours.'

'I heard that!' Dot came bursting in. 'And I'll up the stakes. I'll give Beth a pound in the hand if she'll swap Andy for my Bill.'

'Shame on both of yer,' Lizzie said, shutting the door behind her. 'Sure, I wouldn't swap my Paddy for all the money in the world, and that's a fact, so it is.' She pulled out one of the dining chairs and sat next to Hannah. 'And how are you this morning, me darlin'?'

'I'm feeling a lot better, thank you. I had a good night's sleep, thanks to your bottle of brandy. And while ye're all here, I want to thank yer for what yer did last night. I'll never be able to pay yer back, but I want yer to know how grateful I am.'

'It was nothing, girl,' Dot said, sitting down. 'You'd have done the same for any of us.' She glanced at Beth, her eyes asking if she'd had time to talk to Hannah.

'I know ye're all wanting to know what's been arranged,' Beth said. 'So let's all sit down and talk it through.'

Flo pointed to the only vacant chair. 'Are you and me going to have a game of musical chairs, queen? If we are, I'd better warn yer that my backside is twice the size of yours. Yer wouldn't stand a chance 'cos I'd knock yer into the middle of next week.'

'There's a chair in front of the window, that'll do. But first I'll clear the dishes away.'

'You see to the dishes, queen, and I'll get the chair.'

'No! You sit here and I'll get the other chair. It's a bit wonky, yer see, and yer have to be careful yer don't move around on it too much.'

'Yer wouldn't be hinsinuating that it wouldn't stand my weight, would yer? I'll have yer know there's not much difference between you and me, so don't be so bleedin' sarcastic.'

Dot let out a loud guffaw. 'Only about five stone, girl! And I've had the misfortune of sitting on that chair, and it creaks like nobody's business. If it saw your backside coming down on it, it would give up the ghost and cave in.'

That sounded like a dare to Flo, and she wasn't one for refusing a dare. She would sit on that chair if it killed her, and if it gave one little creak she'd break it up with her bare hands and Beth could use it for firewood. So, with her mouth clamped tight in determination, she made a move towards the window, and the chair.

But her neighbour saw the look and hurried to stand in front of her. 'Flo Henderson, yer'd cause trouble in an empty house, you would.

Now stop acting daft and be yer age. Go and sit at the table and I'll have this chair when I've taken the dishes out.'

Flo would have stood her ground, but Hannah intervened. 'Come and sit next to me, Flo, it's right by the fire and yer'll be nice and warm.'

The little woman weighed up her options. She had two choices. A wonky chair that might collapse and make such a fool of her, her pride would be dented, or a seat by a warm fire. 'I'll do that, queen, and I'll be away from these sarky buggers. Anyone would think they had figures like Venus.'

Dot waited until her friend was seated before asking, 'What makes yer think Venus had a good figure, girl? I saw a statue of her once and she had no arms.'

Beth put the dirty dishes on the draining board before hurrying back into the living room. 'Yeah, I was told Venus had no arms. I wonder how that came about? People talk about her as though she was the most beautiful woman that's ever been, with a figure no other woman has ever matched! It doesn't make sense'

When Flo grinned, her chubby cheeks moved upwards to make her eyes look like slits. 'One thing about her, queen, she's 'armless enough.'

While there were hoots of laughter around her, Hannah was asking herself where she would be if these four women weren't her friends? Even if she'd eventually found her way home last night, which she doubted, she'd have been all alone in her house and not knowing where to turn. They were her saviours. And right now she was glad of their warmth and humour, because it kept her mind from dwelling on the death of her beloved son.

'All right now, let's have a bit of order so Hannah can tell you what's happening.' Beth smiled across the table. 'The floor's yours, sunshine.'

'You tell them, sweetheart, 'cos ye're much better with words than I am.'

Dot sat back in her chair after Beth had told them the story, leaving nothing out. 'Well, girl, some good has come out of it, hasn't it? With yer daughter-in-law and grandchildren living with yer, yer'll be a real family.'

'There's one snag, though,' Beth said, 'and I'm hoping we can help Hannah out. Yer see, her grandson is sixteen and the girl fifteen. They can't be expected to sleep in the same room, not at their age, and the back bedroom hasn't been partitioned off. So I was wondering if our four husbands would help? I remember when we did ours, everyone got stuck in and helped each other. Between the four of them, it wouldn't be such a big job.'

'Paddy will help, me darlin',' Lizzie said. 'Sure, I know the man well enough to say he'll be only too happy to do all he can. And isn't the man clever with his hands, so he is.'

'And yer can count on Bill.' Dot nodded. 'Like Paddy, he's pretty nifty with his hands.'

'That makes three, with my Andy.' Beth stared at Flo. 'Ye're very quiet, sunshine, have yer nothing to say?'

'My Dennis is not only good with his hands, queen, he's also good at getting things cheap. One of his mates works in a wood yard, and he's well in with the manager. So yer'll get all the wood yer want for about half-price.'

Beth rounded the table and hugged her. 'What are yer, sunshine? Ye're a little cracker, that's what yer are.'

Flo beamed at the compliment. 'It's not what yer know, queen, it's who yer know. So I do come in handy sometimes, eh?'

'You sure do, girl!' Dot stretched across the table to pat her hand. 'Yer always manage to come up trumps.'

The mischievous devil in Flo was hard at work. 'While I'm at it, I'll ask my feller to get a few short lengths of hardwood for Andy.'

'And what, pray, would my husband need short lengths of hardwood for?'

'To strengthen the legs on that bleedin' chair! What's the use of a chair that no one can sit on? Flamin' ridiciless, if yer ask me. A waste of space.'

'What did yer say it was, sunshine? Ediciless?'

'No, I didn't, smart arse. I said ridiciless, so there!'

When her four friends burst out laughing, Flo decided to join them. She hadn't a clue what they found so funny, but what the hell? If yer can't lick 'em, join 'em.

Beth glanced at the clock and was surprised to find it was half-eleven. 'I'd better get that letter to Claire done, so it will catch the one o'clock post.' She rooted in the sideboard drawer and found some paper and an envelope, but no pen. 'Yer wouldn't believe it, would yer! I can't find a ruddy pen! The ink bottle is here, but no pen.'

'I can help yer out there, me darlin',' Lizzie said, reaching down for her handbag. 'I've got a fountain pen without any ink in, and you've got ink without the pen! Together we've solved that problem, so we have.'

'I'm not going to write a long letter, Hannah. I'll just say yer were heartbroken at the news, and that ye're not up to the journey to Birmingham. You and some neighbours would like Claire to buy a wreath with the enclosed postal order, and we'd like her to know we'll all be thinking of her and the children on Monday. Then I'll tell her you can't wait for them to come back to Liverpool, and they're more than welcome to stay with yer.' Beth sighed. 'How does that sound, sunshine?'

'Fine, sweetheart. Short and to the point. I do wish I could be there with them, but I'd never make that journey on me own. And anyway, I'll need what bit of money I've got for other things.'

'While I'm writing the letter, would you ladies get yer shillings ready to save time? Mine is on the mantelpiece.'

'I'm sorry to be a nuisance, sweetheart, I seem to be causing yer nothing but trouble. But I can't give any money 'cos me purse is in me handbag and that must still be in me house,' Hannah explained.

'I'll go and get it for yer, girl,' Dot said. 'Give us the key, Beth, and I'll be there and back before yer know I've gone.'

'I'll come out with yer.' Flo put her palms flat on the table and pushed herself up. 'I've just remembered a little message I was supposed to give to someone, but it'll only take me a few minutes.'

Dot came back with Hannah's handbag and, when asked, said she hadn't set eyes on Flo. The letter was written, the envelope addressed, and Beth had washed the few breakfast dishes, swilled her face and combed her hair. Still her next-door neighbour hadn't put in an appearance. 'She'll get a piece of my mind when she turns up. Yer know what she's like, she's probably standing jangling to someone while we're waiting here like lemons.'

They sat for another ten minutes becoming very impatient. 'If she's not here in five minutes I'm going to the shops without her,' Beth said. 'She's a ruddy nuisance.'

'She's here now, girl, she's just passed the window.' Sure enough, a knock followed Dot's words. 'I'll open the door.'

Flo came bursting in, her face alight with excitement. 'I know yer've been calling me fit to burn, but I've done a bit of collecting. Yer see, when yer wouldn't let me in this morning, queen, Sally next-door was wiping her window sill down and I told her about John. She asked if anyone was making a collection for a wreath, 'cos as yer know that's what we always do when someone dies.' Flo stopped and took a deep breath. 'Anyway, she said most of the neighbours would want to contribute because John was well liked in the street.'

Hannah looked a bit upset. 'Yer didn't go asking for money for me, did yer, Flo? I'd be too embarrassed to show me face if yer did.'

'I didn't have to ask, queen, 'cos the word had got around the street and the neighbours came to Sally's to pass the money to her. They wanted to give to show their respect for a man they remember as being a nice polite kid who grew up to be a real gent. And I don't have to tell yer, queen, that everyone around here has the greatest respect for you.'

Flo's round chubby face looked like a rosy apple as she dug deep into a pocket to bring out a handful of coins. 'Some of the women whose husbands are working gave a shilling, and some gave sixpence. But I wouldn't take no more than tuppence from the houses where the men aren't working.' She delved into her pocket once again and brought out more coins. 'I don't know how much is there, but if we all count it together to prove I didn't cheat, then I can tell everyone how much we collected.'

Beth nodded to Dot and Lizzie. 'I'll take the copper, one of you take the tanners and the other the threepenny pieces.'

It wasn't often that Flo showed her serious side. In fact, only the people in this room knew she had one. But there was more to her than jokes, laughter and the occasional swear word, and she showed it now, as she curled her fists, leaned them on the table and looked at Hannah. 'In case ye're worried, queen, I did think twice about taking money off women whose husbands were out of work, but they'd have been upset if I hadn't. They may be skint but they have their pride, I wouldn't want to take that away from them.'

The other women had been putting the coins into piles, but they'd all heard what Flo said and it brought a lump to their throats. They'd all known what it was like to be skint, and the last thing they'd have wanted then was pity.

'There's seven shillings and threepence here, sunshine, yer did very well and we're proud of yer.'

Hannah didn't know what to say, she was amazed her neighbours had given so generously. 'That's a lot of money.'

'I suggest we stick to our original plan and send a five-bob postal order with the money we've put together. That's enough for a wreath, and you can use the rest for the wood yer need.' Beth scooped the money from the table into the glass bowl off the sideboard. 'We can see to that later. If we don't make an effort we'll miss the dinnertime post.'

'I may as well take me nightdress and slippers with me, sweetheart, to get them out of your way. Yer don't want to come back from the shops and find them still on yer couch.'

47

'And why d'yer want to take them to the shops with yer? There's no point in yer carting them around with yer.'

'I thought it would save me coming back to your house, sweetheart. Yer must be fed up with the sight of me, so I'll go straight home.'

'Not on your life yer won't!' Beth patted Hannah's wrinkled cheek. 'If you aren't here when our Ginny comes home from school, there'll be murder. I promised her faithfully that yer'd be sleeping here tonight.'

'I can't impose on yer any longer, Beth, it wouldn't be fair. Yer've done more than enough for me as it is.'

'Put that nightdress and slippers down, sunshine, 'cos there's no way ye're going back to yer own house tonight. In a couple of days, perhaps, but not just yet. And don't think I'm being a martyr, far from it! I enjoy having yer, and so do Andy and the kids.'

When Hannah turned to put the nightdress and slippers back on the couch, she was thanking God for giving her such good friends. The truth was, she was dreading going back home to sit alone with her heartache. There she'd have nothing else to think about but the death of her beloved son. Whereas, with these women, she wouldn't have time to think, and that was a blessing. With each day that passed she would get a little better.

Hannah gave herself a mental shake. What was she talking about, she'd have nothing else to think about? Her daughter-in-law and grandchildren would be coming back into her life – that was certainly something wonderful to look forward to. And if Beth would let her stay here for another couple of nights, just until she got her confidence back, then she'd be ready to go home and start getting the place ready for her family.

She tapped her neighbour on the shoulder. 'Thank you, sweetheart.'

'Think nothing of it, sunshine, ye're more than welcome.'

Chapter Five

Miss Jackson rapped sharply on her desk with a wooden ruler. 'Can I have silence, please? I know you are all getting excited about the holiday and what Father Christmas might put in your stocking, but you are nearing the end of your school days now and I would have thought it was more important you should concentrate on your future working life. So I intend to interview you in groups of three when we can discuss any preference as to employment you may have. I will also give you instructions on how to conduct yourself during an interview and how the Labour Exchange can help you.'

She opened a side drawer in her desk, took out a lined pad and wrote a name on each of the first three lines. 'While I am interviewing I want absolute silence so I'm setting the class an essay to do. The subject is the festive season. I want you to write what it is you like about Christmas, what happens in your family . . . anything that is interesting. And just because you only have two more weeks here, please don't think you can lower your standards. No smudges, crossing out or bad spelling. Is that understood?'

Thirty-four voices answered as one: 'Yes, Miss.' Desk lids were lifted and exercise books and pens taken out. There were three particularly bold girls in the class who were afraid of no one. The threat of the cane meant nothing to them and even detention was greeted with a smirk on their less-than-clean faces. They'd become more unruly since they'd turned fourteen several weeks ago and their mothers had told them they shouldn't have to wait until the end of term to leave, not when they could be bringing in some wages. Miss Jackson would be glad to see the back of them and dreaded to think how they would fare in an interview with any prospective employer. They'd wasted their school years, learning very little, which saddened her. But at least she had the consolation of knowing she'd done her very best for them.

'Will Sally McGuire, Wendy Burton and Virginia Porter please bring their chairs to my desk?'

Sally and Wendy looked apprehensive, but Ginny was all smiles.

The idea of being grown up enough to be looking for a job filled her with pleasure. And she knew now what she'd like to work at, so she wasn't afraid of any questions the teacher might ask.

Sally Maguire was hoping to get a job at the British Enka, where her father worked. She'd filled in an application form and her dad said there was more than a good chance of her being taken on. When Miss Jackson asked if that was what she wanted, the girl appeared surprised by the question and said it was a job like any other. Wendy Burton said there was a Lune Laundry near where she lived, and her mam had already been in to see the boss. He said he would be taking on two school leavers, and would interview Wendy the following week. If she was suitable, she could start work the week after Christmas.

'You two seem halfway to gaining employment, and I hope everything works out for you. If you are polite, pleasant and willing, I'm sure you'll do well.' The teacher turned her attention to Ginny then. 'And you, Virginia, what are your hopes and aspirations?'

'I'd like to work in a shop, Miss, rather than a factory. I like meeting people, and I'd certainly meet plenty standing behind the counter in a shop.' Ginny grinned. 'And I'd always be polite, pleasant and willing. That's if I ever get the chance, like.'

'A small local shop, Virginia, or one of the large stores?'

'I don't mind, but if I was lucky enough to be given a choice, I'd pick one of the big stores in Liverpool.' Again her grin appeared. 'Not asking for much, am I, Miss? But me dad said I should go for whatever I think would be right for me.'

'He has a point,' Miss Jackson agreed. 'Sadly it isn't always possible to get what you would like, but if you are ambitious, you should set your sights high and do your best. And I think you'd be very suitable for shop work. I'll discuss it further with you tomorrow, after I've seen the Headmistress. I have to report to her when I've interviewed all the girls in the class because she's very keen that our pupils should become gainfully employed and like Miss Bond, I'd prefer to think the nine years you've attended this school haven't been wasted.' She wrote a few words alongside each of their names on her pad then waved a hand to dismiss them. 'No talking when you get back to your desks, please, I need quietness to interview three more girls. Start on the essay I've set you, and make it interesting. There might possibly be a small prize for the writer of the most interesting one.'

Ginny picked up her chair and made her way towards her desk. She had to pass Joan on the way and her friend contorted her face to mouth, 'How did yer get on?'

'Fine, no problem.' Ginny was grinning as she placed the chair behind her desk and sat down. Joan had the knack of contorting her face to any shape, just like her mother. But it was wasted this time because she was to find out for herself what the interview involved when she was called, together with Patsy Booth and Doreen Forrester. The three of them looked petrified and Ginny couldn't understand why because Miss Jackson was really nice.

'Oh, well, let's get this essay started,' Ginny muttered under her breath as she took out her exercise book. It had to be about Christmas, and interesting, so where should she start? Then she had a brainwave. She wanted to work in a shop, and all the shop windows around where she lived had been decorated with tinsel and were displaying Christmas stockings, board games, dolls, balls and fairies to go on top of a tree. There were lots of other things too that parents would be buying to put in their children's stockings, and in every window there was a Father Christmas figure of some kind, in his red outfit and moustache and beard made of cotton wool.

Ginny remembered going to a grotto once when she was very young. It was in a big shop in Liverpool called Blackler's where they'd had a real-life Father Christmas who let you sit on his knee while he gave you a present. She'd thought he was a lovely, jolly man, but many of the younger children were frightened and wouldn't go near him. Their Joey was one. He'd screamed the place down when an over-zealous Father Christmas had tried to get him to sit on his knee. Even the offer of a brightly wrapped gift didn't shut the boy up. He'd taken a dislike to the man and nothing anyone said would get him to change his mind. But his tears ceased and there was amazement in his eyes when they got to the grotto, which was, to their young minds, a real wonderland. Elves, pixies and fairies were all hard at work there, making toys for Santa Claus to put on his sleigh ready for Christmas Eve when he would climb down chimneys to leave the presents. They'd all looked so real, Ginny hadn't realised that the creatures were mechanical. Mind you, she was only about four at the time and had really believed there was a Father Christmas. She knew different now, but it was still a magical time of the year for her. She loved it.

'I've got plenty to write about, but I want to be sure Miss Jackson finds it interesting.' Ginny bit on the end of her pen and looked thoughtful. This might be the last essay she'd ever be asked to write and, although she always got a good report for her work and her

51

behaviour, she wanted this to be extra special. So, after much nibbling on the end of her pen, she decided to go back in time to when she was four years of age.

'I told Miss Jackson me dad was getting me a job in Dunlop's, and she was very pleased because she's heard they're a good firm to work for.' Joan had her arm linked through Ginny's as they walked home. 'What did you tell her?'

'Only that I'd like to work in a shop. She said she'd talk to me about it tomorrow, after Miss Bond has had a chance to see her report.' Ginny was swinging a satchel which she'd had for years. It was scratched and scuffed now, but she'd had good wear out of it. She wasn't going to throw it away, she'd keep it to remind her of her school days. 'Me mam said she'd ask in the local shops if there was anything going, but not to build me hopes up. She reckons if anyone was of a mind to take on an assistant, they'd pick someone with experience who would be of help to them in the busy days leading up to Christmas. They certainly wouldn't want an inexperienced school-leaver under their feet, I'd be more hindrance than help.'

'I wish yer were coming to work in Dunlop's, we could travel there and back together.' Joan had a habit of pouting if things weren't going exactly as she wanted them to, and Ginny knew her well enough to know she would sulk all the way home if she was allowed. So she sought to nip it in the bud now.

'I'm glad you've got a job that yer seem keen on, and pretty soon I might be kicking meself for not taking yer dad up on his offer, but I've set me heart on shop work, Joan, and I'm going to do me best to make it come true, even if I have to go in every shop from here to Liverpool.'

Joan, who was now walking with one foot in the gutter and the other on the pavement, began to feel a bit guilty. Just because she was happy to be going to work in Dunlop's, it didn't mean her friend had to. 'I hope yer get one then, kid, I really do. We'd still see each other every night and we'd have loads to tell each other.'

'Keep yer fingers crossed for me then, and say a little prayer tonight. God will probably have more important things to do than finding me a job, but it doesn't hurt to ask and I'll be reminding him every night until I find one.'

Joan changed the subject. 'Ah, how did yer get on with the essay? I couldn't think of anything interesting, like Miss Jackson said, so I thought, what the heck, and I wrote about getting me first job and how excited I was.'

They turned into their street and Joan, tired of walking hop-along, joined her friend on the pavement. 'What did you write about, kid?'

'Oh, shops mostly,' Ginny told her. 'How they're all decorated up for Christmas, and a bit about a grotto I saw when I was four.'

'Trust you to come up with something like that! I mean, I see the same things as you, but it never entered me head to write about them. The trouble with me is, me mam's always telling me, I've got no imagination.'

'Everyone is different, Joan, it wouldn't do if we were all alike. Everyone has a talent of some description but not everyone gets the one they want. Take me, for instance. I would love to be a painter, making beautiful pictures that people would buy, but it's not likely to happen, is it?'

'Well, if everyone has a talent, what's yours?'

'I don't know, Joan, I haven't found it yet. That's why I want to serve behind a counter, so I can meet different types of people. If I find I'm able to communicate with them, and really get on with them, then I've found what I'm good at. And that will be the talent I've been blessed with.'

'And what about poor me?' Joan put on a woeful face. 'If I've been blessed with anything, it's not half hiding itself.'

'That's where ye're wrong, kid, 'cos I've always known what your talent is. Like yer mam, yer have the ability to make people laugh. Ye're very quick-witted when it comes to humour, and yer do very good impressions. And that really is a talent. I mean, I've got as good a sense of humour as most people, but I'll never be in the same league as you or yer mam.'

When they stopped outside Joan's house, she slung her satchel over her shoulder with one hand, and placed the other on Ginny's arm. 'Yer haven't half cheered me up. I might even ask the Metropole if they'd give me a job as a comedienne.' She chuckled. 'It would beat working in a rubber factory any day.'

'Yer never know yer luck in a big city,' Ginny told her with a smile on her face. 'Now I'm going 'cos I want to see if Mrs Bailey is still staying with us.'

'Ay, that was terrible about her son, wasn't it? She must be feeling very sad about it.'

'I know, I feel really sorry for her. She's got no family here, she's all on her own. That's why I want her to stay with us, so she's got company.' Ginny walked to the next front door and rapped on the knocker. Then she called to her friend, 'I think I'll have a night in, it's too cold to be

53

out. And your mam must be sick to her back teeth of me sitting there every night.'

'Don't be daft, of course she's not! She doesn't mind, honest!'

'No, I'll have a night in. I'll call for yer at half-eight in the morning.' When Beth answered the door, the first words out of Ginny's mouth were, 'Is Mrs Bailey still here, Mam?'

'Yes, sunshine, she is. I've persuaded her to stay for a few nights.'

'Oh, goody-goody!' Ginny entered the room with a broad grin on her face. 'I'm glad ye're going to stay for a while, Mrs Bailey, it's nice to have a visitor.'

'A visitor that turfs yer out of yer bed, sweetheart, is a visitor yer can do without.'

'I don't mind sleeping on the couch, really I don't.' Ginny tilted her head. 'Yer hair looks nice, have yer had dinky curlers in?'

Hannah patted her snow white hair. 'Yer mam was kind enough to use the curling tongs on it, and now I've got as many curls as Shirley Temple. And she took me home to get a change of clothes so I feel much more presentable now.'

Beth watched as her daughter put her satchel down at the side of the couch before hanging up her coat. 'How was school today, sunshine?'

'It was great! Miss Jackson interviewed us in groups of three, and she wanted to know if any of us had thought about what sort of work we'd like to do. The two girls I was with, Sally and Wendy, they're expecting to be interviewed for jobs – Sally in the British Enka and Wendy at Lune Laundry. I told Miss Jackson I'd like shop work, and she said she'd have a word with me tomorrow about it. Then she set us a composition to do and I really enjoyed that. At first I didn't know what to write about, then I remembered going to a grotto when I was very young so I told a story about that. I think it's good, but I'm bound to, seeing as I wrote it. There's a small prize for the essay judged to be the best.'

'Well, I hope yer win it, sweetheart.' Hannah patted the girl's knee. 'And I hope the teacher will let yer bring whatever yer wrote home with yer so we can all read it.'

'I'll bring it home tomorrow and yer can tell me what yer think. If I come in with a long face yer'll know the teacher gave me two out of ten for it. But if I'm smiling from ear to ear, that means I got an eight or a nine.'

'If she doesn't give yer a ten, sweetheart, I'll go down and see her meself.'

'Ginny always gets good marks, Hannah, she's pretty clever. A damn sight more clever than I was at school.' Beth rose from her chair. 'I've got the dinner on the go so I'll make us a cuppa and I can rest me legs for ten minutes. I may as well enjoy the peace while I can. Once Joey comes in, there'll be none for anyone until he's in bed.'

As Beth left the room, Ginny linked her arm through Hannah's. 'I'm glad ye're still here, Mrs Bailey, I hope yer stay for a long time.'

'Only till Friday, sweetheart, then I'm going home to light a fire to warm the house through. The men are coming to see to the partition in the back bedroom for me on Saturday, and I don't want them freezing to death. I've got a paraffin stove which I can put up there while they're working, that should take the chill off the place.'

'I'll come and give yer a hand, if yer like? I can make cups of tea for them, or run any messages yer want.'

'Yer'll be welcome, sweetheart, as long as I'm not taking yer away from yer mam. She might want yer to get messages for her.'

Beth came in carrying a wooden tray with three cups and a plate of biscuits on. 'Muck in before our Joey comes. If he sees the biscuits he'll scoff the lot.' She placed the tray on the table before handing the cups out. 'I'm going to sit back and enjoy this. And if yer feel like a laugh, sunshine, I'll tell yer what yer Auntie Flo got up to at the shops today.'

Hannah put a hand to her mouth as she chuckled. 'Oh, dear, she's so funny. Not that I thought it funny at the time, like, but afterwards we all had a good laugh.'

Knowing what tricks her Auntie Flo could play, there was laughter in Ginny's eyes when she asked, 'What's she been doing now, Mam?'

Beth had her hands around the cup for warmth. 'We all went out together this morning, all five of us. After posting the letter off to Claire, we called into the butcher's. I wanted some liver to have with the bacon I've got over from yesterday, and mashed potatoes. Bill the butcher asked me first what I wanted, and I said three-quarters of liver. While he was weighing it, Flo told me that she'd like to get a pound of liver because her feller was partial to it.'

Beth could feel the laughter bubbling inside of her and she played safe by putting her cup down. 'Anyway, Bill handed me liver over and asked me for one and tuppence. After I'd paid him, he weighed some more then wrapped it up and held it out to Flo with a request for one and sixpence. What happened then was priceless. Yer know how dramatic me mate can be? Well, suffice it to say she excelled herself this morning. With her folded arms pushing up that great big bosom of hers, her chin jutting out and her eyes narrowed, she said, "One and six!

What's the matter with yer, d'yer think I was born yesterday or something? Yer've just charged me mate one and tuppence and now yer've got the nerve to try and diddle me! Well, ye're not on, see, 'cos ye're only getting the same as me mate gave yer."

'The butcher was flabbergasted as he stood there holding out the parcel with a look of bewilderment on his face. And the rest of us didn't know where to put ourselves. I mean, yer never know what she's going to get up to next, and I wasn't going to get involved. I was surprised at Bill, though, 'cos she's pulled his leg dozens of times over the years. Anyway, he said, "Yer asked for a pound of liver, Flo, and that's one and six. Beth here only got three-quarters, that's why she was charged less. Now can yer pay me, please, so I can serve the other ladies?" But it wasn't that easy 'cos Flo was in good form. "I didn't ask yer for no pound of bleedin' liver! I want the same as me mate, one and tuppence worth!" Then Bill appealed to her to be reasonable. "Yer said yer'd like a pound of liver 'cos yer husband's partial to it. I heard yer with me own ears, Flo, so don't be coming it." And didn't the bold one start rolling her coat sleeves up as though she was ready for a fight! "I never said I wanted a pound of liver! I told me mate I'd *like* a pound, same as I'd like a leg of lamb, if I had the money to pay for it! Which, for your information, I haven't got. So it serves yer bleedin' well right for listening in to private conversations. Let that be a lesson to yer in the future, Mr Bill Symonds, 'cos some people might not be as understanding as me. But in the meantime, take a bit of liver out of that parcel and I'll give yer the one and tuppence I owe yer." '

Ginny gasped. 'She didn't say that, did she? Ooh, I bet Mr Symonds was mad having to do that for her.'

'Well, he didn't have to, sunshine, 'cos Lizzie said she'd take the pound of liver 'cos that's what she came in for. And that would have solved the problem if Flo hadn't been acting daft. She glared at Lizzie and said, "Do yer mind, Mrs O'Leary? This is a transaction between me and our family butcher, who I have been dealing with for years, and who I'm on very hintimate terms with." ' But Beth thought she'd better not go any further down that road, not to a fourteen-year-old girl. What Flo had gone on to say had set the other four women blushing, and the poor butcher wishing it was closing time. 'Anyway, sunshine, after causing all that trouble, our next-door neighbour only managed to put an angelic look on her clock and ask if none of us had any bleedin' sense of humour! "God, but ye're a miserable lot! Yer wouldn't know a joke if it jumped up and hit yer in the face! Bill knew I was joking, didn't yer, lad? Yeah, of course he did! So give us that ruddy liver and put the one and six on the slate until pay day." Now everyone knows Bill won't give anything on tick, and he kept tight hold of that parcel with a look of determination on his face. "No money, no liver, Flo, so please yerself." '

Ginny was all ears. 'And what happened then?'

'Tilly Mint had had the right money in her hand all along, and she passed it over, saying, "The butcher in Stanley Road gives tick, I'll go there in future 'cos he'll welcome me custom." And Bill said, "I hope that's not an idle threat, Flo. I know I should feel sorry for the bloke in Stanley Road, but every man for himself. At least my wife wouldn't have to put up with me having nightmares every night." '

Beth was startled when there was a hammering on the front door then. 'My God, anyone would think there's a fire!' She hastened to the door, saying, 'If it's our Joey, I'll kill him.'

His cheeky face grinned up at her. 'I heard that, Mam! I hope yer don't kill me before I have me tea 'cos I'm starving.' As he passed her, he winked. 'After all they don't send anyone to the gallows on an empty tummy.'

Joey greeted Hannah warmly. 'Hi-ya, Mrs Bailey! Has me mam been looking after yer today?'

'I've been more than well looked after, sweetheart! I've had four very kind ladies watching over me. With yer mam, there was Mrs Flynn, Mrs Henderson and Mrs O'Leary.'

'Blimey! The terrible four! I bet yer've got earache! One on their own is bad enough, but four of them . . . yer deserve a medal.'

'Watch it, sunshine,' Beth told him, 'ye're not too old for a smack.'

He spied the almost empty plate. 'There's two biscuits there, are they for me?'

Beth told a little fib. 'Yeah, we saved them 'specially for yer.'

Joey eyed the contents of the plate, then his sister. 'How many have you had, Ginny? And this is scout's honour, so no telling lies.'

'Seeing as I'm not in the scouts, that rule doesn't apply to me. Anyway, if yer must know, we've all had ten each.'

His face split into a grin. 'Ah, I've caught yer out there! Yer see, when I looked in the biscuit tin this morning there was only twelve. That's wiped yer eye for yer, hasn't it?'

Beth gasped, 'You cheeky article! I hope yer didn't touch the biscuits with yer dirty hands?'

'No, I just shook the tin a bit.' His eyes bright with stifled laughter, he said, 'I've had me suspicions for a long time that I've been missing out on things by not coming straight home from school, and I've proved meself right now. So, in future, I'll race yer home, Ginny, and beat yer to the biscuit tin.' He picked up the plate and held it out to Hannah. 'Seeing as yer've had ten, Mrs Bailey, yer may as well make it the even dozen.'

Hannah could see he was joking, and went along with it. 'No, thanks, sweetheart, I'll have no room for me dinner if I eat any more. Yer see, besides the ten biscuits, we also had a cream slice each and a jam doughnut.'

'Yer greedy beggars! In that case I might as well eat these biscuits, save them from being thrown in the bin.'

Beth chuckled. 'What bin is that, sunshine? We don't need a bin with you here.' She happened to glance at the clock then and a cry of surprise left her lips as she jumped to her feet. 'Holy suffering ducks! Yer dad will be in soon and I haven't got the liver on! He'll think I've been sitting on me backside all day.'

As she was passing her son on the way to the kitchen, he put his arms around her waist. 'I won't snitch on yer, Mam. If he finds out yer've been eating biscuits while yer were sitting on yer backside, it won't be me what's told him.'

She dropped a kiss on his head. 'Only thirteen and a blackmailer already! Well, two can play at that game, me laddo. You snitch, and yer'll only get a scrap of liver.'

The smell of liver and bacon wafted towards the living room, and when Andy came in, rubbing his hands from the cold, he let out a sigh of pleasure. 'That smell was worth working all day for. Don't bother putting it on a plate, love, I'll eat it out of the frying pan.'

Beth came through, wiping her hands on a tea towel. She lifted her face for a kiss and shivered. 'Yer nose is like ice, sunshine, it's a wonder it hasn't dropped off.'

'I'm frozen through to the marrow, love, it's not just me nose. The wind is bitter and it gets everywhere. But five minutes in front of the fire and I'll be fine.' He held out his hands to the flames and looked sideways at Hannah. 'I walked up the street with Dennis, and he said to tell yer his mate will be dropping the wood off tomorrow at your house between two and three. He got the lot for five bob, which is very cheap. Particularly as it's being delivered.'

'I'll go down and sit with yer until it comes, sunshine,' Beth said. 'They can leave it in the hall and our husbands will take it upstairs on Saturday.'

'Everyone has been so kind to me. I'm lucky to have such wonderful friends.' Hannah hugged herself. 'I can't wait to hear when Claire and the children are coming, I'm dying to see them.' Her eyes clouded over briefly as she remembered the reason for the family's return home. Then she pulled herself together, not wanting to sadden these people who had been so good to her. 'Five years is so long.'

'Yer'll have plenty of time to make it up, sunshine, and it's something to look forward to.' Beth made for the kitchen. 'That ruddy liver will be calling me for everything for letting it burn. It's a wonder it hasn't jumped out of the frying pan and on to the plates by now. I bet it'll spit fat at me for spite.'

'Don't let it get the better of yer, Mam,' Ginny called. 'Just send for Auntie Flo, she'll sort it out.'

Chapter Six

When Miss Bond, the headmistress, came into the classroom, the whispering and chattering stopped immediately and there was complete silence. She seldom had to raise her voice to naughty children; the lifting of a single eyebrow was enough to frighten the living daylights out of the cheekiest pupil. 'Carry on with what you're doing while I have a few words with Miss Jackson,' she told them.

All heads were immediately lowered, but not before they'd glimpsed the exercise books held in her hands. She must have read the compositions they'd written, and curiosity had the most daring girls sneaking a look while hoping they were the one to win the prize. The odds on being the winner were thirty-four to one, but there was hope in each heart that they would be the lucky one. They weren't to find out just yet, though, because the headmistress left the room with the exercise books still in her hand.

Miss Jackson rapped on her desk for attention. 'Miss Bond wishes to speak to the four girls who said they would like shop work. That's Virginia, Alice, Doreen and Marie. Please go along to her office now. The rest of you, carry on with what you were doing.'

The four girls slipped from behind their desks and walked quietly into the corridor. Once out of earshot of the teacher, they all began to talk at once. 'I wonder what she wants us for?' Doreen asked, while the others shrugged their shoulders. 'There's only one way to find out,' Ginny said, 'let's go.'

Miss Bond nodded her head in greeting. 'There aren't any chairs, I'm afraid, so you'll have to stand.' She tutted when she saw two of the girls slouch. 'Alice and Doreen, straighten your shoulders, please, and hold your head high. When you go for an interview you will be judged on your knowledge, politeness and deportment. If you are considered lacking in these qualities, it will be very difficult for you to find rewarding employment.'

The headmistress searched through some papers on her desk before finding what she wanted. 'When being interviewed by Miss Jackson, each of you said you would like to work in a shop. Now it so happens that I have information regarding Woolworth's in the city centre. They intend to take on two school-leavers after the Christmas period is over, and they will be interviewing applicants for the job over the next two days. To be eligible for an interview, you need cards from the Labour Exchange. I've been in touch with the local office and you are to present yourselves there at eight-thirty in the morning. After filling in the questions on these cards, you will take them to Woolworth's in Church Street where the interviews will take place. You shouldn't have any problem answering the questions, but if you do a clerk at the Exchange will assist you. Of course, you won't be the only ones being interviewed for the two positions, there will be girls from other schools, so you'll have to give a good account of yourselves as competition will be fierce. Oh, you will need to ask your parents for the tram fare into the city and back again. You can return to school when the interviews are over.'

Miss Bond studied the four girls standing before her. 'I must stress that appearances are important, so please make an extra effort. And now, are there any questions you would like to ask? Don't be afraid, I won't bite your head off.'

'Will we be getting a reference from the school to take with us?' Ginny asked. 'Whoever interviews us might ask for one.'

'You will be given one before you go home. It will be in a sealed envelope and under no circumstances are you to tamper with that. Make sure there are no finger marks on it either or that may count against you. Now, are there any further questions?'

'No, Miss Bond,' said four voices in unison. 'Thank you, Miss Bond.'

'Very well, you are dismissed. Close the door behind you.'

When the girls had left, the headmistress sat perfectly still staring at the closed door, her brow furrowed. Two of those pupils were in with an even chance. They hadn't wasted their years at school, forever working diligently to be near the top of the class in every subject. They were always clean and tidy in appearance, polite and pleasant. They would acquit themselves well in any interview, and be a credit to the school. The other two, however, didn't stand an earthly and would end up in a job that would never get them anywhere. They had no drive or ambition and had spent their school life being bottom of the class in every subject. The pity of it was they didn't care, and neither did their parents who had never questioned the end-of-term reports which showed their children weren't making the progress necessary to equip them for a decent future.

Miss Bond sighed. The school report these two girls would be taking to their interview would be a true account of their years here and signed by teachers who had taken them in their various subjects. That would hardly help them when they went to Woolworth's tomorrow but one could not falsify a reference, it wouldn't be fair on an employer. But even though she knew they didn't stand a chance, she had to give them the same opportunity as any other pupil.

The dinnertime bell sounded and while there was a mad scramble as some of the girls couldn't get out of the classroom quick enough, others looked at each other and shrugged their shoulders. They'd waited all morning to be told who the winner of the best composition was, but it had never been mentioned. A couple of Ginny's friends coaxed her to ask Miss Jackson, so when she was passing the teacher's desk she cleared her throat and ventured to ask, 'Will we find out today who won the prize, Miss Jackson?'

The teacher nodded. 'Sometime this afternoon, Virginia. Miss Bond took them home with her, but thirty-four essays can't be read in a couple of hours so she's finishing them off this morning.' She smiled at the pupil who was a particular favourite of hers. 'In a little while there will be a lot of disappointed faces in the classroom, and one happy one.'

Joan dug her friend in the ribs as they left the room. 'I bet it won't be my face that's the happy one.'

'Now how d'yer know? Yer can be a right misery guts sometimes, Joan, yer put a jinx on yerself. We all stand the same chance of winning, so have a little faith in yerself.' Ginny linked her arm as they walked through the school gates and turned in the direction of their street. 'I'm more excited about going to Woolworth's for an interview than I am about who wins the prize. Just think, working in such a big store! It would be brilliant.'

'I don't know why they're bothering to send Alice and Doreen for an interview, they can't spell for toffee and they certainly can't add up! You and Marie should walk it, no problem.'

'Ay, we're not the only ones applying for the jobs, there'll be hundreds of girls after them. The Labour Exchange notify every school in the neighbourhood, so me and Marie will be lucky to get a look in.' Ginny wagged her head from side to side. 'Ooh, I won't half be saying some prayers tonight, I can tell yer. I never in me wildest dreams thought I'd get an interview for one of the biggest shops in Liverpool.'

'If yer get put on the sweet counter I'll be coming down to get a free slab of chocolate.' Joan slipped her arm through her friend's and pulled her close. The wind was bitter and penetrated their many layers of clothing. 'It's no good having a mate working in a shop if yer don't make use of her.'

'Yer can forget that, it would be stealing!' Ginny said with some force. 'I've never stolen anything in me life and I've no intention of starting now.'

'Keep yer hair on, I was only joking! Anyway, it would cost me more to get the tram there and back into Liverpool than it would be to buy meself some chocolate.'

Ginny had a fit of the giggles and her shoulders began to shake. Chuckling loudly, she said, 'They make car tyres in Dunlop's – yer'd have a job putting one of them in yer pocket without anyone seeing yer.'

Joan's imagination took over. 'Ay, I could put one up me jumper and people would think I had a big bust.' Her hazel eyes, so like her mother's, were bright with laughter. 'Mrs Henderson would have nothing on me, I'd have twice as big a bosom as she's got.'

'Ah, yes, but Auntie Flo's breasts move up and down, and they're soft. A tyre wouldn't move, it would be rigid. And if yer bumped into anyone yer'd leave them with a bruise!'

They were still laughing when they turned into Edith Road. 'I'll see yer later,' Ginny said. 'I hope me mam's got a good fire going, me feet are like ice.'

'Mine too! But we'll soon warm up with a hot cup of tea and a few sandwiches.' Joan slipped her hand from her pocket to knock on her door. 'I'll see yer later.'

'Be ready when I knock,' Ginny warned, knowing how hard it was to prise her friend away from a warm fire. 'If ye're not, I'll go on without yer 'cos I don't want to be late.'

Joan's mam was standing behind her when she answered Ginny's knock. 'I've just been hearing about yer getting an interview at Woolworth's tomorrow, girl, and I'm over the moon for yer.' Dot Flynn shivered and wrapped arms around her slim waist. 'I bet yer mam's pleased for yer?'

'She's almost as excited as I am, Auntie Dot, and so was Mrs Bailey. The trouble is, they're talking as though I've already got the job! I told them there'll be hundreds of girls applying and there's only two jobs going, so they shouldn't get their hopes up. But yer know what me mam's like, she thinks it's in the bag. I wish it was, but we could all end up disappointed.'

'I'll keep me fingers crossed for yer, girl, and say a few prayers. It would be a real feather in yer cap if yer got it.'

'Ye're not kidding, I'd be walking on air. I'll not sleep tonight, that's a dead cert.' Ginny eyed her friend. 'Come on, Joan, I don't want to be late.'

'Walk quick and yer won't feel the cold,' Dot called after them. 'Ta-ra.'

The friends linked arms before setting off at a brisk rate. 'Are yer coming up to ours tonight,' Joan asked, 'or will yer be too busy?'

'I'll be too busy. Me mam's going to press me clothes and I want to wash me hair and polish me shoes. This is one time I want to look me very best.'

The school bell was ringing as they walked back through the gates. 'Just in time,' Ginny said as they joined the line of girls waiting to be let in. As soon as the double doors were opened, she grabbed Joan's hand and they elbowed their way through the scramble to get to Miss Jackson's classroom. She grinned when she heard her friend mutter, 'It's stupid having to do this, anyone would think we were kids.'

'To all intents and purposes, Joan, while we're still at school we *are* kids. When we draw our first week's wage packet, then we'll be young ladies.'

That brought a smile to her friend's face. 'Yeah, won't it be the gear? Long stockings with a seam up the back and high-heeled shoes. And once me mam's got over the shock of them, I'll be buying a bright red lipstick.'

A loud rap on the teacher's desk had Ginny scurrying to sit down. 'Quiet now, girls, so I can hear myself speak. Miss Bond will be along in about an hour to announce the winner of the prize for the best composition. Until then, I'm going to write some sums on the blackboard for you to copy into your exercise book.' Miss Jackson took up a piece of chalk and began to write numbers on the board. 'You see there are simple additions, subtractions and multiplications. I want them written neatly and, as most of them are fairly easy, I expect many of you to get them all right.' She moved away from the board so all the girls had a clear view. 'Copy them into your books and the task should keep you going for an hour.'

Arithmetic was one of Ginny's strongest subjects so she had no problem and had finished in less than half the time allotted. But she kept her head down, bit on the end of her pencil as many of the girls were doing, and pretended that, like them, she was having difficulty with some of the sums. To sit back now and look around would make it seem as though she was big-headed and swanking, and would make the other girls annoyed. So she concentrated on the one thing that was uppermost in her mind and which was causing her tummy to turn somersaults, and that was the interview tomorrow.

She'd only ever been in the Woolworth's store in Church Street the once, and that was a few years ago when her mam took her into town for a treat on her birthday. They'd gone to the Kardomah first, for a pot of tea and a toasted tea-cake, and she could still remember how she'd sat wide-eyed with wonder when they were served by a waitress in a black dress worn with a white lace pinny and headdress. That was a thrill and an experience she'd never forgotten. And when they'd come out of there, they'd crossed the busy road, dodging tram cars, to the large-fronted store which was Woolworth's where nothing in the shop cost more than sixpence. Her mam had only bought a reel of black cotton, and as she was in a hurry to get back home and start on the dinner there wasn't much time for Ginny to look around as she would have wished. But as she was being led by the hand past the many counters, she was amazed to see such a variety of things on sale. There was the longest sweet counter she'd ever seen in her life, one with combs and hairbrushes, and another with mirrors and purses. She didn't have time to look properly as she was being pulled along, but she'd say the counter she liked best of the ones she saw was one selling little animals made out of lead. How she would have loved to look at them properly and hold them.

Ginny was miles away in her thoughts. When she felt herself being prodded sharply, she was startled. She turned to see Kathleen, the girl sitting next to her, rolling her eyes and jerking her head towards the front of the classroom. Ginny followed her eyes and sat up straight when she saw Miss Bond facing the class. The headmistress was looking quite pleased with herself, and her usually harsh face was wearing a wide smile.

'I know you are all eagerly waiting to see who has won the prize for the best composition, but I would like to say a few words before announcing the result. I was very impressed with the quality of your work and would like to congratulate each and every one of you for using your imagination so well. I was so impressed, I found it very difficult choosing a winner. In the end I was left with two which were both excellent and impossible to choose between. So there are two worthy winners. The prize was a pair of warm woollen gloves, very acceptable in this cold weather, and Miss Jackson kindly went to the shops in her dinner break to buy an extra pair.'

Miss Bond paused. Although she didn't do it on purpose, to add drama to the situation, that was precisely what it did do because there wasn't a girl in the class whose heart wasn't pounding and who wasn't sending a silent prayer up to heaven asking that she be one of the lucky ones. 'The two worthy winners are Sally Hunter and Virginia Porter. If they will come forward, I will present them with their well-deserved prizes.'

Ginny wished the floor would open and swallow her up when she felt all eyes on her. Some were filled with envy, some were even hostile, as though it was her decision to name herself the winner. But mostly they seemed happy for her. She didn't look at Joan because she knew she'd burst out laughing if her friend pulled a funny face, and when she reached the teacher's desk she could tell Sally was embarrassed too because her face was bright red. Fortunately the prizes were handed over without a fuss, and a couple of minutes later the two girls were back in their places.

'Nice work, Ginny,' said Kathleen from the next desk. 'I had a feeling you'd be in with a chance.'

'I'm over the moon! First the interview for a job, and now this. I can't believe it! Me luck seems to be in, all right.' Ginny was feeling very happy and proud. All she longed for now was the day to end so she could run home and tell her family the good news. And Mrs Bailey, of course, 'cos she was almost part of their family now.

'Ye're a jammy beggar, you are,' Joan said on their way home. 'I bet yer any money yer get that job as well.'

'I'm not betting on that, it would be asking for trouble. There'll be some clever girls there tomorrow, the best from all the local schools, so it won't be a walkover for anyone.' Ginny turned her head. 'Any news about your application for Dunlop's yet?'

'Me dad said he should have some news tonight. I hope so, 'cos I can't wait to start work and earn some money.'

Ginny giggled. 'Those long stocking with the seams down the back, and the high-heeled shoes, they're getting to yer, aren't they?'

'Yeah, I'll say! I can't wait to walk down our street all dolled up.' Joan turned her head to make sure there was no one behind them before leaning towards her friend's ear and asking softly, 'Ay, will yer be opening that letter to see what it says in yer report?'

'I certainly will not! We were told not to open them, and I'm doing as I was told. Anyway, yer can't open an envelope what's been stuck down without it getting torn, so I wouldn't even think about it.'

'Yer could steam it open and no one would know. Me mam's done that before today and yer definitely couldn't tell. All yer've got to do is hold it over a steaming kettle and the flap comes open dead easy.'

'You're terrible, you are, Joan Flynn! Yer'll never get to heaven when yer die.' Ginny managed to look horrified, but inside she was laughing. In her mind's eye, she could see Auntie Dot standing over a boiling kettle, her tongue hanging out of the side of her mouth as she concentrated on keeping her fingers away from the steam. And not for one moment would she see any wrong in what she was doing. If the contents of the letter had anything to do with her or one of her family, then she would consider she had more right to know than anyone. 'My mam certainly wouldn't open it, nor would she let me. So I'll just have to wait until after the interview to find out.'

'Oh, I couldn't, I'd be a nervous wreck.' If you weren't looking at Joan while she was speaking, you would really think it was her mother. 'I mean, what if it's a lousy report? Yer could be sitting there, like a lemon, watching someone reading that yer were as thick as two short planks! Ooh, I'd be mortified!'

'I don't think I need worry about that, Joan, I'm far from being as thick as two short planks. And neither are you, so stop running yerself down. Keep telling yerself ye're as good as the next one.'

'But I'm not as clever as you. Ye're in the top three and have been since we started school. I've never been able to catch yer up, I'm too thick.'

'Ye're not thick at all! There's thirty-four in the class and yer've never gone below ninth, so if you're thick, what does that make the other girls? Stop feeling full of self-pity, or yer'll talk yerself out of a job.'

Joan grinned. 'Ay, yer sounded just like Miss Bond, a proper bossy boots. If yer were interviewing me for a job, I'd have wet me knickers by now.'

'Oh, charming, I must say.' They turned into Edith Road and Ginny could see her mother standing outside on the step talking to Mrs Henderson. 'Come on, let's run. There's me mam and I can't wait to tell her.' She took to her heels with Joan running beside her. 'I bet she'll be tickled pink.'

'D'yer know what I'm frightened of, kid? That ye're turning into a bighead. I couldn't stand having a friend who thought she was the cat's whiskers.'

'If yer ever think there's any danger of that, just take me to one side and give me a good talking to. And if I'm not too busy bragging, I'll listen to yer.'

Beth smiled when her daughter stopped in front of her, panting and gasping for breath. 'What's the big rush for? Is it the cold or are yer hungry?'

It was Joan who laughingly told her, 'Yer daughter wants to show off, Auntie Beth, that's all. Honest to God, she's never stopped bragging since we came out of school. It's been so bad I had to go down an entry twice to be sick.'

Flo's arms were folded under her bosom for warmth, and for a second she deliberated on whether to bring one out to wipe her nose, or leave them where they were nice and warm. In the end she decided that if this conversation turned out to be interesting, she couldn't stand there with her nose running. Mind you, it wouldn't worry her, she wasn't fussy. But Beth was a stickler for manners and clean habits. Not that she'd say anything, like, but her eyes would speak volumes. So an arm was pulled free and a hand quickly swiped across her nose before being returned to its warm spot. 'Oh, aye, queen, which entries were these, then?'

Joan wasn't her mother's daughter for nothing, and her reply came quickly. 'I couldn't tell yer, Auntie Flo, 'cos I was too busy being sick to notice the names of the streets. But I can find out for yer tomorrow if yer like.'

Cocky little article, Flo thought, her face looking the picture of innocence. 'That's good of yer, queen, I'd really appreciate it.'

'Why d'yer want to know that, Flo?' Beth asked with a twinkle in her eyes. 'Are yer thinking of taking a mop and bucket to clean up the sick?'

'Curiosity, queen, that's all. I mean yer've got to keep up with the news, haven't yer? Otherwise yer get left behind.'

Ginny stamped her foot in mock impatience. 'Will yer all shut up and listen to my news, please, before the novelty wears off?'

'What is it, sunshine?' her mother asked. 'I'm all ears.'

Ginny opened her satchel and brought out the bag with the gloves inside. 'I won the best composition and these gloves are me prize.'

'Yer weren't the only winner,' Joan reminded her, thinking this swanking could get out of hand if it wasn't nipped in the bud. 'Sally Hunter won as well.'

'I was going to tell me mam that if yer'd given me the chance.' Ginny watched her mother examining the black woollen gloves. 'They're nice, aren't they, Mam? Just what I need for this cold weather.'

Before Beth could answer, Flo had decided that the news wasn't worth freezing to death for, especially as she had a fire roaring up the chimney. And anyway, her feller wouldn't be interested in a pair of woollen gloves. He was only ever interested if someone won on the gee-gees. 'I'd better get in and see to the dinner. But yer've done well, queen, and I hope yer luck holds out for the interview tomorrow. Ta-ra for now.'

'Ta-ra, sunshine, I'm getting in out of the cold meself,' Beth said, rubbing her arms. 'Come in and tell Hannah yer news, Ginny, she'll be made up for yer. And she's got some news of her own, which she's been waiting to tell yer.'

'Ooh, what is it, Mrs Porter?' Joan asked, afraid she was going to miss something. 'Go on, tell us.'

'It wouldn't be right for me to be giving Mrs Bailey's news out, sunshine, she might not like it. So wait until tomorrow and Ginny will tell yer.'

Her daughter was eager to hear what Mrs Bailey's news was, and to pass on her own. So she patted her friend's arm, saying, 'I'm going in. But don't forget I won't be calling for yer in the morning 'cos I've to be at the Labour Exchange for eight-thirty. But I'm to go into school after the interview, so I'll tell yer everything then. Are yer going to wish me luck?'

'Yeah, of course I am. I hope yer amaze them with yer brilliance.'

Hannah was waiting with her arms outstretched when Ginny entered the room. 'Come and give us a kiss, yer clever girl. I told yer yer'd win, didn't I?'

Ginny gave her a hug. 'See the posh gloves I won? There'll be no flies on me tomorrow, they'll all be bluebottles.' She hung her coat up and then sat next to Hannah on the couch. 'Me mam said yer had some news to tell me?'

'Yes, some wonderful news. I had a letter from Claire to say her and the children will be coming on Wednesday, and they'll be staying in Liverpool for good.'

'That was quick, wasn't it? Yer weren't expecting an answer for another few days.'

'She got my letter by the morning post, wrote a letter back and had it in the pillar box in time for the dinnertime collection. She says she can't wait to get back up here, and the children are really looking forward to coming back to the place they call home. They're only renting the house so there's no problem there, and what furniture they've got she's going to sell. Yer see, it would cost a lot of money to have it sent from Birmingham to here, so she's going to sell the lot. Except personal things, like photographs and ornaments, she intends to bring them with her.'

'I can tell by yer face that ye're really happy now, and I'm pleased for yer. It's been a good day for both of us, hasn't it?'

Beth could feel tears stinging the backs of her eyes as she watched. Her daughter so young, yet so understanding and caring, had found a place in her heart for this woman who was old enough to be her grandmother. A strong bond had grown between them over the last few days, and it was that bond which had helped Hannah through the darkest patch in her life.

'So, Mrs Bailey, we've both been lucky today, eh?' Ginny pressed her face close. 'Let's hope my luck stays with me tomorrow.'

'It will, sweetheart, I know it will.'

'Well, I intend to give it everything I've got. I'm going to wash me hair now and put it in pipe cleaners, then I'm going to polish me shoes until I can see me face in them. And I'm going to try and get around me mam to lend me her handbag so I can keep the envelope with me report in clean. I don't think I'd stand much chance if I walked in with me old school satchel. Mind you, if I did, they might give me the job because they feel sorry for me.'

'I've got a small black handbag in the wardrobe, sunshine, yer can borrow that,' Beth said. 'I never use it 'cos it doesn't hold very much, but it's really smart.'

Ginny's blue eyes lit up in her pretty face. 'Oh, boy! Oh, boy! Oh, boy! Am I going to look glamorous or am I going to look glamorous? Watch out, Mr Woolworth, 'cos here comes Miss Virginia Porter.'

Chapter Seven

Ginny had arranged to meet her classmates outside the Labour Exchange at half-past eight, but because she was afraid of being late she'd set out very early. There was no one else standing outside the building and she regretted not spending an extra ten minutes in front of the fire. But she really wouldn't have enjoyed those ten minutes because her heart was racing and her tummy felt as though there were hundreds of butterflies flapping their wings inside it.

She glanced up and down the road, hoping for a sight of the other three girls, and sighed when there was no sign. If they didn't come soon, they stood no chance of getting into town in time for the interview. But she wasn't going to be late because of them, so if they weren't here in five minutes, she'd go into the Labour Exchange building on her own. The new woollen gloves, of which she was very proud, were keeping her hands nice and warm, but her feet were beginning to feel the cold with standing still. It was a real wintry morning, damp and foggy, and the people who passed were well wrapped up against the cold. Many of them had huge mufflers wrapped around their neck and covering most of their face, leaving only noses and eyes exposed. Their breath hung suspended in the cold air for seconds after they'd moved on.

'Hi-ya, Ginny.' Marie Whittaker's voice startled Ginny, who was looking in the opposite direction. 'Haven't the other two turned up yet?'

She gave a sigh of relief before saying, 'I was beginning to think none of yer were going to turn up.' Then she grinned. 'Yer nose is so red yer could warm yer hands on it.'

'I can't feel it so it must be numb.' Marie was a pretty girl with naturally curly mousy hair and a winning smile that showed off a set of perfect white teeth. 'In fact I don't feel anything! I don't know if it's with the cold or fright.'

'I'm nervous myself so ye're not on yer own,' Ginny admitted. 'But me mam said everyone is afraid when they go after their first job. And

73

she also told me there was no point in worrying 'cos it wouldn't alter things. The worst that can happen is that we don't get the job, and even if that does happen, at least we'll have gained a little experience and won't be so frightened next time.' She glanced nervously up and down the road before shaking her head.

'They should be well here by now. And what happens if they've no intention of turning up, and we're stood here like a pair of lemons wasting our time? In fact, because of them, we could miss the chance of getting a job. A good job, at that! One I'd give me eye teeth for.'

'Miss Bond won't be happy with them if they don't turn up,' Marie said. 'In fact they'll be in serious trouble.'

'Yer don't think that'll worry them, do yer? There's only another week at school so they're not going to lose any sleep over Miss Bond.' Ginny did two quick turns of her head then took Marie's arm. 'They mightn't care about getting themselves a decent job, but you and I do! So let's go in and get the cards we need for the interview. If we leave it any longer we might just miss out.'

Marie nodded. 'Okay, let's go! But I'm surprised their mothers didn't make sure they set off early enough. Mine did. She had me out of bed by seven and made me get stripped off and washed in the kitchen sink before she'd give me any breakfast.'

'Like my mam, she's probably looking forward to yer bringing a wage in. I know we won't be earning much, but even a few bob will make a difference to my mam. She won't have to rob Peter every week to pay Paul.'

Marie leaned closer and whispered, 'I wonder if that's the same Peter and Paul that my mam has dealings with?' They were in the entrance hall of the building now, with double doors facing them. 'Ooh, I wonder where we're supposed to go?'

'All the people I've seen coming in have gone through those doors, so as they're the only ones, I imagine that's where we need to go.' As Ginny pushed open the doors and strode through them confidently it was her mother's parting words ringing in her ears that bolstered that confidence and put an extra spring in her step. 'We'd better ask at this counter.'

There were two clerks sitting behind the counter, one busy talking to a man and making notes, the other riffling through a pile of papers in front of him. 'Excuse me,' Ginny said, 'we've been told by our headmistress to come here to collect cards we need to go for an interview at Woolworth's. Can yer tell us what we have to do?'

The young clerk nodded. 'I can help you. Is it the Woolworth store in Church Street?'

'Yes.' And feeling proud of having got this far, Ginny couldn't help adding, 'Me and me friend are dead excited.'

The clerk grinned. 'There's only two jobs going, and dozens of girls will be after them. But the two that are taken on will be lucky 'cos it's a good firm to work for.' He bent down to reach under the counter and was lost to view for a few seconds. When he reappeared, he had two white cards in his hand. 'These are no good without your school references. Do you have them with you?'

With more than a little pride, Ginny tapped the neat patent leather clutch handbag which had been a present from her father to her mother about five years ago. But because it wasn't serviceable, only fit for if you were getting dolled up, it had never been used. 'Mine's in here, being kept nice and clean.' She looked enquiringly at her classmate. 'Have yer got yours, Marie?' When the girl nodded, Ginny smiled. 'All present and accounted for.'

Two white cards were passed across the counter. 'You can fill them in here, and when you've completed them, I'll check to make sure the questions have been answered correctly.'

Ginny looked past the clerk to the large round clock on the wall behind him. 'It's turned half-eight, we're going to have to hurry. It wouldn't look good if we turned up late for an interview.'

The clerk pulled one of the cards back. 'I'll fill it in then. I want your full name and address, and your date of birth.' He was writing quickly. 'School and name of headmistress?' In a matter of minutes, both cards had been completed and the young man was wishing them luck.

'Thank you.' Ginny took care putting the card in her bag. That was to be kept as clean as the letter. 'Yer've been very kind.'

'Just be pleasant, but not forward, and keep those smiles on your faces. Then you won't go far wrong. Those are the main things an employer will be looking for when taking on someone who will be working with the public.' The clerk looked at the queue building up behind the girls and could see heads being shaken impatiently. 'Good luck.'

Once they were out of the building, Ginny took to her heels. 'Come on, Marie, let's make a run for it.' They reached the bottom of the street and turned the corner into a busy main road where they would catch a tram. And who should they see sauntering along as though they had all the time in the world but their two classmates, Alice and Doreen?

'Hey, where d'yer think ye're off to?' Alice asked. 'We were supposed to be sticking together, and here's you two sneaking off.'

'We're not sneaking off,' Ginny said, a look of disgust on her face when she noted the other girls' uncombed hair and unpolished shoes. No effort had been made to smarten themselves up for what should be an important event in their lives. 'Why should we sneak away from you? To hear you talk, anyone would think we're frightened of yer.'

Alice brazened it out. 'Well, yer can just come back to the Exchange with us or we'll tell Miss Bond on yer.'

'I don't care who yer tell, I'm not coming back with yer. If you can't be bothered getting out of bed on time, that's your worry, not mine. I'm going after a job, and I'm not turning up late because of you two lazy beggars.'

'Me neither,' Marie told them, taking some of Ginny's courage on board. 'We're getting the first tram that comes along whether yer like it or not.'

Alice, the bolder of the two girls and a noted bully, pushed her face close to Ginny's. 'If we get into trouble through you, yer snotty-nosed cow, yer'll be sorry. I'll get yer in the playground and by the time I've finished belting yer, yer'll be running home to yer mammy, crying like the baby yer are.'

While Marie backed away a little, Ginny tutted and shook her head. 'Oh, dear, oh, dear! Aren't you feeling brave this morning! Well, yer don't frighten me with yer threats. In fact, it wouldn't worry me if yer brought yer mam and dad to me.' She caught sight of a tram trundling towards them and pulled on Marie's arm. 'Come on, here's our tram. Let's leave these two to figure out what excuse they can make to Miss Bond for being too late for the interviews.'

About the same time as her daughter was hopping aboard the tram, Beth was seeing her son off to school. 'Yer could do with a new coat, sunshine, that one's on its last legs. It's practically threadbare. But it'll have to do yer for a while longer, I'm afraid, 'cos I couldn't afford one now, not with Christmas only days away. But it'll be my priority after the holidays, I promise. Keep that muffler tight around yer neck and stick yer hands in yer pockets. If yer run quick enough, yer could be in school before the cold gets to yer.'

'I'm all right, Mam, don't be worrying.' Joey at thirteen considered himself almost grown up. 'Anyway, I don't feel the cold.'

'I know yer don't, sunshine, ye're tough like yer dad.'

Her son's chest expanded about six inches. His father was his hero, and Joey wanted to be just like him when he was a man. He already had the raven hair and deep brown eyes, all he needed now was to grow about eighteen inches, upward and outward. 'Yeah, I'm going to be just like me dad.' He gave her a beaming smile. 'I'll see yer later, Mam.'

Beth waited until he reached the corner of the street, and gave a final wave before shutting the door. 'He's a little love, that son of mine,' she told Hannah, 'never moans or asks for anything he knows we can't afford.'

'Yer have two wonderful children, sweetheart, yer have every right to be proud of them.' The older woman made her way towards the kitchen. 'I'll wash the dishes while you do whatever else is to be done.'

'No, we'll do them between us. I'll wash and you can dry.' Beth turned up the gas under the kettle. 'The water won't be long.'

They'd finished the dishes and Beth was putting them away in the cupboards when she turned to Hannah. 'Ye're very quiet, sunshine, yer've never said a word since we started the dishes. Are yer feeling all right?'

'Yes, I'm fine.' Hannah forced a smile to her face, but not before Beth had heard her let out a low sigh.

'Come to think of it, yer've been quiet since yer got out of bed. Not that ye're ever very noisy or talking all the time.' Beth wiped her hands on the towel hanging on a nail behind the kitchen door. 'Come and let's sit by the fire, it's freezing in this kitchen. There's a dirty big gap under the door and I'm fed up asking Andy to put a strip of wood across the bottom. He keeps putting it off, but there's no point in me having a big fire in the living room when there's a ruddy draught coming through that could blow yer off yer feet.'

Hannah took her usual speck in the corner of the couch. Although she was doing her best to look as though she hadn't a care in the world, it didn't quite come off. Beth, who had been in her company for nearly four days now, and keeping a close eye on her, could tell there was something on the old lady's mind. 'Come on, sunshine, out with it. And don't tell me there's nothing bothering yer 'cos it's sticking out a mile. My ma's got a saying about a trouble shared is a trouble halved, and she's right. So tell us what's niggling yer and I'll see if I can help in any way.'

'It's nothing really, and yer couldn't help anyway.'

'How d'yer know I couldn't? If yer don't ask, yer'll never know, will yer? So get it off yer chest and yer'll feel better.'

'Well, it's like this, sweetheart – I'm worried about the sleeping arrangements when Claire and the children come. Apart from my double bed, there's only the single one that our John used to sleep in. If the children were the same sex it wouldn't matter, they could snuggle up together and make do for a while. But Bobby's sixteen and Amelia's fifteen, so there's no way they can share a room, never mind a bed.'

'Well, the room will be sorted out at the weekend when the men put the partition up, but I don't know how ye're going to manage for sleeping arrangements. Claire can kip in with you, but yer could do with another single bed.'

'I know that, but I can't afford to buy one. I want them to feel welcome when they arrive, instead of me saying there's nowhere for them all to sleep. That would sound as though I don't really want them to stay with me. It's been going around in me head for a day or two now, giving me a splitting headache.'

'I can't help yer out with money, sunshine, 'cos it's going to take me all me time to manage over Christmas as it is. And I know for certain Dot, Flo and Lizzie are in the same boat. Even though Lizzie's two eldest lads are working, they only earn buttons and she's got the two girls to keep. We get our Christmas Tontine money next week, but mine's all spoken for, otherwise I'd try and help yer.'

'Isn't there a woman in one of the streets who lends money out? I heard about her once but I don't know her name or where she lives. Apparently she lends money to people who are stuck, and they pay her back a few bob a week.'

'Ye're talking about Ma Maloney, sunshine, and yer'd do well to keep away from her. She might be sweet as anything to yer face, but you miss a week's payment and she'll be round to your house and make a holy show of yer. I've heard she pulled a woman out of her house by her hair 'cos she didn't have the money to pay her. If yer get in her clutches, yer'll never get out. Anyone will tell yer that Ma Maloney doesn't have a heart, she's got a swinging brick in its place.'

'I could pay her back, 'cos Claire said she was going out to work, and Bobby and Amelia will be getting jobs. So she'd get paid.'

'She'd make sure of that, sunshine, believe me! Even if she had to take it out of yer face. No, I wouldn't be doing yer no favour by introducing yer to Ma, she's not a nice person to know. I don't want her to be the cause of us falling out with each other.' Then Beth suddenly drew her legs in from the fire and sat up straight. 'Ay, the best person yer can talk to is Flo! She's the only woman in the neighbourhood that Ma Maloney's afraid of! Oh, why didn't I think of her before? I'll give a knock on the wall and she'll be here within minutes.'

'I'd rather yer didn't, Beth, I don't want it broadcast that I'm trying

78

to borrow money. It's something I've never done in me life, and I wouldn't be humiliating meself now if I wasn't so desperate.'

'Hannah, Flo Henderson may have a big mouth, but she knows when to keep it closed. And she's got a big heart, she'll help anyone if she can. So it wouldn't hurt to ask what she thinks of yer going to Ma Maloney for a loan. Yer've got a choice of two worries, sunshine, and that's whether yer go to Ma Maloney or be a nervous wreck 'cos ye're stuck for a bed for yer grandson to sleep in. We all need help sometime in our lives, and we shouldn't be too proud to ask. So I'll give Flo a knock and she can put yer wise.'

Beth used the heel of her shoe to bang on the wall which separated the two houses. 'I'd better put the kettle on 'cos she's a tea tank is Flo. She can drink it until it comes out of her ears.'

When she came back from the kitchen, Beth was wearing a smile. 'I'll get her to tell yer about the set-to she had with the Maloney woman. It was a few years ago and the talk of the neighbourhood for weeks. Yer see, no one had ever crossed swords with her until the day she rubbed Flo up the wrong way. Most of the women were terrified of her 'cos they'd borrowed money without telling their husbands and lived in fear of them finding out. Which is daft, really, because the poor beggars only borrowed to put food on the table. But yer know what some men are like, they've no idea how hard it is to try and make ends meet every week.'

A loud rap on the window heralded the arrival of Flo, in all her glory. She was wearing a wrap-around pinny that didn't quite wrap-around, a mob-cap that fell down to her eyes because the elastic had perished, and there was a huge smudge of soot on the end of her nose.

Beth burst out laughing. 'Ah, yer shouldn't have bothered getting dressed up, sunshine, there's only me and Hannah here.'

'It's too bleedin' early in the morning to be sarky, queen, 'cos me brain's not in motion yet. But no doubt I'll have an answer to yer remark in an hour's time.' Flo turned to Hannah with sweetness in her smile and voice. 'How are you this morning, queen? I hope we find yer well and hearty?'

'Actually, it's Hannah who wants to ask yer something, sunshine, so sit yerself down while I pour us a cuppa.' Beth turned at the kitchen door. 'Seeing as I'm nosy and don't want to miss anything, will yer talk about the weather until I come back?'

'That should take us all of ten seconds, queen, 'cos the weather's bleedin' awful.' Flo dropped on to one of the wooden dining chairs, thinking it would be easier to get up from than the low couch. After a sly glance to the kitchen, she whispered, 'What is it yer wanted to ask me about, queen?'

'I heard that!' Beth shouted. 'Keep yer mouth buttoned until I bring the tea in.'

'Nosy cow,' Flo muttered. 'And she can be wicked, too! I bet if I asked yer again what yer want me for, she'd be bad enough to give me a cup of tea with no sugar in.'

Beth bustled in carrying a tray. 'There yer are, that didn't take long. There's no biscuits, but even if I had any, it's too early in the morning for luxuries.'

When they were all settled with cup and saucer in hand, Hannah appealed to Beth. 'Will you tell Flo about me problem?'

The little fat woman feigned horror. 'Yer haven't got a bun in the oven, have yer?'

'This isn't funny, sunshine, it's dead serious.' Beth explained Hannah's dilemma over sleeping arrangements. 'She could do with another single bed, but hasn't the wherewithal to buy one. So she was asking me about Ma Maloney, and wondering whether she should borrow from her?'

Flo put her cup on the table for safety. 'Oh, yer want to keep away from her, queen, she's a bad bugger. She must be loaded with the money she rakes in every week, but she walks around like a tramp. And talk about being tight-fisted – she wouldn't give yer a spot if she had the ruddy measles! Mind you, I've got to hand it to her for being clever money wise. She knows exactly to the bleedin' penny how much everyone owes, and she'll not let them off with a farthing. She'd take the bread out of kids' mouths, she's that bad.'

'I don't know where else to turn, Flo, and I really am desperate. I'd only be borrowing for a couple of weeks, then she'd be paid back.'

Flo snorted. 'Oh, she'd be paid back all right, she'd make sure of that. Yer'd be well advised to steer clear of her, queen, I'm warning yer.'

'Tell her about the time you borrowed off her, sunshine,' Beth said. 'How she ran after yer for the money, and how much interest she charges.'

'Yeah, she stopped me in the bleedin' street, the hard-faced cow! Right outside the butcher's shop, she starting yelling at the top of her voice how much I owed her and when was I going to pay it back? I was mortified, queen, I can tell yer.'

Beth wanted to get to the part which would bring a smile to Hannah's face, so she egged her neighbour on. 'She didn't get away with it, though, did she? I can remember it as though it was yesterday. Funniest thing I've ever seen.'

Flo chuckled. 'Yeah, it was funny. And it worked, too, 'cos she never bothered me again. She got her money back, but it was in me own time.'

Hannah leaned forward, her eyes bright with interest. 'What did yer do, sweetheart?'

'I'll show yer what I did.' Flo got to her feet and held her arms away from her sides. 'Yer can see the width of me, queen, I mean, a pig wouldn't get past me in an entry. Anyway, I put me basket on the ground and walked like this towards Ma Maloney. Yer've seen the way boxers walk? Well, that's what I did. I got right up to the woman and pushed her with me tummy. She had to move back a few steps or she'd have keeled over, then I pushed me tummy into her again and she bounced back. By this time we had a big audience, 'cos Ma isn't a very popular woman in these parts, and they were clapping and cheering me on. The butcher even left his customers standing in his shop while he came out to referee.' She wiped away the tears of laughter rolling down her cheeks. 'Oh, God, but it was funny.'

'It was a damn sight funnier than you're making out,' Beth said. 'The woman bounced back at least six times. Her feet left the ground and I don't know how she kept her balance.'

Hannah looked from one to the other. 'And what happened then?'

Flo walked slowly back to her chair. 'Well, I looked down me nose at her, didn't I?'

Beth hooted. 'Yer looked down yer nose at her? Sunshine, she's head and shoulders over yer! What yer should have said was that yer looked *up* her nose.'

Flo looked to Hannah and rolled her eyes. 'She's a sarky cow, this one. The best of it is, she stood with all the others cheering me on, but not one of them offered to help.'

'Yer didn't need no help, sunshine, yer were doing very well on yer own. In fact, yer could have taken the lot of us on without turning a hair.'

Flo was quite happy with that. After all, she knew a compliment when she heard one. 'It ended up with me telling Ma Maloney that if she ever made a holy show of me again, or broadcast my private business, I wouldn't be responsible for me actions. She never came after me for the money I owed. I did pay it back, but I used to take it to her house when it suited me.'

'She's still me best bet,' Hannah said. 'I've no one else to turn to.'

81

'How much were yer thinking of asking her for, queen?'

'I don't know what a new bed would cost. Probably about four pound.'

'Yer don't need to pay that much out!' Flo shook her head in disbelief. 'There's a shop in Stanley Road sells second-hand furniture, and when I was passing there last week, they had an iron bedstead outside which looked in good nick. They were only asking five bob for it, and yer wouldn't have to worry about it being dirty 'cos yer could give it a good wash down. All yer'd need then is a mattress, and yer can get a cheap one from TJ's for ten bob. It won't be a thick one, mind, but it'll serve its purpose.'

'So Hannah would only need to borrow fifteen shillings, then?' Beth could see the old lady looking a bit more cheerful. 'That wouldn't be so bad.'

'Ma Maloney only lends out in pounds. Yer see, she charges yer a shilling a week for every pound yer owe. That's why some people can't get out of her debt. By the time they've paid the interest, they can't afford to pay anything off the loan. That's why I said the old witch must be coining it in.'

'Will yer take me around to her or are yer daggers drawn?' Hannah wanted everything doing quickly to ease her mind. 'Today if possible.'

'No, I'm not daggers drawn with her, queen, so I'll take yer around and introduce yer.' Flo's chubby face creased with mirth and her narrowed eyes sparkled with mischief. 'In fact, we'll ask for the loan of three pounds, that's a pound each. What d'yer think, Beth? It wouldn't half come in handy for a few extra bits for Christmas.'

'No, Andy would go mad if he thought I was borrowing from a moneylender.' But even as Beth spoke she was thinking what she could do with an extra pound. The first thing that came to mind was an overcoat for Joey. He badly needed one in this weather, and she'd get quite a decent one from Great Homer Street market for ten bob. 'Mind you, what he doesn't know can't hurt him.'

Flo's smile was one of satisfaction. 'Ay, I can't wait to see Ma's face when she sets eyes on me, she won't know whether to laugh or cry. We'll go after we've been to the shops, eh?'

Several miles away, Ginny and Marie were sitting in a room with seven other girls. It was an office on the top floor of the Woolworth building in Church Street. They'd handed in their white cards and school reports, and been told to wait until their names were called. There was no sign of their classmates, Alice and Doreen, but they were too full of nervous excitement to worry or care. Three girls had been called since they'd arrived almost an hour earlier, and as they'd been there when Ginny and Marie arrived, it appeared they were interviewing applicants on a first come, first served basis. It was very quiet in the room, with girls talking in whispers, so when the door was thrown open, nine hearts started to beat faster. 'Marie Whittaker, would you come with me, please?'

Ginny touched her friend's arm and said softly, 'Good luck.' Then she sat back in her chair and wondered if she would be called next. She hoped so, the suspense was terrible. To take her mind off things, she promised herself to look around the store before taking the tram back to school. She may as well make the most of it while she could because she'd only been into the town centre a couple of times in her life before. That was because her mam couldn't afford the tram fare. But things would be a bit easier, money wise, when she started earning. How proud she'd be when she handed her wage packet over every week, knowing it would make life a lot better for her mam.

Ginny could no longer keep her mind off the impending interview. She wondered how Marie was faring. She hoped her classmate would wait for her because she was dying to hear how Marie had got on. Not that there was any chance of their both being taken on, that would be stretching the imagination too far even to think that two girls from the same class in one school would get the only two jobs on offer. It was a lovely thought, but that was all it was.

'Virginia Porter, will you come with me, please?'

Ginny jumped to her feet. She felt absolutely terrified, her legs unwilling to move, her teeth chattering and her face stiff. But into her hazy mind flashed the words of the clerk at the Exchange. 'Be pleasant and keep that smile on yer face.' So she approached the lady who was holding the door open for her with a tremulous smile. 'Thank you.'

As they stepped outside the room and into a corridor, Ginny caught sight of Marie going into a room a few doors down. It was just a glimpse and more likely than not her classmate hadn't seen her. 'Will my friend be going home now, or can she wait for me?'

'I couldn't tell you that, my dear, you'll have to wait and see. But come along, Miss Ormsby is waiting for you.' They passed a door and Ginny could hear the clicking of typewriters, and the ping when the carriages reached the end of a line. When they came to the next door, the woman halted Ginny by placing a hand on her arm. 'Stand here.' With a flourish, the door was opened and the woman called, 'Virginia Porter, Miss Ormsby.' Then a hand was being pressed into her back and

Ginny was propelled into a well-furnished office. She had never felt so frightened in her life as when she stared at the woman seated behind the desk. Her heart was thumping, her legs felt like jelly, and although she clamped her teeth together to stop them from chattering, they wouldn't behave themselves. But through all that, she managed to keep a smile on her face. That it was a forced smile was not lost on Miss Ormsby, but she gave the girl full credit for trying. Nearly all the girls she'd interviewed over the years had been nervous and apprehensive, which was only to be expected as they were still schoolchildren. The ones who weren't nervous, who stared her out as though to say she held no fear for them, were never offered a job. They were too bold to act as sales assistants because they'd clearly have no patience with customers, and in Woolworth's all the staff were taught that the customer might not always be right but it was not their place to tell them so.

Miss Ormsby waved to a chair facing her across the desk. 'Sit down, please, Virginia.'

Chapter Eight

When the door closed behind her, Ginny eyed the expanse of floor she had to cover to reach the chair. She thought her legs would buckle before she was halfway there. But she did make it, the smile still fixed on her face, and when she was seated she placed the patent leather clutch bag on her lap before lacing her fingers together to stop her hands from shaking.

'There's no need to feel nervous, Virginia,' Sarah Ormsby said. 'I'm only going to ask you a few questions, nothing very terrible.'

'Yes, Miss Ormsby,' Ginny managed to croak as the woman scanned the card from the Labour Exchange before picking up her school report. This held no fears for the girl because she'd never had a bad report in all her years at school.

'I've just interviewed a pupil from the same school, Marie Whittaker, do you know her?'

'Oh, yes, me and Marie are in the same class. We don't live far from each other and I remember us starting in the infants on the same day.'

'So she's quite a good friend of yours?'

Ginny was beginning to realise this woman wasn't an ogre and she relaxed a little. 'She is one of me friends, yes, like a lot of other girls in the class. But she's not me very best friend. That's another girl from our class whose name is Joan. She lives next door to me. We've been friends all our lives.'

'Tell me about your home life, Virginia. About your parents and how many brothers and sisters you have?'

'I've only got one brother, Miss, that's our Joey and he's thirteen.' Ginny was on home ground talking about her family, and although she wasn't aware of it, her smile had softened and her eyes were aglow. 'Then there's me mam and dad. I take after me mam in looks, she's got fair hair and blue eyes. But our Joey is the image of me dad, with jet black hair and dark brown eyes.' Her face became more animated as she spoke of the people she loved. 'My mam is very pretty and me dad is really handsome.'

'You get on well with your parents and brother, then?'

Ginny looked surprised by the question. 'Oh, yes, I've got the best parents and brother in the whole world. We get along fine because we love each other very much.'

Miss Ormsby nodded. 'I'm glad to hear that. Not all children have good parents and a loving home so you are very lucky. And now can you tell me why you want to work as a shop assistant in this store?'

There was no hesitation. 'It's what I want to do more than anything, Miss! And I think I would make a good shop assistant because I like people. I like talking to them and saying things that bring a smile to their face. And working in a big shop like Woolworth's, well, I'll be really proud.'

Ginny realised what she'd said and a hand flew to her mouth. 'Oh, I didn't mean it to sound like that, Miss, I wasn't being forward. I meant if I was lucky enough to get a job here as an assistant, or in any other shop, I would be over the moon.'

Sarah Ormsby kept back a smile only with difficulty. 'You do realise that it isn't the same as playing at shop when you were little? Serving behind a counter is an occupation which requires many skills, and in a store as large as this one, you would be required to observe for several months before being allowed to approach a customer. You would be working under strict supervision until such time as your supervisor considered you were capable of coping with customers unaided. That would depend on how quickly whoever is finally chosen for the position learns the many things that are to be learned. For instance, deportment, speech, appearance, ability to handle money and attitude towards customers – some of whom, I must say, can be very difficult and need to be handled with kid gloves. No assistant should ever answer back or treat a customer with indifference. Such behaviour would not be tolerated.'

Miss Ormsby rested her elbows on the desk. 'So you see, Virginia, working in a big store like Woolworth's is a far cry from standing behind the counter in a corner shop. No doubt you are having second thoughts now?'

'Oh, no, Miss! No matter where yer go to work, yer have to learn and do as ye're told. My mam has drummed that into me. You get paid to do a job and you must earn your wages by making sure you do it well.'

'Your mother sounds a very sensible woman, my dear, and she has obviously done her best to prepare you for work.' Sarah Ormsby lifted the fob watch hanging from a small chain pinned to the breast of her dress. She grimaced. 'I'm running late, I'm afraid, so I'm going to ask Miss Harper to take you to a room where you will stay until I call for you again. I will hold on to your school report for now, but it will be returned to you before you leave the building.' There was a brass bell at the side of the desk which she hit with an open palm. The door was opened so quickly Miss Harper must have been hovering outside.

'Yes, Miss Ormsby?'

'Please take Virginia to Room Four then kindly bring in the next girl to be interviewed. And will you arrange for Virginia and Marie Whittaker to be given a cup of tea and some biscuits? Their wait could be quite a long one.'

'Yes, Miss Ormsby.' The woman inclined her head. 'Please follow me, Virginia.'

Room Four turned out to be the room opposite, the very one Ginny had seen Marie going into. And, sure enough, there was her classmate, sitting all alone and looking rather down-hearted. She obviously had no idea why she'd been put into the room, and her expression said she hoped Ginny could enlighten her.

'Please sit down, I'll come back to you shortly.' Miss Harper was halfway out of the door when Ginny followed her, saying, 'Can I ask yer what we've to wait here for, Miss? I mean, wouldn't Miss Ormsby have said we could go back to school if she'd decided we weren't right for an assistant's job?'

'I'm sorry, I can't tell you that. All I know is that she will interview every applicant before coming to a final decision. And now I must go.'

Once the door was closed and they were alone, Marie's eyes narrowed. 'Well, where are the three girls who were called before us, then? I haven't seen sight nor light of them, so unless they're stuck in another room somewhere, they must have been sent back to school.'

'It would be nice if that were the case, kid, 'cos that would mean we're still in with a chance. Oh, I hope so, 'cos I'd love a job here. Imagine telling everyone yer travelled into the city every day to work. Gosh, wouldn't yer feel important?

'Ay, ye're in danger of getting big-headed, you are, Ginny Porter. If my mam could hear yer, she'd tell yer that a doctor and a docker might do very different work, but one is every bit as good as the other.'

'I know that, soft girl! Anyway, between you and Joan Flynn, there's not much chance of me ever getting above meself 'cos yer wouldn't let me.'

'That doesn't mean that I wouldn't like to work here, though,' Marie said. 'I think it would be smashing. But I don't stand a chance 'cos I'm not very good at sums.'

'Well, we'll just have to wait and see. I'm keeping me fingers crossed, and saying a few prayers. I'm sure God must be sick of the sound of me voice by now 'cos I've never prayed so much in all me life.'

There was a light tap on the door before it was opened and a girl who looked to be about seventeen came in carring a tray set with two cups of tea and a plate of digestive biscuits. She was dressed in a plain navy blue cotton dress with short sleeves and a round white collar, a white pinny tied around her waist. She seemed pleasant enough and this encouraged Ginny to ask, 'Is there a cafe in the shop?'

'Oh, I don't work in the shop, I work in the staff canteen.' The girl was curious. 'Have yer been taken on?'

'We don't know what's happening, worse luck,' Marie said, her winning smile having deserted her again. 'I wish we'd been told straight away, this waiting is turning me into a nervous wreck.'

'Look on the bright side, girl, 'cos if it's anything to go by, yer must be still in the running. If yer weren't, yer'd have been sent home by now.'

Then Ginny had a thought. 'Are there any girls in other rooms? I mean, have yer taken tea to anyone else? Yer see, there were three girls interviewed before us and we don't know where they've disappeared to.'

'Yer've got me there, kid, 'cos I haven't seen no one else. I certainly haven't taken tea to anyone and I know no one else has 'cos I'm the skivvy in the canteen, being the youngest, yer see. The general dogsbody in other words.'

'Don't yer like yer job, then?' Ginny asked, thinking skivvy and dogsbody didn't sound very nice.

'Oh, I love it! Wouldn't swap it for any other job. I get on with all the women in the canteen and we have a good laugh.' She was a tall slim girl, with black hair and brown eyes which she now rolled to the ceiling. 'I'd better get back to work. I'll be sent later to pick up the tray so drink the tea while it's still hot.'

'What's yer name?' Ginny asked as the girl was about to close the door behind her. 'Just in case we see yer again.'

'Me Sunday name is Marjorie, but I get Margie. And yer will see me again 'cos I'll be back for the tray in about fifteen minutes. So hurry up and get cracking on those biscuits.'

'Ay, she seems nice, doesn't she?' Marie lifted a cup and saucer from the tray and her usual smile reappeared. 'I feel proper posh now, getting waited on. This is how people with money live all the time. Waited on hand and foot, and they take it for granted.'

'They're welcome to it.' Ginny helped herself to a biscuit. 'I'm happy with me family being just as we are. Although, I must admit, I'll feel a lot happier if I get this job.'

'What will yer do if yer don't?'

'Start looking around other shops in earnest. I'd like to get fixed up somewhere before Christmas. Oh, I don't mean I want to start work before the holiday, that's not possible, but at least I'd like to have the promise of a job to start the week after.' Ginny tutted when she saw part of Marie's digestive biscuit break off and fall into the cup. 'Ye're a dirty beggar, look what yer've done! Yer dunked yer biscuit so long, yer've lost half of it. That cup will be in a right state by the time yer've finished.'

'No, it won't, clever clogs, 'cos I'll fish it out with the spoon.' But Marie's intentions didn't work because the biscuit had disintegrated. 'Oh, dear, what am I going to do? Yer were right, I've made a mess and I feel ashamed.'

Ginny was sorry she'd said anything. 'Don't worry, no one of any importance is going to see the cup. If that Marjorie comes back, just explain and say ye're sorry. In fact, if it'll stop yer from worrying, we'll swap cups when we've finished and I'll pretend it was my fault.'

'Oh, that's the gear, Ginny, thank you.'

They had no way of knowing the time, except that for them it was dragging. It was only when Marjorie came to collect the tray that she told them it was around eleven o'clock. 'The shop staff get fifteen minutes break morning and afternoon, and they take it in four shifts.' She giggled. 'They couldn't all come together otherwise there'd be no one to serve the customers so the breaks start at ten and finish at eleven. And when I left the canteen the fourth shift were getting ready to go downstairs, so I knew it was nearly eleven.'

'That means we've been here over two hours,' Ginny said. 'I wonder how much longer we're going to have to wait?'

'Listen, kid,' Marjorie picked up the tray, 'if there's a job at the end of it yer shouldn't mind if yer've got another two hours to wait.'

'I know.' Ginny pulled a face. 'I'm not usually a moaner, it's just that this means so much to me. I'd sit here for twenty-four hours if I thought it would help.' She saw the waitress reaching for the knob on the door and remembered her promise. 'Oh, before yer go, I've got a confession to make. I was dunking one of the biscuits and half of it fell off into the cup. I tried to get it out with the spoon but it all broke up. I'm sorry.'

'There's worse things happen at sea, girl, so don't worry yer head about it.' With that the girl left and the two classmates were once again on their own.

'Miss Bond will be wondering where we've got to,' Marie said. 'She will have expected us to be back by now.'

'That's just what I was thinking, but it can't be helped.' Ginny leaned forward, and in a conspiratorial whisper asked, 'Ay, what are we going to tell her about the other two, Doreen and Alice?'

'The truth, of course! I'm not telling lies and getting meself into trouble over them. If Miss Bond asks, I'm going to tell her . . .' Marie's words were cut short when the door opened and Miss Harper popped her head in.

'Marie Whittaker, Miss Ormsby will see you now.'

Left alone, Ginny was wishing her friend well while at the same time wishing she'd been asked to go first. In her head she was telling herself she wasn't being selfish, it was just that she wanted to get the ordeal over. But she wouldn't have long to wait now, and even if Marie couldn't speak to her when she came back, she'd know by her face whether she'd got a job or not because that wide, winning smile would be in evidence.

Ginny expected to have a long wait, so she was surprised when after ten minutes the door opened and Marie walked in, her smile reaching from ear to ear. You could see she was bursting with excitement and dying to tell her friend what had happened, but she was told by Miss Harper to take a seat. 'Wait here and I'll be with you in a moment. Come with me, Virginia.'

Miss Ormsby nodded to the chair facing her. 'Sit down, Virginia, I won't keep you long now.' Interviewing young people was the one part of being Personnel Officer that Sarah Ormsby disliked. To see the eagerness on young faces being replaced by disappointment, and even the threat of tears, was something she didn't enjoy. Today had been no exception. Twelve or thirteen applicants, she couldn't remember now exactly, and of those at least nine had left the building full of despair. But in this job you had to put your own feelings to one side, and this she did willingly now as the task in front of her was a pleasant one. There was a smile on her face when she leaned forward and met Ginny's eyes. 'It has been decided to offer you the position of counter assistant. Your employment will start the Monday after New Year.' She pushed the envelope containing Ginny's school report across the desk. 'You can take this with you, but not the card from the Labour Exchange. We will be notifying them that the positions have now been filled.'

'Oh, thank you, Miss Ormsby! I won't let yer down, I promise. I'll be punctual and hard-working, you'll see.'

'I don't doubt you, Virginia, that's why you have been chosen. Now, at this moment, Miss Harper will be giving all the details of employment to Marie Whittaker so wait in the corridor until she's free to see you. She will explain to you what being a junior assistant in the firm of Woolworth's entails. The hours you will be working, your wages, everything you need to know. And if there's anything you're not sure of, don't be afraid to ask questions.' Sarah Ormsby put her palms flat on the desk and pushed herself to her feet. She held out her hand and smiled. 'I'm sure you'll be a very valuable member of the staff, Virginia, and I wish you well. I also hope you and your family have a very happy Christmas.'

Ginny gripped her hand. She was so happy she felt like giving the Personnel Officer a hug and kiss, but she restrained herself. 'Oh, I'll have a wonderful Christmas now, Miss Ormsby. Yer've just given me the best present I've ever had. Thank you.'

Once again Ginny faced the expanse of floor from the desk to the door. Only an hour ago she could barely walk across it because her legs had turned to jelly with fear. Now she felt so happy she wanted to skip across. Do cartwheels even. But she settled for walking sedately and turning back at the door. 'Merry Christmas, Miss Ormsby.'

There was a separate entrance to the stairway leading to the offices above Woolworth's store, so when the two girls were leaving they came straight down on to Church Street. It was a wonder they managed to get down safely because they were both waving their arms about in excitement, their voices trying to drown each other out and their eyes everywhere but on the steps.

'The way we're going on it's going to take us all day to tell each other what happened.' Ginny glanced briefly at the front of the big store. She would have loved to have gone in and had a good look at the place where she'd be working very soon, but Miss Bond's face was imprinted on her mind. The headmistress would be wondering how they'd got on, and they owed it to her to let her know as quickly as possible. 'You go first, Marie, and tell me all about the job you've been given, then I can tell yer about mine.'

'I'm to start off working in the stock room because Miss Ormsby said I wasn't good enough at arithmetic to be put as a sales girl. But she said she'd give me a chance to improve meself, and she's going to review the situation in six months' time.' Marie was walking sideways so she could see the expression on Ginny's face. 'The wages are only six shillings a week in the stock room, but if I bring me sums up to scratch and I get taken on as a counter assistant, the wages will go up to seven and six. Plus a shilling a week to help with the tram fares.' She did a hop, skip and a jump. 'So you must be starting on seven and six, yer lucky beggar.'

Ginny nodded. 'Yeah, plus the shilling for the tram fares. I've to clock on at a quarter to nine, I'll have two tea breaks and a half-hour lunch break. The store shuts at five-thirty, but we have to tidy the counter before we can leave so it'll be a quarter to six before we get away. But it's only half day on a Wednesday, so we'll be on our way home before half-one.'

'Yeah, everything's the same for me, except I'll be working in the stock room and getting eighteen pence a week less than you. But it won't be for long 'cos I'm determined to get behind a counter. I'll ask me mam to give me some sums to do every night, and she won't have to shout at me no more about going on a message for her. She'll think I'm sickening for something when I offer to go to the shops, but it's one way of learning if I keep me eye out and count the change proper.'

'This is our tram coming,' Ginny said. 'I can't wait to tell Miss Bond 'cos after all if it wasn't for her we wouldn't have got the jobs. I bet she'll be proud of us. Two job vacancies and they both go to girls from her school – that's a real feather in her cap.' She boarded the tram and made for the stairs. 'Let's sit on top 'cos it's not usually crowded up there.'

As they flopped on to the hard wooden seat at the very back of the tram, Marie said, 'It was only supposed to be two jobs, kid, but Miss Ormsby decided to make it three. It was Miss Harper what told me. She said I was a borderline case, not quite good enough from the school report to be offered a job behind the counter. But as it was only me sums what let me down, Miss Ormsby decided to give me a chance. She said it was up to me whether I wanted to be someone in life and have a decent job. So I'm going to show them I can do it, I'm determined.'

'Of course yer can do it, Marie! It's not as though ye're thick like some of the girls in class. Yer've just been too lazy and couldn't be bothered. But now yer've got a goal, something to aim for.' Ginny giggled. 'And just think, kid, yer'll have the honour of travelling backwards and forwards to work with me. Now the thought of that should make yer work twice as hard!'

92

'I said yer were getting big-headed, Ginny Porter, and that just proves it. Yer don't half think ye're someone.'

'And that just proves you've no sense of humour, Marie Whittaker! Yer'd better hurry up and find one if yer want to travel with me every day. I can't stand a misery guts.'

The walls of the two-up-two-down houses were very thin, and Dot could hear voices coming from next door. Especially Flo Henderson's. Now what was she doing there at this time of the morning? Perhaps there was something wrong with Hannah? Then Dot shook her head when she heard the low voice of the elderly woman. She couldn't make out the words, but it didn't sound as though there was anything wrong with her. Probably Flo had run out of something and was on the cadge. That was it, Dot told herself, and went on cleaning out the grate. Many's the time she'd been caught short herself and had to go to Beth's on the cadge.

But fifteen minutes later, when the sound of Flo's voice could still be heard, Dot told herself there was definitely something going on. The prospect of a long, cold, bleak day loomed large in her mind. She wiped her hands on the towel hanging behind the kitchen door, then reached for her coat. If there was something happening that could liven up her day, then she wanted to know what it was.

Beth looked surprised when she opened the front door. 'You're early, aren't yer? There's another hour at least before our usual time for the shops.'

'I heard voices, girl, and I wondered if there was something up?'

Flo waddled to the front door and peeped over Beth's shoulder. 'Oh, blimey, yer might have known. It's that nosy cow from next door.'

'I came in good faith, girl, to offer help if help was needed, so we'll have less of the nosy cow. And I'd like to be asked in, if yer don't mind. Apart from me being ruddy well freezing, it's bad manners to keep anyone standing on the step.'

Beth moved aside. 'Yer'd better come in or I'll never hear the end of it. But God knows when I'm going to get me housework done at this rate.'

'Oh, blow on it for one day,' Dot said, stepping into the hall. 'No one will notice the difference.'

Observing the goings on from across the street was Lizzie O'Leary. She had been polishing the sideboard which stood in front of the window, but when she saw Dot Flynn knocking on Beth's door, she stopped polishing and peeped through her net curtains. There seemed to be a lot of activity going on over there this morning. First she'd seen Flo going in, with her pinny and mob-cap still on. This signified there was something up, otherwise she'd never leave the house in her working clothes. And now Dot Flynn was being invited in, the mystery deepened. There was definitely something in the wind, and Lizzie, like all women, hated to miss anything. So the duster was left on the sideboard while she donned her coat and slipped the front door key into her pocket. The polishing could wait, her curiosity couldn't.

Beth was really taken aback when she saw Lizzie too. 'What's got into everyone this morning? I've hardly done a tap of work yet, and I've got a houseful!'

'Sure, curiosity is a terrible thing, me darlin', so it is! But if yer tell me that all is well, and there's nothing amiss, then I'll be crossing the road again to carry on with me own housework.'

Flo's voice drifted out to them. 'Yer might as well come in now ye're here, queen. It wouldn't do yer heart no good sitting over there wondering what's going on over here.'

'Yes, yer'd better come in, sunshine.' Beth stepped to one side. 'The more the merrier, I suppose. And I can always do me housework tonight when the family are in bed.'

'There's no need for that, queen, just 'cos yer neighbours are interested in yer welfare. Besides, yer asked me to come in, I didn't invite meself,' Flo protested.

'Yes, I did, sunshine, just to ask yer a quick question. But that was a good half-an-hour ago, and ye're still here.'

'Why didn't yer knock for me instead?' Dot asked. 'I could probably have told yer what yer want to know.'

Flo was squinting now as the mob-cap threatened to cover her eyes, and she was pushing it back up her forehead when she said to Dot, 'Why should she knock for you when I'm only next door?' As soon as she took her hand away, the mob-cap fell down again, making her more irate. I mean, how could she put forward a good argument when she couldn't even see the person she had a cob on with? 'Anyway, yer'd have been no good to her, 'cos yer don't even know Ma Maloney.'

Hannah grimaced. It was bad enough Beth and Flo knowing she wanted to borrow from a moneylender, but now it seemed the whole street would hear about it before the day was out She should have thought of another way of raising money, like pawning her wedding ring. She wouldn't want to do that, though, 'cos it was the only thing she had left that her husband had bought her.

Dot was standing with her arms folded across her chest. 'What d'yer mean, girl, that I don't know Ma Maloney? There's no one within a mile of this street that doesn't know the old witch. Scrooge isn't in it. Bleed yer dry, she would.'

'Yer do surprise me,' Beth said, forgetting her housework while she digested the latest piece of news. 'I never knew yer borrowed from her?'

'Oh, it's years ago now, long before we all got so pally. I would never have done it if I hadn't been really down on me uppers. Bill had been laid off work for a few weeks and I was at me wit's end. I'm not proud of it, but I'm not ashamed either! As they say, it's any port in a storm.'

'Who's Ma Maloney?' Lizzie asked. 'I've never heard of her.'

'She's a moneylender, sunshine, and I was asking Flo what she knew about her. Yer see, I know someone who could do with a loan to help her out.'

'Blimey, couldn't we all?' Dot said. 'I did me list of shopping for next week, and what I've paid into the Christmas clubs, plus me Tontine money, won't come anywhere near covering it.'

'Same here.' Beth decided to bite the bullet. There was no sense in pussyfooting around, they were all good mates in the room. 'That's why me and Hannah have decided to ask the Maloney woman for the loan of a pound.'

'Ay, don't yer be leaving me out, seeing as I'm the one what's going to take yer to her.' Flo was thinking what a cheek they had. They asked for her help and then left her out! 'The three of us are asking for a loan.'

'I deliberately left yer out, sunshine, in case yer didn't want anyone to know. It's not up to me to tell everyone yer business. But I don't mind them knowing about me. Our Joey is badly in need of a warm coat for the winter, and I'll get one from the market for him for about ten bob. Then there's our Ginny leaving school. She'll have to have long stockings to go to work in, I couldn't expect her to go in school socks and navy blue fleecy knickers. So whether she's a nice person or not, a pound off Ma Maloney would come in very useful.'

'Ooh, aye, that's a thought,' Dot said. 'I'd forgotten about our Joan coming out of school clothes. I think I'll join the club and come with yer to see the Maloney woman.'

'She'll think it's her birthday, four new suckers coming for a loan.' Flo didn't realise how comical she looked with the mob-cap all askew and the blob of soot on the end of her nose. 'I bet she'll rub her hands with glee when she sees us.'

'Make that five suckers, me darlin',' Lizzie said. 'Sure, it's meself that's not going to be left out. An extra pound will come in very handy, so it will.'

When Flo started to shake, the floorboards began to creak in protest. She pressed her hands on the table for support while she doubled up with laughter. 'Ooh, me imagination is running riot. If old Ma Maloney sees five of us marching towards her, she'll think it's a bleedin' lynch mob! Perhaps it would be better if we went in twos.'

'Not on your life, sunshine, it's all or none. And anyway, we need you to show us where she lives and to introduce us.' Beth told herself if she wasn't firm with her friends, the day would be over and still the housework wouldn't be done. 'So will yer all go back to yer own houses now and leave me and Hannah to get on with making the place presentable? And say we all meet here again at half-past one to go and find this Maloney woman? We can see for ourselves what she's like, and what we're letting ourselves in for.' She opened the front door. 'Come on, ladies, let's be having yer.' When Flo was passing, Beth grinned at her. 'And wash that soot off yer nose before we go visiting, will you, sunshine, 'cos yer look like the squaw of Big Chief Sitting Bull.'

Chapter Nine

'What shall we do after we've hung our coats up?' Ginny asked as she walked across the empty playground with Marie's arm tucked in hers. 'Go straight to the classroom or go and see Miss Bond first?'

'I don't know, kid.' Marie's nerves were taut as she tried to keep her excitement under control. Never in a million years would she have thought she stood a chance of getting that job in Woolworth's. Ginny, yes, she was a clever girl, but not Marie. Now she was so proud of herself she could hardly contain her enthusiasm. 'I'll do whatever you want to do.'

'We'd better go straight to our class and see what Miss Jackson says. Miss Bond might have someone with her in the office and she wouldn't like to be interrupted.' Ginny was just as proud and excited, but she'd made up her mind not to let it show until she got home. After all, she and Marie were the first girls in the class to have landed a definite job and she didn't want her classmates thinking she was sticking her nose in the air at them. Even though she did feel like shouting it from the roof-tops. 'I'm sure of one thing, though, Marie, I'm not half hungry.'

'Oh, yeah, me too! Me tummy's beginning to rumble.'

The corridors were empty and the only sound to break the silence was their footsteps as they headed for the cloakroom. After hanging up their coats, they had to pass one classroom to get to theirs, and they could hear the voice of the teacher shouting out a question, and then the murmur of pupils who were lucky or brainy enough to know the answer. 'Well, here goes,' Ginny said as they stopped outside Miss Jackson's classroom. And taking a deep breath she opened the door.

There was a look of optimistic expectancy on the teacher's face when the two girls walked in, and all the pupils raised their heads, eager to know how their mates had fared. All except for two . . . Alice and Doreen. They'd been hoping to see Ginny and Marie before the teacher did because they'd told lies and intended to bully the other girls and frighten them into corroborating their story.

Miss Jackson beckoned the new arrivals towards her desk. 'Well, how did you get on?'

'We both got taken on, Miss Jackson,' Ginny told her. 'I'm to be a counter assistant and Marie is going in the stock room.'

'Oh, that's wonderful news! I am so pleased for you!'

'I won't be staying in the stock room for long, Miss, only till I'm better with sums. And I'm going to work very hard on them so I can serve in the shop with Ginny.'

The classroom was buzzing as the girls sitting at the front desks relayed the news to those behind. But when the teacher rapped sharply on the desk with a ruler, heads dropped and silence reigned. 'Patricia Cornwall, I'm going to leave you in charge while I take Virginia and Marie to see Miss Bond. You will report any girl who misbehaves.'

'Yes, Miss.' Patricia was top of the class in every subject, and also a monitor She was a big girl, a head above anyone else, and very well made. She was more than capable of keeping order, and she wouldn't hesitate to report any girl who took advantage of the teacher's absence because she knew they wouldn't try getting their own back on her.

Miss Jackson tapped on the headmistress's door before popping her head in. 'I've brought Virginia and Marie to see you.'

'Oh, good, bring them in.' Miss Bond swept aside the papers in front of her. A break from writing school reports was just what she needed. 'And how did the interviews go?'

The girls had been pleased with their teacher's reaction when they'd told her their news, but nothing could have prepared them for Miss Bond's. She had been known to smile on occasion, but never before had they heard the sound of laughter coming from her lips. She was really overjoyed. The girls were a credit to the school, she told them, while thinking how well it would look when the school inspectors next came. She listened attentively to all they had to say, smiling and nodding her head at the right times. Virginia she was pleased for, but it wasn't a complete surprise that she'd been taken on because of her exemplary record. On the other hand, Marie's appointment was like a bolt out of the blue. 'I hope you mean what you say about improving your arithmetic, Marie, because it would stand you in good stead in the future.'

'Oh, I intend to, Miss Bond.' And because she had never seen the headmistress so relaxed and pleasant, Marie dared to add, 'I can't have Ginny getting eighteen pence a week more than me.'

'Miss Jackson and I were quite concerned when we were told neither of you had turned up at the arranged time outside the Labour Exchange.

And when you didn't appear in class we assumed you were playing truant, even though we agreed it would have been quite out of character as both of you have always been reliable and punctual.'

'But we did turn up!' Ginny told her. 'I was there fifteen minutes early, and Marie came five minutes after me! Why would you think we were playing truant? Me mam would have me life if I did that!'

'Alice and Doreen said they were there on time but you didn't show up. They didn't like to go ahead without you so they waited and waited. In the end they were too late to present themselves at Woolworth's.'

Marie's mouth opened wide. 'Oh, the fibbers! They won't go to heaven when they die, they won't! Me and Ginny waited for them, then when it was getting late we went into the Exchange and filled in our cards. We were running along County Road to the tram stop when we saw them. They had no intention of meeting us, they were strolling along looking in shop windows.'

The teacher and headmistress exchanged glances before Miss Bond said, 'Never mind, I'll sort out the misunderstanding later. Suffice to say I am absolutely delighted for you both, you are a credit to the school. And now, have you had any lunch?'

'No,' Ginny said, shaking her head. 'And we're both hungry.'

'Then I suggest you take the rest of the day off, you deserve it. Go home, have something to eat and tell your families the good news. We'll see you on Monday morning for the start of your last week at school.'

The two girls looked at each other and grinned broadly. Oh, what a wonderful day this was turning out to be! And the best was yet to come. Just wait until they told their families. They'd be so proud when they knew their daughters had landed a job in Woolworth's.

'This is the street.' Flo had walked ahead of her friends, marching with a straight back and leading them like a sergeant would lead his men. And when Flo straightened her back, her bosom was thrust forward and was a force to be reckoned with. 'She lives halfway down on the right. Come on, follow me.'

She walked a few steps then turned to see the other four women standing motionless. Hannah had moved a step forward, because although she was as nervous as anyone this trip was one of necessity for her. But to Beth, Dot and Lizzie, while an extra pound in their pocket for Christmas had sounded wonderful this morning, the means of getting it weren't so appealing now.

'You go on,' Beth said, speaking for herself and her two mates. 'It looks a bit much for five of us to knock on her door.'

When Flo tutted and shook her head, her chins swayed from side to side. 'Don't be so bleedin' daft! If yer want the money yer've got to ask for it. Ma Maloney isn't Lady Bountiful, she doesn't go handing cash out to everyone she sees. Anyway, if her front door's not open we go around the back 'cos she does most of her business in the entry. And she does that for two reasons. A lot of women don't want it known they borrow off her so they use the back entry, and she doesn't want to be seen handing money over because of the police. Like the street-corner bookies, what she's doing is against the law and she could find herself in trouble. Not that anyone would snitch on her 'cos they need her, and they'd be cutting their nose off to spite their face. Now, are yer coming or not?'

Hannah moved forward. 'I'll come with yer.'

Beth quickly followed. Come hell or high water she was going to keep an eye on the elderly woman who wouldn't be up to the ways of any Smart Alec. 'We'll all come, but we'll walk a bit behind, in pairs, so we don't stick out a mile.'

When Flo came abreast of Ma Maloney's house and found the door closed, her footsteps didn't falter and she kept on walking to the nearest side entry. They turned into it and sure enough, halfway down, they could see three women talking and nodding their heads to someone who was hidden from view. Arms were stretching out and it was obvious that money was changing hands. 'We'll hang on until they're finished,' Flo said. 'They won't be long because Ma isn't one for gossiping. Time is money to her.'

'If Bill could see me now, he'd do his nut,' Dot said. 'He doesn't believe in borrowing or lending money.'

'Neither does Andy,' Beth said. 'And it's only the thought of seeing our Joey going to school this morning without a decent coat on his back that is keeping me from turning tail.'

'What the men don't know won't hurt them, and I'll not be telling Paddy,' Lizzie comforted herself with saying. 'Sure, we can have it paid back in a couple of weeks.'

'You might, I won't!' Flo only had her husband's wages coming in because her two children were still at school. Amy was thirteen and Wendy twelve. 'I'll be lucky if I can pay her one and six a week, and as a shilling of that will be interest, it means I'm only paying sixpence off me loan.' But Flo could never be serious for long, and she began to chuckle. 'Of course I could go down Lime Street one night, and earn enough to pay her off in one go.'

'Ye're being optimistic, aren't yer, sunshine?' Beth, in her mind's eye, could just see her little fat friend walking along the street which was the haunt of prostitutes. 'Yer'd end up having to pay the men, not the other way round.'

'There's no need to be so bleedin' funny, queen, 'cos every woman looks the same down an entry on a dark night with a sack over her head.'

Faces were beginning to look a bit brighter now. After all, yer couldn't be worrying and laughing at the same time. 'It would have to be some sack in your case, sunshine, 'cos an ordinary coal sack wouldn't fit yer.'

'Ho, ho, very bleedin' funny.' Flo noticed some movement down the entry and said, 'Ay, out, the women are finished. Shall I go first, or would one of you like the honour?'

There were no takers for that offer so Flo marched gallantly forward. Her bosom stood to attention, her hips swayed and a look of determination was fixed on her chubby face. She reached the door of Ma Maloney's just as it was being pushed to, and her hand shot out to prevent its closure. 'Hang on, Ma, there's some more customers for yer.'

The look on the moneylender's face when she saw who it was confirmed the story Flo had told. The woman obviously didn't know whether to laugh or cry, but it would be fair to say she was not best pleased to see who her visitor was. 'I'm in a bleedin' hurry and haven't time to mess around, so yer can sod off.'

'Now is that any way to greet an old friend?' Flo's attitude was cocky. 'Here's me, thinking yer'd be glad to see me.'

'Well, I'm not, so buzz off.' Ma Maloney was eyeing Flo's tummy and remembering the time she was bounced by it. Better not be too unpleasant or she could end up being bounced down the cobbled entry. Her eyes like slits, she asked, 'What are yer doing here anyway?'

'If yer'd care to step forward, yer'd see I've got four friends with me, and we've all come on a peaceful mission – to ask your good self if we could borrow a pound off yer. A pound each, that is.'

Ma poked her head out a bit further. 'I haven't got no five pounds on me! What d'yer think I am anyway, yer silly bitch? I'm not lending money to no strangers 'cos I might never see them or me money again.'

'I'm not a stranger, yer know where I live,' Flo said, feigning a hurt expression and being prepared to give way a little so as not to lose face before her friends. 'I know we had a little set-to last time I borrowed off yer, but yer must admit yer asked for it by making a show of me in front of all me neighbours. But that's over and done with now, and these are all respectable women who will not let yer down.'

'I haven't got five pounds on me, yer'll have to come back another day. And one of yer will have to take on responsibility for making sure the others pay.' The calculating eyes landed on Hannah and were quick to sum her up. Here was a woman who would be too frightened of the consequences if she didn't return the loan, with interest. 'You, whoever yer are, can collect the money off yer mates and bring it to me every week. And I hope yer know that there's a shilling interest every week on every pound owing.' When Hannah nodded, Ma Maloney said, 'As I told yer, I haven't got five pounds on me, yer'll have to come back next Monday.'

Because she'd been reluctant to come out of her yard into the entry, Beth couldn't see the woman from where she was standing. The voice alone told her they were dealing with a harsh woman who mustn't be allowed to get her claws into Hannah. But because it was many years since she'd last seen her, Beth moved to stand next to Flo so she could get a good look at the woman they called Ma Maloney, and she didn't like what she saw. It would have been hard to guess her age, she could be an old-looking fifty or a young-looking seventy. Straggling, greasy hair hung down to her shoulders; hard, calculating dark eyes stared unblinkingly from a face to which a smile would be a stranger. The coat she was wearing looked as old as the hills. It was a tweed mixture, which many, many moons ago had been beige and purple. Now the only colours that could be made out were the variety of stains all down the front which suggested she never took the coat off to eat. The elbows, cuffs and pockets were frayed, and Beth couldn't help thinking she'd seen better dressed tramps.

'I'll be the one to make sure yer get yer money every Saturday. Me name's Beth Porter and I live next door to Flo Henderson here so yer don't have to worry about getting yer money back. But a couple of us are desperate, so could yer let us have a couple of pounds to be going on with?'

'I can let yer have two now, that's all. The rest on Monday. And I want all the names and addresses before I hand over anything.' The moneylender began to close her door. 'I'll get the two pounds for yer.' When she was sure she couldn't be seen, she undid the shabby coat to reveal the two side pockets she'd stitched into the lining. The pinny she was wearing had a wide deep pocket which contained the money she'd collected in that morning, but she hadn't had time to count her takings yet, or mark her books, so she didn't want to touch that. Instead, she lifted the pinny to get to a money belt she had tied around her waist. She knew exactly how much was in there so she could take two pounds out and still know where she was up to. After extracting two notes from the belt, she made sure the fasteners were safe, then smoothed down her pinny so the bulge wouldn't be noticed. One could safely say, without fear of contradiction, that Ma Maloney was not a trusting soul.

She opened the entry door and held out the two grubby pound notes. 'I want the names of whoever's having these.' Then she pulled a small tattered book from her pocket and a stub of pencil. 'Names and addresses?'

'Beth Porter and Hannah Bailey. And we all live in the same road as Flo, so we're not likely to do a bunk.'

'Just remember, if yer can't pay anything off it one week, yer've still got to pay the shilling interest.' Ma Maloney didn't speak normally, she growled out her words as though they were begrudged. 'I'm not a bleedin' benevolent fund.'

None of the women liked the look or sound of Ma, but until they had their pound in their hands they weren't going to upset her. But Lizzie was stung into saying, 'Sure, isn't it meself that's noticed ye're not given to acts of charity! But then, it's safe to say yer don't get very far in life being soft-hearted, and that's a fact.'

Dot spoke for the first time. 'Did someone mention the word heart? Only I think we're entering strange territory here 'cos I don't think she has one.'

Flo quickly decided if they stayed any longer, and the insults kept flying, the three unlucky ones wouldn't be getting their loan on Monday. 'That's about it then, Ma, so we'll leave yer in peace to go about yer business. Yer must be busy this time of the year. So we'll give yer a knock on Monday, eh? Front door or entry, which is the best?'

The moneylender stepped back into her yard, and through lips that were barely parted, said, 'Here, ten o'clock sharp. I can't afford to be hanging around so if ye're not here on time that's yer own bleedin' fault.' With that the entry door was firmly closed and the women could hear a bolt being shot, then footsteps shuffling over the cobbled yard.

'My God, whoever said she was a witch wasn't far wrong,' Dot said. 'Did yer see the state of her coat? She wouldn't even get a balloon off the rag and bone man for it.'

Flo jerked her head to get them moving away from the back door. 'Come on, let's go.' And keeping her voice low, she said, 'I wouldn't care but no one can tell me she isn't loaded. She must be bleedin' rolling in money! Just think, she's going to get five bob a week interest off us alone! Add that to the dozens of other women who borrow off her, and she's got to be raking in a fortune every week.'

'Yeah, why didn't one of us think of it first?' Beth slipped her arm through Hannah's as they neared the main road. 'We could have been rolling in it.'

'Oh, you'd have made a fine moneylender, I don't think!' The very idea had Flo laughing. 'Ye're too soft, you are, yer'd only have to hear a sob story and yer'd fall for it. Yer have to be tough in that game. Tough, fearless and without friends. It would cost you money, queen, yer'd never make any.'

'I wouldn't want to be one,' Beth replied, squeezing Hannah's arm. 'What do you say, sunshine? If Ma Maloney is a typical moneylender, then I'd rather be skint. I think if she tried to smile her face would crack. She's one sad, miserable woman.'

'She's a sad, miserable, rich woman, queen, and she's probably laughing her little cotton socks off right now because she's got another five suckers on her books.'

'Not for long she won't,' Hannah said. 'I'm going to pay her off as quick as I can. I don't want to be in debt to the likes of her.'

'I wouldn't worry yer head about that, girl, until after Christmas,' Dot said. 'When are yer going to look for a bed?'

'Flo said there's a good shop on Stanley Road so I might take a trip down there now. I've only got a few days, I've got to move meself.'

'I'll come with yer,' Beth offered. 'Two heads are always better than one.'

Dot wasn't going to be left out. 'I'll come, too!'

'Oh, I was going to ask yer to watch out for Ginny and Joey. Just in case I'm not back when they get home from school.'

'No, I'm coming with yer. Yer know I hate to miss anything. Anyway Flo will watch out for the kids for us, won't yer, girl?'

A look of amazement came over Flo's face. Well, the flamin' cheeky beggars! She was the one who'd mentioned seeing the bed, and here they were trying to fob her off! 'How soft you are! Yer can take a running jump, that's what yer can do. I'll go with Hannah and Beth, and *you* can watch out for *my* kids.'

'Before any blows are exchanged, can I suggest that I'll make me way home now and keep an eye out for all the kids?' Lizzie the peacemaker suggested. 'I'll bring them in out of the cold if ye're not back in time.'

'Thanks a million, sunshine, ye're a pal,' Beth said. 'But doesn't it seem a bit much for four of us to go looking for a second-hand bed?'

'Nah, the more the merrier, queen!' Flo was in her element. Anything that kept her out of the house was fine by her. She'd peeled the spuds this morning, so it wouldn't take her long to get the dinner on the go. 'It's not a big shop, so with a gang of us the poor man could easily get confused and sell the bed for less than he intended.'

'If you make a holy show of us, Flo Henderson, I'll break yer ruddy neck for yer.' Beth knew she was wasting her breath, because her neighbour couldn't resist showing off in the spotlight. And in all fairness, it had to be said she was a dab hand at getting a bargain. 'Unless, of course, yer get the bed for half the price.'

'Oh, I can't promise half the price, queen, but I might wangle the odd shilling off.'

Lizzie chuckled, more than a little sorry she was going to miss a treat. But someone had to be there for the children. 'I'll be wishing yer the best of luck, so I will. And don't worry about the kids, they'll be fine. I'll see yer later, ta-ra for now.'

Lizzie had her head bent against the bitterly cold wind as she turned the corner of the street. Her eyes were watering from the cold, and she wiped the back of her hand across them to clear her vision. It was then she saw a familiar figure knocking on the Porters' door and then trying to peep through the curtains. Lizzie quickened her steps. What was Ginny doing home at this time of the day, and how long had the poor thing been standing around in the cold?

Ginny saw their neighbour walking up the street and hurried to meet her. 'D'yer know where me mam is, Mrs O'Leary? I can't see any sign of her, and I can't get in! I've been around the back but that's locked as well!'

Lizzie thought before she spoke. She must not mention the money-lender. 'The usual gang went out to the shops, and they'd all have been home by now if Hannah hadn't wanted to look for a bed she'll need when her family come next week. And, of course, we all wanted to go with her.' They had reached Lizzie's house and she was quick to insert the key. 'Inside with yer, me darlin', and we'll soon have yer nice and warm.'

Ginny's spirits sank. She was so looking forward to telling her mother about her job, now she felt let down. 'D'yer know where they've gone, Mrs O'Leary, so I can go after them?'

'Ah, now, sure, I'd not be knowing that, me darlin'. I offered to come home to make sure there was somewhere for all the children to shelter, just in case the women took longer than expected. But it's yerself that's very early, and yer mam wouldn't be expecting yer, otherwise she would have come home. Are yer not feeling well, me darlin', is that it?'

Ginny sighed. 'No, Mrs O'Leary, I'm fine. But me and another girl went for an interview at Woolworth's, and when we got back to school the headmistress said we could come home early because we'd had nothing to eat and were starving.'

Lizzie could sense the disappointment in the young girl. 'Oh, of course, I knew about the interview, and yer mam mentioned a few times that she wondered how yer were getting on. But she didn't expect yer home at this time, me darlin', 'cos yer were supposed to go back to school for the rest of the day.' Lizzie was torn. If she asked how the interview had gone and the girl hadn't got the job, she would be embarrassed. And if she had been successful, perhaps she wanted her mother to know before anyone. But she'd known Ginny since she was a baby, so surely it was only natural to show interest? 'Take yer coat off, me darlin', and those nice warm gloves ye're wearing. Then yer can sit down and tell me how yer got on.'

'I got the job, Mrs O'Leary! I start the Monday after the holidays.'

'Oh, glory be to God!' Lizzie threw her arms in the air before wrapping them around Ginny. 'Now isn't that the best news I've had for weeks?' She didn't need to pretend or put on a show, she was genuinely delighted for the girl. 'Wait until yer tell yer mam and dad. Sure, they'll be over the moon, so they will. It's not everyone who is clever enough to get a job in such a foine shop as Woolworth's, and yer have every right to be feeling proud of yerself, so yer have.'

The sincere pleasure in the Irish woman's voice, and the beaming smile on her face, cheered Ginny up and she began to chuckle. 'Well, I'd be telling a lie if I said I wasn't chuffed with me little self, Mrs O'Leary. I really did want to work in a shop, but I thought it would be a local one, sweet shop or greengrocer's perhaps. I never dreamt me first job would be in such a big shop in the city centre. I can thank our headmistress for it because she's the one who put the opportunity my way. And she's as pleased as I am.'

Lizzie slapped an open palm to her forehead. 'The reason she let yer home early is because yer'd had nothing to eat all day, and here's me keeping yer yapping while yer starve to death! It's meself that's losing the run of me senses, right enough. But if you'll poke a bit of life into the fire for me, I'll put the kettle on and make yer a butty. Then we can sit by the fire with a nice cup of hot tea and a jam butty while yer tell me everything that's happened to yer today. And I want to know every word that's been spoken, and what the people who interviewed yer were like. All the ins and outs, me darlin', I'll settle for nothing less.'

And as today was a big milestone in her life, Ginny had no intention of letting anyone settle for less.

Chapter Ten

'Ooh, it's quite big, isn't it?' Beth and her three friends stood in a tight group outside the large, glass-fronted second-hand shop. 'I've passed it dozens of times but never really taken any notice of it.'

'The shop's been here for donkey's years.' Flo was happy to fill them in with all the information. Mind you, she thought, if they didn't go around with their eyes shut, they'd know these things for themselves. 'It's changed hands a few times to my knowledge. Our Elsie bought a three-piece suite from here when she got married, and she didn't half get her money's worth out of it.'

'They've got stacks of furniture in there,' Dot said, 'I'd love to have a good root around to see if there's any bargains. Some of my furniture could do with replacing.'

It was all too much for Hannah who was very quiet. For the first time in her life she'd met and borrowed from a moneylender, and she didn't like the experience one little bit. Now she was standing outside a second-hand shop, and this was a first for her too! But, as she told herself, beggars can't be choosers.

'Come on, let's get it over with, we can't stand here gawping all day.' Beth propelled Hannah forward and pushed open the shop door, setting off a bell that was attached to the top of the door frame. The sound was another thing that added to Hannah's apprehension and had her clinging tighter to Beth.

The tinkle of the bell had no sooner stopped than a man appeared from somewhere at the back of the shop. He was small and thin with dark hair and a thick neat moustache which was not only his pride and joy, but which he thought made him look like a certain heart-throb film star. Rubbing his hands together, he said, 'Good afternoon, ladies, can I help you?'

By this time Flo and Dot were in the shop, and the man raised his brows. 'Are you all together?'

Beth nodded. And without giving a thought to the fact that not one of them had a shopping bag with them, she said, 'Yes, we're all mates.

109

We've been out shopping and as we were passing we wondered if yer happened to have any decent single beds for sale? One of our neighbours has visitors coming for Christmas and she's a bed short.'

The shopkeeper, a smooth-talking ladies' man who thought he was God's gift to women, focused the full force of his charm on Beth as she was the most attractive. 'Ye're in luck, love, 'cos I've got two single beds in at the moment and both are in good nick. And seeing as ye're such a pretty woman, I'll do yer a good price on them.' Still rubbing his hands together, he said, 'If yer come with me, I'll show them to yer.' His eyes were inviting Beth, but to his dismay when he turned around he had four women on his heels.

They came to a bedstead leaning up against the wall with the bars and bedhead lying in front of it on the floor. 'This one has no mattress but it's in good condition. It wouldn't cost very much for a mattress if yer know the right place to go.'

Beth was eyeing the springs. 'How much are yer asking for it?'

'Only ten bob.' Again his hands were rubbed together and he gave her his film star smile. 'And that's a bargain.'

'What!' Flo pushed herself forward, and because he wasn't a tall man, she was able to meet his eyes. 'What have yer done to it since last week that's upped the price from five shillings to ten bob?'

The salesman was knocked off course, but only for a second. 'I don't know where yer got that from, Missus, but that bed was never five shillings.'

'It bleedin' well was! There's nowt wrong with my eyesight, Mister, and the tag yer had tied on it said five shillings. It wasn't in the shop that day, yer had it outside with some other bits and pieces.'

'Not this bed, Missus, that was another one.'

'Another one, me eye! What d'yer take me for! It was this bleedin' bedstead all right, with two brass bulbs on the headboard. So don't be coming it, Mister, 'cos we're not daft, we weren't born yesterday.'

'All I can say then is that me partner must have put the wrong price tag on it.' The man was wishing all sorts of bad things for Flo, but he still managed to give them his best smile. 'Anyway, seeing as how it's Christmas, the season of goodwill and cheer, I'll let it go for seven and a tanner. Now I can't say fairer than that.'

Hannah hadn't spoken since they'd entered the shop. She was more than content to leave matters in the hands of her friends as she wouldn't have the nerve to haggle over prices. But she needed to speak up now. 'Yer mentioned yer had two beds for sale, where's the other one?'

Once again the hand-rubbing started. 'Ah, well, yer see, the other comes complete with a good clean mattress, so naturally it's a lot dearer than this one. I paid over the odds for it 'cos it's in cracking condition and I need to recoup some of me money. I've got a wife and three children to keep, and they expect Christmas presents like everyone else.'

Beth decided to play him at his own game. She put on her sweetest smile. It came complete with fluttering eyelashes. 'Ooh, yer do surprise me. I didn't think yer were old enough to have three children. Yer don't half carry yer age well.'

Dot thought she'd add a little bit of flattery. 'I was just thinking the same thing! I don't know what ye're taking that makes yer look so young, but I wouldn't mind some of it meself.'

The man's chest expanded about six inches. He was beside himself. He didn't know whether to flash his smile, rub his hands or stroke his moustache. And Flo thought the whole thing was so hilarious, she couldn't help adding her twopennyworth. Anyone as vain as this man, she thought, deserved to have his leg pulled. So she heaped more praise on the poor bloke's head. 'If yer could put whatever it is in bottles and sell it, yer wouldn't have to worry about flogging second-hand furniture, yer'd be a ruddy millionaire.'

Hannah wasn't used to the humour of the three friends or the antics they got up to. She just wanted to get a bed sorted out as quickly as possible. 'Could we see the other bed, please, and would yer tell us how much ye're selling it for?'

The salesman moved an old-fashioned screen out of the way, and there was the bed. The spring base, the mattress and the wooden headboard were standing up against a wall, while the iron bars were lying across the floor, tied together with string. 'It's practically brand new, there's not a mark or stain on the mattress.' Then began the sales talk. 'The house it came from was like a little palace, yer could eat yer food off the floor.'

'Can yer let the mattress down, so me friend can have a good look at it?' Beth was feeling confident that this was the bed Hannah would end up with. It certainly looked in excellent condition. It all depended now on the mattress and price.

Hannah nodded, well satisfied with the cleanliness of the mattress. It would certainly be the answer to her problems, if she could afford it. 'How much are yer asking for it?'

'Only a pound, love, and yer'd be getting a bargain. It's worth twice that.'

'A pound!' The sound of Flo's voice had the man creasing his face as though to say, oh, not that one again. 'No one in their right mind would give yer a pound for it! She'd be better off taking the seven and six one and buying a brand new mattress from TJ's for ten bob. She'd be two and six in pocket.'

The man sighed. 'Okay, I'll drop it two and six, even though I'll be losing money on the deal.'

Flo shook her head. 'No, yer'll have to do better than that. If my mate's got any sense, she won't give yer a penny more than fifteen bob. And that's being generous with yer. But if yer can't see yer way clear to doing that, well, I'll have to take her to another shop I know where the bloke is more understanding.'

Hannah's heart stopped beating, and Beth and Dot held their breath. Flo had never let them down before but this time Hannah's peace of mind depended on it.

Harry Partridge, for that was the shopkeeper's name, did some quick thinking. He wasn't likely to sell the bed to anyone else as most people were spending what money they had on food and presents for Christmas. And he would still be making a profit at fifteen bob. But he could strangle the little fat one with his bare hands. He was sure he'd have got what he'd asked for if she'd kept her ruddy nose out of it. If he ever saw her coming to the shop again he'd put the closed sign up. 'Oh, go on then, seeing as it's Christmas and the time of goodwill, yer can have it for fifteen shillings – even though it means me losing money on the deal.'

Flo threw her head back and tutted. 'Me heart bleeds for yer, Mister, and I'll be thinking of yer on Christmas Day with no turkey on the table and yer kids starving.' She gave him one of her mischievous smiles which almost made him change his mind about her. Almost but not quite. She had just lost him five bob. 'If me turkey was a bit bigger, I'd invite you and yer wife and kids to our house. I hate the thought of anyone going hungry on Christmas Day.'

While this was going on, Hannah had noticed a small chest of drawers standing next to the bed. It was in need of a good polish, but that was neither here nor there. It would be really useful because when the men put the partition up in the back bedroom, it would mean she'd have a chest of drawers for each of the children's bedrooms. At least they'd have somewhere to put their clothes and it would make the rooms look more homely. She tugged on Beth's coat. 'I wonder how much that chest of drawers is? It would be ideal for when the back bedroom is made into two.'

Beth could see the salesman talking to Dot, so she put a finger to her lips to ask Hannah not to say anything yet. If she appeared too interested, the price would go up. 'Excuse me.' She tapped the man lightly on the arm. 'Do yer deliver?'

'We do sometimes, love, but we couldn't do nothing before Christmas, not now. Yer see we've only got the one small van and we've dozens of deliveries to make. There's no way we could fit yer in until after Christmas.'

'Oh, dear,' Hannah said. 'I need it before then.'

'I'm sorry, love, but no can do. Where d'yer live anyway?'

'Only off County Road, not very far away.' Beth wondered if they'd gone all through that rigmarole for nothing. 'Is there no way yer can help?'

The man scratched his head, careful not to move a hair out of place. 'There's a young lad lives at the back, he's got a handcart he uses to do odd jobs. He'd do it for yer, but he wouldn't do it for nowt, he'd want paying.'

'I wouldn't expect him to do it for nothing,' Hannah told him. 'But how much d'yer think he'd charge?'

'If yer'd like to hang on, I'll go and see if he's in. I won't be a few minutes.'

When the four women were left alone in the shop, they all began to talk at the same time. 'Yer've got a real bargain there, Hannah,' Dot said. 'It's as good as new.'

'It certainly is.' Beth nodded knowingly. 'Yer can thank Flo for getting it so cheap. I wouldn't have had the nerve to bargain him down.'

'I know.' Hannah reached out and gripped Flo's arm. 'I'm beholden to yer, sweetheart, yer've done me proud.'

The little woman preened. 'Think nothing of it, queen, I don't like to see no one getting conned. And the swine would have conned yer if he'd been let. He'd have charged yer a pound and laughed all the way home. And he'd have slept with a clear conscience.' Flo nodded to the chest of drawers. 'Have yer got yer eye on that?'

Hannah shook her head from side to side, saying, 'I've got me eye on it, but I can't see me getting it. I don't think the man will be bargained down twice in one day.'

'I'll tell yer what to do, queen. Don't you mention that yer've got yer eye on the chest, just see what he says about having the bed delivered first. Would yer be prepared to spend the whole pound note if it meant yer could have the bed and the chest of drawers delivered to yer front door?'

'Oh, of course I would! I'd be over the moon!'

'Don't be building her hopes up, sunshine, 'cos that's not going to happen,' Beth said. 'As the man told us, he has to buy the furniture and he needs to make a profit.'

'Yer'd fall for the bleedin' cat, you would, queen! Yer don't take no notice of his sales patter, 'cos he'll blind yer with science! Yer can take it from me that he wouldn't let anything go out of this shop without him making a few bob on it. After all, he doesn't stand here day after day just for the sake of his ruddy health. So let's play our cards right and see what we can come up with. When he comes back, let Hannah pay him for the bed and the delivery, and when that's all settled I'll see what I can do about the chest. I'll know by then how much Hannah has got to play with, so I'll pretend I'm interested in the chest and see what I can get it for.' They heard a movement coming from the back of the shop and Flo whispered, 'Let's all act daft, shall we, and see where it gets us?'

When Harry Partridge came back, he let his eyes run over the stock in the shop, causing the women to wonder if he thought one of them was hiding a sideboard under her coat. But they do say that thieves don't trust anyone, 'cos they believe everyone is like themselves.

'I've seen young Billy and he'll deliver the bed tonight for yer. But he wants a shilling for his trouble.'

'That's fine, thank you very much.' Hannah opened her handbag and took out her purse. 'I'll settle up with you for the bed, but what about the boy with the handcart?'

'You pay him yerself, Missus, when he makes the delivery.' The man took the pound note from Hannah. 'I'll get the change for you. We keep our money in the back room for safety. I won't keep yer long.' He was back within minutes with two half-crowns. 'I forgot to tell yer, Billy said it would be about half-six before he got to your house 'cos he's busy. So don't think he's not coming because he won't let yer down.'

'That's fine,' Beth said to Hannah, 'we'll have our dinner over by then, so I can come and sit with yer until he comes.'

This was where Flo stepped in. 'I've been looking at that chest of drawers. It's not worth writing home about, but it would do for one of the kids. How much d'yer want for me to take it off yer hands?'

Harry Partridge closed his eyes and put a hand over his mouth so they wouldn't hear him groan. Why did there always have to be a fly in the ointment? Particularly such a large one with a big mouth? And why did she have to come into his shop and give him a headache and indigestion? 'There's nothing wrong with that chest that a good polish wouldn't put right.'

'Go 'way, it's on its last legs!' Flo was sailing close to the wind but was still confident. Hannah, on the other hand, could see her chances of getting the chest fading. 'But my feller's a carpenter by trade, so he could fix it that it didn't wobble any more.'

The man pinched the bridge of his nose between two fingers, and with as much patience as he could muster ground out the words, 'It doesn't wobble, it's in good nick, and the price is four bob.'

Flo folded her arms and hitched up her bosom. 'I'll give yer three for it, and that's me last offer.'

Harry Partridge was known to have quite a temper at times, with a colourful vocabulary to match. But with three pairs of eyes watching him with interest he counted up to ten before saying, 'All right, Missus! To get rid of yer, I'll let yer have it for three.'

Flo became all sweetness and light. 'I knew you and me could strike a deal. Will yer see that it goes on the handcart with the bed, please?' She turned to Hannah and held out her hand. 'Be an angel and lend us three bob, queen. I'll sort yer out when we get home.'

The salesman watched the four women leaving the shop, and had a sinking feeling in his stomach that he'd been well and truly taken to the cleaner's. He stood scratching his head, his mind so distracted he didn't realise he was making a mess of the hair he'd spent ten minutes on that morning, standing in front of the mirror over the mantelpiece combing it until he was satisfied every strand was in place.

Ginny was back and forth to the window looking for any sign of her mother. 'They're a long time, aren't they, Mrs O'Leary? They should be well back from the shops by now.'

'Yer mam will be here any minute, me darlin',' Lizzie said. 'Whatever it is is taking longer than they expected, but I know what it's like when ye're eager to see someone and the fingers on the clock don't seem to be moving.' She cocked an ear. 'If I'm not mistaken, I can hear Flo's voice now.' She stood up and went to the window. 'Sure, will yer just feast yer eyes on them? The four of them are doubled up with laughter, so they are.'

'I'll go now then.' Ginny picked up her coat from the couch. 'Thank yer for having me, Mrs O'Leary, it was very kind of yer.'

'It's meself that's coming with yer.' Lizzie took her coat from a hook and was putting it on while she followed Ginny across the cobbles. 'Something's tickled their fancy, and sure I enjoy a laugh as well as the next woman.'

Beth looked surprised to see her daughter. 'What are you doing home? It's only a quarter to four, I wasn't expecting to see you.'

'Miss Bond let me and Marie Whittaker come home early 'cos we'd had nothing to eat and were starving.'

'Why didn't yer come home at dinnertime, like yer usually do? Joey ate most of the sandwiches I made for you.' Beth was teasing. She could tell her daughter was bursting with excitement and wanted to build it up so Ginny got the reaction she wanted. 'How come yer didn't get anything to eat?'

'Well, yer see, it was like this.' The girl was thrilled all the neighbours were here, it added to the special occasion. 'Me and Marie were nearly four hours in Woolworth's. The reason for that was a Miss Ormsby, who is the Personnel Officer, didn't know whether to start me on as a supervisor or make me the general manager!'

Beth was laughing inside but kept her face straight. 'And what did this Personnel Officer finally decide?'

'To start me as a junior sales assistant, starting on Monday the second of January. And the other girl from our class, Marie, she got a job in the stock room.'

Beth held her arms wide and when Ginny ran to her, lifted her daughter in the air and spun her around. 'Oh, you clever girl, that's brilliant! I am so pleased yer got the job that yer wanted, and I'm so proud I feel like crying.'

'Don't you dare cry,' Flo said, kissing Ginny's cheek. 'It's a bleedin' celebration, queen, not a ruddy funeral.'

'I'll say!' Dot was next in line to hug the laughing girl. 'Just don't go all posh on us, or get too big for yer boots.'

'I'll be serving behind a counter, Auntie Dot,' Ginny told her. 'I didn't get the general manager's job.'

'Give yerself time, sweetheart.' Hannah was last with her congratulations. 'There's many a true word spoken in jest.'

Lizzie was getting impatient. 'Can we come in your house for five minutes, me darlin', so I can be brought up to date with the day's events?'

'Five minutes only, ladies, 'cos I've got to get the dinner on early. Me and Hannah have to be at her house by half-six.' Beth gave her daughter another big hug. 'Today's been a good day all round, sunshine. Wait until yer dad finds out, he'll be delighted.'

The atmosphere around the Porters' table that night was boisterous to say the least. The whole family shared in Ginny's good fortune as she told them in detail what had been said at the interview, then of the long wait before being told she'd got the job. 'I start on seven and six a week, plus an extra shilling travel allowance that they give to those who have a certain distance to come. And I'll have company every day 'cos Marie only lives a few streets away.'

Andy wasn't a man given to tears, but seeing his daughter so happy brought a lump to his throat. He was so proud of her and what she'd achieved off her own bat. Fourteen years old and never caused them a moment's worry. 'Yer've done well, love, and yer'll get on in life. I bet yer end up with a good job 'cos yer've got the confidence to go for what yer want.'

Ginny rolled her eyes. 'I might sound confident now I know I've got the job, but yer should have seen me this morning, I was a nervous wreck. Me legs were like jelly, me heart was in me mouth and something in me tummy was doing cartwheels.'

Beth's mind went back to the day she'd gone for her first interview. She didn't have the confidence her daughter possessed and she'd been terrified. And the job was only in a small factory making up cardboard cartons, nothing so grand as Woolworth's. 'Yer've done very well for yerself, sunshine, and as yer dad said, yer'll get on in life, please God.'

Joey had been listening intently, but hadn't said a word. Not that he wasn't pleased for his sister, 'cos inside he was feeling very emotional that she'd done so well. But he didn't know the right words to use that wouldn't make him sound like a cissy. 'When yer get this general manager's job, Ginny, yer can put a good word in for me. I wouldn't mind a supervisor's job to be going on with and I can work me way up,' he said gruffly.

His sister laughed. 'I'll keep yer in mind, kid.'

'Well, now we've heard all your news, I'll tell yer what sort of a day me and Hannah have had.' Beth saw the old lady start, and stretched across to pat her hand for reassurance. There was no fear of her slipping up and bringing Ma Maloney into the conversation, not when she knew Andy would go mad. 'When Flo heard Hannah was a bed short for her grandchildren coming, she told us she'd seen a really good second-hand one in a shop in Stanley Road. So when Lizzie said she'd come home and keep an eye out for the children if we weren't back by the time they got home from school, we decided to walk down to the shop and have a look at this bed. There was me and Hannah, and Dot and Flo. And what a lark it turned out to be.' Beth started at the beginning and left nothing out. Actions, expressions and words, she gave them the lot. Even Hannah, who hadn't found Flo's antics a bit funny at the time because she'd feared they were going to lose her the bed and the chest

117

of drawers, could now see the whole scene in an entirely different light. And her shoulders shook as her laughter joined that of her adopted family.

'I didn't think it was a bit funny at the time 'cos the man was giving her daggers and I thought he would throw us out of the shop. Me and Beth and Dot had very little to say for ourselves because I think we were all too embarrassed.'

'Oh, yer soon learn not to get embarrassed at anything Flo does!' Beth chuckled. 'If yer did, then yer couldn't be friends with her. And I couldn't imagine life without Flo in it to cheer me up when I'm miserable. She never pays the price she's asked for anything! Oh, in a food shop she will, but not in a second-hand shop or down at the market. She's saved me and Dot a few bob over the years, I can tell yer. And Lizzie as well!'

Hannah nodded. 'I'll know who to ask in future if I'm looking for a bargain. She got the bloke to knock five shillings off the bed, and then a shilling off the chest of drawers. I still can't believe it!'

'She did yer proud, Hannah, but that's Flo all over. She's got a heart as big as a week and is a good one to have as a friend.' Andy was pleased for their elderly neighbour. She'd been a widow for years so she must be scrimping and scraping every week to make ends meet. Six shillings was a lot of money to her. 'And the furniture's being delivered tonight, is it?'

It was Beth who answered. 'It's coming about half-six, so as soon as we've finished our dinner I'm going down with Hannah to keep her company until it comes. And between yer, yer can tidy up and wash the dishes while I'm gone.'

'Yer won't let them take the bed upstairs, will yer?' Andy asked. 'We don't want it in our way tomorrow while we're putting the partition up. It'll have to go in yer living room for now, and we'll take it upstairs when we've finished.'

Hannah's eyes found and held his. 'What would have happened to me if you hadn't seen me wandering that night? And if you and yer family and friends hadn't cared for me? I'd have been in Queer Street, with no one to turn to for help. In fact, they'd have probably locked me up in one of the lunatic asylums.'

Ginny was horrified at the thought. 'No, they wouldn't, Mrs Bailey, we wouldn't have let them! And we've loved having yer here, haven't we, Mam?'

'Of course we have, sunshine, it's been a pleasure. Hannah is welcome to come any time she likes.' Beth smiled at the woman who had been, only a week ago, just a neighbour who lived at the top end of the street. They'd always been friendly with her, passed the time of day and perhaps chatted for a few minutes. But now their closeness was more than mere friendship, she was like one of the family. 'And she's still got a few more days with us, before her family come.'

'That'll be a happy day for you, won't it, Hannah?' Andy's deep brown eyes were understanding. 'And I bet they can't wait to see you. It'll be nice for them to have a granny back in their lives.'

'Talking about grannies,' Beth said, 'I'll have to get up to see my mam and dad in the next few days. The trouble is, Speke is a hell of a long way to go so I can't afford to visit them as often as I'd like. But I can't let Christmas go by without seeing them, they'd never forgive me and I'd never forgive meself.'

'It is a long way to Speke, sweetheart, it's right out in the country.' Hannah had met Beth's parents when they lived in the next street, but they were passing acquaintances, they'd never really been friends. 'What possessed them to move so far away?'

'My sister Elsie persuaded them. Yer won't remember Elsie, she's very religious and spends a lot of time in church. She never had any intention of marrying, never even had a boyfriend even though she was a good-looking girl. Me mam always said she was married to the church. Anyway, she talked them into moving to a parlour house so she could have a downstairs sitting-room of her own. I know me mam regrets the move, although she'd never admit to it because Elsie has a grand job and is very good to them. But it's not half lonely, out in the country and miles away from shops.' Beth saw the plates were empty now and started to stack them together. 'Both me mam and dad miss the neighbours they'd had for years. There was nothing the old girl enjoyed more than a good gossip, and me dad liked his pint of bitter in the corner pub. I think moving was the worst thing they ever did but it's too late now, we can't turn back the clock.'

'Leave the dishes, love, we'll do them,' Andy said. 'Yer'd better be going 'cos if ye're not in when the delivery comes they're not likely to come back again.'

Beth glanced at the clock and quickly pushed her chair back. 'Come on, Hannah, we're cutting it fine.'

'I'll light a fire when we get in,' Hannah said, cuddling up to Beth for warmth as they walked down the street. 'I can bank it up and it'll take the chill off the house for the men coming tomorrow. If I put the fireguard around, it should be safe.'

'I'll give yer a hand.' Beth shivered at the thought of going into a house where there had been no fire for several days. 'We'll soon have the place warm.'

They stopped outside Hannah's house and she took a key from her pocket. 'We'll have to leave the front door open so I can see what I'm doing. The street lamp sheds quite a bit of light into the hall.'

'Give me the key and you stand by the door until I light the gas.' Beth wasn't taking a chance on the old lady standing on a chair. 'I've brought a box of matches.'

Hannah heard Beth mutter and knew she'd walked into the table. Then the light streamed out of the living room into the tiny hall. It was then Hannah saw the letter lying on the floor. As she bent down to pick it up, she called, 'I've got a letter, and it's from Claire.'

'Oh, that's lovely! Bring it in and let's see what she's got to say.'

'I'll put a light to the paper and wood in the grate first, shall I? Otherwise you and me are going to freeze to death. It won't take long, there's coal in the scuttle.'

'You read the letter and I'll light the fire. I know it's none of my business, but I want to hear what Claire has to say as much as you do.'

Hannah ran her thumb under the flap of the envelope and tore it open. 'Oh, she's put a pound note in it! She didn't have to do that.'

'Read the letter, sunshine, and yer might find out why.' Beth was on her hands and knees in front of the grate. She'd put a light to the balls of newspaper, and was encouraged when the wood caught fire. A few decent-sized cobs of coal and with a bit of luck they'd have a roaring fire in no time.

'They're still coming on Wednesday. They get into Exchange Station about two o'clock, but I haven't got to worry about meeting them 'cos she hasn't been away from Liverpool so long she's forgotten where the tram runs from. And the pound is to help buy a few extra groceries in.' Hannah was giving the news as she read it. 'Oh, Claire says she's sending a tea chest by a removal firm that delivers all over the country. She's sending bedding, linen, crockery and ornaments, and it should arrive here on Tuesday, in time for the bedding to be of use. She says that should put me mind at rest 'cos I'm probably worried in case I don't have enough.'

Beth sat back on her heels and took the newspaper away from the fire as the flames were now licking merrily around the coals. 'I'd been thinking about whether yer'd have enough bedding, sunshine, but I didn't like to mention it. Anyway, I don't need to now 'cos yer've been sorted out.'

'Oh, it's been on me mind, sweetheart, 'cos I haven't got loads of spare bedding. We'd have got by, but only just.'

When a knock came on the door, Hannah shoved the letter back in the envelope. 'Young Billy, whoever he is, is nice and early. I'll open the door.'

Billy was a young man of about eighteen. Tall and well-made, with blonde hair and laughing blue eyes, he was a handsome lad. And he was a worker. With the help of his twelve-year-old brother, he had the bed and chest of drawers in Hannah's living room within minutes. Beth was very impressed. 'Ye're a quick worker, sunshine!'

'Yer can't afford to stand still if yer want to earn a few bob, Missus. Time is money, and it's hard to come by. I want to give me ma a few bob extra, with it being Christmas. There's eight of us at home, and trying to feed that many is no joke.' He pocketed the shilling Hannah handed to him and showed a set of strong white teeth when he smiled. 'Have a nice Christmas, ladies, and the best of good luck in the coming year.'

'What a nice lad,' Hannah said, after closing the front door. 'I bet his mother's proud of him. Good worker and very pleasant.'

'Yeah, I was quite taken with him.' Beth pushed herself to her feet. 'Now if yer can get a shovelful of slack, I'll bank the fire up and it'll last through the night.'

Hannah turned at the back door. 'This has been a very lucky day all round for me and Ginny. She's got the job she wanted, and I'm over the moon for her. And me, well, I've got the bed and the chest of drawers which I needed but couldn't see my way clear to getting. And now this letter from Claire has just rounded things off. I'm a very lucky lady.'

Beth smiled at her, thinking that now wasn't the time to mention a certain lady who went by the name of Ma Maloney, and who would haunt them all until she got her money back.

Chapter Eleven

After breakfast on the Saturday morning, Beth managed to get Hannah alone in the kitchen as she was putting the plates away. It was the only chance she'd had, with Ginny sleeping on the couch. She was there when they went to bed at night, and still there when they got up, so a private conversation had been impossible. With a finger to her lips first, Beth whispered, 'I'd like to get down to the market this morning if I can, to look for a coat for Joey. I don't want the children to know, 'cos they'd be bound to mention it to Andy and he'd wonder where I'd got the money from. He doesn't get paid until Saturday morning so it'll be after one when I get his wages.' She raised her eyes to the ceiling. 'I hate telling him lies, but he'd be really upset if he knew I'd borrowed from a moneylender.'

With an ear to the door, to make sure Ginny and Joey were still at the table talking, Hannah said, 'But how are yer going to manage that? Yer can't hide a coat from the children, they'd be bound to see it.'

'By being crafty and telling more lies, I'm afraid, sunshine. I'll ask Flo if she'll nip to Great Homer Street with me, and if I'm lucky enough to find a decent coat for Joey, she can take it in her house until this afternoon. Then I can bring it in with me when I've done me weekend shopping and Andy will think I bought it out of his wages.' Beth put her hands together as though in prayer. 'May God forgive me for my sins.'

'But where are yer going to tell the children ye're going this morning? And what'll yer do if they want to go with yer?'

'I've got it all figured out, sunshine, and I'm getting more devious and sly by the minute. But I want yer to know that every word out of me mouth isn't a lie, and I don't spend me days being dodgy and crafty.'

'I know that, sweetheart, yer don't have to explain anything to me. Whatever yer do, it'll never be anything to hurt anyone. And all ye're doing now is for the good of yer son.'

'Well, I want yer to help me out, if yer will? I was going to come down with yer to get the fire going so the house is warm for the men coming this afternoon, but would yer mind taking Ginny and Joey with yer? They're both good workers, and they wouldn't get in yer way. Our Joey will go shopping for yer if yer want to stock up. And for his age, he's got a good little head on his shoulders. He wouldn't let anyone overcharge him.'

Hannah chuckled. 'He's another Flo in the making, is he?'

'He's got a long way to go before he's that good. But talking of my next-door neighbour, I'm going to slip out the back way and give her a knock to see if she feels like coming to the market with me. I won't be two minutes.'

Flo saw Beth walking up her yard and hurried to open the back door. 'What's up with yer, why didn't yer bang on the wall like yer usually do?'

'What I've got to say is a secret, that's why.' Beth stepped into the kitchen and peeped through into the living room to see if Flo's children were there. There was no point in telling a secret while children were listening, 'cos it wouldn't remain a secret for very long. 'Where's Amy and Wendy?'

'I've let them go to our Helen's with a Christmas card. They were pestering the life out of me to let them go, 'cos the crafty buggers know they'll get a penny off her. Any minute now, my dearly beloved sister will be calling me fit to burn on several counts. One, that I'm too tight to pay for a stamp to post her card, and second that I've got the girls from under my feet and put them under hers.' Flo's chubby face creased. 'I bet any money that some time today or tomorrow I'll be getting a visit from my nephew and niece. They'll hand me a Christmas card and then sit on the couch until I give them a penny each. Mind you, I can't blame our kid for playing silly beggars, 'cos I started it.'

Beth was getting impatient. 'Yer can tell me all about it on the tram.'

'On what tram? I'm not going on no tram.' Flo looked into Beth's eyes. 'Or, if I am, where the bleedin' hell am I going to?'

'Great Homer Street. I want to go to the market to look for a coat for our Joey, and I'd like a bit of company. Also, when we get back, I'd like yer to hide the coat in your house until we come back from the shops this afternoon.'

'Oh, aye! Pulling a fast one on your Andy, are yer?' Flo ran her fingers through her dishevelled hair. 'I don't think I should get involved in anything underhanded.'

'Yer what! Well, the cheek of you! If I'm underhanded, who was it taught me? Florence Henderson, that's who! The most underhanded person I know.'

'Ah, ay, queen, fair's fair. Yer must know someone who's more underhanded than me. I'm sure if yer racked yer brains yer'd come up with someone.'

'I'll do that on the tram, too, sunshine.'

'Yer'll do what on the tram, queen?'

'Rack me brains, soft girl, that's what. And if I come up with anyone, I'll let yer know.'

'I haven't said I'm going on the tram with yer yet! I've still got loads of housework to do, and see about something for our dinner.'

Beth knew her friend so well, she knew exactly how to go about bringing things to a conclusion that would suit both of them. 'Okay, sunshine, I understand. I'll get Dot to come with me, if she's not too busy, like.'

Flo bristled. 'Of course she'll be busy! She'll tell yer to get lost 'cos Saturday is a very busy day for everyone.'

Beth opened the kitchen door. 'I'll ask her first, but if she is too busy then I'll nip down to the market on me own.' She stepped down into the yard. 'I'll give yer a knock after dinner, sunshine, to go to the shops.'

'Hang on a bit, queen! What's the bleedin' rush? I haven't said I wouldn't go with yer so don't be taking the huff.'

'I'm not taking the huff! It's just that I haven't much time if I'm to be back to have Andy's dinner ready. It's a case of putting me skates on.'

'Bloody hell! Give us a chance, will yer?' Flo slipped the straps of her pinny over her head. 'It won't take me two minutes, I've only got to comb me hair.' She didn't bother folding the pinny, just threw it on the draining board. 'I'll be at yours before yer've got yer coat on.' And as a parting shot, she called, 'And before yer say owt, I have washed me face and me neck so I haven't got no tidemark.'

Beth smiled as she walked down the yard. 'Don't be in too much of a hurry, sunshine, 'cos first I've got to talk the children into going with Hannah. So shall we say fifteen minutes, to be on the safe side? But just in case Ginny and Joey are still in when yer come, don't mention where we're going, for heaven's sake, or yer'll be letting the cat out of the bag.'

'Listen, queen, why don't yer just tell me to keep me bleedin' mouth closed?'

''Cos I'm too much of a lady, that's why.'

'Well, I'll be buggered!' Flo stood on the top kitchen step with her arms folded. At least they must have been folded under her mountainous bosom because they were nowhere to be seen. 'Lady indeed! The state of you, and the price of bleedin' fish!'

'Flo, can we leave our falling out until we're on the tram, sunshine? It'll save us time and give us something to talk about. I'll see yer in a bit, ta-ra.'

'Ye're wasting yer time looking on those stalls, queen, 'cos most of the stuff is rubbish. It's like what the rag and bone man who comes around our street collects. And yer know he only gives the kids a balloon for it 'cos it's not worth no more.'

'I can't afford to buy Joey a new coat, sunshine, it's as easy as that. It's got to be a second-hand one, like it or lump it.'

'But I keep telling yer about the stall at the far end of the market! The woman what has the stall, her name's Mary Ann, she sells some smashing stuff. Her feller collects from the posh areas, and gives money for quality stuff.'

The market was heaving with people looking for bargains for Christmas presents and bits and bobs to put in the stockings their children would be hanging over the mantelpiece on Christmas Eve. The two friends were being pushed from all sides. Now Flo didn't take too kindly to this, and if it hadn't been for Beth some people would have gone home with bruises which were not acquired accidentally.

'Okay, let's try this Mary Ann's stall, if it'll keep yer quiet.' Beth hung on tightly to her mate's arm so they wouldn't get separated in the crowd. 'Then I want to look for long stockings for our Ginny, and some nice knickers and an underskirt, if they're not too dear. I can't send her to work in the navy blue fleecy lined ones she wears for school. Apart from the fact that they're worn out and only fit for the midden, she needs clothes that are more grown-up now, so she can hold her own with the people she'll be working with.'

Flo pulled her to a halt. 'Here yer are, this is the stall.'

Beth gasped. She hadn't been expecting anything like this. All the other stalls had one or two trestle tables, but this one had four, and they were arranged to form a square, with a woman and a young girl in the centre, moving quickly to serve the many people who were holding items up that they wished to purchase. The woman, Mary Ann, had bright red hair which was piled up on top of her head and kept in place by a tortoiseshell comb. She wore the traditional black woollen shawl, long black skirt and a black apron with a wide, deep money pocket in the front. And all the time she was serving, she was talking and cracking

126

jokes with the many people pushing against the trestle tables. It seemed everyone knew her, and she knew her regulars by name. Beth enjoyed the jovial atmosphere, it was really Christmassy, and there wasn't a face in the heaving throng that didn't have a smile on it. It wasn't hard to understand why because the stallholder was hilarious. Beth forgot she was pushed for time, and stood still to listen.

'If ye're not going to buy that blouse, Aggie, put the bleedin' thing down before yer wear it out,' the stallholder called out.

'I can't make up me mind whether the colour will suit me, Mary Ann.'

'Oh, aye, Aggie, what mind is that then?'

'My mind, of course, yer soft cow!'

'I didn't think yer had a mind, Aggie. If yer did, yer'd know that bright green definitely wouldn't go with that bright red complexion of yours.'

'I haven't got no bright red complexion, Mary Ann, yer hard-faced cow. My feller says I've got a very healthy colour.'

Mary Ann shook her head from side to side. 'Your feller has been as blind as a bat since he broke his glasses, he can't see a hand in front of him. He probably doesn't even remember what yer look like. It was only last week he walked into the house next door to yer by mistake, sat down at their table and they felt so sorry for him they gave him some dinner.'

Even the woman, Aggie, was laughing now. 'Ye're a cracker, Mary Ann, yer really are. And now, how much is this blouse?'

'It was fourpence ten minutes ago, Aggie, but I've had to put it up to sixpence 'cos I've lost trade with yer keeping me talking.'

'Yer can sod off, Mary Ann. Here's yer fourpence, that's all ye're getting.'

Mary Ann took the money and smiled at the woman. 'I'll give yer a word of advice which I won't charge yer for, Aggie. Remember yer said the other week yer were going to buy your feller a pair of reading glasses from Woolworth's? Well, don't give him them for Christmas if yer intend wearing that blouse, 'cos the colour will blind him again.'

Aggie shoved the blouse into her basket. 'Ye're a hard-faced cow, Mary Ann, and if it wasn't for this table between us I'd knock yer into the middle of next week.'

The stallholder grinned. 'Have a nice Christmas, Aggie, and all the best to you and yer family.'

'Oh, yer'll see me before then, Mary Ann, 'cos I'll be needing a skirt to go with the blouse.'

Mary Ann turned and shouted to the young girl who was moving like greased lighting to meet the demands of customers, 'Ay, Sadie! Keep yer eye open for a bright green skirt will yer? It's for Aggie, so it needs to be big enough to go around the gas works.'

While Aggie was mumbling what she'd do to the stallholder if she could get her hands on her, another woman was becoming very irate and more than a little jealous. 'Is there any chance of getting served here, Mary Ann? That big mouth isn't the only customer yer've got, yer know. And seeing as it's only a week to go before Christmas, I'd like to get home in time to put the turkey in the oven.'

Mary Ann was taking money from people as she talked, and it all went into the deep pocket in her apron. 'Hello, Tilly! I'm glad to see yer in a good mood and looking very happy. And just for yer information, out of all me customers, Aggie hasn't got the biggest mouth. *You* can lay claim to that fame. Yer can knock her into a bleedin' cocked hat. And that's on a day when yer've got a bad headache and are disinclined to talk.'

Beth was chuckling with the rest of the customers when Flo gave her a dig in the ribs. 'I hate to spoil yer pleasure, queen, but we've got to have dinners on the table for our fellers' coming in from work so can yer bear to tear yerself away?'

'I could stand here all day,' Beth said. 'It's as good as a pantomime.'

Flo grabbed her mate's arm and tugged hard, paying no heed to those standing behind who were pushed and shoved and had their toes trodden on. 'There's only women's clothing up here, we need to be at the other end. So move yerself.' As they elbowed their way through the crowds, she said, 'If they've got one, yer'll have to be satisfied with getting the coat for Joey and leave the other things. We can always come back next week for the rest. Don't forget, we get our Tontine money on Tuesday.'

'I'm not likely to forget, sunshine, not when it's all spoken for. Without that there'd be no presents for the kids or Andy. And I mustn't forget meself, I've got to have something new to wear on Christmas Day.'

They got as near to the end table as they could, pushing in when a customer was served and there was an empty space. They'd been there about five minutes when the young girl helping on the stall caught their eye. She was a pretty girl, was Sadie, with bright blonde curly hair and eyes the colour of the sky on a summer's day. She gave them a big smile. 'Yer'll have to shout out if yer ever want to get served. It's no good being polite or they'll walk all over yer.'

Beth liked her on sight. 'I'm looking for a coat for me son, a nice

128

warm one. Have yer got anything in that line, sunshine?'

Sadie pointed to the back of one of the trestle tables where there was a clothes rack standing. 'Yer might find something on there. How old is yer son?'

'He's thirteen, but I'll say fourteen so he'll get some wear out of it. And he's pretty big for his age.'

'Hang on for a few minutes while I serve a couple of women who've been shouting till they're blue in the face. If I don't serve them soon they'll have a heart attack. And one thing that makes Mary Ann mad is someone dying by her stalls. She says it's bad for business.'

With a smile that would melt the hardest heart the girl left them, and they could hear her holding her own with the impatient customers. But true to her word she was back with them within a few minutes, and ducked under the trestle table to stand beside them. 'There's one I think might suit yer, and it's in very good condition. Come on, I'll show it to yer, then I'll have to get back to serving or Mary Ann will have me life. We've been rushed off our feet since half-eight this morning.' The girl was moving the clothes along the rack as she spoke. 'Mind you, yer don't feel the cold so much when ye're busy.' She came across what she was looking for and pulled a hanger from the rack. 'This is it, and as yer can see it's hardly been worn.'

Beth's hopes rose. The coat was navy blue and made of a very good material. There was no sign of wear on it anywhere. 'Ooh, ay, Flo, that looks just the ticket, doesn't it? Right size, I'd say, good colour, and as the girl said, it's hardly been worn.'

Flo was impressed. 'It looks good to me, queen. Nice thick material to keep the cold out, and yer can tell it's come from a posh house 'cos I bet it cost a few bob when it was bought.'

'How much is it, sunshine?' Beth had her fingers crossed. Their Joey would think he was the bee's knees in a coat like this. 'Me money will only stretch to so much.'

'I'm not sure, I'll have to check with Mary Ann,' Sadie said. 'Have a look through the rest of the clothes on the rack, there might be something else that would do if this one's out of yer price range.' She grinned. 'That means if yer can't afford it.'

'Ooh, I hope I can, sunshine, 'cos me son would be over the moon swanking around in a coat like that. Run and ask her, and put me out of me misery.'

When the girl had gone, Flo asked, 'Aren't yer going to look on the rack, queen? Yer never know, there might be another coat that would do Joey. Yer'll not find one as good as that one, 'cos that's a cracker, but

129

there might be something that would tide him over.'

But Beth shook her head as her eyes followed Sadie. She could see Mary Ann listening first, then stroking her chin and pondering. Then she aimed a pretend blow at the girl's chin, and Beth could just make out what she was saying above the din. 'Oh, go on then, but yer'll have me in the bleedin' workhouse.'

Sadie's pretty face was a joy to behold. As Beth was to say to Flo on the tram going home, it was as if they'd been friends of the girl for years. 'Mary Ann said yer can have it for seven and six, seeing as it's Christmas. But will yer visit her when she's in the workhouse?' The girl threw her head back and her laughter filled the air. 'She said more than that, but I've left the swear words out. Anyway, if yer want it, the coat is seven and six, and a real bargain at that price.'

'I'll take it, sunshine.' Beth passed over the pound note she'd got off Ma Maloney the day before. But she was too happy to let her mind dwell on the moneylender. 'And I want to thank you, and Mary Ann, 'cos I know a bargain when I see one. And I'll certainly be back to see yer after the holidays.'

Sadie dipped into her pocket and brought out a ten-shilling note and half-a-crown. 'I hope yer son likes the coat. Yer can tell him it belonged to a very clever boy who hadn't had it long before he went on to high school.'

This time Flo was very impressed indeed. 'Go 'way! How did yer find that out?'

Again Sadie's laugh tinkled. 'I didn't, Missus, but a little lie doesn't hurt if it makes someone happy. Anyway, if I don't get back to work, Mary Ann will have me guts for garters. Have a nice Christmas and come back and see us again sometime.' With that, the girl ducked under the trestle table and approached one of the many pairs of hands being held out to her.

Beth jumped down from the tram platform and turned to help her mate. Getting on and off trams was the bane of Flo's life. With her short legs she couldn't get down from the high step without swearing to high heaven or being given a hand down by a friend. Sometimes a sympathetic conductor would be her saviour, and that would put her in a good mood for the rest of the day, but the one on this tram was busy collecting fares upstairs so Beth had to take the strain. 'Come on, sunshine, put yer weight on me arm and I'll lower yer down.'

Once she was safely on the pavement, Flo breathed a sigh of relief. 'D'yer know what, queen? I'd rather clean the house from top to bottom than get off a bleedin' tram.' She linked arms and nodded to the coat over Beth's arm. 'If one of the kids happens to see yer passing Hannah's window, what are yer going to say about the coat?'

'I've got it all figured out, sunshine, have no fear. We're not walking up the street, we're walking up the entry. And you can take the coat in with yer.'

'And I'm the underhanded one, am I, queen? Yer don't do so bad yerself. I've heard yer telling more lies today than I'll tell in a month of Sundays.'

'Oh, now let's not get carried away! I'd say that was a bit of an exaggeration. There's lies and there's lies, sunshine, and mine have only been little tiddlers compared to the ones you can come out with. In fact, compared to you, I'm just a babe-in-arms.'

'Yer do all right, in any case. Yer ruddy face would get yer the parish.' They stopped outside Flo's entry door and she held her arm out for the coat. 'This seems a right bleedin' carry on to me. Why can't yer take it in yer own house, there's nobody there to see it!'

'How d'yer know? Our Ginny and Joey could be back by now. And I'm not taking any chances, so ye're getting lumbered with it, sunshine, until after we've done our shopping.' Beth leaned forward until their noses were nearly touching. 'I don't know why ye're moaning, it's no skin off your nose to mind the flaming coat for a couple of hours.'

'I know that, queen, and I'm not really moaning. It just seems daft going through all this cloak and dagger stuff for a bleedin' second-hand coat! Still, if that's what yer want, I'll take the coat and put it in me wardrobe until later.'

Beth was smiling as she pinched her friend's chubby cheek. 'I wouldn't have that coat but for you, sunshine, and I'm really grateful to yer. And when we've got more time, I'd like to know how yer knew about that market stall. Ye're a flaming mystery to me, the things you know that I don't, even though we seldom go anywhere without each other.'

Flo tapped the end of her nose. 'The difference between you and me, queen, is that I keep me eyes and ears open. And as yer can see, it pays off.'

'It certainly does, sunshine, I'll give yer that. And now, I'd better get in and start on the dinner. I'll give yer a knock at the usual time.'

'Hang on a minute so I can get this straight. Are Lizzie and Dot going to be let into the secret of this coat, or do I have to lie to them, as well?'

'No, I'm going to tell them. And I'm taking them down to see the

131

stall next week, if we've got time. It's a good place to know about and keep in mind.' Beth began to walk away. 'If I didn't tell them, they'd soon find out. When our Joey gets that on his back he'll be strutting up and down this street as though he's king of the castle.' She turned and waved a hand. 'Ta-ra, I'll see yer later.'

Andy pushed his plate away, licking his lips on the taste of bacon. 'I enjoyed that, love, it was tasty. The mashed potatoes were nice and creamy, just as I like them.'

'I aim to please, sunshine.' Beth picked up his empty plate and placed it on top of hers. 'What time are yer going down to Hannah's?'

'We're meeting down there at two o'clock. If we left it any later we'd never get it done in the one afternoon. Dennis has got all the nails we'll need, Bill is bringing a hammer, and Paddy a saw. All I've got to take is a screwdriver and meself.'

Joey grinned. 'I'll take the screwdriver down for yer, Dad, and yerself can stay here.'

'Yer won't be cold, 'cos Mrs Bailey's got a fire roaring up the chimney,' Ginny told him. 'And she took one of those paraffin heaters upstairs as well.'

Joey's eyes nearly popped out of his head at what he thought was a great injustice. 'Don't yer mean *I* took the heater upstairs? It took me all me time, but I lugged it up.'

'Ah, I'm sorry, brother, I should have mentioned that,' Ginny said. 'Yer did a good job, 'cos I certainly couldn't have lifted it, it was too heavy.'

There was affection in Andy's eyes. 'Women will rarely admit that men are much stronger than they are, will they, son? They'll make use of us for things they can't do, but yer'll almost never hear them say we are the stronger sex.'

'Physically yer might be,' Beth conceded. 'But when it comes to raising a family and keeping a house going, ye're not in the meg specks. None of yer would last a week.'

Andy laughed. 'I don't know so much. I can make beds, and I believe Paddy is a wizard in the kitchen, so there'd only be the shopping and Dennis and Bill could manage that.'

'Oh, so yer won't be washing or ironing yer clothes, then?' Beth asked. 'And I noticed yer didn't say who was going to peel the spuds, make a pan of scouse, or get on their knees and scrub the kitchen floor?'

Andy winked at his son. 'One thing women are better at than men is talking their way out of sticky situations. So before I get meself involved in an argument I don't stand a snowball's chance of winning, I'm going to put me overalls back on and give the lads a knock. The sooner we make a start, the sooner we'll be finished.'

'It shouldn't take yer long with the four of yer, should it?' Beth was crossing her fingers under cover of the tablecloth as she prepared to tell a lie. 'Not that it makes any difference to me, we're only having sandwiches for our tea. I've got a lot of shopping to do, but I should be home by the time you are.'

'It won't take us long to put it up, just a matter of two hours at the most. But if ye're going to take into account the number of times we stop for a warm, a cuppa and a fag, yer can add another hour on to that.'

'Don't forget yer've got to put the new bed up when yer've finished,' Beth reminded him before giggling. 'Being the weaker sex, we women couldn't manage it.'

Andy pushed his chair back and said to Joey, 'See what I mean, son? When it suits them, they're the weaker sex. If it doesn't suit them, they're good at hitting yer on the head with the rolling pin.'

'Me mam would never do that to yer,' Ginny said while Joey nodded his head in agreement. Neither of them favoured one parent over the other, their love for both was equal. 'Me and Joey are going down to give Mrs Bailey a hand with making yer cups of tea and taking them up to yer. It'll save her legs, she said. And Joey's going to keep the coal scuttle full so she doesn't have to go down the yard.'

'That means we've all got a busy afternoon,' Beth said. 'So let's clear away and get the dishes done. Many hands make light work.' Then she raised her voice so it would carry through to the kitchen where Andy was. 'Yer see, sunshine, there are some jobs men and women do very well together.'

But he had other things on his mind. His head popped around the door and he asked, 'Ay, love, does Hannah know the partition is going to be plain bare wood?'

'I haven't said anything to her, and I doubt if she's given it any thought. But it's no big deal because me and Dot can put some wallpaper up for her. It only takes three strips each side, it should be a doddle.' Then as though to press home a point, Beth added, 'Even if we are the weaker sex.'

Andy reached for his donkey jacket. 'I'm on me way before we start all over again. I'll see yer later, love.'

'Will yer tell Mrs Bailey me and Joey won't be long?' Ginny called. 'Tell her we're washing the dishes together to prove it's possible for both sexes to work together in harmony.'

Andy chuckled as he opened the front door. 'I'm not as poetic as you, love, and I'll never remember all that. I'll just tell her ye're washing the dishes, that'll do.'

'And yer got that for seven and six?' Dot asked in disbelief. 'It's got to be the best ruddy bargain I've ever seen.'

'Sure, yer never spoke a truer word, me darlin'.' Lizzie was feeling the material of Joey's coat. 'It'll have cost a pretty penny when it was bought, right enough.'

The four friends, together with all their shopping, were crowded into Flo's tiny kitchen as Beth proudly showed off her bargain. 'I wouldn't have got it only for Flo, though, she must take all the credit. I would never have found the stall if she hadn't been with me.'

Flo's bosom stood to attention while the wagging of her head from side to side told of her pleasure at the compliment. But she knew her two daughters, Amy and Wendy, were in the living room and they had a tendency to repeat everything they heard. So she put a finger to her lips. 'Little pigs have big ears.'

Beth's hand went to her mouth. 'Oh, lord, I'm that thrilled with meself I forgot anyone might be listening. Anyway, ye're all agreed I got a good deal?'

'If I thought they had another one that would fit our David, I'd be down there like a shot,' Dot said. 'He could do with a good winter coat.'

'Come with me and Flo one day through the week, sunshine, 'cos yer never know, yer might just touch lucky.'

'And it's meself that'll be joining yer, right enough.' Lizzie was thinking of her two sons, Mick and Seamus. 'I'll not be missing a bargain if I can help it.'

'Right, the four of us will go down the day we get our Tontines.' Beth was very pleased with herself and couldn't wait to see her son. 'But don't forget I bought the coat this afternoon, while yer were out with me. Don't slip up or I'll be in trouble.'

Dot crossed her heart. 'Scout's honour, girl, I won't let yer down. And I'm damned sure Flo and Lizzie won't.'

'I know none of yer would, sunshine, ye're me best mates, aren't yer?' Beth lifted her basket from the floor. 'I'm going to put me shopping in the house and then go down to Hannah's. I can't wait to see our Joey's face.'

'Tell him to give us a knock so we can see it on him,' Dot said. 'He'll be a proper little gentleman.'

Flo was leaning back against the sink with her arms folded across her tummy. 'I think the word ye're looking for is swank.'

'And who would blame the lad, in a coat like that?' Lizzie's head was busy agreeing with her words. 'There'll not be another one in the neighbourhood as well dressed.'

'Don't tell Joey that, Lizzie, 'cos he's big-headed enough.' Then Beth shook her head. 'No, I take that back. If he does swank, it won't be because he's the best dressed in the neighbourhood, it'll be because he's never in his life owned such a fine coat.'

Joey's reaction to the coat had Beth telling herself it was worth all the lying she'd done, and was still doing. Her son was so pleased he could hardly speak, and when the men downed their tools to admire the material, the make and the fit, he was so excited Beth thought he would faint. She looked at Andy. 'What d'yer think, sunshine?'

'I think yer've done very well, love. If yer only paid seven and six for that coat, then whoever sold it to yer were practically giving it away.'

'That's all it was, ask any of me mates, they were with me. Anyway, I might tell the odd little white lie, but I'm not telling fibs now.'

'Did they have any girls' things, Mam?' Ginny asked. 'I could do with a new coat.' Then she realised she sounded jealous of her brother, and that wasn't what she'd intended. After all, she did have a decent coat while Joey didn't. 'I don't mean for now, the coat I've got will last a while. But I could start saving up out of me pocket money when I start work, and get one for next winter.'

'I'll take yer to the stall and yer can look for yerself. Yer'll be having every Wednesday afternoon off, so we could go then. In the meantime, there are three women all waiting to see Joey in his new coat – Auntie Flo, Auntie Dot and Auntie Lizzie. So how about it, sunshine?'

The boy's eyes were like saucers. 'Yer mean I can put it on now?'

'Of course yer can, that's what I got it for, to keep yer warm.' Beth held the coat wide and he slipped his arms into the sleeves. 'Oh, boy, oh, boy, oh, boy! I feel like James Cagney in this.'

And when he set off up the street, there were four grown men watching plus his proud mother and sister, and Hannah. And before darkness descended there were few in that little street of two-up-two-down houses who hadn't seen and admired Joey's new coat.

135

Chapter Twelve

'Alone at last!' Beth said on the Monday morning after seeing the children off to school. 'Ginny's all excited 'cos it's her last week at school, and Joey's a bundle of excitement over his new coat.' She chuckled as she pulled a chair out from the table and sat down facing Hannah. 'He'll thump any kid that looks sideways at it, never mind lays a finger on it.'

'There's not many boys can boast a coat like that, sweetheart, it's a very good make.' Hannah nodded for emphasis. 'If yer'd bought it new, in a shop, it would have set yer back about four guineas. If not more.'

'Yeah, I hopped in lucky all right, thanks to Flo. She did us both a good turn last week, God bless her.' Beth laid her arms flat on the table and sighed. 'A quiet fifteen minutes and then I'll see to the clothes in the dolly tub. I've always hated Monday mornings and the big wash, but it's worse in this weather 'cos there's nowhere to dry them off.'

'I'll give yer a hand, sweetheart, 'cos there's some of my washing in there.'

Beth shook her head. 'No, there's no room in that kitchen to swing a cat, we'd only be in each other's way. Yer can make the beds for us, sunshine, or give this room a dust, that would be a big help. But neither of us is doing anything until we've had a quiet fifteen minutes, so let's talk about where you're up to. The men did well on Saturday getting the partition up and seeing to the bed. Are yer happy with it?'

'More than happy, sweetheart, everyone has been very kind. I never thought that back bedroom could be made into two, but although there's not stacks of space, there's enough and both rooms look nice. They'll look more cosy when the wood is covered by wallpaper, but I'm sure Claire will see to that. If I remember rightly, she's handy around the house.'

'There'll be no need for that, sunshine, 'cos that job is in hand for today. If you'll nip to the shops and get a roll of paper that doesn't clash with the paper already up on the other walls, we can do it today. I'll have to see what me three mates have got planned, but I promise yer that whatever happens, the bedrooms will be ready for occupation by tonight.'

'There's no need for that, it can wait until Claire comes. I've taken enough off you and yer friends as it is.'

'Oh, but ye're not upsetting me plans, sunshine. I promised meself that everything would be done before yer family arrive, so yer wouldn't be worrying that head of yours.' Beth took hold of the old lady's hand. 'I'm doing it because I want to, Hannah, and so are me mates. We all think ye're one smashing lady, so please let us help yer? When Claire and yer grandchildren are living with yer, we'll know ye're being well looked after and won't interfere. But yer know ye're always welcome in this house.'

There were tears in Hannah's eyes. 'And you in mine, sweetheart. And all yer family and friends. I'll miss seeing Flo every day, and Dot and Lizzie. But it's not as though I'll be living at the other end of the world, I'm only down the street and can come for a cup of tea if I'm feeling lonely, or invite yer to mine.'

'I doubt yer'll be lonely with two youngsters in the house, sunshine, they'll keep yer on the go. Keep yer young in heart as well.' Beth sighed as she glanced at the clock. 'Break over, time for work. If you'll make the beds for us, I'll start taking the clothes out of the dolly tub and rinse them in cold water in the sink. Then I'll get as much wet out of them as I can with the mangle before hanging them on the clothes rack on the kitchen ceiling. There'll be damp everywhere for a day or so, but it can't be helped.' She pushed herself to her feet. 'I don't want to sound like a slave driver, but needs must when the devil drives. Me three mates will be here as soon as they've finished their work, to see what the arrangements are for the day. I don't want to be caught napping.'

'You see to the washing, sweetheart, and leave the beds and the living room to me. I may be getting on a bit in years, but I'm still capable of keeping a house clean.'

Beth leaned across the table to kiss her cheek. 'Ye're on, sunshine! I'll meet yer here in an hour's time, please God.'

'So what's on the agenda for today?' Flo was sitting on one of the wooden dining chairs, but looking at her you would think she was sitting on fresh air, for there was no sign of the chair. 'We three have all been to see Ma Maloney, and we've got our pound off her. So we could do a bit of Christmas shopping with it, and do the rest tomorrow when we get our Tontine.'

'I'd like to go to the market and have a look at this stall yer were raving about,' Dot said. 'But it's what the majority want to do.'

Beth had thought all this through when she was rinsing the clothes, but didn't want her mates to think she wanted everything her own way. So she went about it in a roundabout way. 'I'd like to go to the market, too, but I'd rather go with enough money in me pocket to buy everything I want. I thought today perhaps I'd try me hand at papering that partition the men put up for Hannah. A bit of wallpaper would brighten the place up and make it look warmer. But if you lot have set yer minds on going to the market today then you go, don't let me stop yer. I can always go tomorrow after we've been paid our Tontine money. At least then I'd have enough to buy most of the things I want for presents.'

Flo's legs were too short for her feet to touch the floor, and she had a habit of swinging them backwards and forwards. When she heard what Beth had to say, she left them dangling. 'I'll leave the market until tomorrow as well, 'cos as yer say we'll have all our money. So I'll give yer a hand with the papering.'

'You can't wallpaper to save yer life!' Dot said. 'Yer can't stand on a ladder because yer say ye're afraid of heights!'

'It doesn't stop me from cutting the border off the paper, or mixing the bleedin' paste, smart arse! And I can paste each piece and hand it to Beth when she's ready. You go about yer business and leave us to go about ours.'

'No!' Dot sounded quite definite. 'I can put paper up, I've done our living room a few times and didn't make a bad job of it. So I'll skip the market until tomorrow and give Beth a hand.'

'Yer mean yer'll give Beth and Flo a hand, don't yer, queen?' Flo put on her hard done by expression. 'Seeing as I was the first one to offer me services.'

'Well, I'll not be going to the market on me own, and that's a fact,' Lizzie said. 'It's much more fun when ye're in company. So shall we all give a hand with the papering today, and say for certain we'll go to the market tomorrow?' She looked from one face to another. 'Sure, I know we don't need five of us to put a few strips of wallpaper up, but I'm sure there is plenty we can help Hannah with. Like cleaning the windows ready for her family coming, or polishing the furniture, brushing the yard – there must be loads we can do.'

Beth was over the moon but tried hard not to show it. She knew there hadn't been any work done in Hannah's house for a week now, so the whole place could do with a good clean right through. 'That's a good idea, it would be nice to have the house shining for Claire and her children coming. And we could all go to the market tomorrow with a clear conscience and some money in our purses. All except Hannah, 'cos she's got a tea chest being delivered so she'll have to wait in for it.'

'I wouldn't be going anywhere tomorrow anyway 'cos I want to get the house warmed through and the bedding aired off. Besides I only want to buy a couple of little things to give Bobby and Amelia for Christmas, and perhaps a pair of stockings or something for Claire.'

'We could get those for yer from the market.' Beth didn't know Hannah's financial situation and certainly wasn't going to ask. But being a widow for so long, and no wage coming into the house, she certainly couldn't be flush with money. 'Stockings are a lot cheaper there than they are in the shops, sunshine, so yer'd save a few coppers. And we could get socks for the lad, save you bothering.'

Hannah would never admit it, she was far too proud, but she did have to struggle for money every week. She had tried not to let her standards slip, either in the house or with clothes, but it had been hard going over the years. All she had to her name now was the shilling change from the pound she'd borrowed off the moneylender, and the pound Claire had sent to buy groceries in. Oh, she had her rent money put away, that was one thing she wouldn't miss. When she was young, her mother had drummed it into her that you could go without coal or food, but you couldn't go without a roof over your head. 'I'll have to see how I'm off for money after I've paid for the roll of wallpaper.'

'I bought a roll of wallpaper more than I needed last time I decorated,' Dot said. 'So ye're welcome to that 'cos I'll never use it. That's if yer like it, of course. If yer don't, there's no harm done and no hard feelings.'

'Is it the same as yer've got in yer living room?' Beth asked, her hopes rising. You could buy a roll of paper for a shilling, but Hannah was probably counting her coppers, never mind her shillings.

'Yeah, that's it,' Dot said. 'Light beige with a tiny pink flower on.'

'What colour is the paper yer have up, me darlin'?' Lizzie asked.

'It's hard to tell because it's been up so many years. But it's very plain and doesn't have any pattern on at all.'

'Then it wouldn't clash with whatever is put up.' Beth smiled with pleasure. 'Blimey, you and our Joey are definitely enjoying a lucky streak. I wish some of it would rub off on me.'

'You used all yer luck up the day yer married the most handsome man in Liverpool.' Dot winked. 'So don't be getting greedy.' She rose to her feet. 'I'll fetch the paper and yer can see for yerself, Hannah, whether yer think it will do.'

She was back within minutes, with a roll of wallpaper that everyone agreed was very pretty. Hannah was overwhelmed by all that was happening so quickly. She wasn't being given time to be embarrassed by the generosity of these people. It was only a week ago, when she'd heard that her beloved son was dead, that she had wished she too could die. There didn't seem any point in living. But these women, and their families, had never stopped letting her know, in their different ways, that she still had a lot to live for. So there was a smile on her face when she said, 'As your Ginny would say, I'm going to be proper posh.'

It was Lizzie who decided it was time to start work. 'I'll go across and mix some flour and water for paste. I'll make it in the bucket, so I will, me darlin's, and by the time the paper's trimmed and cut to size, the paste will be well set.'

'Who's got a decent pair of scissors?' Beth asked. 'The only ones I've got wouldn't even cut butter.'

Flo put her hand in the air. 'I've got a smashing pair of scissors. At least they belong to Dennis, but what's his is mine, and what's mine is me own.'

'Mine are not bad, either,' Dot said. 'And two pair would come in handy, so I'll get them. Now I think we should all start making a move if we want to get anything done.'

'I'll second that,' Beth said. 'It's all hands to the pumps.'

'So, yer've had a busy day, you and yer mates?' Andy glanced down the table and his eyes held that look that always made Beth go weak at the knees. It was the look that said even after seventeen years of marriage he was still crazy about her. 'Did they do a good job for yer, Hannah?'

'An excellent job, Andy.' The old lady didn't know whether she was on her head or her heels or cloud nine. 'Yer wife did an expert job on the papering, helped very efficiently by Flo and Dot. They had the papering done in no time, then cleared up after themselves before helping Lizzie, who was cleaning me house from top to bottom. It's like a little palace now, shining like a new pin. And I don't know how to start thanking everyone, there aren't enough words to express how grateful I am.' She could feel a lump forming in her throat and a voice in her head warned her that she was in danger of becoming maudlin and making everyone miserable. 'I'm so used to having servants waiting on me hand and foot, I don't know what I'm going to do after tomorrow.'

'I'll come down and wait on yer during the holidays, Mrs Bailey,' Joey said. 'I can go on messages for yer, and bring yer coal in.'

'And I can wash yer dishes,' Ginny said. 'And I'm a dab hand at dusting.'

Beth smiled, proud that her two children had a caring nature. 'I don't think that will be necessary, not when Claire and the children are there. After all, Bobby is sixteen and Amelia fifteen, so they'll be a big help.'

Ginny's face dropped. 'I can still come and see yer, can't I? I mean, yer'll want to know how I'm getting on in me new job, won't yer?'

'Of course I will, sweetheart, I'll be eager for yer news. And the children will be pleased to see yer. They'll have to start from scratch here 'cos they'll have no friends. They've been away so long they won't know a soul.'

'I'll introduce Amelia to my friends,' Ginny said, her eyes bright. 'And Joan's brother is about the same age as Bobby, so perhaps they'll become mates.'

'Just let things take their course, sunshine,' Beth said. 'The children are bound to feel strange at first, so give them a chance to find their feet. And I don't want you or Joey to make nuisances of yerselves when me back's turned, either. Let everyone get settled first, and Christmas over, then we can take our time in getting to know each other.'

'New Year's Eve is a good time to get to know each other,' Andy said. 'Usually the whole street is out, and all very friendly after having had a few drinks.' He chuckled. 'Some will be the worse for wear, but it is only once a year and yer can't blame them for making merry.'

'That's an idea, that, Hannah,' Beth said. 'We'll probably meet up a few times before then, but pass on our invitation for them to come here on New Year's Eve for a drink. The house will be full to bursting point, 'cos the families on both sides come in, and Lizzie and her lot. At one time we used to take turns in having a party, but somehow over the years it's been whittled down to ours every year. I don't mind, though, 'cos they all chip in with sandwiches, cakes and beer. And Flo, Dot and Lizzie come round the next morning and help me clear the mess away.'

'Oh, that will be lovely!' Ginny clapped her hands together. 'I can't wait to meet them. And don't forget I'll be at your house straight from school tomorrow to help yer empty the tea chest that's coming.'

'A busy day all round from the sound of things,' Andy said. 'My dear wife draws her Tontine tomorrow and can't wait to get to the shops to spend it on presents for us. I have hinted that a bike would be useful for getting me to work, but she told me Father Christmas said he'd never get a grown-up bike on his sleigh. So I guess I'll have to make do with socks and hankies again.'

This was a standing joke among their neighbours. Andy would say to Dennis, 'Yer'll never guess what Santa brought me? A pair of socks and a packet of three hankies.' And Dennis would nod his head and say,

'Same here.' This would be repeated by Bill and Paddy, and followed by loud guffaws. Beth was determined to do a bit better this year, and had informed her mates of her intentions so the four men were in for a pleasant surprise. Although she worried that the surprise wouldn't be pleasant if someone let it slip that Ma Maloney had made the gifts possible.

'It's the thought that counts, sunshine, not the present. And anyway, there's another reason for celebrating Christmas other than giving presents, and we should never forget that.'

'But there's no harm in giving presents, sweetheart,' Hannah said. 'It's part of the celebration of Christ's birth. Didn't the three Wise Men bring gifts to the baby Jesus?'

'I haven't forgotten that, Hannah, but these days Christmas seems to be getting more commercialised. To some it's just another excuse for having a good booze-up. Last year half the men at Midnight Mass could hardly stand on their feet they were so drunk. The whole church reeked of beer.'

'You can't make people believe something they don't want to believe in, love. Something that interferes with the life they want to lead. But it'll all come back to them in the end and they'll pay the price.' Andy wasn't one to preach about religion, and kept his beliefs to himself. He was of the firm opinion that not everyone who went to church was a good person, they just wanted to appear to be so, while many genuinely good-living people never went near a church but spent their lives doing good deeds for others. And thinking about helping others, he said, 'Seeing as yer've had a busy day, me and the children will clear away and wash up. How about that?'

'I would be delighted, love. I'll put me feet up on the couch and wait in anticipation of being brought a nice cup of tea. And I'm sure Hannah would also be very appreciative.' Beth chuckled. 'See, when I want to speak posh, I can do. The trouble is, most of the time I can't be bothered. It comes more naturally to speak as common as muck.'

Four women trying to walk together in a market jam-packed with people was almost an impossibility. 'We'd be better walking in pairs, as long as we don't lose sight of each other,' Beth said. 'Most of us want a stall selling new stuff: stockings, shirts, underwear and socks. And Hannah gave me six shillings to buy something for Claire and the two children. It's not much for three presents, I know, but the poor woman is hard pushed for money.'

'I'll take yer straight to a stall what sells all those things,' Flo said, screwing up her eyes when yet another elbow prodded her bosom. 'Otherwise yer'll end up getting nothing.'

'What about the stall where Beth got the coat?' Dot asked. 'Couldn't we try there?'

'They only deal in second-hand clothes,' Flo said, sending daggers to a woman who had just trodden on her little toe. She wouldn't have minded so much, but it was the little toe that had a corn on. 'We can call there later if yer want, but let's get some of our presents first.'

Beth grinned at her. 'Okay, sunshine, you be in charge and lead the way. Your loyal followers will be right behind yer.'

With that, Flo got herself ready to do battle. With a look of determination on her face, she bent her arms and pushed her elbows out. They would act as a deterrent to anyone who didn't get out of the way quick enough. But they weren't just a deterrent, they were a weapon which left many people, if not mortally wounded, then bruised enough to remember the little fat woman who let nothing stand in her way. Fists were waved in the air at her, curses were called and threats made to her wellbeing. But she forged ahead regardless, with her three mates walking in her wake, not knowing whether to pretend they weren't with her, feel sorry for her victims or laugh their heads off.

When Flo came to an abrupt halt, the three women were caught unawares and nearly fell over each other. 'What did yer stop like that for, yer silly nit?' Dot said. 'I nearly tripped over Lizzie!'

'But yer didn't, did yer? And it'll teach yer to look where ye're going in future.' Flo raised her eyes to the heavens, as though to say some people had no ruddy sense. 'Anyway, this is the stall.'

There were groans from her friends when they saw the customers around it were about five deep. 'Oh, God, we'll never get served there!' Dot said. 'We'll be here all flamin' day!'

Flo folded her arms and her lips thinned to a straight line. 'Do yer intend to moan the whole bleedin' time we're out, Dot Flynn? 'Cos if yer do, I'm going to love yer and leave yer. I'll be quicker on me own and I'll have no misery guts moaning down me ear.'

'There's no need to take that attitude, girl,' Dot said. 'All I said was that there's so many people round the stall we'll be here for ages.'

'If yer look around yer, queen, yer'll see every stall is the same. It's not only us what have got Christmas presents to buy, it's the whole of Liverpool. And no matter where yer go, it'll be the same.'

'She's right,' Beth said. 'So we'll take our chances at this stall. And we'll take a leaf out of Flo's book and push our way in. If we get separated, then so be it, it can't be helped. But don't anyone move far from this stall 'cos we'd never find each other in the crowd.'

But Dot wasn't having any of that. Half the fun of going shopping with Flo was to see how she got around shopkeepers to knock the odd ha'penny or penny off things. 'We'll stick together, even if it takes ten minutes to get to the front to see what they're selling.'

'We've all got lists,' Flo said, 'and I'll guarantee that on this stall they sell everything on those lists. Now, because there's four of us, and we'll be spending a good few pounds, I suggest we work it like this . . .'

And so it was that when the four friends finally got to the front, and could see all the goods on sale, they had a plan to set in motion. They let Flo go first. 'Here ye're, lad, I'm next to be served.' She smiled sweetly at the man who ran the stall with his wife. Today he had his thirteen-year-old daughter helping out as well. 'Could yer pass me one of those men's shirts over, please, so I can see the quality?' She felt the material and pursed her mouth. 'How much are yer asking for them?'

'Two and eleven, Missus, and that's a good price. They'll wash and wear well.'

'I don't doubt yer for a minute, lad, but I'm counting me coppers. Yer see, I need four of them and me purse won't run to that.'

The stallholder was doing some quick adding up in his head. Four shirts was too good a sale to lose, and he was making a shilling profit on each, so he could afford to be generous. 'Well, seeing as ye're buying four, Missus, I'll knock tuppence off each of them. How does that suit yer?'

'That's mighty kind of yer. What colours d'yer have them in?'

'Just the white and blue. But we've got them in all sizes.'

Flo brought a scrap of paper out of her pocket. 'I'll have two white, both size seventeen neck, and two blue in a size sixteen.'

When he'd gone, Flo turned to her mates. 'We've got a bargain there. Now, d'yer want me to try with the stockings and underskirts?'

There was a chorus of, 'Oh, yes, please!' And for added measure Dot said, 'Ye're doing fine, girl, I take me hat off to yer.'

'Give us yer lists then, and I'll see what I can do.'

The man came bustling back with the shirts in a bag. 'Here yer are, Missus, that's eleven shillings exactly.'

Flo passed a ten bob note and a silver shilling over. 'Ta, very much, lad. But I've been having a word with me mates here, and we might be able to do more business with yer. They were going to buy ladies' stockings and underskirts from one of the stalls we passed, but I told them to try here first 'cos yer might be cheaper.'

'How much were they selling the stockings for?' the stallholder asked, thinking he was being crafty. Little did he know that when dealing with Flo, he wasn't in the meg specks.

'They were ninepence on one stall, and elevenpence on another.' She kicked back sharply with her foot when she heard the gasps of surprise from her mates. If they kept that up, they'd give the game away. She herself had no qualms about telling fibs because if the feller was any good as a businessman he'd know that ladies' stockings were a shilling in the shops and elevenpence in the market. Decent ones that is. Seconds were a lot cheaper but you took a chance on them. Sometimes they'd have ladders in, or no ruddy heels.

'And how many of each d'yer want?'

'Eight pair of stockings and four underskirts. But it all depends upon the price 'cos like most other folk, we've got to go careful.'

'I'll do yer a good deal, seeing as ye're spending a few bob. Yer can have the stockings for tenpence a pair and the underskirts for one and six. That is the best I can do, Missus, so what d'yer think?'

Flo was delighted but had to ask first, 'Do the underskirts have lace at the top?'

The stallholder nodded. 'Yes, they've got lace on, and they're in four colours so I can give yer one of each.'

'That's fine, thank yer. I'll get the money off me mates while ye're seeing to them. Oh, can we have two blue and two pink, please? We don't like yellow or green.'

Beth handed over a pound note. 'I get it to twelve shillings and eightpence, so pay him out of that and we'll find somewhere to have a cup of tea and settle up.' She placed a kiss on Flo's cheek. 'Friends don't come any better than you, Florence Henderson.'

After goods and money had been exchanged, the friends were moving away from the stall when Beth saw some men's woollen scarf and glove sets and she called after the stallholder, 'Excuse me, but could yer tell me how much the scarf and glove sets are, please?'

'Two bob, love.' He grinned. 'No, I can't knock anything off them, I'm selling them at rock bottom prices as it is.'

'Can I have two sets, please? One in navy and one in black.'

'Who d'yer want them for?' Flo asked, along with a sharp dig in the ribs. 'Yer'll have no money left the way ye're going on.'

'I know what I'm doing, sunshine, don't worry. I've got Ginny two pairs of stockings and an underskirt, Andy a shirt and one of the scarf sets, Claire a pair of stockings and underskirt and the same for Amelia. The other scarf is for the boy, Bobby. So that's Hannah sorted out for her family and one thing off me mind.'

'I thought she only gave yer six bob! It comes to more than that.'

'Only coppers, sunshine, and I'm not going to lose any sleep over that. There's only our Joey and meself to see to now. Oh, and me mam and dad, I'd forgotten about them. I could have got a pair of stockings for me mam if I'd thought on, but it's too late now. Me dad's easy, he's happy with a packet of fags.'

'Here yer are, love.' The stallholder passed a bag over. 'That'll be four bob.'

As she was rooting in her purse, Beth asked, 'Would yer get us another pair of stockings, please? And I don't suppose yer've got any boys' woollen gloves, have yer, for a lad of thirteen?'

'Yeah, a tanner a pair. I'll get them and the stockings for yer.'

'I suppose yer know ye're spending money like a man with no hands, don't yer?' Dot said. 'By the time we get home yer'll be skint.'

'Yes, but I've got nearly all me Christmas presents. All I need to get now is a comic book for our Joey, to go with the gloves, twenty Woodbines for me dad, and then there's only little old me to worry about. I would like something new to wear on Christmas Day.'

'Will yer pay the man, me darlin', and let's find somewhere to sit and have a cuppa.' Lizzie was looking fed up with herself. 'Sure, I'm not thinking straight at all. So far, all I've bought is a shirt for Paddy. If I'd had me mind on it, I could have bought scarf sets for the two boys and that would have been them seen to. And I'm sure there'd have been something for the two girls. I'm slowing down in me old age, and that's a fact, so it is.'

They found a cafe and were lucky enough to get there just as four people were vacating a table. They sighed with relief when they sat down, glad to take the weight off their feet. Then they noticed there was no one serving on the tables, so Dot volunteered to take her turn at the counter and ordered a pot of tea for four and scones.

While they were waiting, Beth took a piece of paper from her handbag and a stub of pencil. 'Now, while it's all fresh in our minds, let's make a list of who's bought what, how much they owe and who they owe it to.'

'I've only bought the shirt so far,' Lizzie said, disgusted with herself for not being quicker off the mark. 'So I'll pay Flo my two and nine, and that makes us quits. I'll have to go back to the stall when we've had a cuppa, though, I can't go home with just Paddy sorted out.'

Beth felt much happier when she'd been paid all the money owing to her. She'd started to get worried when she saw the cash in her purse dwindling, but it looked more healthy now she knew exactly how much

147

she had to play with. 'All things considered, I think I've done very well. The money I've got in the butcher's and the greengrocer's club will sort me out for dinners over the holiday, and I've still got money on me sweetshop card. I'm feeling quite chuffed with me little self.'

'I'm nowhere near finished, so I'll go back with Lizzie.' Dot was counting the money in her purse. 'I've got Joan's things, but nothing for David. I bet he'd be made up with one of those scarf sets so I'll get him one. And seeing as Beth's got two presents for her feller, I'll have to do the same or there'll be blue murder. Men are worse than women for jangling when they get in the ruddy pub.'

Flo used the table to push herself to her feet. 'The woman behind the counter is waving her bleedin' hand off, trying to tell us our tea's ready. Who's coming to give me a hand?'

Dot snapped her purse shut and put it in her bag. 'I'll come with yer to stop yer moaning about me.'

Flo put her hands on her hips and looked her friend up and down. 'Well, can yer tell me why yer've put yer money away and left yer bag on the table? Which means I'll be the sucker left to pay for it all!'

'We're all paying our share today, so we'll square up when yer let us know how much it is.' Beth grinned. 'And no licking the butter off the scones, Flo Henderson, 'cos I'll be keeping me eye on yer.'

'All I can say is, it's a bleedin' pity yer've got nothing better to do.' With that, Flo waddled towards the counter, knocking elbows as she went, spilling tea down customers' coats and on to the tables. 'How much, queen?'

The girl behind the counter looked at the tray and did some mental arithmetic. 'That's one and four, girl.'

Flo handed over the right money. 'Thank you, queen.' Then she turned to Dot and raised her brows in a haughty expression. 'I paid, so you can carry the bleedin' tray.'

Tempers were calmed as the friends sipped their tea and ate the scones which turned out to be delicious. Beth thought this was a good time to organise themselves. If they didn't, tempers would become frayed again and they'd end up going home with only half the things they needed. 'Lizzie, why don't you and Dot go back to the stall, get what yer want and meet me and Flo back here?'

'But Flo's only bought a shirt so far, there must be a lot more things she wants,' Dot said. 'So why don't we all go back to the same stall?'

'Not me,' Flo told her. 'My girls are too young for long stockings and lacy underskirts, so I'm going to see if that Mary Ann has any decent second-hand dresses. They'd be easy enough to wash and the girls wouldn't know no difference.'

'Oh, I'll come with yer, sunshine,' Beth said, her face alight. 'They might have something that takes me eye. In fact, I could get two for the price of one.'

Dot shook her head. 'Don't even think of going there without me and Lizzie, girl, 'cos that wouldn't be fair. If there's any bargains going, we want to be there.'

'Yer can't have it all ways, queen,' Flo told her. 'If we have to sit here waiting for yer, the day will be over. So I suggest you and Lizzie get off yer backsides right now, and run like the clappers back to that stall. Yer know exactly what yer want so yer don't have to arse around. Me and Beth will have another cup of tea, and if ye're not back by the time we've drunk it then we're off.' Even as she was speaking, Flo knew it was a load of rubbish. There was no way she or Beth would let their two friends down. 'Go on, get yer bleedin' skates on! Ye're too ruddy slow to catch cold, the both of yer.'

The two women were quickly off their chairs and out of the door. As she watched them disappearing, Beth clicked her tongue on the roof of her mouth and said, 'Well, that was certainly telling them, sunshine! I bet they're quaking in their shoes now.'

'Don't be so bleedin' sarky, queen, there's no need for it. At least I got them off their backsides, which is more than you did.'

'Ay, wouldn't it be the gear if we could get some nice dresses off that Mary Ann's stall? It would save us a lot of money.'

'It'll be interesting, queen, and a good laugh if nothing else.'

And as the ladies were to find out, Flo had never spoken a truer word.

Chapter Thirteen

'Oh, my Gawd!' Dot's eyes nearly popped out of her head when she saw the crowds around Mary Ann's stalls. At least Flo had said there were stalls there but they couldn't be seen for the people around them, pushing and shoving, were about ten deep. The noise was deafening as each one tried to make themself heard above the others, and it had to be said that all the people weren't full of Christmas cheer or goodwill. In fact there were several arguments going on between women who each swore they were the first to pick up the pink blouse or the black knitted cardigan. 'We'll never get through that lot, we'd be trampled underfoot if we tried.'

Lizzie was equally amazed. 'Sure, it's meself that's been to this market a hundred times, but never in me life have I seen anything like this.'

Above the babble around them, Flo shouted, 'That's because we never come to this end. I only heard about it from some woman I got talking to in the shops. Apparently this Mary Ann is well known all over Liverpool and does a roaring trade. Everything is second-hand and it's all just thrown on the stalls, yer have to sort through it yerself. But she sells good stuff and doesn't try to fiddle yer, like some do. It was crowded when me and Beth were here the other day, but not quite as bad as this. Beth got what she was after, though, and we weren't that long getting served.'

'Is it worth staying?' Dot asked, looking very doubtful. 'We could stand here for an hour and end up with nothing.'

'That's up to you, sunshine, but I'm going to see if there's any dresses going cheap, even if I do have to wait an hour,' Beth said. 'Remember I got our Joey's coat here and what a bargain that was! You and Lizzie don't have to stay if yer don't want to, but don't start moaning if me and Flo come home with some real bargains.'

Lizzie was beginning to enjoy the atmosphere. She couldn't see who was serving, but whoever it was, she was causing a lot of laughter. 'We're not in that much of a hurry.'

'Let's go down to where that rack was, queen. There were clothes hanging on it the other day, but we didn't bother looking when yer got the coat.' Flo was thinking she could do with a decent dress herself for Christmas. 'And it might not be so crowded down there.'

It was just as busy, but the people seemed to be moving quicker, and it wasn't long before the women could see the stalls and the clothes piled up on them. It was a case of spotting a colour or a piece of material that caught your eye, and hoping for the best when you pulled the garment out of the stack. Often two or three women would spot something at the same time, and there'd be ructions, with the garment being pulled in different directions. And that was when Mary Ann would get involved and the four friends began to enjoy themselves as they listened to her.

'That'll be eightpence each, ladies, please,' said Mary Ann to three women who were fighting over a dress.

'I saw it first, Mary Ann, and I had me bleedin' hand on it when these cheeky cows tried to take it off me,' said one customer.

Mary Ann stood in front of them behind the stall. 'As I said, that'll be eightpence each, ladies, so let's be having it.'

'I'll give yer the eightpence, Mary Ann, if these two will take their thieving hands off the thing.'

'Oh, no, Tilly, yer've misunderstood. The price of the whole dress is two shillings. But if ye're having a third each, then that works out at eightpence.'

The second irate customer joined in now. 'Tell her to take her bleedin' hands off it and I'll give yer the money. But I'm not parting with a penny while these two have got their paws on it.'

The stallholder held out her hand. 'Give me the bleedin' dress here and none of yer can have it. Come on, hand it over.'

'Ah, that's not fair, Mary Ann, I saw it first,' protested Tilly.

Mary Ann was sorry for Tilly, who was a good customer, but now wasn't the time to show favouritism. 'Tilly, Maggie and Nellie, hand me the dress over before yer tear it, then I'll be forced to tear the three of yer limb from limb. And believe me, ladies, I'm in the right mood for it.'

The three customers knew better than to argue with the stallholder so they took their hands off the dress and used them as fists to belt each other. They were only light blows, not really in earnest, but Mary Ann knew how to put a stop to it before it developed into full-scale warfare. She held the dress above her head and shouted, 'Anyone want to buy this lovely blue dress for two bob? It's a bleedin' gift at that price. Going to the first one who shouts.'

'I'll have it!' Beth surprised herself by shouting at the top of her voice. But the dress looked very pretty, appeared to be near enough her size, and if three women were prepared to come to blows over it, it couldn't be bad. 'Over here, Mary Ann.' She had the silver coin ready in her hand to pass over.

Mary Ann narrowed her eyes as she took the money and dropped it into the deep pocket of her apron. 'Ye're not one of me regulars, but I seem to know yer face from somewhere.'

'I was here with me mate last week, I bought a coat for me son.'

The stallholder snapped her fingers. 'That's it, I never forget a face even if I can't remember where I saw it. Sadie served yer, didn't she?'

'Yeah, and me son was made up with it. He walks up and down the street, swanking like no one's business. That's why all me mates came with me today, to see if we could get anything for ourselves and our daughters.'

Mary Ann turned to where the three customers were still pulling and pushing each other. 'They're going to end up knocking spots off each other. And if they intend to draw blood, they'll not do it on my merchandise. I'll have to sort them out, but you stay where yer are and I'll ask Sadie to come and attend to yer when she can. We haven't had time to breathe today, we've been rushed off our bleedin' feet. And on top of that, yer get stupid buggers like those three women. Just look at the size of that dress, and the size of them. The ruddy dress wouldn't go near them. But you try telling them that. They all think they've got figures like Jean Harlow.'

As she was walking away, Flo called, 'Yer haven't gone all this time without a cuppa, have yer?'

'Can't afford the time to go for one, sweetheart! I've got to make the money while I can, 'cos after Christmas trade will fall right off and me and the family will be living on bread and drippin'.'

Beth was holding the dress up for her mates to see. 'I can't believe me luck! Two bob for a dress which will look nice when it's been washed and ironed.'

'If you fell down the bleedin' lavvy, queen, yer'd come up with a gold watch,' Flo said. 'I told yer, yer face would get yer the parish.'

'If another one like that comes up, I'll grab it,' Dot said, thinking how near she'd come to missing out. It would have been the price of her for being so impatient. 'In fact, if I can get a bit nearer this stall, I wouldn't mind having a root through the things.'

'Go on then,' Beth said, wanting to share her good luck with her friends. 'Yer'll be better on yer own, rather than us all trying to keep together. I'll hang on till Sadie comes over.' She pointed to where the pretty blonde girl was serving half-a-dozen people at once and smiling as she did so. 'Come back if yer see her talking to us, she might tell us where it's best to look.'

Lizzie opted to go with Dot, leaving Flo with Beth. 'It's terrible if they haven't had a cup of tea all day.' The little woman's face showed concern. 'I'd do me nut if I had to go without me cuppa. It's the one thing that keeps me going, so I know how they must be feeling. I'd even go to the cafe for them, but the tea would be cold before I got it back here.'

Beth tried to keep the grin off her face as she imagined Flo walking down the street with a cup of tea in each hand, shouting for everyone to get out of the way so she wouldn't spill any. Her intentions were good, but not very practical. 'The people in the cafe wouldn't let yer bring their cups out anyway, sunshine,' she said. 'They don't know yer from Adam, so yer couldn't blame them for thinking they'd never see their cups again.'

'They wouldn't think that, queen!' Flo's eyes twinkled. 'Just one look at me open, honest face, and they'd willingly oblige. I bet they'd even carry the bleedin' cups for me.'

It was at that point Sadie appeared before them, her smile welcoming. 'Hi-ya! I didn't expect to see yer back so soon. How was the coat?'

'It went down a treat, sunshine, yer made one young lad very happy. So me and me mates thought we'd like a bit of the same treatment. I've just bought this dress off Mary Ann, and I'd like another if yer've got one. And yer know Flo, she was with me the other day, she'd like something for herself and her two daughters.' Beth was pushed forward when Dot and Lizzie turned up, having seen the arrival of Sadie. 'Blimey, I hate to say it, but these two ruffians are also me mates and they're looking for some bargains.'

'Most of the good stuff has gone now 'cos we've been open since eight o'clock and have been mad busy. But Mary Ann's husband is bringing another load in about half-an-hour, so if yer take my advice, yer'll hang on.' Sadie glanced at Flo. 'How old are yer daughters?'

'They're thirteen and twelve, queen, and just about the right size for their age. And Lizzie here, she's got two daughters the same age.'

'Try and push in a bit further along and I'll empty a bag in front of yer. But yer'll have to be quick 'cos there'll be a stampede. Most of our regulars are smashing and we do try to give them preference. We've given them the wire about more stuff coming in, and told them where to stand so they'll have first chance to go through the clothes. Anyway, push yerselves in further up and wait.' With that Sadie turned away to answer some of the urgent calls. But Flo's voice called her back.

'Listen, queen, I'd go and get yer something to drink, 'cos yer must be dying for a cuppa. But I've nothing to put it in, and me mate said the cafe wouldn't let me bring cups out.'

Sadie smiled. 'We've got a billycan, but I don't think yer'd like to walk along the street with it, it's a disgrace. Half of the enamel has been chipped off.'

Flo straightened her back, thrust out her bosom to its full extent and gave a sharp jerk of her head. 'I'm not too proud to walk down the street with anything, queen, I'm not a bleedin' snob. Go and get it and I'll take it to get filled.'

'Hang on.' The girl ran across the square made by the stalls, and grabbed hold of Mary Ann's arm. The women could see her mouth moving, then the red-headed stallholder turned to them and gave them the thumbs up sign. Sadie delved into one of the boxes under a stall near the clothes rack and brought out the enamel billycan. 'Mary Ann said she'd pay yer when yer get back. And she said to thank yer and tell yer she'll be yer friend for life.'

'I'll come to the cafe with yer, sunshine,' Beth said. 'Save yer going on yer own.'

The billycan turned out to be no stranger to the owner of the cafe. He took one look at it and grinned. 'Will yer tell Mary Ann that I said to buy a new one? That thing standing on me counter is lowering the tone of me cafe.' He picked up the offending billycan and handed it to his wife to fill. Then he let out a loud guffaw. 'When yer tell Mary Ann what I said, make sure ye're standing well clear of her. She's only small and thin, and yer wouldn't think butter would melt in her mouth. But she didn't get that red hair for nothing, and when she lets fly, she packs a hefty wallop. She's the salt of the earth, though, and as straight as they come.'

When the full billycan was placed on the counter, it was Beth who asked, 'How much is that, please?'

'Fourpence, seeing as it's for Mary Ann. And yer can tell her it's got the right amount of milk and sugar in, and comes with the compliments of Joe.'

Flo was beginning to feel left out, and she couldn't have that. After all, she did have a tongue in her mouth. 'Well, Joe, would yer butter two scones for us, please? One each for Mary Ann and Sadie, which will be given with the compliments of Flo and Beth.'

155

On the walk back to the market, Beth said, 'I'll pay for the scones, 'cos I'm a bit better off for money than I thought I'd be. I'd put ten bob aside for a dress for meself, and I've got one for two bob! And, if me luck holds, I'll get another one.'

'And I'll pay for the tea, in the hope that some of your luck will rub off on me.'

Beth put her arm across her mate's shoulders and squeezed. 'I bet yer any money, sunshine, that yer get a dress that'll put us all in the shade. A real bobby dazzler that will make Dennis fall for yer all over again.'

And Beth's words turned out to be true. The tea and scones were so welcomed and enjoyed by Mary Ann, she put on a show for her customers. With her skirt lifted, she did an Irish jig in the middle of the square, while customers clapped, whistled and sang. And while she was dancing, the stallholder kept shouting to customers she knew. 'Keep yer hands off that jumper, Sarah, it wouldn't fit yer and the colour would make yer look like death warmed up.' Another twirl, and, 'Fanny, I'm watching yer! Just because I'm singing doesn't mean I'm in such a good temper I'll forget the tuppence yer owe me from last week.' It was happy interlude that cheered everyone and put smiles on their faces.

Flo and Beth were amply rewarded for their thoughtfulness when the stallholder's husband delivered a dozen more bags on a small handcart. And because Sadie had helped sort the clothes out into the very good, the good and the not really worth having, she knew the bag she put in front of Beth and her mates contained ladies' and girls' clothes. The four women had a rare old time going through the assortment while being pushed and shoved by hordes of women wanting to get right by the table. The language from some of them was enough to bring blushes to most faces. Men down on the docks swearing was one thing, but coming from women it sounded dreadful.

There were two women behind the friends whose language was that of the gutter. While Dot was no angel, she drew the line at filth and blasphemy, and she knew she wasn't the only one offended because she could tell by the expressions on the faces near her, particularly Lizzie to whom blasphemy was a sin.

Clutching to her chest the items she intended to purchase, Dot turned her head. 'I'm not used to language like that, so would yer mind keeping yer mouth shut?'

'Oh, aye, listen to Miss Hoity-Toity talking. Thinks she's too good for us.' There followed a string of blasphemy which brought protests from everyone around. 'Are you going to make me keep me mouth shut, yer stuck up cow?'

Flo wasn't going to have a mate of hers spoken to like that, so she excused herself and squashed past a few customers to reach the woman who was standing with a sneer on her face, defying anyone to take her on. And it was that sneer that really brought up Flo's dander. 'My friend is too much of a lady to fight with the likes of you, she wouldn't dirty her hands on yer. She's not used to people what are as common as muck, yer see. But she's not the only one insulted by yer language. Everyone that can hear yer is insulted, me included, and I'm quite capable of making yer shut yer mouth. So any time ye're ready, I'm willing to oblige.'

'Don't stoop to her level, sunshine,' Beth said, having visions of it turning into a free for all, with people getting trampled underfoot. Not that she didn't agree with Flo, 'cos she did. It was only days to Christmas, and the woman with a voice like a fish-wife was taking God's name in vain. 'She obviously doesn't know any better, so she's more to be pitied than anything.'

While these words brought forth nods and murmurs of agreement from all those within hearing distance of what was going on, they also brought forth a roar of rage from the woman concerned. And with the rage came enough bad language to turn the air blue. But it also sent her friend scurrying away, fearful of getting involved. Not to mention being fearful of her husband finding out that the woman he'd warned her to keep away from, had been the cause of her getting caught up in a fight.

The cursing woman, named Fanny Mason, put her basket on the ground between her legs and began to roll up her sleeves. 'Okay, who wants to be first? The little fat one with the big mouth, let's start with you, eh? Yer won't last two minutes.'

Those words just happened to be the woman's undoing. She didn't have time to think about it, though, because the blow Flo aimed at her tummy had her doubled up and gasping for air. There wasn't a person near by who felt any pity for her. She'd been asking for it, and now she'd got her comeuppance.

Beth had taken the clothes Flo had chosen from her, and put them over her arm with her own. 'Dot, have yer finished buying?'

'Yes, girl, I've finished. And delighted into the bargain 'cos I've got some really good stuff.'

'What about you, Lizzie? I notice yer've got a few things for the girls as well as yerself.'

'I've done well, me darlin'. Today's been an eye opener, so it has.' Lizzie glanced over to where the big-mouthed woman was beginning to get her breath back and was giving Flo daggers. 'Sure, it was only spoilt by that heathen of a woman who doesn't know why we celebrate Christmas.'

'That's her loss, Lizzie, she's not worth bothering with. So let's get our clothes sorted out and I'll call Sadie over. I'm hoping to get the dresses in the tub tonight before Ginny has the chance to see the ones I've got for her. By the time I've washed and pressed them, she won't be able to tell they're not new.' Beth put a hand on Flo's shoulder. 'Come on, sunshine, we're ready to go. Take these dresses off me and pay for them yerself, otherwise we'll get all mixed up.'

The woman with the foul mouth and equally foul temper was eyeing Flo up and down in a manner designed to cause more aggravation. 'Come on, d'yer want to try yer chances now, yer bleedin' fat cow? I'm ready for yer when I wasn't before.'

As quick as a flash. Flo bent her knee, pushed her leg back, then brought it forward with all the force she could muster, aiming a kick at the woman's shin. A shriek of pain came first, then as the woman hopped on one foot there followed threats of what would happen when she got her hands on 'the fat cow's neck'. And even when people standing near by said she'd only got what she deserved, the woman would certainly have gone for Flo's neck if she'd been able to put her foot on the ground.

'Some other day, perhaps, when I've got more time.' Flo's grin was cheeky. 'And as for me being a fat cow, well, at least I can look in the mirror every morning without frightening meself to death. I bet that's more than you can do. Of course, yer might not have a mirror in your house, yer've probably cracked them all by now 'cos it would have to be a ruddy strong mirror to stand up to looking at your ugly clock every day.'

With a cry of rage the woman lunged forward. But the crowd standing near by had been expecting her to try something, and without a word being spoken they moved as one to fill the empty space between her and Flo. They wouldn't have had the guts to tell the big-mouthed harridan to shut up, but the least they could do was unite behind someone who did. And what a bit of excitement they had to tell their husbands over the dinner table that night! They'd add a bit more to it, like, to spice it up and make it more interesting. But there was no harm in doing that, was there?

Beth caught Sadie's eye. 'Can we pay yer, sunshine?'

The girl's eyes widened when she saw they each had several dresses over their arms. In fact, Lizzie and Flo had six, two dresses for each of their daughters, and two for themselves. 'Ooh, er, yer've done well, haven't yer?'

Flo said, 'We've done very well, queen, thanks to you. And now we've found yer, we'll be back regularly to see what yer have to offer. Now, can yer tell me what I owe yer?'

Sadie took the clothes from her and laid them down one at a time. 'The girls' dresses are one and six each, so that's six shillings. This dress for you is two bob, but this other one is four bob, I'm afraid, 'cos it's a very fashionable style, fine material and as good as new. Is that too much for yer to pay?'

You could almost see Flo ticking the prices off in her mind. 'I was never any good at sums in school, but I get it to twelve shillings, is that right?'

Sadie nodded. 'Can yer afford that much?'

Flo nearly nodded her head off, causing her chins to think they were on the big dipper. 'Of course I can afford them! Six dresses for twelve bob, queen, that's marvellous!'

Lizzie came next. She was expecting to pay the same as Flo, seeing as she too had six dresses. But Sadie said hers were two shilling less because although her two dresses were of good quality, they weren't made by a famous fashion designer. 'Sure, that'll not be worrying me at all, so it won't. Who'll know the difference, begorrah, unless they peep down the back of the dress?'

Dot owed seven shillings, for two dresses for herself and two for Joan. Beth had the same, but as she'd already paid for one dress, her bill was only five bob.

'I haven't enough loose money to give yer change, so I'll have to ask Mary Ann to change this ten bob note. I won't be long,' Sadie said, pleased that the ladies had spent so much money. In fact, a lot of money had been passed over the stalls today, much more than usual. Mary Ann would be delighted they'd had such a good day, as would her husband, though like herself they'd be glad when it was over. It was hard on the feet standing for nine hours without a break. But Sadie had something to look forward to when she got home to her grandma's. Her boyfriend Harry would be there waiting for her, and when her grandma and granda were in bed, she and Harry were going to talk about buying an engagement ring.

Mary Ann tied up a loose strand of her red hair and smiled at the young girl she loved like a daughter. 'What are you looking so happy

159

about? There's another couple of hours to go before we can even think of getting away.'

Sadie giggled. 'Which means in a couple of hours I'll be seeing my Harry!'

Mary Ann tutted. 'What it is to be young and in love, eh? I'll be getting a bit of time alone with my feller tonight, too, but I'll be too bleedin' tired to do anything about it. Anyway, what are yer waving that ten bob note at me for?'

'I need change. D'yer know the woman who bought that boy's coat, and her and her mate got us the tea and scones? Well, with their other two mates they've spent quite a few pounds between them. They're nice, too, very friendly.'

Mary Ann took the note, put it in a separate pocket reserved for paper money, then dug deep into her pocket for change. 'Wish them all the best for me, and say we hope to see them again.' She chucked Sadie gently under the chin. 'We could do with four new customers, especially if they're nice and friendly.' A movement caught her eye and she turned to see a young boy pulling a pullover from the stack of clothes. 'When yer get home with that, Frankie Stewart, tell yer mam I said it's sixpence and she can pay me tomorrow. If she doesn't pay tomorrow, then interest will be added and it goes up to a shilling. Now you tell her what I said, or one of us will box yer ears for yer.'

Sadie put her face close and grinned. 'That'll be the day when yer box Frankie's ears for him. Yer love the bones of him, and his baby sister. Ye're getting soft in yer old age, Mary Ann. Pretty soon yer'll be giving the clothes away for nothing.'

'If yer ever see me doing that, queen, then that's the time for yer to bring in the men in white coats. Now go and give those nice friendly women their change so yer can put a move on and help get this crowd thinned out a bit. I know they're me bread and butter, and most of the time I'm pleased to see them, but nine hours of grasping hands and loud voices, well, it gets yer down. Especially when yer chilblains are playing yer up.'

The four friends were in a very happy frame of mind on the way home. The happiest being Flo, who kept reminding them that her four bob dress was the classiest of the lot. Hadn't it been made by a posh bloke for a very rich woman? And hadn't the man had his name sewn in the dress to prove it was no ordinary one that could be bought cheaply in the likes of TJ's? No, she'd bet any money that the woman who had owned the dress before had bought it from Cripp's, the posh shop in

Bold Street, where there was a man in uniform standing outside to help the rich people from their cars. And if it was raining, he'd hold an umbrella over their head while they walked from their car to the shop door.

Dot was sitting with Lizzie on a seat in front of Flo and Beth, and as the tram had trundled along she'd listened patiently until she could stand no more. Turning her head, she said, 'Flo?'

The chubby face creased into a smile. 'Yes, queen, what d'yer want?'

'I want yer to shut up about that ruddy dress 'cos ye're beginning to get on me nerves. And if I hear much more of it, I personally will take it upon meself to cut it to pieces with that very sharp pair of scissors yer said yer had.'

'Ooh, I wouldn't recommend that, queen, 'cos yer'd have two of us to contend with. Me because I've taken a liking to that fashionably styled dress which is made from the finest material and is as good as new, and my feller 'cos he'd be very unhappy with yer for touching his scissors what he's very proud of.'

'I'll bring me own ruddy scissors then,' Dot said. 'Or yer could do us all a favour and shut up about the blasted dress.'

Beth rubbed her elbow over the window of the tram to see whether they were near home. 'Only two stops to go,' she said, then tilted her head to look at Flo whose backside was half on the narrow seat and half in mid-air. 'It's a lovely dress, sunshine, and it will look nice on yer. But isn't it a pity that yer can't wash it?'

Flo forgot she was only being held in place by grasping tightly to the back of the seat in front. When she took her hand away to look at Beth in surprise, it was only her quick thinking that kept her from landing in the aisle. 'What d'yer mean, I can't wash it? Of course I can wash it!'

'Didn't yer see the label on the inside which says that the garment should be dry cleaned only? It's made of soft wool. Yer can't just stick it in the dolly tub with the rest of yer wash, yer'd ruin the thing!'

Flo's eyes narrowed. 'Are you having me on, Beth Porter? 'Cos if yer are I don't think it's a bit bleedin' funny.'

'Now would I do that to you, sunshine? Ask these two if yer don't believe me.'

'Beth's right, me darlin', so she is,' Lizzie said. 'I'd have mentioned it to yer, but I was sure yer must have seen it, the way yer had the dress inside out inspecting it.'

Dot didn't turn her head because the grin on her face would have given the game away. But when Flo tapped her on the shoulder, she couldn't not turn her head so she bit hard on her lip to take the smile away. 'I thought yer'd seen the label, girl, otherwise I would have said something. But there's a dry cleaner's on County Road, yer can take it there when it gets dirty.'

'I'm not taking it to no dry cleaner's! They'd charge more than I paid for the flamin' dress!' Flo's face was the picture of injured pride. 'Of all the bloody stupid things I've ever heard . . . well, that beats the lot. Fancy making a dress what yer can't wash! It doesn't make any sense.'

'Well, yer see, girl,' Dot said, 'the posh lady that yer said bought it at Cripp's on Bold Street, she'd be rolling in money, wouldn't she? I mean, what's a couple of bob to her? She could afford to get it dry cleaned every time she wore it.'

'This is our stop.' Beth put her hand under Flo's elbow to help her to her feet. 'Come on, sunshine, don't keep the driver waiting.'

As she swayed down the aisle, the little woman was muttering under her breath. 'I've a good mind to take the bleedin' dress and ask for me money back. The silly buggers should have known the likes of us can't afford to have clothes dry cleaned. Coats, yeah, I can understand that, but not ruddy frocks what yer have to kneel down in to clean out the grate.'

The conductor was one who knew Flo's dilemma when it came to getting off the tram so he was on hand to help her down. His chivalry restored her humour somewhat. 'Thanks, lad, ye're a proper gentleman.'

Not for the world would the man tell her he felt as though his back was broken from taking the full weight of her body. 'It was a pleasure, love, set me up for the day it did. You take care now and have a happy Christmas.'

For a full thirty seconds the dress was forgotten as Flo sang the man's praises. 'That's what I call a real gentleman. Yer don't get many like him these days. If I hadn't had me hands full, I would have given him a Christmas tip.'

Beth's jaw dropped. 'But yer haven't got anything in yer hands, only yer purse! I'm carrying yer shopping.'

Angelic was the word to describe Flo's face. 'D'yer know what, queen? I clean forgot about that. But it's too late to run after the tram now, I'd never catch it up. But I'll look out for him next time we get on.'

'I can tell yer where he lives if yer'd really like to give him a Christmas box.' Dot knew her words wouldn't be welcomed. And anyway, she hadn't a clue where the man lived, she was just winding Flo up. 'He only lives off Rice Lane.'

'I've no time to be going to Rice Lane, I've got too much to do.' Flo's nostrils flared and her lips set in a straight line. 'Anyway, who

162

asked you to stick yer nose in? Why don't yer just mind yer own business?'

'Now let's not have any arguments,' Beth said. 'We've had a nice day and done very well for ourselves, so let's be merry and bright.'

'You all did very well for yerselves, but what about me?' Flo asked with a bulldog expression on her face. 'Yer don't think about me, do yer? I'm the one what's bought a dress which is no good to me.'

They were turning into their street now. 'The dress will be fine,' Beth said. 'Yer'll look like a real toff in it on Christmas Day.'

'Four bob for a dress I can only wear for one day! I don't think that's a bleedin' bargain. And if my feller finds out I'll never hear the last of it.'

'Don't tell him then!' Dot said. 'We won't say nothing to him.'

'What if he sees the label, clever clogs? He can read, yer know.'

'Oh, aye, what label is that, sunshine?' Beth asked.

'The one you smart arses saw, but I didn't. The one about dry cleaning.'

'I don't remember seeing any label! Did you, Dot?'

She shook her head. 'Not that I noticed. What about you, Lizzie?'

Lizzie's shaking head came at the same time as the penny dropped. 'Why, you lying cows! Fancy playing a trick like that on me!' Flo got on her high horse, but she didn't stay there long because she started to see the funny side of the situation. 'It was me own bleedin' fault for falling for it. But I'll get me own back on yer, so watch out.'

They were passing Hannah's house on the opposite side of the street when Beth came to a standstill. 'You lot go on, I want to call at Hannah's to see if the tea chest has been delivered. I'll see yer in the morning.' As she crossed the cobbles she could hear Flo threatening to get her own back with a vengeance, and there was a smile on Beth's face when Hannah opened the door. 'Has the chest arrived yet?'

The old woman looked all flustered. 'Come in, sweetheart, but don't look at the place, it's in a right mess.'

Beth gasped when she saw the state of the living room. The couch was piled high with bedding, cushions and coats, and all sorts of scarves and things. And the table and sideboard were covered in ornaments, crockery and pans. The newspaper these had been wrapped in for the journey was ankle-deep on the floor. 'In the name of God, Hannah, what's happened here?'

She wiped a hand across her forehead as though tired and weary. 'I expected them to leave the tea chest, but they made me empty it right away and took it with them. They were very nice about it, but they said the chest was only hired and they had to take it back or they'd be in trouble.'

Beth put her shopping down on one of the dining chairs. 'You look worn out, sunshine, it's too much for yer. Sit down and I'll make yer a pot of tea before I run home to get our dinner on the go. You can have yer dinner with us, then me and Ginny will come back with yer and between us we'll have this lot cleared away before yer can say Jack Robinson.'

Hannah sighed. 'I can't work like I used to. A few years ago I would have had all this put away in no time. It doesn't pay to grow old, sweetheart.'

Beth bent to kiss her cheek. 'Growing old is something no one can change. It happens to everyone, rich or poor. All the money in the world can't keep yer young. But it's the way yer grow old that makes the difference. Some people give up the ghost in their fifties and sixties, while others grow old gracefully. And you, sunshine, have found the secret of growing old with dignity. Yer don't look anywhere near yer age, and me and me mates are not going to let yer put yer feet up yet. Yer've got years ahead of yer and there's still plenty of mileage left on yer clock. Once yer grandchildren are here yer'll get a new lease of life, you'll see. There'll be no stopping yer, yer'll leave us all standing.'

She patted a wrinkled cheek and made her way to the kitchen. 'And now for that cuppa. We could both do with one. And while we're drinking it I'll give yer something to laugh about.'

Hannah called after her, 'Is it about Flo?'

'Of course it's about Flo! Who else can make yer laugh when ye're down in the dumps and don't think yer'll ever laugh again? Florence Henderson, that's who.'

Chapter Fourteen

As soon as Ginny walked through the door, she asked, 'Has Mrs Bailey's family arrived yet, Mam?'

'I couldn't tell yer, sunshine, 'cos I'm not long in meself.' Beth lifted a cheek for her daughter's kiss. 'I've been to see yer grandma and granda, and as I don't see them very often I can't just dash in and out. I did call at Hannah's when I was passing this morning, but it was just to see if she'd got herself sorted out for Claire and the children coming. I wasn't expecting them to be there, not that early in the day, 'cos it takes a long time to come from Birmingham to Liverpool. Especially if they've got to change trains.'

'Can I go down and see if they've come now, before I take me coat off?'

'Certainly not! I don't want yer making a nuisance of yerself. Just give them time to settle in after that long journey. I did tell Hannah that she could bring them up tonight if they weren't too tired, to make our acquaintance, like, so at least they'll know a couple of faces in the street.'

Ginny threw her satchel on the couch and hung up her coat. 'Did me grandma and granda like the Christmas card I made them?'

'They were over the moon and told me to thank yer. They also said yer were very clever, but I'm not going to tell yer that in case yer get big-headed.'

'I wish we could go and see them more often. It's months since the last time.'

'I know, I feel guilty about it meself. But yer know money's always been tight, and some weeks it takes me all me time to manage. I was only thinking, coming home on the tram, that when you start bringing a wage in, we could all go up about once a month, on a Sunday when yer dad's not working.'

'What did they think about me getting a job in Woolworth's? I bet they got a surprise.'

'They said I was to tell yer they were very proud of yer. And they asked me something we haven't given any thought to which is what are yer supposed to wear for work? Yer can't go in yer gymslip, yer'd look daft.'

'Miss Harper, the one who told us all about our hours of work and that, she said it would be all right to wear the gymslip, seeing as it's dark navy, with a white blouse. Just until yer had the money to buy me a dark skirt and blouse.'

Beth hadn't intended telling her daughter about getting the dresses from the market, not until they'd been washed and ironed and looked respectable. But she changed her mind now. Perhaps the market was also the place to get a neat skirt and blouse for Ginny to start work in. She might not like the idea, but it was Hobson's choice. She could either wear her school clothes, or get some suitable second-hand ones. That's all the money would stretch to.

Beth took a seat next to her on the couch. 'I didn't mention last night that me and the gang had been down to the market in Great Homer Street. You know, where I got our Joey's coat from. The reason I didn't was because we'd all bought second-hand dresses and we wanted to wash them before anyone saw them. I've got two smashing ones for meself, and two for you. I put them in steep in the dolly tub overnight, and then through the mangle this morning. They're dry now, but they need ironing.'

Ginny's blue eyes lit up. 'Are the dresses yer bought for me grown-up ones?'

'Of course they are! Yer'll be a working girl soon, so there wouldn't be much point in buying yer children's clothes.'

Ginny was excited now. 'Will they do to wear for work?'

'No, sunshine, they're floral cotton. They'll be nice for Christmas, and in the summer, but not suitable to wear for work. What I was thinking, though, is that yer might get a decent navy blue skirt from there. If yer did, it would tide yer over until we could afford to buy yer a new one. And yer'd feel better than yer would going to work in yer gymslip.'

'Can I see the dresses?'

Beth pushed herself to her feet. 'I'll get them. But don't forget they'll look a lot different when they've been ironed. And if our Joey comes in, then run up the stairs with them and put them on me bed. I want us to surprise him and yer dad on Christmas Day.'

When Beth came back from the kitchen with the dresses over her arm, Ginny jumped to her feet. 'Which are mine, Mam?'

'The blue floral and the pink spotted are yours.' Beth handed them over and waited for her daughter's reaction. 'Well?'

Ginny was like a cat on hot bricks as she held one dress and then the other up to her neck and waltzed around the room. 'Mam, they're gorgeous! Oh, I'm going to be the belle of the ball in these. The blue for Christmas Day and the pink for Boxing Day. Oh, thank you, Mam, thank you. Ye're the best mam in the whole world.'

Beth caught a shadow crossing the window. 'Here's our Joey. Run upstairs with them and don't breathe a word 'cos yer know what he's like for repeating things. I suppose everyone in the street knows where his coat came from and how much it cost.'

Joey came in rubbing his hands together, his nose bright red with the cold. 'I hope there's a pot of tea on the go, Mam?'

'I haven't been in meself for long, I haven't had time to make tea. But I'll put the kettle on to shut yer up.'

'Yer've no right to stay out so long.' There was a cheeky look on Joey's face. 'If yer were a good mother yer'd be home for yer children coming in from school, and yer'd have a roaring fire going in the grate and a pot of tea on the table.'

'If it's a servant yer want, son, then yer've come to the wrong house. It's you what should be waiting on yer old mam, not the other way around.'

Joey took his coat off with great care. It was his pride and joy and while he used to throw his old one on the couch, this one was hung on the hook properly, using the label sewn into the back of the neck. 'Oh, yer poor old woman. You sit down and put yer tired feet up while I put the kettle on and make yer a cuppa.'

Ginny came running down the stairs. 'Was I hearing things, or did you just tell me mam to put her feet up and you'd make a pot of tea?'

'Yeah, but I didn't say there'd be a cuppa for you.' Then Joey remembered it wouldn't be long before his sister was working and he'd be earning pocket money. 'Nah, I was only kiddin'. I'll make a cup for you too.'

'Well, wonders will never cease! Are yer sure ye're feeling all right, brother? Ye're not sickening for anything, are yer?'

'Don't knock it, sunshine,' Beth said. 'Never look a gift horse in the mouth.'

'No, I won't! I'll sit back and enjoy me drink. I bet the tea will taste better 'cos it was made by me kid brother.'

'Well, whoever makes it, get on with it or yer dad will be in before I've even started on the dinner.' Beth flew up the stairs so she could remove the dresses from the inquisitive eyes of her son. After folding them on the bed, she opened the wardrobe door, thinking if she hid them on the bottom in the corner even Joey wouldn't find them. It was a double wardrobe with a mirror in the dark oak middle panel, and because the children's rooms were too small for a wardrobe, some of their best clothes were hanging in it next to hers and Andy's. Not that any of them possessed what you would call Sunday clothes, but their spares were an improvement on the ones they wore daily.

Beth knelt down, and after pushing the hanging clothes out of her face, leaned forward to put the dresses on the bottom. It was then her eyes lighted on a bundle stuck in the corner out of sight. She sat back on her heels, remembering the time she'd thrown the black skirt in there because it had got too tight around the waist for her. That was a few years ago, and she'd completely forgotten about it. At the time she had intended to let the waist out if she could, but she'd never got down to it and it had gone out of her mind.

She pulled out the crumpled skirt and flung it over her shoulder out of the way. Then when she was satisfied she'd found a good hiding place for the dresses, she got to her feet and picked up the skirt which at one time had been her favourite. It had six shaped panels, which fitted neatly over the thighs before falling into folds. It had fitted her like a glove at one time, until she'd started putting on a bit of weight. She gave the skirt a good shake, and told herself that it would come up nice if it was washed and pressed. It probably wouldn't go near her, but perhaps it could be altered to do Ginny a turn until they could afford a new one. But would her daughter think it was too old-fashioned for her? There was only one way to find out, and that was to ask. If Ginny didn't want it, there'd be no harm done.

So after nodding her head in agreement with herself, and giving the skirt another good shake, Beth folded it over her arms and tripped lightly down the stairs. 'Look what I've just found at the bottom of the wardrobe. I haven't worn it for ages 'cos it had gone too tight around the waist for me. I'd clean forgotten about it until I just spotted it.' She held the skirt to her. 'I didn't half like it, it was me favourite. I used to think it gave me a figure like a film star.'

The two children were sitting at the table with their hands around the cups of hot tea. There was a cup poured out ready for their mother. 'Perhaps it'll fit yer now, Mam,' Ginny said. 'Try it on and see.'

Diplomacy was called for here, Beth told herself. It would be better for her daughter to want it herself, without having it pushed on to her. 'I'll try it on in the kitchen.' She was only gone a matter of seconds, and when she came back there was a look of disappointment on her face. 'Look, it won't go near me. I'd need at least another two inches around the waist. It's sad, really, 'cos I do like it.'

'Yeah, it's a nice skirt,' Ginny said, feeling sorry that the skirt wouldn't fit her mother when she liked it so much. 'I love the way it flares out.'

And who should come to the rescue but Joey? 'Why don't you have it then, Sis? It should fit yer 'cos ye're thinner than me mam.'

Ginny's eyes showed interest. 'I would do, but it would be too long for me.'

'That would be no problem, if yer like it.' Beth kept her voice casual. 'Yer Auntie Dot is a dab hand at alterations, as yer know. If all it needed was taking up, then she'd have it done in an hour. That's if yer asked her nicely.' Beth turned to go back into the kitchen to take the skirt off. 'I've just had a thought. If it's no good to you, sunshine, Dot would jump at it. She always liked it, and she's thinner than me.'

Once more Joey came to the rescue. Not that he knew it, mind, 'cos if he did he'd charge for his help. 'Charity begins at home, Mam, so give yer own daughter the chance first.' He jerked his head. 'Go on, Sis, try it on before somebody else beats yer to it.'

Ginny didn't need telling twice. She ran out to the kitchen and Joey could hear her and his mam laughing. And it made him feel good. He was lucky having parents and a sister who liked to laugh, and whose faces were never far from a smile. Two of his mates who lived in the street had mothers who were always bawling at them. Yer never heard them laughing or being loving towards their children. And they used bad words, too, which his mam never did.

Ginny came in, slinking like she'd seen film stars do. With a hand patting her hair, she did an impersonation of Mae West. 'Come up and see me some time, big boy.'

Joey's eyes bulged out of his head. 'Ay, yer don't half look different, our kid. Yer look dead grown-up.'

Ginny giggled. 'It feels good. And it fits me except it's miles too long.'

'It needs about three inches taking off it, that's all,' Beth said. 'If it was just a plain straight skirt, I could do it meself, but with it being flared I'd only make a mess of it. I'll nip next door after we've had our dinner and ask Dot to do it for yer. Then I can wash and press it, ready for yer to start work in.'

Ginny threw her arms around her mother's neck. 'Thanks, Mam! There's such a lot of nice things happening, I think we're very lucky.'

And Joey, thinking of his new coat, endorsed that. 'We sure are.'

169

* * *

'How did yer find yer mam and dad, love?' Andy asked, looking down the table at his wife. 'Both well, I hope?'

'Yeah, they seem fine. Glad to see me as always. I told them we'd try and get up to see them one Sunday soon. I don't think they see many people with there being no houses for miles around. After living in a street like this for most of their married life, with plenty of friends and neighbours, they must feel lonely and isolated where they are.'

'I think ye're right. We should make the effort to see them more often. Perhaps when the weather improves, eh?'

'Guess what, Dad?' Ginny couldn't keep still, her bottom was sliding back and forth over the seat of the wooden chair. 'One of me mam's old skirts fits me and I'm going to wear it for work.'

'Go 'way! Yer mam's always telling me that she gets so much wear out of her clothes, by the time she's finished with them they're only fit for the muck midden.' Andy's deep brown eyes sparkled. 'Mind you, I never really notice what she wears, 'cos if she wore a coal sack, she'd still be beautiful to me.'

Beth blushed. 'Don't act so daft.'

'Me dad's not daft, 'cos I think ye're beautiful as well,' Joey said. 'Yer knock all the other women into a cocked hat.'

'There isn't a child in this street who doesn't think their mother is beautiful, sunshine, don't ever forget that. And there's not a mother who doesn't think her children are beautiful.'

Joey lowered his eyes to his plate and kept his mouth shut. But his mind was asking how could Jimmy Bowling think his mother was beautiful when she had long hairs growing out of her chin and only two yellow teeth in her mouth? He didn't voice his thoughts, though, 'cos the last time he'd mentioned Mrs Bowling, his mam had told him that God made everyone, and He gave everyone beauty of some kind. You couldn't always see it, because it could be in the mind or the heart. He tried to think of that every time he called for his mate, but he still couldn't understand why the woman couldn't cut the hairs off. Surely God wouldn't stop her from doing that? Otherwise, why were scissors and razors invented?

'Any sign of Hannah's family yet?' Andy asked, changing the subject.

'I think they should be there by now, but I couldn't say for sure. If they're not, Hannah will be a nervous wreck because she was bad enough this morning. Ginny wanted to go up when she came in from school, but I think they should be given time to settle down first. Hannah knows she can bring them up if she wants to, but I don't want

170

to push meself where I might not be welcome.' Beth turned to her son and tutted. 'Joey, will yer stop pushing that carrot around the plate, please, and put it in yer mouth?'

With a cheeky grin, he speared the carrot and popped it into his mouth. 'It was playing hard to get with me.'

'I'll play hard to get with you if yer don't finish that dinner. I want everywhere tidied away, just in case Hannah does bring her family. And I want to nip next door to ask Dot to alter the skirt for Ginny. With a bit of luck she'll do it tonight and I can have it washed, dried and pressed for Christmas. It'll be one thing off me mind.'

'Leave the place to us, Mam, we'll tidy it up,' Ginny said. 'I'll clear the table and shake the cloth out. Then our Joey can help me with the dishes. Me dad can supervise.'

'I think I'll take yer up on that. It seems to have been a long day, even though I haven't done much. It's that flipping long journey to me ma's and back. So I'll be glad to have a natter with Dot. I won't stay, though, just ten minutes or so.'

Andy's guffaw was deep and throaty. 'How many times have I heard yer say that? It's always going to be only ten minutes, yet yer can bet yer bottom dollar we won't see yer for at least an hour.'

'You're a fine one to talk,' Beth said. 'Every time yer go out with yer mates to the pub, it's only ever going to be one pint. Except it never is.'

'That doesn't happen very often, love, so yer can't throw that up in me face. It's over a week since I had a pint.'

Beth looked surprised. 'It never is, is it?'

Andy nodded. 'More than a week.'

'Well, why don't yer go to the pub tonight, Dad?' Ginny asked. 'Me and our Joey can look after ourselves till me mam comes back.'

Her father shook his head. 'No, I'm saving me money until Christmas Eve. Then me and the lads are going to push the boat out.'

'I've got a tanner to spare if yer feel like a pint,' Beth offered. Her husband worked hard, never took a day off and always handed his wage packet over. He deserved some pleasure out of life. 'D'yer want me to ask Bill when I take the skirt next door? And I'm sure Dennis and Paddy would be all for it.'

'No, I've got more to do with me money with Christmas only days away. Besides, me and me mates made a pact a week ago that we'd save our money and have one really good night out to celebrate.'

Beth stood behind her husband's chair and put her arms around his neck. 'Ye're welcome to the price of a pint if yer want one, sunshine, yer know that.'

'No, I'll hang out until Christmas Eve, love, but thanks all the same. You poppy off next door and have a natter with yer mate. Me and the kids will sort this place out.'

'Well, if ye're sure yer don't mind, I'll just slip me coat on 'cos it's bitter. And I won't say I'll only be ten minutes, then yer can't throw it up in me face.' Beth ruffled his thick, dark hair. 'When I come back I expect to see a fire up the chimney and everywhere nice and tidy. You have been warned.'

Joan Flynn opened the door to Beth, and her eyes looked either side for sight of her friend. 'Hasn't Ginny come with yer?'

'No, she's washing the dishes and tidying up for me.' Beth shivered. 'Ye're not going to keep me standing on the step, are yer, sunshine?'

'I'm sorry, Auntie Beth, come on in.' Joan quickly closed the front door to keep out the cold. 'I was just surprised Ginny wasn't with yer.'

'Her and Joey volunteered to wash up so I could come and have a natter with yer mam.' Beth entered the living room and made straight for the fire. Holding her open hands out to the flames, she grinned at Bill and young David. 'Good evening, gentlemen. I hope the weather is warm enough for yer?'

Dot came through from the kitchen wiping her hands on a tea-towel. 'We were just talking about you, and here yer are! That's what I call a coincidence.'

'Oh, aye, what were yer saying about me then?'

'Well, it wasn't about you, actually.' Dot rolled the tea-towel into a ball, and not wanting to break the conversation, she threw it into the kitchen where it landed in the sink. 'I was just asking Bill why he didn't give Andy a knock to see if he fancied a pint.'

'And what did yer say to that, Bill?' Beth asked. 'Did yer give the same answer as I got from Andy, that yer were saving yer coppers so yer could paint the town red on Christmas Eve?'

Bill folded the *Echo* and laid it on his knee. 'Something along those lines, love. But I don't think I mentioned anything about painting the town red. Not in front of the Missus, anyway. It wouldn't go down well, yer see.'

'No, it ruddy well wouldn't!' Dot picked up the poker from the brass companion set and rattled it between the bars of the grate to liven up the fire. 'I'm not having you and yer rowdy mates rolling home on Christmas Eve, staggering down the street shouting and singing.'

'Yer can't half exaggerate, love.' There was fondness in Bill's eyes

172

when he smiled at his wife. 'I have never in me life staggered home drunk. And I can't sing for peanuts.'

Joan was hovering in the background, waiting to get a word in. Then when she realised she could be waiting for ages, she butted in, 'Auntie Beth, can I go down to see Ginny? Just for an hour or so?'

'Of course yer can, sunshine, she'll be glad to see yer.' Beth wagged a warning finger. 'But don't stop her from getting the dishes done. I'd hate to have to start on those when I get back.'

After the door closed on her daughter, Dot said, 'She's got an appointment for an interview at Dunlop's tomorrow, and she can't wait to tell Ginny. She's a shivering wreck now, so God help her when her name's called to go into the office tomorrow. They'll be lucky to get a word out of her.' She touched Beth's arm. 'What's that ye're carrying?'

Beth held the skirt up. 'Doesn't this take yer back a few years? I've just come across it at the bottom of the wardrobe. It won't fit me around the waist, but it looks fine on Ginny except it needs three inches taking off. I'm hoping yer'll be an angel and do it for us.'

'Yeah, of course I will! I've got some black cotton in so I'll start it tonight. Anyway, sit down, will yer? Ye're making the place look untidy.'

'Here yer are, Mrs Porter, yer can have my chair,' David said, leaving the comfort of the fireside chair. 'I'll sit on the couch.'

'That's nice of yer, sunshine.' When Beth sank into the chair, she grinned. 'Yer've left it nice and warm for me.'

The words had no sooner left her lips than there came a hammering on the front door. 'In the name of God, who can this be?' Dot jumped up. 'Whoever it is will get a piece of me mind for making that racket.'

Joey didn't give Dot a chance to tell him off, he got in before her. 'Me dad said to tell me mam that Mrs Bailey and her family have come.'

'Okay, lad, I'll tell her.' Dot was already reaching for her coat. 'We'll be there in no time.'

Beth, who had heard all this and left her chair, asked, 'What d'yer mean, we'll be there in no time?'

'Because I'm coming with yer! Yer don't think I'd miss out on a thing like this, for heaven's sake. A little bit of excitement will do me the world of good.'

'But me house will be full!' Beth complained. 'Can't yer leave it for another time to meet them. Tomorrow, perhaps?'

'No, I can't!' Dot was crafty and quickly saw a way to settle the argument. 'Do yer want that skirt doing, or not?'

Beth shook her head at Bill. 'Your wife is a sly beggar. She's resorting to blackmail now.'

He feigned a weary sigh. 'Take it from one who's had years of experience, Beth, and give in gracefully. Because yer'll never win with her.'

Dot grabbed her mate's arm. 'Don't be standing there gabbing when yer've got visitors. It's bad manners to keep them waiting.'

But Beth stood her ground. Two could play at blackmail. 'Did yer say yer'd definitely do that skirt tonight?'

While young David shook with laughter, Bill chuckled. 'Yer've met yer match there, Dot, she's as crafty as you.'

Beth raised her brows. 'I learnt it from her! Her and Flo Henderson. And now, what were yer saying about the skirt, sunshine?'

'I'll do it tonight, even if I have to stay up all ruddy night! Now, can we go, please, I'm dying to see what they're like.'

Claire was shaking hands with the two women before they were even through the door, and thanking them profusely for the help they'd given to Hannah. 'My mother-in-law has told me everything, and I can't find words enough to thank yer. And yer husbands, too! I could hardly believe me eyes when I saw what they'd done to the back bedroom in such a short time. Everywhere looks nice and homely, and I really mean it when I say Mrs Bailey is lucky to have such good friends and neighbours.'

Beth and Dot were thinking the same thing: that Claire looked older than they'd expected her to look. Then again, the tragedy of losing her beloved husband was enough to put that haunted look in her eyes and the lines etched on her face. Beth hugged her close. 'We were glad we could be of help, sunshine. Yer see, we are very fond of yer mother-in-law, who is respected by everyone in this street. And yer can thank me other two friends, and the men, when yer see them. Which I'm sure won't be long.'

As she was speaking, Beth's eyes were on Hannah. She had never seen her looking so happy. Her face was aglow, and her eyes shone with love and pride for the two grandchildren standing either side of her. It was as if they wanted to be as near as possible to the grandma they hadn't seen for over five years. The scene was enough to bring a lump to the throat.

'This handsome young man is my grandson, Bobby, and the pretty young lady is my granddaughter, Amelia,' Hannah said with a hand on each of their shoulders. 'Children, this is Mrs Porter and Mrs Flynn.'

Beth rushed to hug them, followed quickly by Dot. 'Yer can call me Auntie Beth, it sounds much more friendly. That's if yer want to, of course?'

Dot winked at the two children who were looking a bit shy and overwhelmed. 'Don't make up yer minds on that yet, not until yer get to know her. She's got a nice face, but she's also got a ruddy awful temper. But ye're quite safe calling me Auntie Dot, I'm as sweet as sugar candy. Never lose me temper or argue. In fact, I'm too good to be true, really.'

'Dot's got a son about your age, Bobby, and me friend over the road has two. So yer won't be short of mates. And those two girls standing there, as quiet as mice and looking as though butter wouldn't melt in their mouths, are Ginny and her mate Joan. They'll show yer around, Amelia, and I promise they're not always as bashful as they are now.' Beth jerked her head at Joey and her eyes were telling him to show his manners and stand up to make room for the visitors. 'Sit yerselves down and I'll put the kettle on. And Ginny, don't stand there like a dummy, bring Joan over and keep the children company.'

Ginny's face went bright red. Each time she looked at Bobby she caught him looking at her. And he wasn't half nice-looking. Better than any other lad in the street. 'Mam, why don't you sit down and we'll make the tea? Bobby and Amelia can help us and we can get to know each other.'

When Joey saw Bobby's face go crimson, he came to his aid. 'Girls only talk about stupid things that wouldn't interest Bobby. He'd have a headache in no time with them giggling and nattering away. Why don't I save him from a fate worse than death and take him to meet David? At least they'd have something in common.'

Andy had been quiet, listening with interest. 'Why don't I ask Bill if he feels like a pint after all, then I'd be out of yer way? And perhaps all the children would like to visit David, and they could get to know each other over there. That way everyone would be happy.'

'That's a very good idea, sunshine,' Beth said. 'Then we women can have a good old gossip.'

'What sort of a job did yer have?' David asked. 'Were yer an apprentice?'

Bobby nodded. 'Yeah, an apprentice gas fitter. I've done two years, so I'm hoping when I get a job they'll take that into consideration.' His eyes kept straying to where the girls were sitting around the table. 'What do you do?'

'Apprentice plumber, I work with me dad. The money's lousy, but if

175

yer want to have a skill at yer finger-tips, then yer've got to put up with it. It pays in the end, when ye're twenty-one and on full money.' David was happy having someone his own age to talk to. 'Will yer be looking for a job after Christmas?'

'Yeah, and so will me mam and our Amelia. We'll have to now we don't have me dad's wages coming in.' There was a catch in the boy's voice. 'I know I'm too young to be much help to me mam, but she did tell me I was the man of the house now.'

David was sensitive enough to steer the conversation down another avenue. 'Where did yer sister work?'

'In a factory that made overalls. She'll probably get a job quicker than I will.'

Joan had her ear cocked to where the boys were sitting. He was dead handsome was Bobby, but he probably looked on her and Ginny as schoolgirls. So she took it upon herself to put him wise. 'I'm going for a job interview tomorrow, in Dunlop's, where me dad works. Why don't yer try there for a job, Bobby?'

'Do they have gas fitters there?'

Joan didn't have a clue. 'I'm not sure, but I could ask me dad to find out for yer.'

'What about you, Ginny?' Bobby asked. 'Have you got a job lined up?'

Her face coloured. She was dying to show off and tell him she was going to work in one of the biggest shops in Liverpool, but that wouldn't be nice when he'd just lost his dad and must be feeling very sad and unhappy. 'Yeah, I'm going to work in a shop. I start the first Monday in the new year.'

'I know where you could try for a job, Amelia.' David was being very daring. At sixteen he was awkward with girls, didn't know what to say to them. In fact, he didn't know any but his sister and her friend Ginny. 'One of the men at work said his daughter's been for an interview at Hartley's Jam Works, and she got taken on. So it might be worth yer trying.'

Now it was Amelia's turn for pink cheeks. She'd been sneaking glances at David, and thought he looked nice. He had a lovely smile and fine white teeth. 'I'm going to the Labour Exchange tomorrow so I could ask about Hartley's. Thanks for telling me.'

Joey was beginning to think he'd have been just as well staying at home with the old people because the young ones were hardly a bundle of laughs. Then he remembered the circumstances which had brought Bobby and Amelia here tonight. He couldn't imagine what he'd feel like if his dad died, he'd probably want to die as well. 'Do you and yer sister play cards, Bobby?'

There was a slight hesitation before the boy replied, 'Yeah, we used to play a lot.'

'Well, why don't yer come down to ours one night and we can all play? We've got snakes and ladders if yer don't like cards.'

'I hope that invitation includes me and our Joan?' David said. He didn't have many real friends, and had taken a fancy to Bobby and his sister. 'We could all come to yours one night, then here another night.'

Ginny and Joan smiled and nodded. No more playing with a skipping rope or hopscotch, they were past that stage now. Young ladies they were, and cards were for grown-ups. 'That would be nice,' Ginny said. 'Except I'm not a very good player.'

'I'll teach yer,' Bobby said. 'It's easy when yer know how.'

Joan wasn't going to let her mate get away with that. 'Yer can teach me, too, Bobby, 'cos I'm hopeless.'

Ginny thought Amelia was being left out, so she asked, 'I suppose you're very good at cards, are yer?'

'Am I heck! The only time I win is when they let me 'cos they feel sorry for me.'

'I'll teach yer, Amelia,' David offered, much to his own surprise. 'And Bobby can teach the other two.'

Joey sat back in his chair and smiled as he scratched his head. Something told him that playing cards was going to be much more fun in future than it had ever been.

Chapter Fifteen

'This is how life should be every day.' Andy stretched out his long legs and gave a sigh of pleasure as he sipped on a glass of sherry. 'It's a pity Christmas Day only comes once a year.'

'Yer wouldn't say that if yer had the worry of it.' Beth looked at the floor, strewn with paper which had been ripped from presents by hands eager to find out what goodies were concealed inside. Andy had been delighted with his new blue shirt and the scarf and glove set, and Ginny was beside herself with joy when she saw the grown-up stockings and underwear. She was upstairs now trying the underskirt on with one of the second-hand dresses. As for Joey, he was sitting on the couch with his head buried in a comic. He'd been told not to expect anything for Christmas because his coat had cost a lot of money so he was well pleased with the gloves and comics he'd found in the pillow case hanging from the mantelpiece, along with an apple, tangerine, nuts and a small Cadbury's selection box.

Beth fingered the string of pearls around her neck. Of course they weren't real ones, only cheap imitations, but they looked very pretty. They were a present from Andy, along with a bottle of Evening In Paris perfume. And when she'd finished her glass of sherry, she'd have a good wash, put on one of the new dresses and dab a spot of the perfume behind her ears. 'Which one of me mates did yer ask to get these presents for yer?'

'Oh, yer can't catch me out there, love, 'cos knowing how you and yer mates tell each other everything, I knew nothing would be a surprise to yer. So one of the men I work with, he got his wife to buy them. I hope yer like them?'

'They're lovely, sunshine, yer did well. And as soon as I can gather enough energy, I'm going to get washed and doll meself up.'

'You relax while yer can, there's no rush today.'

So Beth dropped her head back and let her mind wander over the events of the last few days. She'd managed well for money and was pleased with herself. Some weeks it was hard going to put a few coppers in all the clubs, but it was worth it come Christmas. She'd have been lost but for the sweetshop club, and the butcher's and greengrocer's. Her mates seemed to have just about managed, too, and Hannah had been helped out with money by Claire, who had been paid her husband's two weeks wages in hand. The bit of insurance he'd had was just barely enough to bury him and pay their fares to Liverpool. But it was a relief to Beth to know the old woman had her family around her for Christmas, and wasn't going short.

She took a sip of her sherry. Everything had gone smoothly until yesterday morning when Flo had reminded them all that they owed Ma Maloney a shilling interest on the pound they'd borrowed. And when Dot said the moneylender could wait until after the holiday, Flo warned that she wouldn't think twice about knocking on their doors on Christmas Day asking for what they owed her. It was no use threatening to tell their husbands on her because she was afraid of no one, man or woman. So their purses were emptied on Beth's table and a shilling was counted from each of the four stacks of coins. And while they were counting, who should knock on the door but Hannah? She'd remembered the moneylender, and to get out of the house without her daughter-in-law suspecting anything had made the excuse to Claire that she'd borrowed a shilling off Beth days ago and must just nip up and pay her debt.

The closing of a door brought Beth to her feet and over to the window. 'It's the O'Learys on their way to Mass. Just look at them, Andy, all in their Sunday best and walking in line. Lizzie and Paddy in front, Mick and Seamus behind, and the two girls, Molly and Eileen, bringing up the rear. They're a credit to their parents those kids. Not one has ever been a ha'porth of trouble. They never give cheek or answer back, not like some of the kids in the street.'

Andy came to stand beside her and slipped an arm around her waist. 'They were at Midnight Mass with us, why do they need to go again?'

'I'm sure they don't need to, sunshine, they're going because that's what they want to do. They're not doing anybody any harm. They're good-living people but never shove religion down anyone else's throat. Yer never hear them arguing or shouting or using bad language. There's a few in this street could do with taking a leaf out of their book. Thoroughly nice people who yer could trust with yer life.'

The O'Learys were out of sight now, and Andy pulled her close. 'Aren't I a thoroughly nice man yer could trust with yer life?'

Bright blue eyes met deep brown ones. 'I trusted me life with you some sixteen years ago, sunshine, and yer've served me well.'

He nuzzled her neck, and whispered, 'I've done me best, love, but if it was in my power I would give yer the moon, the sun and the stars.'

Joey was at an exciting part in his comic, where the hero was confronting the baddie, and at first he was torn between carrying on or listening in to what his mam and dad were saying. His parents didn't know he was, of course, or they would have moved apart, afraid of being thought soppy. But as far as the boy was concerned there was no real contest between them and the comic because he was never happier than when he was watching his mam and dad showing their love for each other. He could go back to the comic any time, and anyway it was a dead cert that the hero would win. Otherwise he wouldn't be a hero, would he?

After making up his mind, and putting his finger on the line he was up to in the comic, Joey found himself thwarted by his own sister. She came running down the stairs as happy as could be. 'How do I look, Mam?' Ginny did a twirl to show off the blue floral cotton dress, then lifted the skirt a little to show off her first grown-up underskirt.

'Yer look lovely, sunshine, the dress really suits yer.'

'Yer look like a million dollars, love.' Andy was thinking how quickly children grew up.

Now that was going too far for Joey and he pulled a face. 'If I had a million dollars, I'd want more for me money than that.'

Nothing was going to dampen Ginny's spirits, and she smiled at him. 'Ah, well, yer see, our kid, I've got the dress but you haven't got the million dollars. So that must tell yer something.'

'I'll give yer all something to think about,' Beth said. 'I was up very early this morning to put the turkey in the oven and make the stuffing, and all the potatoes and veg are ready to put on. I think yer'll agree I deserve a break? So I'm going to make meself look as glamorous as I can so as to compete with me daughter, and yer dad's going to dickie himself up in his new shirt. And while we're doing that, you two can get stuck in and tidy this place up. I want all this paper picked up and put in the bin, and yer presents taken up to yer rooms. Except the dress yer've got on, Ginny, and the comic you're reading, Joey. And when all that's done, we can sit back and relax for the rest of the day.' She rolled her eyes. 'Is everyone in favour, or are there any complaints?'

'No, we'll do it, Mam,' Ginny said. 'And when we've finished, can I go down to Mrs Bailey's to show her me dress?'

'Oh, I don't think so, sunshine, not on Christmas morning. They'll be busy seeing to the dinner and things.'

Joey folded the comic up neatly and put it under the cushion of his chair. 'It's not Mrs Bailey she wants to show off to, it's Bobby!'

The colour flooded Ginny's cheeks. 'No, it's not, yer daft nit! I want to see Mrs Bailey.'

But nothing was going to stop her brother from saying what he thought. 'Go 'way! I saw the sly looks yer were giving him the other night. And every time he spoke to yer, yer face went the colour of beetroot and yer couldn't speak for stuttering.'

'You big fibber!' Ginny appealed to her mother. 'Mam, will yer make him shut up before I clout him one?'

'On this day of all days, I'll have no arguments or clouts in this house. So both of yer set to and tidy this place up while me and yer dad get dressed. Surely yer don't begrudge me half an hour on me own after the week I've had?'

'I don't begrudge yer nothing, Mam, 'cos I know how busy yer've been. And I bet yer've gone without things yerself to give us our Christmas presents.' Ginny picked up one of the squashed cushions from the couch and began to plump it up. 'And there'll be no fights because I don't care what our Joey says, I'll just ignore him.'

'Yer can't take a joke, you can't.' The boy could feel tears smarting at the back of his eyes, and so no one would see them, he bent down and began to pick up some of the paper from the floor. 'I was only pulling her leg, Mam, I didn't mean nothing by it. There was no need for her to act like a big soft baby.'

'Not everyone has the same sense of humour, sunshine! What you think is a joke might not be funny to someone else. Just think before yer speak in future.' Beth winked at Andy. 'I'll let you have the sink first, love, while I get me clothes ready. Give me a shout when the coast is clear.'

When both parents had left the room, Joey sidled over to Ginny. 'There was no need to take the huff, yer've upset me mam now.'

'Well, you shouldn't tell fibs.'

'I've told yer, it was just a joke. If Joan Flynn had been here, I'd have said the same to her, 'cos she was giving Bobby cow eyes too.'

Ginny giggled. 'She wasn't, was she?'

'Yeah, she was worse than you! She even offered to try and get him a job!'

Upstairs, Beth cocked an ear before moving to the bedroom door. In the kitchen Andy raised his head from the sink. And a smile crossed both faces when they heard the laughter of their children coming from the living room.

* * *

Andy undid the top button of his trousers and let out a sigh of relief. 'My old ma, God rest her soul, used to say me eyes were bigger than me belly, and she was right. I've eaten far too much and I am absolutely stored. But it was a really good meal, love, and there was certainly plenty of it.'

'There sure was, Mam, I'm full to the brim.' Joey rubbed his tummy and rolled his eyes. 'One more mouthful and I'd have burst.'

'Me too!' Ginny gazed at the two roast potatoes left on her plate. 'I couldn't eat them, Mam, even though I love roasties and these are nice and crisp, just the way I like them.'

'Well, leave them, sunshine, it's no use making yerself sick.' Beth was feeling full to bursting herself. 'I won't do so many tomorrow, 'cos I hate waste. There's lots of carrot and turnip over as well, but I can do a fry-up with that tomorrow.'

'That's some turkey, love,' Andy said, eyeing what was left of the bird on a meat plate in the middle of the table. 'It's the biggest we've ever had. How much did yer say it weighed?'

'I didn't say, sunshine, because I don't know meself. I ordered one about four pound, which I always do, and I nearly died when I saw Bill the butcher wrapping it up without bothering to put it on the scales. He gave me the wire to take it and say nowt, and just charged me for a four-pound bird. But as me and Flo were leaving the shop, he whispered that some woman had ordered it, then changed her mind and said she wanted a goose instead.'

'Ay, yer hopped in lucky there, love. I'd say that bird was at least seven pound if it was an ounce.'

'Oh, I know how lucky I was, 'cos it'll do us three days at least.' Beth put her hands on her tummy and pressed gently. 'There's something else I haven't told yer about the bird, but I couldn't tell yer without laughing, and if I laugh I'll be sick.'

'I'll get yer a drink of cold water, Mam, then yer won't be.' Joey was off his chair like a shot. He loved it when his mam had a funny tale to tell them. He came through with a cup full of water. 'There yer are, Mam, if yer drink that yer'll be able to laugh.'

Beth took a few deep breaths to compose herself. 'I told yer Flo was with me in the butcher's? Well, she didn't say a dickie bird when she saw me getting this turkey which was twice the size of hers but only cost the same. It was when we got outside the shop that she started, and it was so comical I don't know how I kept me face straight. Yer all know that when Flo has anything of importance to say, she always folds her arms, straightens her back and gives a sharp shake of her head.

Unfortunately, she couldn't fold her arms because she had her turkey in them, and she was floundering, couldn't get herself comfortable to take me on. In desperation, she put the turkey on the ground and went through the usual arms, shoulders and head routine. Then she felt better and eyed me up and down.

' "I hope yer know Bill didn't mean yer to keep all that turkey to yerself," she said. "He gave me the wink as if to say, she's yer mate, she'll see yer all right." I told her Bill certainly hadn't intended me to share the bird with anyone, and anyway, how could I? And d'yer know what she said? "One leg of that bleedin' bird will feed my family for a whole day. So I'll pick it up on Boxing Day, and it had better have plenty of meat on it. If I see teeth marks, I'll know yer've been having a nibble, and that would be cheating." '

Andy looked from the bird to his wife's face. 'D'yer mean to tell me that's why yer said yer didn't feel like a leg, yer'd have some breast instead?'

Beth nodded. 'Yer know what Flo's like, she won't think for one minute that I'll keep a leg for her. But I'm going to, just to see the look on her face. We won't go short, there's enough meat left on that bird to last us a few days.'

'Mam, can I take it round with yer in the morning?' Ginny asked. 'I'd love to see her face.'

Beth held up her hands. 'The part about the butcher, the bird and Flo is all true. Every word, I swear. But Flo makes a joke of everything – she was just being herself, having a laugh. Not for one second would she think I'd take her seriously about expecting me to give her one of the legs. She made a joke about it, so now I'm doing the same. When she sees that bird with one leg still on it, and I tell her I had some of the breast, she'll think I've lost the run of me senses. But it'll give her something to laugh about.'

'So yer won't be taking it to her, then?' Ginny said, looking disappointed.

'I won't need to, will I, sunshine? Her and Uncle Dennis always call on Christmas Day to wish us the compliments of the season, so I can show it to her then. And we can all have a laugh together.'

'Have yer got enough sherry left for the ladies?' Andy asked. 'Don't forget, Dot and Bill always call, and so do Lizzie and Paddy. I've got enough beer for the men, but what about the women?'

'There's nearly a full bottle of sherry! We've only had the two glasses out of it so we've enough to keep the ladies going. Besides, they usually bring a bottle of something with them, even if it's only milk stout, so we won't go short. When I feel able to stand up, I'll get these dishes out of the way and then get cracking on making a couple of dozen fairy cakes. They should be enough with a plate of biscuits, 'cos no one will be hungry. Or they shouldn't be if they've eaten as much as we have. If they are, then they must be gannets, and I can't be expected to feed gannets.'

The dishes were washed and put away, and the smell of fairy cakes just taken from the oven filled the air. 'Now to sit down and put me feet up for an hour,' Beth said, stretching out on the couch. 'I might even close me eyes and have forty winks.'

'That's a very good idea,' Andy said. 'But why can't we go to bed for an hour? It would be much more comfortable.'

'Yeah, and we wouldn't have to listen to your snores.' Joey lifted his head from his comic long enough to give his views. 'Me mam's not so bad, but I'm sure they must be able to hear you at the bottom of the street.'

'I don't snore,' Andy said, chuckling because his snoring was so bad he sometimes woke himself up. 'I just breathe heavily.'

'If yer breathed any heavier, sunshine, yer'd bring the ceiling down.' Beth wriggled her toes and her blue eyes became alive with laughter as her vivid imagination took over. 'Yer woke me up one night in the summer, and it was light in the room. I looked up, and for a minute I thought it was snowing in the bedroom because flakes of plaster were falling softly from the ceiling and they looked just like flakes of snow.'

'I'd say that was more than a slight exaggeration, love. I admit to snoring but . . .' Andy's voice faded as a knock came on the door.

Beth quickly swung her legs off the couch and slipped her feet into her shoes. 'Just when I was beginning to relax. Who the heck can this be? It's not Flo because her knocking nearly brings the door down. And it's too early for them, anyway.'

'I'll go, Mam,' Ginny said, on her way to the door. 'You stay where yer are.'

Beth rolled her eyes at her husband when she heard her daughter's warm welcome and invitation to the visitors to come in. 'Oh, lord, she's asking them in.' She smoothed down the front of her dress while hissing to her husband, 'Fasten that top button on yer trousers.'

'Go on in, they won't eat yer.' Ginny pushed Amelia and Bobby ahead of her. 'Look who's here, Mam!'

The youngsters looked so shy, Beth's heart went out to them. The poor kids had gone through so much in the last two weeks, their whole lives had been turned upside down. 'Come and get near the fire, yer must be freezing.'

'We're not cold, Mrs Porter, it's only a stone's throw from Grandma's to here.' Bobby nodded to his sister who was holding a parcel in her gloved hands. 'Amelia has a present for yer, from me mam and grandma.'

'It's just a little thank you for all yer've done.' The girl handed the parcel over. 'Me grandma said to tell yer it wasn't much, just a token to let yer know how much she appreciates all yer've done and how kind yer were to her.'

'Oh, she shouldn't have bothered! I only did what anyone else would have done in the circumstances.' Beth smiled at the two youngsters who were obviously hoping she'd be thrilled with what they'd brought. 'I'm not going to say I'm not pleased, though, 'cos everyone likes to get a surprise, don't they? But I'm not going to open it until yer've taken yer coats off and are settled down comfortably.'

'I'll take their coats,' Ginny said, 'and hang them up.'

As she passed her brother on her way to the tiny hallway where the hooks were, Ginny noticed he was wearing a cheeky grin. 'One word out of you, our Joey,' she warned, 'and yer can forget pocket money.'

He shrugged his shoulders and held out his hands. 'I haven't even opened me mouth!'

'Yer'd better keep it that way if yer know what's good for yer,' Ginny hissed. 'Make a fool out of me and I'll never speak to yer again.'

As Joey's eyes followed his sister, he told himself that girls weren't half two-faced. Just look at the way Ginny was smiling now at their visitors when less than a minute ago she'd nearly bitten his head off. The best thing he could do when he grew up was to ask his dad's advice. He'd been lucky finding Mam, who never lost her temper over silly things and was never childish. There must be others like her, so he'd bide his time until one came along. Mind you, there was something to be said for never getting married, so he might even try that.

Beth held the present in her hands until they were all seated, and because Hannah's grandchildren had a look of expectancy on their faces, she acted as though she was very eager and excited. 'It feels heavy, I wonder what it can be?' Then as she was tearing the paper she giggled and said, 'Ooh, isn't this lovely? I don't half love surprises.'

They all sat forward in their chairs as the paper fell to the floor. And when Beth looked down and saw what was in her hands, she didn't have to pretend to be pleased. It was a vase shaped like a jug with a beautifully curved handle. It had been hand-painted, its background a very pale green, with the rim and base painted in gold and a flower pattern in delicate shades of blue, lilac, pink and yellow on the rest of it. It was so pretty, Beth was lost for words. She'd never owned anything as delicate as this in her life. 'I don't know what to say, it's wonderful!' She was feeling quite emotional. 'I didn't expect anything as lovely as this, it really is beautiful and I adore it. But it must have cost a lot of money and your grandma and mam shouldn't have spent so much on me.' She passed the vase to Andy. 'Isn't it beautiful, love?'

'It's a lovely present, no doubt about that.'

Ginny asked, 'Can I hold it, Mam, so I can see it properly?' She handled the vase with great care. 'Where will yer put it? On the sideboard or mantelpiece?'

'I'll have to give that some thought,' Beth told her. 'I'd like it on the sideboard where it would show up better, but I'd be frightened of it getting broken. But we'll put it there now until I make up me mind, so no one is to throw things on to the sideboard, like yer usually do.'

When his mother was pleased, Joey too was pleased. And because it was Mrs Bailey's grandchildren who had put that look of pleasure on her face, he was going to be extra nice to them. To Bobby anyway, though he'd have to think about Amelia seeing as he'd just reviewed his feelings on girls and would have to decide which group she came under. 'When are yer going to be looking for a job, Bobby?'

'Me and me mam are going to the Labour Exchange the day after tomorrow to see if there's anything going. We went last week, but there was nothing doing, too near Christmas. Amelia's a lucky blighter, though. You know David from next door told her about Hartley's Jam Works, well she mentioned it to the bloke at the Exchange. He must have liked the look of her 'cos she came away with a card, and instructions to take it to the Personnel Office at Hartley's.'

'That sounds hopeful, sunshine!' Beth was happy for the girl. They needed some good fortune after what they'd been through. Only once had they mentioned their father, Ginny had told her, and that was when Bobby had said he was now man of the house. She wasn't going to bring the subject up and upset them. 'We'll keep our fingers crossed for yer.'

Amelia lifted her hands to show she had fingers on both of them crossed. 'I won't be able to sleep for the next two nights, so I'll have time to say plenty of prayers.'

'I believe yer've put two years in as an apprentice gas fitter, Bobby?' Andy said. 'Is that the trade yer want to stay in?'

'Well, yeah! I'm too old now to be taken on as anything else. Anyway,

I enjoy the job and am quite experienced after two years.' He grinned. 'I stopped being the can lad last year when a new boy started.'

'There's one place yer could try, it's on Stanley Road. Yer probably remember Parr's Aunt Sally from when yer lived in Liverpool? Everyone uses it. But George Parr owns a lot of property around Stanley Road and he employs builders, plumbers and gas fitters. Not on a big scale, like, so I'm not saying there'll definitely be a job going, but it's worth a try.'

'I'll remember that, Mr Porter, thanks. My boss gave me a very good reference, so that should help me when I go for an interview.'

Beth was only half listening as she placed the vase in the middle of the sideboard and stood back to admire it. Satisfied, she asked, 'Would anyone like a drink of lemonade?'

'That would be nice.' Amelia seemed less shy and more relaxed now. 'I suppose yer noticed the scarf and gloves our Bobby was wearing? Grandma said you were the brains behind buying them. And my nice underwear.'

'Well, it's not easy buying for someone yer don't know.' Beth smiled at them before making for the kitchen. 'I'll pour yer a drink.'

Andy followed her out. 'Why don't we go next door to Dot's and let her kids come here?' He jerked his head towards the living room. 'They'd be far better off with kids their own age. Yer can tell they're putting on a brave face, which isn't natural. But if they were with other young people, they would probably come out more. Besides, Dot's always saying David hasn't got many mates, so it wouldn't hurt for him and Bobby to team up.' He slipped his arms around her waist. 'As for the girls, well, they make friends more easily, don't they? They'd talk to anyone about any subject under the sun.'

'Hey! What are you insinuating? That everyone of my sex is brainless and talks too much?'

'Those are your words not mine, sweetheart.' He squeezed her tight. 'What I should have said is that you women have got us men beat by a mile. Yer could take us to the cleaners and we wouldn't even notice.'

'Aye, well, as long as yer know yer place.' Beth pressed her cheek against his and they rocked together gently. 'Ye're right about Bobby and Amelia, they are putting on a brave face. It's only when they drop their guard yer can see in their eyes that the shock and heartache has taken a heavy toll. And they would be better in the company of young people, where they don't have to pretend. So we'll do as yer say and slip next door for an hour while David and Joan come here.' Beth picked up two glasses of lemonade and carried them through. 'Here yer are, kids, the other two glasses are following.' When Bobby and Amelia smiled their thanks, she told them, 'Me and Mr Porter are going next door for an hour to wish them the compliments of the season, like. So we'll send David and Joan here, to keep yer company.'

Joey let out a long wail. 'Oh, not Joan! Anyone but Joan! She's the only girl I know who never stops talking yet doesn't say anything.'

'Ay, you, she's my friend!' Ginny reminded him forcefully with a dig in the ribs. 'And she doesn't talk as much as you.'

'That's enough now.' Beth handed her husband his coat. 'And there'll be no arguments while we're next door. Don't forget, yer can hear everything through these walls.'

'We'll be good, Mam, I promise.' Ginny glared at her brother. 'If he starts any of his shenanigans I'll send him next door, to you.'

Beth grinned when she saw the look of rebellion on her son's face. She knew it was all show because he and Ginny never fell out for longer than five minutes. 'Be careful with the glasses because we haven't got many. Oh, and don't knock the sideboard, for heaven's sake, or yer'll tip the vase over and break it.'

Joey waited until his dad was out of the door, and his mam was following. Then he called, 'Mam, is it all right if we breathe?'

Beth turned and lightly cuffed his ear. 'As long as yer don't breathe heavy and bring the plaster off the ceiling.'

He grinned and nodded. 'I'll breathe as light as a snowflake falling, Mam, I promise.'

Beth and Dot were relaxing on the couch, discussing the usual things women talk about: the price of food and clothes, and what the neighbours had been up to. It was nice and quiet, and peaceful. Andy and Bill were sitting in the comfortable fireside chairs facing each other across the hearth. With a Woodbine in one hand, and a glass of beer in the other, they were content to swap thoughts on work, wages and the weather. And putting the world to rights, of course.

Occasionally they would hear raised voices and laughter coming through from next door. 'Just listen to our Joan,' Dot said. 'Yer can hear her voice above all the others.'

'They seem to be enjoying themselves, that's the main thing.' Beth let out a sigh. 'I keep thinking of those two poor children. I mean, no one could possibly know how they feel unless they've been through it themselves. And Claire, God love her, must be beside herself with grief. Same as Hannah! So who comforts who?'

Andy had been listening. 'The children will come to terms with it

189

quicker when they start work and are meeting people. And when they make new friends. Kids are very resilient, they're the ones that will pull Claire and Hannah through this difficult time. Claire will be finding it the most difficult – she'll be heartbroken and angry that her husband's died so young. But from what I've seen of her, I'd say she'll hide her grief and concentrate on making life as normal as possible for the children.'

'Yeah, she struck me as being a good mother,' Beth said. 'She'll put the needs of the kids before her own. But she has to try and make something of her own life, otherwise she'll end up an old woman before her time.'

Andy tilted his head and those brown eyes of his caused Beth to go weak at the knees. 'I'm sure you and your mates won't let her shut herself away, will yer? She's about the same age as you two, and Flo and Lizzie, so I've got a feeling yer'll soon be a fivesome, instead of a foursome. I can't see yer all sitting back and letting her fade away, that wouldn't be like you.'

'Of course they won't,' Bill said, taking a puff on his cigarette. 'She'll be one of the gang in no time.'

Beth and Dot exchanged looks. 'If yer hadn't been so busy sorting the world out, yer would have heard us making plans to bring Claire into the fold.' Dot told them. 'Isn't that right, girl?'

'That's right, sunshine. While the two men have been busy talking about what they'd like to achieve, we've got everything under control. As me mam says, if yer want a job doing proper, then get a woman to do it.'

Chapter Sixteen

Ginny tried to open her mouth to chew on a piece of toast, but found she couldn't. The toast tasted like sandpaper and she seemed to have lost the ability to function properly. She'd been so looking forward to this day, her first day as a grown-up going to work, and now the time had come she was so filled with dread she had no control over her movements. The cup of tea looked inviting, and would help take the dryness from her mouth, but she was even afraid to pick up the cup because she knew her hand would shake so much the tea would spill over. And the worst of it was, she'd been so excited last night she'd asked her mam to get her up at the same time as her dad this morning. She was going to have her breakfast with him, then take her time getting dressed for the big occasion. It was important to be dressed properly because first impressions counted for a lot. So her clothes and shoes were going to be immaculate and her blonde hair brushed until it shone. Oh, she'd had such great plans for today, imagining herself walking out of the house all neat and tidy, as befitting a shop assistant from Woolworth's. And here she was, unable to eat, drink or even speak.

Andy had watched his daughter as he ate his breakfast, and recognised the signs. He could still remember being petrified the day he had started work. His mam, God rest her soul, had physically to throw him out of the house and had shut the door on his pleas for her to go with him, just to the gates of the factory. What a cissy he must have been!

Beth came through from the kichen. 'Have yer got time for another cuppa, sunshine?'

'No, I'd better be on me way.' Andy pushed his chair back and stood up. 'I don't want to be late or they'll think I overslept after a boozy New Year.' When he kissed his wife, he whispered, 'I think Ginny's got the jitters. Sit down with her and see if yer can talk her out of it. The poor kid looks scared to death.'

Beth nodded. 'I'll see to her, she'll be all right.'

Just then help came from an unexpected quarter. They heard Bill next door shouting goodbye to Dot, and it gave Beth an idea. 'Ginny, yer haven't forgotten that Joan starts her job in Dunlop's today, have yer? She's just coming out with her dad and David so d'yer want to wish her good luck? She's probably nervous, it being her first day, so come on.' Acting as though she didn't know there was anything amiss, Beth pulled her daughter to her feet. 'Hurry, or yer'll be too late.'

If anything Joan looked even worse than Ginny. Her face was white, her lips were quivering and her eyes showed signs of recent tears. 'Ginny, I'm frightened. Me legs and everything are shaking.'

Ginny had never seen Joan like this. Her friend was usually very sure of herself, even too cocky at times. She gave her a quick hug. 'I'm terrified meself, kid, but we'll be all right. Nobody is going to bite our heads off or strangle us.'

'I've told her that,' Bill said. 'There's nothing to be frightened of. Now come on or ye're going to make us all late.'

His son had less sympathy for his sister. 'Stop acting like a big baby,' David said, 'and put a move on.'

Ginny linked her mother's arm as they watched Andy and the three Flynns walking down the street. 'I thought I was bad enough, but Joan looks worse than I feel! I'll be glad to get today over so we know what to expect tomorrow.'

Beth squeezed her arm. 'Across the country, right this very minute, there'll be thousands of young lads and girls feeling exactly the same as you and Joan. And when they come home tonight, like you, they'll be wondering what they were worried about. It's a big day in yer life, sunshine, so enjoy it.' She pushed her daughter towards their step. 'Let's get in and have a hot cup of tea, I'm freezing. And when yer come in tonight, I want to see yer all happy and pleased with yerself. And me and yer dad and Joey will want to know everything that's happened to yer during the day. So get yer memory cells working so yer don't forget any little details.'

When the front door was closed behind them, Ginny gave her mother a big hug. 'I love you, Mam, and me dad and our Joey. I'm a very lucky girl, and I'm going to be lucky today with everything going right and me loving me new job.'

'That's the spirit, sunshine! Keep that up and yer'll pass with flying colours.'

Marie was waiting for Ginny at the end of the street, and they linked arms to walk to the tram stop. 'Let's keep talking, Ginny,' Marie said. 'Then we won't have time to think. Tell me what yer got for Christmas?'

So the tram ride was spent talking about everything but what lay ahead. Even when they were walking up the stairs to the Personnel Office at Woolworth's, they were chatting away as though their life depended on it. It was only when they saw Miss Harper waiting for them outside the office that their tongues were silenced.

'Ah, Miss Porter and Miss Whittaker. We'll wait here for a while as there is another new girl starting today. As soon as she arrives I'll show you where the cloakroom is and then take you to the department where you'll be working.' Miss Harper relaxed her expression and smiled. 'Did you have a nice Christmas?'

'Oh, yes, Miss.' Two voices answered as one. Then Ginny said, 'I hope you did, too, Miss Harper?'

'It was a quiet one, Virginia, but pleasant and peaceful.' When a young girl came hurrying towards them, she said, 'Ah, here is Miss Hayes.' She introduced the girls, then said, 'I'll take you to the cloakroom, then to the supervisors you'll be working under. Virginia and Patricia in the store, and Marie in the stock room. Follow me, please.'

Patricia Hayes was an attractive girl with long dark hair and lovely green eyes. She was eyeing the other two up as they followed Miss Harper, then smiled when they caught her doing so. 'I'm Pat,' she whispered. 'What's your names?'

Ginny whispered back, 'I'm Ginny, and this is a mate of mine, Marie.'

That was all they had time for because they were told to hang their coats up quickly and remember the number over the hook as this was to be the one they used each day. Then they were marched down a different staircase which took them into the main body of the store. The girls found it all very interesting as the staff behind the counters took off covers and straightened any item that wasn't just right. They would have loved to dawdle and watch properly, but they weren't allowed as they had to move quickly to keep up with Miss Harper. She had looked very efficient upstairs, but it was nothing to her attitude now. The first time she raised her hand, she beckoned over a woman from the right-hand side of the shop who was supervising the work being done on a counter. The second time it was raised to alert a woman on the left-hand side. Both women wore dark suits which told of their seniority. 'Miss Halliday, this is Miss Virginia Porter. I would like her to start on haberdashery as a junior assistant to Miss Landers. Please take her over there and explain her duties. And Miss Bryan, I would like you to attend to Miss Patricia Hayes. She is to go as junior to Miss Ramsey on cosmetics. Please make sure that both girls know exactly what their duties are. I will take Miss Whittaker to the stock room.' With a smile at the two young soon-to-be counter assistants, Miss Harper walked briskly away, leaving the wide-eyed, very apprehensive Marie to follow quickly in her wake.

'Come with me please, Miss Porter.' Ginny gave a quick wave to Pat then walked alongside the supervisor whose suit was severely tailored, with the skirt reaching almost down to her ankles. Her hair style was also severe, being combed away from the face and twisted into a bun at the nape of her neck. 'The use of first names is not allowed in the store. The rule does not, however, apply to the canteen. You must address the senior assistant with respect at all times, and you will be required to take note of how she deals with customers without getting under her feet or hindering her in her work.' While Miss Halliday spoke, she had her eye on every stall they passed, and Ginny believed nothing would escape her scrutiny. 'You must also acquaint yourself with the merchandise on your counter. However, you will not be allowed to serve for several weeks, or until such time as you are deemed responsible enough to do so. Even then you will not issue receipts or handle cash. All transactions must be supervised by Miss Landers.' They stopped in front of one of the long counters. 'You will have a fifteen-minute break when Miss Landers gives the order, and will then make your way to the canteen for a cup of tea. You will not be required to pay for the tea on the morning or afternoon break, but you will have to pay for your lunch.'

Ginny's voice sounded timid. 'I've brought some sandwiches with me, Miss, will I be able to eat them in the canteen?'

Miss Halliday's face relaxed into a smile which seemed to change her whole personality. 'Of course you can, several girls bring their own lunch. But any drinks you have then will have to be paid for.'

The assistant behind the counter was keeping herself busy by putting buttons back in the right boxes, and tidying the reels of cotton and skeins of various-coloured wool which had been handled by customers and just thrown back anywhere. She stopped what she was doing when Miss Halliday moved to the edge of the counter. 'Miss Landers, this is your new junior assistant, Miss Porter.'

For seconds there was no smile or word of welcome as the woman eyed Ginny up and down. And the girl's heart sank as she thought, She doesn't know me, yet she doesn't like me! And I'm going to have to work with her!

Frances Landers was twenty-eight years of age and a bitter old maid. She had been spurned at the age of twenty-two by a man she'd courted for three years and had taken for granted would marry her. But he'd fallen for a younger girl who was prettier than the rather plain Frances, with her nondescript features and little in the way of personality. She now held a grudge against life in general, and pretty young girls in particular. In fact, she was the reason the previous junior assistant had left to find work elsewhere.

The senior assistant could feel Miss Halliday's eyes boring into her and swiftly collected her thoughts. She couldn't afford to lose this job. A smile which didn't reach her eyes appeared on her face. 'Good morning, Miss Porter, I'm glad to meet you. Would you come and stand behind the counter, please, and I'll answer any questions you may have.'

Mary Halliday's eyes didn't miss anything. The late greeting, the false smile, all put on for her benefit. There weren't many employees she didn't like – some were slow and perhaps lazy, but they were generally honest, pleasant, and got on with the rest of the staff. She wished she could say the same for Miss Landers but didn't like or trust her. She couldn't prove it but she'd bet that young Joyce Connor had left because her life was being made a hell by this bitter woman who had treated her like a skivvy. Well, it wouldn't happen to pretty young Ginny, not if the supervisor could help it.

'I'll leave you now, Miss Porter, but I'll be keeping an eye on you. If you wish to speak to me, at any time, you'll find me either on the shop floor or in the small office at the very back of the store.'

'Thank you, Miss Halliday, I'll remember.'

When the supervisor was out of earshot, a sneer came over Frances Landers' face as she mimicked Ginny. 'Thank you, Miss Halliday, I'll remember.'

A voice in the girl's head told her that if she didn't stand up for herself now, her life wouldn't be worth living. So, taking a deep breath, she said, 'Why didn't yer say that while she was here? I didn't think it was funny, but Miss Halliday might have done.'

'Don't you dare talk to me like that or I'll report you for insubordination! You're here to take orders from me and you'll do as I say or I'll make life very unpleasant for you.'

'I will take orders from yer, and I will do as I'm told.' Ginny was already thinking what a bad start this was. How could she go home and face her family if she got the sack on her first day? 'But only if I think what ye're saying or asking me to do is fair, and ye're not picking on me. Yer seem to have taken a dislike to me so perhaps it would be better for both our sakes if I ask Miss Halliday now to move me to another counter.'

The change in the woman was so quick Ginny thought she'd imagined everything that had happened before. Gone was the sneer, and in its place was something intended as a smile. 'But I haven't taken a dislike to you! What makes you think that? We'll get along fine as long as you don't get under my feet when I'm serving and you're not looking over my shoulder all the time.'

'I'll do as Miss Harper and Miss Halliday told me to do. I will watch and observe, and acquaint myself with the merchandise on the counter. I can't go wrong if I do that.'

The store doors had been opened by now, and customers were coming in. It was a trickle at first, but when Ginny came back from her tea break, the shop was quite busy. She enjoyed the hustle and bustle, and as she stood back so as not to get in the senior assistant's way she smiled at each customer who bought from their counter. There had been little in the way of conversation between her and Frances Landers, but that didn't worry the girl because the difference in their ages was too great for them to have anything in common and she still hadn't forgotten that frosty introduction.

Ginny had been looking forward to meeting up with Marie on the morning break to see how she'd got on, but there'd been no sign of her and one of the girls sitting near by said the stock room often had their times changed. So when she entered the canteen at lunchtime with her carry-out in her hand, Ginny was delighted to see her old schoolmate waving to her.

'I've saved yer a place, Ginny, sit yerself down.' Marie's ever-ready smile was on display. 'How have yer got on?' Then, without waiting for a reply, she gabbled, 'I'm over the moon with my job – it's brilliant. But that doesn't mean to say I wouldn't like a job behind the counter when they'll have me.'

'I haven't done much, only stand and watch. But I know I'm going to like the work 'cos the customers that come in are really friendly.' Ginny took one of the sandwiches out of the neat parcel her mam had made, and took a bite. 'I'm not keen on the woman I'm with, though, 'cos unlike the customers, she's not a bit friendly.'

'Oh, they are in the stock room, they're smashing. There's more men than women and we've had a really good laugh.' Marie was clearly excited and loving every minute of it. 'The men won't let the women lift anything heavy, so the work's easy. It's just a case of knowing where everything is in case anything is needed in the shop. Yer need to know where to put yer hand on it instantly. It won't take me long to get the hang of things 'cos all the boxes are marked and numbered. So yer can't go wrong, really.'

'Have yer seen anything of Pat?' Ginny asked. 'The girl who started with us.'

Marie shook her head. 'You're more likely to see her than I am. Can't yer see her from your counter?'

'No. She's a lucky beggar, though, getting put on cosmetics. I would have loved that.' Ginny was wishing she was as satisfied as Marie, but couldn't help feeling downhearted. And it was all the fault of that Miss Landers, the miserable thing. Even when she smiled at the customers, you could see it wasn't genuine. 'Just think of all the coloured lipsticks and powders. And the nail varnish . . .'

'My mam wouldn't let me wear lipstick or nail varnish, so it wouldn't do me no good. She says I'm too young to be putting that stuff on, and making an old woman of meself.' Marie began to giggle as in her mind's eye she could see her mother wagging a finger in her face and warning: 'Yer'll be old soon enough, my girl, so don't be wishing the years away. Enjoy yer youth while yer've got it, 'cos it doesn't last forever.'

'I don't think my mam would mind a bit of powder,' Ginny said. 'But she wouldn't like me to plaster make-up on, like some girls. There's a girl in our street, I'd say she was about eighteen, and she wears thick powder, with great big spots of bright red rouge on each cheek and lipstick so red yer can see her coming a mile off.'

Marie grinned. 'My mam says girls like that look as common as muck with their faces painted like a clown. Good time girls, up to no good.' The grin turned into a chuckle. 'And if she ever sees me looking like a painted doll, she'll put me across her knee and take her slipper to me. *And* disown me into the bargain.'

Ginny was just beginning to feel more cheerful when she noticed chairs being pushed back and workers getting to their feet. 'Everyone is leaving, it must be time for us to get back to our posts.'

Her friend showed her serious side then. 'Yer looked really down in the dumps when yer came in, and that's not like you. If this woman ye're working with starts picking on yer, don't put up with it. As my mam always says, start as yer mean to go on. If she thinks ye're soft, she'll only pick on yer more. So put yer foot down with a firm hand.'

As the friends left the canteen, Ginny said, 'I did stick up for meself, I didn't just stand there like a lemon and let her get away with it. But I'm frightened that if I go too far she'll report me and I'll get the sack.'

'It would be your word against hers, but if she's been here donkey's years the bosses would probably take her side.' Marie shrugged her shoulders. 'Just see how it goes, kid, that's all yer can do. What's this woman's name, by the way?'

'Miss Landers. I think her first name is Frances, but why I think that I don't know. *She* certainly didn't tell me. Miss Halliday may have mentioned it, or else I'm going round the twist.'

Marie touched her arm. 'Here's where we part company. But I'll wait for yer outside tonight, and we'll travel home together.'

As soon as they parted company, Ginny could feel knots in her tummy and her heartbeat quickened. It had been her dream to work behind a counter, and since she'd been told she had the job at Woolworth's, she'd lain in bed each night practising how she would smile at the customers and make sure they were satisfied with their purchases. She'd always be cheerful, helpful and patient, she had vowed. Or that had been her dream until she'd been introduced to Miss Landers, and then the dream turned into a nightmare. Now she wished she was working in the stock room with Marie where she could be having a laugh and a joke.

Ginny's thoughts were all over the place as she walked back to the haberdashery counter. And when she got there, and saw a strange woman behind it, she thought she was in the wrong place. But she couldn't be because there were the buttons, wools and needles, just as they'd been before she went for her lunch.

The young woman behind the counter could see the confusion on the girl's face. 'Are you Miss Porter?'

Ginny nodded. 'That's me, but where's Miss Landers?'

'Come through here, we can't talk over the counter.' There was a smile on the woman's face and friendliness in her voice. 'She's gone for her dinner break. Didn't she explain it all to you?' A deep sigh was her answer to Ginny's shake of the head. 'Well, my name's Miss Sutherland and I'm senior assistant on the next counter, selling gloves and purses amongst other things. The seniors' dinner break is split into two shifts, which means a shortage of staff for those two periods. So we each have to cover and take responsibility for two counters. I'm surprised Miss Landers hasn't told you this, she's supposed to be training you and filling you in with all the information you'll need in your position as junior sales assistant.'

'Perhaps she'll do it this afternoon, when she gets a chance.' Ginny decided diplomacy was the best way to keep the peace. 'She was busy replenishing the stock this morning.'

Miss Sutherland tutted. 'Did she allow you to help her? That's the best way of learning what goods you actually stock, and their prices.'

Ginny was in a dilemma. This woman was a different kettle of fish from Miss Landers; there were no airs and graces about her, and her voice and manner were friendly. 'I thought Miss Halliday said I was to watch how Miss Landers dealt with customers without getting under her feet or hindering her in her work, and I was to acquaint myself with the merchandise on the counter. So while she was serving and replenishing stock on the counter, I stood back so I wouldn't be in her way. But I have noticed that all the goods have prices on them, anyway.'

'That's a fat lot of good if you're standing behind the counter, dear, because you'd have to stand on your head to read them.' Miss Sutherland felt sorry for the girl for being unfortunate enough to be put on this counter with an assistant who was unpopular with nearly all the staff. Life wasn't going to be a bed of roses for her, that was for sure. And if Miss Halliday decided to do one of her spot checks on how a junior assistant was progressing by inspecting the neatness of the counter and asking her the price of various items, you could bet your sweet life that Frances Landers wouldn't shoulder the blame for her not knowing. No, the supervisor would be told the girl was lazy and slow to learn. Not up to the job, in other words.

'During Miss Landers' lunch break, you will notice I will not be paying much attention to my own counter. This is because I know my junior is quite capable of running it on her own. If she was in doubt about anything, of course she would ask for my help or advice. But I know I have no worries on that score because I taught her properly from the very start and have complete faith in her ability to cope. She is seventeen and has been with me since the day she started three years ago. Her name is Helen Bleasedale. I'm Dorothy Sutherland, though as you are aware first names are not allowed during working hours. But there's no harm in me asking yours, is there?'

'Virginia.' Ginny was thinking what bliss it would be if she'd been put on a counter with this young woman. 'But my friends call me Ginny.'

'Well, Ginny,' this was said in a conspiratorial voice, 'shall we make a start? While I'm serving, you can go to the front of the counter and

199

familiarise yourself with the items we sell and their prices. Make sure you don't get in the way of any customers, though.'

Ginny's face lit up. 'Ooh, can I do that?'

'Of course you can! But don't forget what I said about not getting in the way.' Because the girl looked so pleased, Dorothy Sutherland decided to help her by injecting a warning note into what she was saying. 'You won't be allowed to serve for a while, but if any other jobs on the counter need doing, you can tackle them. For instance, you can start now by putting the buttons in the correct boxes. You see, customers pick them up, then perhaps decide they're not what they're looking for and throw them down anywhere. And you can do the same with everything else on the counter. While you're doing it, you can be making a mental note of all the prices in case Miss Halliday asks. She may come up on you one day when you least expect it, and I'm sure you'd like to have the prices off pat. That would certainly be a feather in your cap.'

The next half hour went too quickly for Ginny, who was really enjoying what she was doing. And she was pleased with herself because she thought she was doing it well. But all too soon Miss Landers appeared on the scene. 'What d'you think you're doing on this side of the counter?'

'I asked her to do some jobs while I've been serving,' Miss Sutherland said, seeing Ginny flinch. 'I've been quite busy and have been glad of her help. She's got a good little head on her shoulders, she picks things up very quickly.'

This wasn't what Frances Landers wanted to hear. She didn't want a junior with a good head on her shoulders who picked things up quickly. There was sarcasm in her voice when she replied, 'I can't say I've noticed it. Probably because I've been too busy.'

As she was squeezing through the gap in the counter, ready to return to her own, Miss Sutherland kept her voice low so as not to embarrass the young girl. 'Well, you wouldn't notice it if you leave her standing by the wall doing nothing. She was taken on to learn a job, not to be a statue.' She passed Ginny and noticed all the eagerness had left her pretty face. The girl looked decidedly downcast at the return of her senior. On impulse, Dorothy put a hand on her arm and squeezed. 'I'll see you tomorrow, Miss Porter.'

Ginny nodded. She felt so miserable she wished she could cry. But she told herself she was a working girl now and tears were out of the question. 'Thank you, Miss Sutherland.'

Slyness being part of her nature, Frances Landers waited a few seconds before saying, 'You are one little creep! First you crawl to Miss Halliday, now Dorothy Sutherland. What have you been saying to her about me?'

Ginny didn't answer immediately, she waited until the unfairness of it all called up her temper. If it wasn't for this woman, she'd be really enjoying her first day at work. 'I haven't said a word about yer. Why should I, and how could I? I don't know the first thing about yer except that ye're supposed to be training me.'

'Are you answering me back? How dare you!'

'If yer can call telling yer the truth answering back, then I suppose I am. But I'm not deaf, dumb or daft, so I'm not just standing here listening to yer calling me for everything when I haven't done nothing wrong.'

Nostrils flared and eyes shot daggers, but there was no immediate retaliation from the senior assistant. The simple reason for this was that she could see she was being watched from the next counter, and Dorothy Sutherland was one member of staff she didn't want to cross swords with. 'Seeing as you're so clever, you can carry on what you were doing. But keep well away from customers.'

This suited Ginny because she didn't even like standing near this woman who seemed intent on doing her harm. So she speedily moved to the front of the counter, smiling at the customer who was waiting to be served with ribbon. She was straightening the cards which had hair nets on, and wasn't really listening to what was being said across the counter, until the woman raised her voice in protest. 'But it's got here that these ribbons are tuppence a yard, not threepence.'

Ginny's eyes slid sideways to where the woman was pointing to the reels of coloured ribbons. They were in three different widths, from one penny to threepence a yard. 'I'm sorry, my assistant must have put them under the wrong sign. The red ribbon you are interested in is threepence a yard. The narrow one is tuppence.'

She's telling lies, Ginny thought, and blaming me for mixing them up! But it wouldn't do for her to interfere, not in front of a customer. But why was Miss Landers trying to overcharge the customer? She wouldn't be gaining anything by it. Or did she just get a kick out of telling lies and being wicked?

The customer looked confused. The narrow ribbon had a ticket on it saying it was a penny a yard, the medium one had tuppence a yard on its ticket, and the wide one threepence. The signs were clear enough, and she wasn't blind or stupid. 'I'm not paying over the odds for anything so don't bother yerself. I'll go to TJ's for what I want.'

Miss Landers was around the counter in a flash. 'Don't be so hasty, dear, wait until I check. I'd be the last person in the world to want to overcharge you.'

Ginny couldn't believe her ears as she listened to the woman being fawned over and apologised to. According to the senior assistant, she'd made a great mistake and hoped she would be believed when she said the prices had been altered while she'd been at lunch, and no one had informed her. So the woman went away with one yard of red ribbon for which she was charged tuppence. As she was walking away, she was asked if she would like a receipt. After being treated so well, the customer smiled when she replied that it wasn't worth a receipt for tuppence. It wasn't as if the ribbon was for someone else and she needed proof.

The whole time this was going on, not once did Ginny lift her head or her eyes. That poor customer would have been diddled out of a penny if she hadn't been alert. Heaven knows why because the ribbons were very clearly marked. Still it was no good arguing with the woman she was disliking more as the day wore on, and who she was beginning to think had a slate loose.

Miss Landers was serving a customer when Ginny went back behind the counter. Although she took care not to move too close, she listened to what was being said. After all, she was here to learn, not stand like a dummy. The woman wanted two yards of the widest ribbon in a pretty pink. Automatically Ginny's mind told her that would be sixpence. She watched the ribbon being measured on the round wooden measure, and then cut with the scissors that were kept under the counter. Then she was all eyes as she took note of how the senior assistant curled it around her fingers before popping it into a bag. She could practise that at home with a piece of string until she got the hang of it.

The sixpence was handed over in exchange for a receipt, then Miss Landers turned towards the till. Ginny carried on watching because the more she learned the better for herself. She saw the till drawer being opened, then the next thing she knew, Miss Landers was bending down to the floor. Thinking the sixpence must have dropped, Ginny moved forward to help. 'Have you dropped something?' Then her senior moved so fast, Ginny wasn't sure afterwards whether she'd imagined it or not. But she thought she saw Miss Landers with her fingers inside her shoe.

'No, I have not dropped something! I thought I'd snagged my stocking on that rough piece of wood. Nothing for you to get bothered about.'

Ginny turned away. The sixpence must have gone in the till without

202

her seeing. Anyway, one good thing came out of it: Miss Landers had snagged her stocking. The girl laced her fingers and looked towards the ceiling. Forgive me, God, but I hope she has three dirty big ladders in them tomorrow, Ginny prayed.

Chapter Seventeen

Ginny stood by the counter watching Miss Landers checking that it was ready for the next morning. She could see some of the staff walking towards a door at the rear of the store where the cloakroom was situated, but was too afraid to follow for fear of falling victim to her senior's vicious tongue. Not one civil or kind word had she heard all afternoon. She felt the woman's eyes on her, and when she met her gaze it was to see the sneer she was getting used to.

'Don't stand there like a fool, take yourself off! You're neither use nor ornament to me, I can work better without you.'

Ginny hesitated, not knowing whether to say 'good night'. She didn't want to, not after the way she'd been treated, but her mam had told her she should always respect her elders. Then the decision was taken from her when something happened to change her outlook on her first day at work. She found herself faced by a young woman she'd glimpsed working on the next counter.

'Hello, I'm Helen Bleasedale, I work with Miss Sutherland.' The young woman turned her head and smiled. 'See, she's waving to yer.'

Sure enough, when Ginny looked there was Dorothy Sutherland waving. As she waved back, Ginny's spirits lifted. 'I'm Ginny Porter.'

'Yes, I know.' Helen was an attractive girl with a mane of dark hair which she wore tied back for work, laughing eyes, a nice set of teeth and a sunny smile. 'Come on, I'll walk to the cloakroom with yer.'

This act of friendliness gave Ginny the courage to say airily, 'Good night, Miss Landers.'

'How did yer first day go?' Helen asked. 'And how did yer get on with your senior, Miss Frances Landers?'

'All right, I guess. But she's not the easiest person in the world to please.'

'That is putting it mildly. I feel sorry for yer being put with her, she's a bad-tempered so-and-so. Wicked, too! I wouldn't trust her as far as I could throw her. But yer've always got me to talk to now, and Miss

Sutherland. So don't think ye're on yer own, Ginny, 'cos we'll always help yer.'

Before Ginny could answer, she found herself being grabbed from behind. And when she turned, there was Pat, the girl who'd started with her and Marie that morning. She was the second person in two minutes who had greeted Ginny with a smile. 'I wondered what had happened to you! Me and Marie were talking about yer at dinnertime.' Then Ginny remembered her manners. 'Oh, I'm sorry, this is Helen Bleasedale who works on the next counter. Helen, this is Pat, she only started this morning.'

'I'm on cosmetics,' Pat said proudly. 'It's the gear, I'm made up.'

'Who's your senior?' Helen asked.

'Miss Ramsey, and she's great. We get on like a house on fire.'

'Yeah, she's very nice,' Helen agreed. 'Very popular with all the staff because she's got a terrific sense of humour.'

'Yer mean she likes pulling people's legs,' Pat chuckled. 'I've fallen for it a few times today. I should have had more sense, I know, but I never thought anything of it when she sent me to the counter selling shoe laces and tins of shoe polish, and told me to ask for a tin of elbow grease. It didn't dawn on me until I saw the face on the girl behind the counter. She called her assistant over and, looking dead serious, told her what I wanted. Then the pair of them burst out laughing and I realised I'd been had.' She grinned at Ginny. 'What about the one you're working with, did she play any tricks on yer?'

Ginny felt Helen squeeze her arm before she answered. 'No, the woman I'm working with isn't like that. She's a bit starchy, real prim and proper.'

They reached the cloakroom and as Helen's coat was at the far end, it was time to part company. 'I'll see yer tomorrow, Ginny, goodnight.' She smiled at Pat. 'See yer.'

'You're lucky making a friend so quick,' Pat said. 'She seems nice.'

'Well, I don't know her very well yet, but I hope we'll be friends.'

They were both startled when Marie appeared before them like a whirlwind, grinning from ear to ear. 'So we've found yer at last,' she said to Pat. 'We wondered where yer'd got to when we didn't see yer here this morning, or at lunchtime.'

'I saw you this morning, but I was with the junior off the next counter and we sat at the other end. And I didn't come here for me lunch, I met me mam outside and she took me to the Kardomah for a cup of tea and a toasted tea-cake.'

Ginny raised her brows. 'Aren't you lucky! We had to make do with cheese butties.'

'It's not something that'll be happening every day,' Pat told them. 'Today was a bit special 'cos it's me mam's birthday.'

'Ooh, er!' Marie did a little dance as she winked broadly at Ginny. 'We'll do that one day when we're getting pocket money. See how the other half live, eh? Mingle with the rich and famous.'

'I said the Kardomah, kid,' Pat said, 'not the ruddy Adelphi.'

Ginny lifted her coat to make sure her handbag was still hanging beneath it on the hook. They weren't allowed to take bags or purses into the shop with them, or money of any description. She could understand why, but was afraid of leaving the few coppers tram fare in her purse in case it got stolen. She'd be in a fine pickle if it did, 'cos it would be a very long walk home. 'Me and Marie get the twenty-two tram, how do you get home?' she asked Pat.

'I could get that with yer, but it would mean a bit of a walk. I live in Westminster Road so I'm better getting the right tram or bus, whichever comes first. I'll see yer here in the morning, though, eh?' With a wave of her hand Pat walked quickly away.

Marie struggled into her coat. 'Yer seem a lot happier than yer did at dinnertime. How did yer get on with misery guts? Was she any more friendly with yer?'

From the time Helen Bleasedale had stood in front of her with a smile on her face, and Miss Sutherland had waved to her, Ginny had decided not to tell her family or friends about how her day had been spoilt by Miss Landers. They probably wouldn't believe her anyway because it would be hard to find the right words to say how worthless she'd been made to feel. And she really did feel much better about the job now. She'd made a few friends, and she was happy in the knowledge that every lunchtime Miss Sutherland would be taking over the counter. It would be childish of her to let Miss Landers ruin her first day, or any other for that matter. 'Oh, she's not so bad. A bit grumpy and has no sense of humour, but I can put up with that. I've been allowed to tidy the counter – putting the buttons in the right boxes and making sure the ends of the ribbons aren't loose, that sort of thing. And I've learned a lot of the prices which I'm very pleased about. I'll be lying in bed tonight going over everything in me head.'

'I'm going to ask me dad to set me some sums,' Marie said. 'If I do that every night until I'm good at it, then I can ask Miss Ormsby if she'll consider giving me a job in the shop as an assistant. D'yer think she would?'

'There's no harm in asking, Marie. But yer want to get yer arithmetic up a bit before yer think about it.'

'I'm going to try very hard, every night. And it's not that I don't like being in the stock room, 'cos the people there are brilliant. But I think I'd stand more chance of getting on if I was an assistant behind the counter. So I'm determined to buckle down and do what I should have been doing all the years I was at school.'

'Is yer dad good with figures, then?'

Marie looked surprised. 'He's bound to be at his age, isn't he?'

For the first time that day, a genuine chuckle left Ginny's mouth. 'It's to be hoped so! But if he's not and doesn't like to say so, he could be ticking yer sums when he should be putting a cross by them. Yer'd better get yer mother to double check.'

Marie's smile was wide. 'Yeah, I'll do that. And just to be on the safe side, I'll ask the woman next door.'

The two girls were laughing when it was time to go their separate ways. 'I'll see yer here in the morning,' Ginny said.

'Yeah, and we won't be so scared 'cos we'll know what's coming.' They'd walked a few steps when Marie turned and called, 'Don't be surprised if I bring me homework with me for you to check. Yer were always top of the class, so yer've probably got more brains than me dad, me mam, and the woman next door put together.'

Ginny waved. 'You do that, Marie, 'cos I wouldn't mind. I could do it on the tram if yer'd keep yer mouth closed long enough for me to concentrate.'

Her friend's smile was wide as she did a little jiggle with her shoulders and bottom. 'I'll be as quiet as a mouse. And I'll even tell the conductor to keep his voice down when he's collecting the fares.'

There was a spring in Ginny's step as she walked down her street. Her friends more than compensated for the dreadful Miss Landers, and she wasn't going to allow the woman to spoil her life for her. She'd put up with the sneers and the sarcasm, she wouldn't let them get to her.

'Do I get me pocket money on Saturday, then?' Joey asked, his eyes eager. 'Yer did promise me, and I have helped me mam today.'

'I don't get any wages this week, Joey, I have to work a week in hand.' Ginny stood her knife up straight while looking across the table at her brother. 'It's me mam yer should feel sorry for, 'cos she's got to give me the money for me tram fares.'

'We'll manage for one week, sunshine, it just means cutting down a bit.' Beth leaned her elbows on the table. 'I'm glad yer enjoyed yer first day at work, it's a load off me mind. And I'm glad yer made friends so quickly.'

Ginny had only mentioned Miss Landers' name once. Instead of dwelling on her she described all the items they sold on the counter, how she was to learn all the prices, and the tea breaks in the canteen where they didn't have to pay for the tea. Then there were the nice things that had happened and the friends she'd made. And she had them laughing over Pat and the tin of elbow grease. 'That Marie Whittaker is a scream. She's never got a smile off her face and some of the things she comes out with are hilarious. She repeats everything her mam says – like girls who wear a lot of make-up look like clowns, and are as common as muck.' Ginny pursed her lips and nodded her head, just as she'd seen Marie do. 'This is what she looked like when she was telling me what her mam said. "Good time girls they are, up to no good. And if I ever see yer looking like a painted doll I'll put yer across me knee and take me slipper to yer. And I'll disown yer into the bargain." '

'She sounds a nice girl, this Marie,' Beth said. 'Yer'll have to ask her round one night.'

Andy put his knife and fork down neatly on the empty plate. 'Yer haven't said very much about the woman yer work with. The one that's over yer.'

'There's not much to say about her, Dad. She's very old-fashioned and seldom smiles, except when she's serving a customer. Even then the smile looks stiff, as though it's forced. I suppose she must be a good worker 'cos she's been there for years, but I can't honestly say I like her. I'll work with her, but she's not the type yer could have a good laugh with or make a friend of. But it won't worry me, I've made four good friends and I'm very pleased with me little self.'

Beth jumped to her feet when a knock came on the door. 'Oh, my God, who can this be? Just look at the state of the place, we haven't even cleared the table.'

'It's Joan Flynn,' Joey said. 'I've just seen her passing the window.'

'Blimey, they got their dinner over quick.' Beth moved fast, stacking the plates. 'You open the door, Ginny, she probably wants to tell yer how she got on at work, and find out how you fared.'

And Beth was right. Joan was no sooner in the door than she asked, 'How did yer get on, Ginny? D'yer like it?'

Ginny grinned. She'd never thought of it before, but Joan was very like Marie in her mannerisms: the way they held their heads, arms folded across their tummies, and the words pouring from their mouths as though they couldn't get out quick enough. 'I got on smashing, and I love it. What about you?'

'Not very impressed, kid, not very impressed. The job wouldn't be so bad but the smell of flipping rubber is everywhere. It gets up yer nose and stays there. And it sticks to yer clothes.'

Beth came through from the kitchen where she'd plonked the plates on the draining board so she could hurry back and not miss anything. 'Yer wear an overall, don't yer, sunshine? That should keep the smell off yer clothes.'

'It doesn't, yer know, Auntie Beth. It's still on me clothes and in me hair.' Then the humour she'd inherited from her mother came to the surface. 'Me mam said I'll never get a feller 'cos they wouldn't come within a mile of me.'

'Yer dad and David have worked there for years, lass,' Andy said, 'and it doesn't seem to have done them any harm.'

'Ah, yeah, I thought of that meself, but me mam helped me solve the mystery.' At that moment, Beth thought Joan looked the spitting image of Dot. 'Yer see, I didn't know it, but me mam's just told me she's got no sense of smell. And as for David, well, he's sixteen and he's never had a girlfriend.' The girl nodded as though the facts that she'd just given proved the point she was making. 'So me dad said the only way out of it for me was either to find another job, or look for a boyfriend what hasn't got no sense of smell.'

There was much laughter as Joan pulled out a chair and made herself comfortable. 'Tell me about your day, Ginny. But if yer've been put on a counter selling fancy perfumes, then I'd better warn yer not to tell me 'cos I wouldn't be able to stop meself from clocking yer one.'

'No, nothing so swanky. I've been put on haberdashery, with the pins and needles, buttons, ribbons and cottons. It's a nice counter and I'm quite happy with it, although I've got to admit that another girl who started with me and Marie this morning was put on cosmetics and I was dead jealous.'

'Can I ask yer to shift yer arms while I take this cloth off?' Beth took the four corners in her fingers and carried the cloth out to shake in the yard. 'Start putting the chenille cloth back on, Ginny, in case we have more visitors. I don't want to be caught napping twice in one night.'

And Beth was thanking her lucky stars she'd just made it when the knocker sounded. 'I'll go, Mam,' Ginny said. 'It's probably one of the neighbours.' But when she opened the door to Bobby and Amelia Bailey, Ginny was wishing she'd combed her hair. She just knew it looked a mess. 'Come on in.'

There was no greeting from Bobby, who looked as though he would burst if he didn't get his news off his chest. He went straight to Andy. 'I did as yer said, Mr Porter. I got a card from the Labour Exchange this morning and went down to George Parr's. And guess what? I got a job!'

Andy and the others in the room acted just the way Bobby was hoping they would. 'I don't believe it! Yer got a job, just like that?

'I was dead lucky, Mr Porter. The man who owns the business doesn't live in Liverpool. There's a foreman runs the building side of it, and a manager in the shop. Anyway, I managed to see the foreman and I gave him the reference I had from me last employer. After reading it, Mr Sellers asked me a few questions about the trade, then he took me to a part of the shop where there was a wash basin. He said, "There's a leak in that tap, show me how yer'd put a washer on." I was surprised 'cos there's not many people who can't put a washer on. Still, I wasn't going to argue, and I did as I was told. Then when I was finished he took me through to his office and explained they already had an apprentice but he was hopeless at the job, and stayed off sick at least one day in every week. He'd actually stayed off today, which was in my favour. Anyway, they'd already decided to give him a week's notice and were going to look for another apprentice.'

Bobby had calmed down a bit now he'd got the most important bit off his chest. And he was able to smile when he said, 'Mr Sellers said my reference was one of the best he'd ever seen, and based on that he would like to offer me the job and could I start tomorrow!'

Four voices chorused, 'Tomorrow!'

'I know, I couldn't believe it meself. I felt like pinching me arm to make sure I wasn't dreaming. But, as Mr Sellers explained, their gas fitter had been mucked around with the other boy being so lazy and taking so much time off. And he really needed, and deserved, a decent apprentice to help him because he had a lot of work on.'

'Oh, I'm made up for yer, sunshine, I really am,' Beth said. 'I bet yer mam and grandma are proud of yer?'

'They both burst into tears when I told them.' Bobby jerked his head as if to say that women weren't half soft. 'But I'm really made up that I'll soon be bringing a few bob in. And Mr Sellers said there'd be a couple of hours' overtime every week. That would be a big help 'cos the flat wage isn't very much.' He held Andy's eye. 'I've got you to thank for it, Mr Porter. I didn't even know George Parr's existed until you told me.'

'I'm glad I told yer then. I didn't think yer'd get a job to start right away, mind, but I'm highly delighted for yer. It'll be a big help to yer mam.'

'And I won't be the only one bringing in a few bob next week.' Bobby turned to where his sister was sitting next to Ginny. 'Our Amelia will be bringing in nearly as much as me.'

'Oh, of course,' Beth said, 'I'd forgotten you were starting work at Hartley's today. How did yer get on, sunshine?'

Attention was now on the shy girl who blushed. 'I'm only on washing jam jars, so the pay is just five bob a week. But I saw the supervisor and explained about me dad, and how I needed a job that paid a bit more, and she's promised to see personnel tomorrow and ask if it's possible to move me to another department. It might only be an extra shilling or eighteen pence a week, but it all helps.'

What caring children they are, Beth thought. Their dad must have been very proud of them. And if he was looking down from heaven now, he'd be proud that they were trying their best to help their mam. Swallowing the lump that was beginning to form in her throat, she said, 'It's been quite a day all round for the young ones. Four of yer get sorted with jobs in the one day. That's pretty good going.'

'I think I've grown a couple of inches since this morning,' Bobby said. 'And if I sound big-headed, well, that's because I feel it right now.'

'I bet yer grandma was pleased with yer,' Ginny said. 'And when ye're going home, I'll go with yer to tell her all about my job.'

'Oh, ye're not leaving me out,' said Joan, looking very determined. 'I'll come with yer as well. But I'd like yer all to come and let me mam and dad know what's going on as well. Yer know how me mam hates to miss anything, she'd give me the rounds of the kitchen if I kept all this away from her.' She looked from Amelia to Bobby. 'I don't suppose either of yer was born with no sense of smell, were yer?' When they looked bewildered and shook their heads, she tutted. 'No, I thought it was too much to ask for. Still, if the smell gets too much for yer, just give me the wire and I'll get a couple of me mam's pegs to put on yer nose.'

'Listen, sunshine, I've been going in and out of your house for years,' Beth said, 'and not once smelled rubber. It's you, ye're imagining things. When yer've been working there for a week or so, yer won't even notice it.'

'Does that mean I'll be able to get meself a feller?' Joan opened her eyes and mouth wide, and held up her hands in a dramatic pose. 'Oh, I'll be saved from being an old maid, living alone with only a cat for company.'

'It doesn't necessarily follow that because yer don't smell of rubber yer'll get yerself a boyfriend, soft girl.' Ginny shook her head. 'I'd feel sorry for any boy who was caught in your trap, 'cos even if yer smelt like a rose, it wouldn't stop yer from being as soft as a flipping brush.'

'Listen, if you don't tell them, they won't know. So if ye're a true friend, yer'll keep yer mouth shut and only you and me will know I'm two sheets to the wind. And now that's been sorted out to our mutual satisfaction, are yer all in favour of going to see me mam before we pay Mrs Bailey a visit?'

'I'll come next door with yer,' Beth said. 'It'll pass an hour away for me, and you can read the *Echo* in peace, sunshine.'

'Oh, so now ye're saying that ye're going out for my sake?' There was a chuckle in Andy's voice. 'Ye're not going to have a good old jangle with Dot, ye're going so I can read me paper in peace and quietness?'

'Yeah, something like that, love. But if yer'd rather I stayed in, then yer only have to say so, 'cos your word is my command.'

'Don't say nothing, Dad,' Joey piped up. 'While ye're reading yer paper in peace and quiet, I can read me comic without going over the same line half-a-dozen times.'

'Come on then, kids,' Beth said. 'We know when we're not wanted. Just make sure that kettle's on the boil at nine o'clock.'

It was noisy in the Flynns' house for the next half-an-hour as each of the youngsters gave their account of the day's happenings. Joan thought it only right, seeing as it was her house, that she should be allowed to shout louder than the others, but her brother soon cut her down to size when he couldn't hear what Bobby was saying to him. 'I don't know why yer don't get a job on the market, our kid, with the voice yer've got,' David said. 'I bet yer could outdo a ruddy foghorn.'

Joan, who was trying to make an impression on Bobby, was cut to the quick. 'Don't you be picking on me or I'll thump yer one!'

David grinned. 'Who would yer get to lift yer up?'

Their father intervened. 'That's it! I've got a headache trying to listen to everyone at once. Now let's see if I've got it straight.' Bill smiled to himself at what he was going to say. 'I've heard Amelia's story, and Ginny's. Bobby I've only heard bits of, and would be grateful for a bit of hush so I can hear it in full. As for you, Joan, all we got when we were having our dinner was your voice complaining about the small of rubber in Dunlop's. Now seeing as it's a rubber factory, it would be strange if it smelt of fish, don't yer think?'

213

Dot sighed and raised her brows to Beth before saying, 'Bill, they're making enough noise without you adding your twopennyworth. And I bet you were just as excited after your first day at work as yer daughter is today. After all, it is a turning point in her life.'

Joan grinned cheekily at the father she adored. 'That's put you in yer place, Dad. This is a day for the young ones, not an old fogey.'

'Ay, that's enough cheek out of yer,' Dot said. 'Yer dad's only a year older than me, so if ye're calling him an old fogey, ye're calling me one, too! Just watch yer lip, young lady, or I'll be giving yer a thick one.'

'While ye're still in one piece,' Ginny said to her friend, 'shall we make our way down to see Mrs Bailey?'

Beth nodded at her daughter. 'That's a good idea, sunshine, before it gets too late. I don't want yer knocking on her door at all hours.'

'Yeah, okay.' Joan was willing. 'Are yer coming, Amelia and Bobby?'

'Our kid can go with yer, but I'll stay and talk to David,' Bobby said. 'Tell me mam I won't be long, half-an-hour or so.'

Beth noticed Joan's smile drop, and thought, Oh, aye, she's got her eye on him. Fourteen and probably noticing boys for the first time. She sighed, thinking that in another couple of years Ginny would probably be courting. Children seemed to grow up quicker these days than when she was a girl. Still, as long as Ginny found herself a good lad, one that would look after her, that's all they could ask for. 'Go on, poppy off to see Mrs Bailey. But mind yer don't overstay yer welcome, and remember she's not a slip of a girl any more so behave yerselves.'

Ginny had a job getting Joan to leave the Baileys; she knew her friend was hanging back waiting for Bobby to come home. In the end she said, 'I'm going whether you are or not. It's nearly ten o'clock and me mam said I hadn't got to stay too long.'

'Ten o'clock's early! We're not schoolchildren any more, we're working girls. My mam won't mind me staying until this time.'

'Well, you please yerself, but I'm going.' Ginny pulled a face at Hannah. 'Yer'll have to throw her out if yer want to get rid of her, Mrs Bailey.'

It was Claire who answered. 'I'm sure it won't come to that. But if it was Amelia who was out at this time of night, I'd be worried. Particularly with it being such a dark night and the street lamp outside seems to be broken.'

'I wouldn't stay out until this time on a dark night,' Amelia said. 'In the summer perhaps, when the nights are light, but not when it's pitch black.'

'Oh, I'll come with yer,' Joan said, knowing when she was outvoted. 'Yer'll only call me for everything if I don't.'

Ginny gave Hannah a kiss. 'Yer look a lot better now yer've got yer family with yer. But as ye're my friend, I'll still keep coming down to see yer.'

'I want yer to, sweetheart,' Hannah told her. 'I want to know how ye're getting on at work, and all about yer friends. In fact, I'm a nosy old so-and-so, and I want to know everything that happens in yer life. So ye're always welcome here.'

Claire showed them to the door and Ginny was just stepping down on to the pavement when Bobby bumped into her. 'Oh, I'm sorry,' she said, 'I didn't see yer.'

'I didn't see you either.' Bobby was wishing he could rub the toe she'd trodden on. 'It's hopeless having a streetlamp that doesn't work.' He glanced up the road. 'I'll walk back with yer, to make sure yer get home safe. Take an arm each.'

Joan was in her applecart. Clinging on tightly to his arm, she started to chatter and didn't stop until they reached Ginny's house. A gaslamp further up the street gave some light, and they could see Bobby smiling when he withdrew his arms and said, 'There yer are, girls, home safe and sound.'

'Ay, I'm not home,' Joan said. 'Yer should do the job proper and take me to my door.'

Ginny was embarrassed. 'Don't act daft, it's only a few steps.'

'If ye're worried about anyone running off with yer,' Bobby said, while thinking anyone who ran off with Joan would regret it very quickly unless they were stone deaf, 'I'll stand here until yer get inside yer door.'

There was nothing Joan could do but walk to her own front door and knock. When it was opened by her mam, she waved to the two figures standing a few yards away before disappearing inside. But she wasn't in the best of moods. At the back of her mind she knew she'd spoilt things by talking too much and showing off, but she wasn't going to blame herself for Bobby's lack of interest so she ignored what that little voice in her hand was saying, and told herself it was Ginny's fault for being so smarmy and goody-goody.

Beth and Andy were having their last cup of tea of the day when Ginny walked in. Joey was in bed and everywhere was quiet. 'How was Hannah, sunshine?'

'She's fine, Mam! I think she's getting well looked after 'cos she

215

looks tons better than she did before her family came.' Ginny hung her coat up before making her way towards a fire that had been banked down for the night but was still giving out warmth. 'Did yer mean it when yer said I should ask Marie to come round one night?'

'Of course I did! That's if yer want to, of course?'

'Oh, yeah, it would be great! Yer won't half like her, she's very funny and is always laughing. She reminds me of Joan, they're both good at impersonating people.' Ginny remembered something and began to laugh. 'How about this, for instance? Marie wants to get a job behind the counter eventually, but it's her arithmetic that's letting her down. Anyway, she said she's going to get her dad to set her some sums every night. And when I asked if her dad was good at sums, she answered, "He's bound to be, at his age, isn't he?" And when I said his age didn't mean he'd be good at sums, she said she'd get the woman next door to double check them.'

'I'll look forward to meeting her,' Beth said. 'She sounds like a tonic.'

'She is! As I said, she reminds me of Joan, but she's got a bit more on top.'

'The trouble with Joan is, she gets her mouth going before her brain,' Andy said. 'But she's a good kid, for all that.'

'Yeah, I know, and she'll always be me best mate. I'll have to ask her in if Marie comes or she'll feel left out. And I was wondering whether I should ask Amelia, 'cos she hasn't had time to make friends with anyone yet.'

'That would be nice, sunshine, I'm sure she'd be made up. It was thoughtful of yer to think of her, but then I shouldn't expect any less from yer, should I?'

'Right, I'll ask Marie tomorrow and see what night is best for her. But I'm going up to bed now 'cos I feel worn out.'

'I've kept the cosy on the pot to keep the tea warm for yer, sunshine. Don't yer want a cuppa before yer go to bed?'

Andy shuffled to the edge of his chair. 'I'll pour yer one out, sweetheart. Let yer old dad spoil yer this once. It isn't often a man's daughter starts her first job.'

'No, thanks, Dad, I'm not fussy about one. I'm so tired it's taking me all me time to keep me eyes open. It must be all the excitement, learning everything on the counter and the prices and meeting new people, me head is spinning. So I'm going to have an early night and in the morning I'll be fresh to start another day.' Ginny gave her mother a hug and a kiss, and then kissed her dad. 'Goodnight and God bless.'

'Goodnight and God bless, sunshine.'

'Goodnight and God bless, sweetheart.'

When they heard the footsteps climbing the stairs, Beth looked across at her husband. 'We've got a good one there, sunshine.'

Andy nodded. 'Aye, we certainly have, love, we certainly have.'

Chapter Eighteen

They were sitting on the tram the next morning when Marie brought a small notebook from her bag. She waved it in Ginny's face and laughingly said, 'I didn't trust me dad, me mam, or the woman next door. But I do trust you 'cos I've seen yer in action.'

Ginny took the notebook from her and opened it up. There were three pages with sums on, but she quickly noticed that they were easy sums, not likely to test the mind of anyone but a child. 'I see yer got them all right. Or were yer parents being kind to yer?'

'Well, if they were, they didn't know they were being kind to me. They wouldn't have been backward in coming forward if they'd thought I'd done any of them wrong. Yer see, they know how much I want a job behind the counter so they wouldn't be soft with me.'

'I'll run over them quickly, shall I?' Knowing Marie wouldn't keep quiet while she did this, she added, 'While you look out of the window at the scenery.'

There was a deep chuckle. 'Listening to you, anyone would think I talk too much.'

'I only know one person who talks more than you and that's my friend Joan. Her mouth is never still. Anyway, feast yer eyes on the shops, or the people hurrying to catch a tram to take them to work.'

'I don't know whether this has skipped yer notice, Ginny, but since we've got on this tram you've done twice as much talking as me.'

'I was just beginning to notice that so if yer'll let me concentrate I'll get on with these sums.' It was only about five minutes later that Ginny was handing the book back. 'They're all right, kid, but ask yer dad to make them a bit harder for yer. And I'll do my bit to help by giving yer some sums to do in yer head. That's what yer have to be able to do behind a counter, Marie. There's pads there which yer can use, but it's easier if yer can add up in yer head. There's nothing over sixpence in the shop, so we're not talking in pounds. A customer might buy three or four things and altogether they'll only come to a shilling. So it's not hard by any means.'

'Not hard to you, perhaps, but very hard to someone who's thick.'

'You are not thick, Marie! If ye're going to think that about yerself, yer'll never get a job as a shop assistant. Look, say a woman comes in to buy four buttons at tuppence each. Then she asks for two yards of ribbon at three pence a yard. Now how much would that come to?'

Marie's tongue came out of the side of her mouth as she concentrated. 'That's eightpence for the buttons, and sixpence for the ribbon.' She used her fingers to add the sixpence to the eightpence. 'I get to one shilling and tuppence.'

'And that's right! Now it wasn't so hard, was it?'

Marie's bottom did a dance on the wooden bench seat. 'That's great! Can yer give me another one to do?'

Ginny shook her head. 'We get off the stop after this, but we'll do it again tomorrow. And there's something I want to ask yer. Would yer like to come round to ours one night and meet me mam and dad? I've told them about yer and they'd like yer to come. I'll get me friend Joan to come in as well. Would yer like that?'

'Oh, yeah, that would be the gear! It's only a ten-minute walk from ours to yours. And can we make it tomorrow night? With it being Wednesday, our half day, I'll have plenty of time to make meself look presentable then.'

Ginny grinned. The more she was with Marie, the more she liked her. 'That's settled then. And tell yer mam not to worry about yer walking home on yer own in the dark, me and me kid brother will walk with yer.'

As soon as they stepped off the tram, Ginny's tummy began to turn over. The thought of having to face Miss Landers wasn't a pleasant prospect. But she said nothing to Marie. The least said, soonest mended. After they'd hung up their bags and coats, she forced a smile to her face. 'I'll see yer in the canteen at break time.'

Miss Landers was checking the counter when Ginny arrived, and although she looked up, she didn't smile or pass the time of day. And it continued like that for the next hour and a half. The only time the senior assistant spoke, or barked would be a better word, was when she was serving and ordered Ginny to tidy the reels of cotton and ribbons in the front of the counter. Or if there were no customers, she would accuse the girl of deliberately getting under her feet.

Ginny was beginning to think the woman she was working with wasn't right in the head. There was no sense in the orders she gave, and certainly no reason because Ginny made sure the counter always looked immaculate. But nothing she did found favour with her senior who was bitter and twisted. It was a great relief when the time came for her morning break. After that, she could look forward to her senior's dinner break when Miss Sutherland took over. So while she sat and enjoyed her cup of tea, laughing at the things Marie came out with, Ginny kept the nice things in the front of her mind and the nasty things at bay.

While she was walking through the store, back to the haberdashery counter, she made a resolution. She would get on with her work and ignore Miss Landers, as she herself was being ignored. If the woman didn't want to be friendly, then that's how it would be.

There was a customer being served when Ginny got back so she walked through to stand behind the counter. She made sure she kept well away from her senior, but she'd have had to be deaf not to hear what was going on. The customer was buying several things, and without even thinking what she was doing, Ginny was adding the prices up in her head. Her very presence seemed to annoy Frances Landers who turned and stared unblinkingly at her until Ginny dropped her gaze. 'Get round to the front and tidy the reels of cotton. And the knitting needles need straightening,' she ordered her assistant.

The customer had been served, paid over two shillings and fourpence and had the receipt in her hand. She gazed from the hard face of the woman behind the counter to the young girl who stood by looking very uncomfortable. 'Was there any need for that?' the woman asked, feeling quite angry that anyone so young should be belittled in front of a customer. 'Were you never taught to say "please" and "thank you"? Anyone with your attitude should not be allowed to work with the public.' With that she walked away with her nose in the air, and Ginny felt like running after her and giving her a hug. She did watch her for a few seconds. When she turned back, there was no sign of her senior.

Filled with curiosity, Ginny murmured, 'Where the heck has she got to?' Then she walked behind the counter and was amazed to find the woman bent double, as she had been the day before. 'Have yer caught yer stocking again?'

Miss Landers sprang up like a jack-in-the-box, her face contorted with anger. 'Don't you ever dare sneak up on me like that again! And don't pry into my affairs, you cheeky little madam, I've a good mind to report you.'

Ginny was completely bewildered by the attack and the look of sheer dislike on her superior's twisted face. 'I only asked if yer'd snagged yer stocking again, there's no harm in that. I certainly wasn't prying.' Then the girl's pride overcame her fear. 'Anyway I think it might be a good idea if yer do report me. They're bound to ask to hear my side of what happened. So shall I go and ask Miss Halliday to come down?'

She watched the transformation come over the other woman in amazement. No one would believe her if she described it, they'd have to see it for themselves. The face of the woman before her was no longer contorted in anger but grimacing in what was supposed to pass for a smile. Shivering inside, Ginny told herself it was like one of the masks she'd seen hanging up in the sweetshop on the corner of her street. They were grotesque, bought by children to frighten their friends.

'I didn't mean to bawl at you, it's just that I got out of bed on the wrong side this morning. You'll have to learn not to take things to heart because I don't really mean to upset you,' Miss Landers cajoled.

But Ginny wasn't prepared to be treated like a skivvy whenever this woman felt like venting her anger on someone. If she had to come in to this every day, being miserable and humiliated, she'd be better off working somewhere else. And all because of this woman who she would swear had a screw loose.

Being too young to deal properly with the situation, Ginny stood lost for words. Then her eyes lighted on Miss Sutherland, who was talking and laughing with Helen on the next counter. What a difference it would make if she'd been put with someone who was easy to get on with. Then she took heart from the knowledge that it wouldn't be long now before Miss Sutherland took over for the dinner break. Perhaps she could have a word with her about the way Miss Landers was treating her. And she could ask was she the only one the woman had taken a dislike to? Surely she must have had other juniors working with her, how had she treated them?

Ginny couldn't bring herself to speak, so she stayed silent and walked to the front of the counter. She'd stay there, even if she had to keep moving things that didn't need moving, anything to keep a distance between her and her senior until Miss Sutherland came to take over. But it shouldn't be like this, it just wasn't right. She'd looked forward so much to starting work, and here she was, more miserable than she'd ever been in her life. Never in that short time had she come into contact with anyone who was so hostile to her. Who openly showed their dislike, even hatred, of her. And she didn't see how she could cope with it day after day. Her life wouldn't be worth living. Yes, she'd have a word with Miss Sutherland, that was the best thing. She'd advise Ginny on what to do.

'I'm coming!' Dorothy Sutherland waved to the senior assistant from the next counter then groaned under her breath. 'Just look at the state of her, Helen, she looks like a bull ready to charge. Honest, she gives me the willies. Anyway, I'd better get up there before she starts frothing at the mouth. I'll see you later.'

Frances Landers didn't even exchange a greeting with her, just turned her back on the woman taking over from her and stormed away. Dorothy grinned at Ginny. 'Was that smoke I saw coming from her nostrils? She looks as though she's ready to do battle.'

Ginny was about to say she'd already been the butt of her senior's bad temper when she saw the customer who had stuck up for her earlier coming towards the counter. 'Hello, dear, I see that dreadful woman isn't here. Has she been given her marching orders?'

'She's gone to her dinner,' Ginny told her, blushing. 'This is Miss Sutherland, she takes over every day, just for the dinner break.'

Dorothy had been listening with interest. 'What's all this? Who is this terrible woman you're talking about?'

'The assistant who was serving behind the counter this morning. I work across the street in Henderson's, and I nipped out in my morning break to buy some ribbon and other bits and pieces. We sell everything in our store but they're more expensive than here. So, although my bosses wouldn't like to hear me say it, I do shop here quite often.'

Dorothy nodded. 'I know, I've seen you. But what happened this morning, weren't you satisfied with the service you received?'

'Oh, I've been served many times by that assistant, and although I can't complain about the service, I've always felt a smile from her wouldn't go amiss. It would certainly attract more customers. No, what horrified me this morning was the way this young lady was spoken to. She was humiliated in front of me, and I find that totally unacceptable. I was very angry and made my views known to the person in question. I wondered afterwards whether this young lady would suffer because of me, and that's why I'm here now, in my lunch break.'

Ginny's lip quivered. Someone being nice to her made her want to cry. 'I'm all right, thank you. After you'd gone, I stuck up for meself. My mam has always drummed it into me and me brother that you should respect your elders so I didn't give her cheek, nothing like that. I just said what I thought, and Miss Landers apologised.'

'Oh, well, no harm done then,' the customer said, smiling. 'I would be devastated if I'd been the cause of more trouble. Now I'll have to put my skates on or my break will be over.'

'Thank you,' Ginny said. 'It was very kind of you to come back.'

Dorothy was concerned that the miserable Frances may have lost them a customer. 'I hope what happened won't stop you from shopping here?'

'Of course not! But I think the assistant concerned should be told a customer has complained about her conduct, and perhaps she'll be more careful in future. Anyway my name is Miss Meadows, Alicia Meadows, if you wish to take the complaint further, and as I said I work in Henderson's.' With a cheery smile, she walked briskly towards one of the two front doors which opened on to bustling Church Street, the main shopping street in Liverpool.

'I bet she's no ordinary shop assistant,' Dorothy said. 'She's very sure of herself, very confident. Anyway, tell me exactly what happened? And I want to know word for word.'

So Ginny recounted the whole episode. 'It's not only what she says, Miss Sutherland, it's the way she says it, and the way she looks at me – as though she hates me. I don't know why because she hasn't even bothered to find out what I'm like. I was going to ask you about the other juniors who have worked on this counter with her. Was she nasty with them or is it only me she's taken a dislike to?'

'I really shouldn't be discussing another senior assistant with you, Ginny, but I think you deserve to know that she's been like that with them all. Some of them have stuck it out for a year, others six months. But the last young girl, Joyce Connor, she only stayed a matter of weeks. The thing is, not one of them went to Miss Ormsby about her, which of course they should have done. And young Joyce wouldn't tell a soul why she was packing the job in. She just said she'd found something she thought more suited to her.' When two customers came to the counter at that point, Miss Sutherland said, 'You put the counter in order while I serve these ladies. We'll talk later.'

There was a steady stream of customers. When twenty minutes had passed, Ginny thought there'd never be time to find out what she needed to know. Another ten minutes and Miss Landers would be back from her lunch break. But fate was on her side for once, and there was a break between customers.

Dorothy pretended to mop her brow. 'That was a busy little spell. It certainly kept me on the move. Still, that's what we need. If there were no customers, we'd all be out of a job.' She raised her brows at Ginny. 'But by the sound of things, pet, you wouldn't worry if you didn't have a job here. Am I right?'

'Oh, no! I want to work here more than anything! I would really love the job if it wasn't for the person I'm working with. She's supposed to be training me in how to be a good counter assistant, but she hasn't told me one thing about the job. All she's done is bawl at me and make me feel like something that's crawled from under a stone.'

'I'll tell you briefly what I know about her. It's no excuse for her behaviour, but it's the reason we all put up with her in the beginning. Why we all felt sorry for her and allowed her to get away with a lot of things.' Dorothy took a deep breath. 'Apparently she was courting a bloke and they'd talked of getting married. So she started a bottom drawer, fully convinced she was to be wed in the near future. However, didn't her intended run off and marry another girl who was prettier than Frances! That was the tale we all got when she first started working here and everyone, from the bosses down, felt sorry for her and she got away with murder. It took a while for us to realise that misery and rudeness are second nature to her. And, of course, the poor bloke we'd called for everything had our sympathy and understanding then.'

Ginny listened in silence. It must have been terrible to have been let down like that, but it didn't give Miss Landers the right to take it out on everyone else. 'Lots of people have bad things happen to them, like one of our neighbours whose son died. Now that is a lot worse than being let down by someone, but Mrs Bailey didn't take it out on those around her. She was very sad, and she cried, but she was never rude to anyone.'

Dorothy Sutherland grabbed hold of her arm. 'She's coming down the store now, so I'm going up to meet her. I want a word with her, but not in your presence. If she says anything to you, just say you didn't hear anything and you know nothing.' As she slipped through the opening in the counter, she said, 'You keep your chin up, pet, and everything will turn out fine. It may not happen right away, but be patient and don't do anything rash.'

Frances Landers was clearly taken aback when confronted by Dorothy. 'Have you left that stupid girl in charge of the counter?'

'Yes, I have left her in charge, and no, she isn't stupid. I want a quick word and you would be wise to listen. A customer has complained about you humiliating Miss Porter in her presence. She had very strong views on the matter, and asked if I would pass her complaint on to the highest authority.' Dorothy Sutherland asked herself what a few little white lies mattered if they had the desired effect – in this case, to frighten someone into treating a young girl with the respect she deserved. 'I haven't reported it, but I must warn you that unless you change your whole attitude, you're likely to find yourself in trouble.'

'All I did was tell the stupid girl to move. She's forever getting under my feet and she'll never make a good assistant because she hasn't even bothered to learn the price of anything. Not even the buttons.'

225

'If she hadn't learnt anything, then the blame would lie at your door because you are supposed to be training her. As it happens, she's picked up all she needs to know without your help. I had quite a rush on while you were away, and for everyone I served she whispered the price of their purchases to me. She knows the cost of everything on the counter, and is quick at adding up in her head. And on top of that, she's a nice kid who I for one would find it a pleasure to work with. If you go too far, and one day get the sack, don't say you weren't warned.'

With that Dorothy spun around and hastened back to her counter where Helen was on pins waiting to find out what was going on. But the version she got was heavily censored, of course, for her senior assistant didn't believe in gossip. If she had anything to say, she said it to your face and then it was over. She did not clat on a work colleague. However, that afternoon her eyes were constantly turning to the adjacent counter. If she'd seen anything amiss, she would have been there like a shot, colleague or no colleague. She would not allow the mind of a pretty young girl to be warped by someone who was bitter and twisted. Nor would she allow the bright smile she'd glimpsed to be hidden away because the girl was too intimidated to show it.

When Beth was waving Ginny off that morning, if she'd had the slightest inkling of the misery and heartache in store for her daughter she would never have allowed her over the doorstep. But as she had no idea, Beth was humming as she gave Joey his breakfast and sat talking to him for a while before it was time for him to leave for school. And once the door was closed on him, she set to on her housework. The grate was always the first job: raking the ashes into the ashcan and carrying them out to the midden, then adding just enough coal to keep the fire alive. Money was tight and to have a roaring fire all day when she was alone in the house would be a waste.

She was on her knees, wiping the hearth over with a floorcloth, when there came a thumping on the window. Sitting back on her heels, she muttered aloud, 'What the hell does Flo want this time of the morning?' She pushed herself up and smoothed down her pinny as she made her way to the front door. 'What in heaven's name are yer doing here so early? I haven't even started to tidy up yet.'

Flo obviously had a cob on because her face was set as she brushed her friend aside and entered the house. By the time Beth had closed the door, Flo was standing in the middle of the room with her arms folded under her bosom. She was wearing a pinny that was a few sizes too small for her and a mob-cap that was hanging down over her eyes.

'What the hell was going on here last night? All the coming and going, and the shouting and laughing, it sounded as though yer were having a ruddy party! But yer never thought of giving me a knock, did yer?'

'Flo, is that the only reason yer've called this early in the morning? Surely it wasn't so important that yer couldn't wait a couple of hours?'

'If yer'd given me a knock last night, I wouldn't have had to bleedin' knock this time of the morning, so don't be trying to put the blame on me.' Flo pursed her mouth and blew her breath upwards to chase away a strand of hair that was tickling her nose. 'Some friend you are, I must say.'

'Yer didn't miss that much, sunshine, so don't be getting a cob on. What yer could hear when yer had yer ear to the wall was Bobby telling Andy about getting himself a job. The lad was over the moon, and we were all pleased for him. Oh, and if ye're that interested, he brought his sister with him.'

Without a by-your-leave, Flo pulled a chair from the table and plonked herself down. This was much to the detriment of the chair which made its feelings known by creaking loudly. 'Seeing as I'm here, and I want to know everything that went on, yer may as well put the kettle on and we can talk over a cuppa.'

'Oh, I may as well put the kettle on, may I? And what about the state of me room, which hasn't been dusted, and me beds which haven't been made? I'd much rather yer went home and came back when I've finished all me housework.'

'To walk home now, and then come back again, would be a waste of good shoe leather. No, as I'm here and sitting comfortably, I may as well stay. And I may as well be sitting with a cuppa in me hand.' Flo jerked her head back, catching her chins unawares. 'If yer were a true friend yer would have the kettle on already, not make me beg for it. Yer'll be asking me to get on me bleedin' knees in a minute.'

Beth pretended to be indignant and tutted as she made her way to the kitchen. 'I don't know, me life's not me own.'

'Stop yer bleedin' moaning, will yer, and see if yer can find any biscuits to have with the tea. Ginger snaps, if yer've got them, I don't half love to dunk them.'

After putting a light under the kettle, and having a little chortle to herself, Beth strolled back into the living room. 'Are yer sure yer wouldn't like me to make yer a few slices of thick toast, dripping with best butter, and a jar of marmalade to complete the picture?'

'Don't be so bleedin' sarky, queen, it doesn't suit yer. And how would yer like it if, the next time yer come to mine for a cuppa, I was sarky with you? Yer'd soon have something to say.'

'Flo, in the sixteen or seventeen years we've been neighbours, I've probably had half-a-dozen cups of tea in your house, so yer haven't really had the occasion to be sarcastic. And not once in those years have I seen sight nor light of a ruddy biscuit!'

'I can't help that, queen, 'cos it's our Amy and Wendy. When me back is turned they scoff the lot.' Flo put a chubby hand across her mouth to hide the smile that was starting to appear, but it was no good, there was no keeping the laughter back. 'God forgive me for telling lies! It's not the girls that scoff the biscuits because there's never any left for them to scoff. If me mind knows I've got biscuits in the pantry, then it nags at me, and forces me against me will to pinch a couple. Then the couple turn into handful, and another handful, until there's none left. Only then is me mind at rest.'

'Yer should be ashamed of yerself, Flo Henderson, yer've got no willpower at all. Ye're worse than a ruddy baby.' Beth suddenly screwed up her eyes and groaned. 'Oh, no! Dot's just passed the window, I bet she's coming here.' And the words were barely out of her mouth before the knock came. 'I don't know, I'm sure you lot think this is an open house.' On her way to the door she carried on talking. 'The dust is an inch thick everywhere, and I've got ruddy visitors!'

Dot stood on the pavement, grinning. 'Yer'll be getting carted away, talking to yerself.'

Beth's hands went to her hips. 'What d'yer want, sunshine, 'cos I'm a bit pushed at the moment?'

'Don't come that with me, girl, 'cos I know yer have a visitor. In fact the whole street knows yer've got a visitor 'cos Flo's knock would wake the dead.' Dot hesitated, not being quite as forward as Flo. 'Are yer going to ask me in, then?'

'Have you finished yer housework?' Beth asked, standing with feet apart in the middle of the top step.

'Most of it, yeah.' Then Dot realised that was perhaps the wrong answer. 'Well, no, I haven't. I've cleaned the grate out, that's all.'

A voice floated out to them. 'Let her in, for heaven's sake, I'm having to hang on to the table so the draught doesn't blow me off the chair.'

'Okay, yer can come in then.' Beth stood aside. 'But only for twenty minutes. One cup of tea and then ye're both getting turfed out.'

Dot nodded to Flo in greeting. 'Was she as rude to you, girl? Honest, I feel like an unwanted tramp what's knocked to try and sell her some pegs.'

'She didn't exactly welcome me with open arms, queen,' Flo said, with a very exaggerated wink. 'But I've got strong shoulders and a thick skin.'

'You might have a thick skin, sunshine, but I'm the one what's thick in the head,' Beth said. 'I want me bumps feeling for letting yer in before I've got me work done.'

'We'll give yer a hand, won't we, Flo?' Dot rubbed her hands together. 'I'll brush the floor and the queer one can dust. That only leaves you with the dishes to do.'

Beth resigned herself. Anyway, having a natter broke the monotony. 'I'll get another cup and saucer out.'

So the three neighbours sat for half-an-hour filling each other in with whatever news they had. And Flo sat swinging her legs under the chair, content now she knew as much as her friends. 'So, Bobby's got himself a job, which I'm glad about. Ginny seems to like her job by what yer say, and your Joan thinks hers stinks!'

Dot tapped her chin. 'I'm sorry I told yer that, Flo, 'cos I know yer can't keep yer trap shut. I can just see it in me mind now. You meeting our Joan in the street and asking her what the smell is. She'd be mortified.'

'I'm going to have to stretch me money out this weekend, with the tram fare I'm having to fork out this week and next,' Beth told them. 'I know it's only two bob, but two bob goes a long way in this house. And there's Ma Maloney to worry about, and her shilling interest.'

'Take a tip from me, queen,' Flo said. 'Pay her, even if yer have to starve yerself. 'Cos sure as eggs is eggs, if yer don't pay her Saturday, she'll be knocking on yer door on Sunday.'

'I daren't let that happen, Andy would go mad. So, as yer say, even if I have to starve meself, I'll make sure she gets her shilling. And I'll have to see Hannah, make sure she pays her pound of flesh. It won't be so bad in two weeks, when Ginny starts bringing her money in, but I'm going to be strapped this weekend.'

'I'll lend yer the shilling, girl, so don't worry,' Dot said. 'I'm not loaded, but I do have our David's money coming in. It's not much, but I'm a bit better off than you. So yer can put yer mind at rest on that score.'

'Thanks, ye're a pal. I'll remember yer in me will, sunshine.'

'Ooh, if yer do, can yer leave me that vase Hannah bought yer?'

Flo's chair groaned when she swivelled her bottom around to confront Dot. 'You can sod off, you can! If anyone gets that vase, it's me!'

'Yer cheeky pair of articles! Well, yer can both sod off, 'cos I ain't going anywhere and that vase stays right where it is. And when I said yer can sod off, I mean right now, so I can get some work done. I said twenty minutes, but yer've been here nearly an hour and it's time for yer to go. I'll see yer at eleven o'clock to go to the shops.'

As they were being escorted out, Flo said to Dot, 'Well, this is nice, isn't it, queen? Talk about "Here's yer hat, what's yer hurry?" isn't in it!'

'She's got no manners at all, girl, so don't let it get to yer. Dragged up, she was, as common as muck.'

That afternoon Ginny was left in peace. No barked orders, no sneers. There was no conversation or smiles, either, but she could put up with that because her family and friends more than compensated. And while she made herself useful on the counter, she had a thought to keep her happy. Marie was coming to visit her house tomorrow night. Joan was coming, too, so it should be fun. Perhaps she should ask if Amelia would like to come as well, seeing as she hadn't had time to make friends yet. That would make four of them, which would be great! They could always have a game of cards if they ran out of things to talk about. But somehow Ginny couldn't see that happening. Not with Marie and Joan there. They could both talk the hind legs off a donkey.

Chapter Nineteen

On Wednesday morning the atmosphere around the haberdashery counter at Woolworth's was decidedly chilly, but even Frances Landers couldn't spoil Ginny's happiness. For the first time in her life she was having invited guests to her house that night, and to her that was a definite sign she had left her childhood behind and was now an adult. A very young one, she admitted to herself, but nevertheless a working adult.

From a box under the counter, Ginny was filling up the button boxes that were running low. When she'd finished with the buttons she would move on to the needles, then the wool, until the whole counter had been topped up. They kept a stock of every item they sold, and when that was running low, the senior assistant would order more from the stock room.

Frances Landers could sense Ginny's high spirits, and decided that as she herself had nothing to be happy about, she'd put a blight on her junior assistant. She'd take care, though, because Dorothy Sutherland's warning had been heeded. Anything nasty she said from now on could be repeated, and she would get into trouble for it. So it wasn't what she said that would upset the young girl, it would be the way she said it.

'Be very careful with those buttons and needles. In fact, be careful with every single thing on the counter. You see, every few months there's a stocktaking, and if there's a discrepancy between the money we've taken and the goods we've sold then you'll be in serious trouble.'

Ginny frowned. 'How d'yer mean, *I'd* be in serious trouble? You're in charge of the counter, not me, so it's you who would be in trouble. Anyway, what do yer mean by discrepancy?'

The sneer was back on that hard face. How easy it had been to burst the stupid girl's bubble. 'It means we are not carrying the stock we should be, and we haven't taken in enough money to cover the discrepancy.'

'But I don't handle any money, that's your job. And I don't refill the boxes under the counter, that's another of your jobs.' Ginny was getting agitated. She didn't trust this woman who was obviously out to harm her. 'This is only me third day here, I'm not allowed to do anything but fill up the counter, so how could I be blamed for anything?' She was so upset she became more outspoken than she would have done if she'd been thinking clearly. 'You're getting paid to keep check on this counter. To make sure the customers are served right and everything runs smoothly. If it doesn't, then it's down to you. And I'm glad I can't serve or use the till, 'cos then yer'd find something else to blame me for.'

Oh, what satisfaction the senior assistant was getting from Ginny's reaction! It didn't enter her head that this was weird. In her mind she was the only sane one. 'Oh, it's not only the till that things can go missing from. Every time there's a stocktake, they find items have gone missing from most counters. Items for which no money has been received and which cannot be accounted for. Which can only mean they have been stolen.'

What's she getting at? Ginny asked herself. Why is she telling me all this? 'Seeing as we're not allowed to bring bags or purses in with us, there's no way staff can steal things. And as I don't touch the till, or handle money, I haven't anything to worry about, have I?'

'If someone is a thief, then believe me they'll find a way to steal. It's in their blood and they can be very crafty.'

She's doing this just to make me feel miserable, Ginny thought. And she's trying to frighten me. Why she would want to is a mystery, but I'm not going to let her. 'I wouldn't know nothing about that, 'cos I've never stolen anything in me life. But I did hear someone say once that it takes a thief to know a thief.'

The senior assistant gasped. Although she felt anything but calm, Ginny forced herself to say, on a lighter note, 'Oh, have yer never heard that saying before? I am surprised, seeing as yer seem to know so much about people who steal. Mind you, ye're a lot older than me so ye're bound to know more. Me now, I've never known a thief in me life. But as I'm only half your age, I've probably only got half your knowledge and still have a lot to learn. Although I've got to say I don't really want to learn the ways and habits of people who steal. That is not why I came to work in Woolworth's.'

Nothing more was said after that, although if Ginny had known the thoughts that were running through Frances Landers' head, she would have had cause to worry. For revenge was uppermost in the mind of this woman who, because of her strange, selfish behaviour and lack of humour, didn't have a friend in the world. But she didn't need a friend, because her one joy in life was hurting people, and seeing that hurt in their eyes. She found that exhilarating and exciting.

Had her mother still been alive, she could have told people that her daughter had been like that from a very young age. At the age of two, when she was barely toddling, she'd take great delight in pinching or biting other young babies in the street. It got to the stage where women used to have to keep a close eye on their children when their prams were put out so they could get some fresh air. Frances had never been a loving child who liked to be kissed and cuddled. Had never shown love or affection to anyone, not even her own parents or the boy she was courting. So being jilted at the altar hadn't turned her into the bitter, wicked woman she was now, for she had never been any different. And that was why the man she'd thought intended to marry her ran off with a pretty girl who knew how to laugh and to love.

For the rest of the morning Ginny kept her distance, even though she thought she'd given as good as she got, for once. The prospect of the evening ahead was soothing to her wounded pride, and she was determined that nothing would mar her first attempt at playing hostess.

'Joey, will yer sit on the couch with yer comic instead of lying sprawled across the table?' Ginny was on pins, wanting everywhere to look nice for Marie's first visit. It didn't matter so much about Joan because she'd been coming in and out of the house since she was old enough to climb the front step on her own, and Amelia had been a few times so she was no stranger. 'Ye're spoiling the look of the room, making it untidy.'

'Let them sit on the flipping couch.' There was a look of disgust on her brother's face. 'Why should I move 'cos yer've got some flipping stupid girls coming?'

Beth let out a soft sigh. She really didn't like taking sides or showing favouritism, but she knew how important tonight was for Ginny. 'Go on, sunshine, sit on the couch, there's a good boy.'

'Ah, ray, Mam! It's coming to something when I can't sit where I want in me own house! She'll be asking me to go and sit in the coal-hole in a minute.'

'Well, this is Ginny's night to have her friends in. You can ask your mates in another night, then yer'll be even.'

Her son gaped, as though she'd gone mad. 'What would I invite me mates in for? They'd think I had a screw loose or was losing me marbles.'

'That's no reason why yer should want to spoil things for me. Honest, ye're like a little baby crying 'cos their dummy's fallen out of the pram.' Ginny saw the hint of laughter in her brother's deep brown eyes and took advantage. Slipping an arm across his shoulders, she bent and whispered, 'Come on, ye're always saying how much yer love yer sister, so prove it.'

'Geroff!' They boy tried to curl his lip like he'd seen James Cagney doing in a film, but he knew himself it wasn't having quite the same effect. 'Ye're a sloppy beggar, you are.' But he was weakening. 'Why d'yer have to invite all girls? Why couldn't yer invite some boys, so I'd have someone to talk to?'

Andy looked up from his evening paper. 'Why don't yer go and ask David to come in then? He'd be company for yer.'

If Beth had been sitting near her husband she would have given him a sharp dig. Men never thought before opening their mouths! Here she was, worried because she'd only been able to afford half-a-pound of broken biscuits, and there he was, inviting all and sundry! She'd had a job trying to pick out the almost whole biscuits, and was satisfied there'd be at least one each. If the girls wanted more, then they'd have to eat the broken ones. 'David wouldn't want to come in if he knew there were four girls coming. He'd run a mile.'

But Joey had perked up by this time and was moving over to the couch. 'He'd come if he knew Bobby was going to be here, I bet yer.'

Beth put a hand to her head and groaned. The plate of broken biscuits was beginning to look pitiful. 'Behave yerself, Joey, there wouldn't be enough chairs to go round. Besides, I've nothing to give them with their cup of tea. I'm not made of money, yer know.'

The idea was beginning to catch on in Ginny's head. 'They won't be expecting anything to eat, Mam, they'll all have had their dinner!' She nearly jumped out of her skin when she heard the knocker. 'Ooh, I wonder who this is? I'll go, Mam.'

Bobby was standing behind his sister and he grinned at Ginny. 'I thought I'd better walk her up, with it being dark. And I'll call for her if yer tell me what time yer'll be throwing her out.'

Ginny didn't know about the broken biscuits and her mother's headache, so she didn't hesitate to say, 'Oh, come in, Bobby! David from next door is coming, I think, and he'd be glad to see yer.'

'Oh, okay, I'll be able to tell him how I'm getting on in me job.' Bobby was very pleased with himself. He hadn't been expecting to find work so quickly, had thought it would be weeks at the earliest. And although it was only his second day working at George Parr's, he knew he'd hopped in lucky. The skilled gas fitter he'd been put with was brilliant, a fast, efficient worker, and a comedian into the bargain. He was dead funny the things he came out with, and he didn't talk down to

Bobby but treated him like an equal. 'And I can tell yer dad, 'cos I know he'd be interested with tipping me off about the firm in the first place.'

Beth had heard all this and decided it was no use worrying, it was out of her hands now. 'Slip next door, Joey, and ask David to come in.'

'He won't come if his talk-a-bit sister's here. He gets enough of her at home.'

'That's for him to decide, sunshine, not you. Besides, you were the one what suggested it in the first place! Remind me to box yer ears in the morning before yer go to school.'

Joey was beaming as he dashed across the room to give her a kiss. 'Ye're a smasher, Mam, and I don't half love yer.' With that he smiled at the first of the visitors before making for the house next door. And while he went the front way, his mother was running up next door's yard.

'Dot, have yer got any biscuits yer can let me have?' Beth shook her head when she was invited in. 'I can't stay, they'll all wonder where I've got to. It's just that things have got a bit out of hand. Our Ginny was inviting a few of her friends, which I could have coped with, but the numbers seem to be growing. Bobby walked Amelia up and Ginny, God love her, asked him to stay as well. And now our Joey's in your living room inviting David. Now I've no objection at all, sunshine, honest. I wouldn't care if the house was full and they were standing on each other's toes, but I would like to be able to offer them a biscuit that's all in one piece.'

Dot grinned. 'I can let yer have half a packet of arrowroot, girl, but that's about me limit until the weekend. Ye're welcome to them, though, honest. And I'll get our Joan to ask some of her mates here next time, save you having all the bother.'

'Ye're a pal, sunshine, and I do appreciate it.' Beth tucked the packet of biscuits under her arm, where they were hidden from view. 'I'll see yer tomorrow.'

As she slipped in through the kitchen door, Beth's son was coming through the front with Joan and David. There were lots of greetings and chatter, and Beth was thankful nobody seemed to have missed her. 'There's only yer friend Marie to come now, sunshine. Are yer sure she knows her way here?'

It was Joan who answered. As soon as she'd set eyes on Bobby, she'd begun to show off. 'Of course she does! She was in our class at school, and I know she was a bit thick, but not *that* thick.'

Ginny gasped. 'What are you talking about, Joan? Marie didn't do badly at school.' She could have made a fool of her friend and said Marie was higher in class than Joan was, but it wasn't in her to embarrass anyone. 'If she hears yer saying that she won't think it's a bit funny so kindly keep remarks like that to yerself. I like her, I invited her here, and I don't want you insulting her.'

David nodded. 'Our kid needs putting in her place, Ginny, she's far too big-headed for no reason at all. She's certainly no brain-box.'

'Well, this is a nice way to start the evening, I'm sure,' Beth said. 'So I'm laying down a few house rules. There'll be no raising of voices, no sarcasm, no insults and no showing off. If yer stick to those rules, we can all have an enjoyable evening.' She cocked an ear. 'That's the door, Ginny, d'yer want me to go?'

But Ginny was already opening the door while her mother was still speaking. 'I thought something had happened to stop yer coming.'

Marie's wide grin was there to cheer Ginny's heart. 'I didn't like leaving me mam with the dishes, so I stayed to give her a hand.'

'I'll believe yer where thousands wouldn't.' Ginny jerked her head. 'Come on, get yerself inside, me mam is waiting to meet yer.'

'She doesn't know what she's letting herself in for.' Marie was laughing as she entered the room, her wonderful smile almost as wide as her face. But she got a surprise when she saw the room was full. Ginny had told her Joan and a girl called Amelia would be there, but she hadn't expected boys as well. She soon gathered herself together and laughed, 'If yer'd told me it was going to be a party, Ginny, I would have worn a long dress and brought me dance shoes.'

Her smile and bubbling personality won Beth and Andy over right away. She looked such a happy, friendly girl, you couldn't help but take to her. And another one who was smitten at first sight was David. At sixteen he'd never had a girlfriend, never shown the slightest interest in the opposite sex. But one look at Marie's happy, smiling face, and he started to take an interest. Secretly he was over the moon because for once he didn't have any pimples. He quickly jumped to his feet and offered her his seat on the couch. 'D'yer want to sit down?'

'We're going to sit around the table so we can have a natter,' Ginny said. 'But first, as your hostess for the evening, it's part of my job to make sure everyone is introduced. Now, there's only Marie who hasn't met yer before, so I'll do the introductions before we sit down.'

So, starting with her parents, Ginny took Marie around and introduced her to everyone except Joan who had spent nine years in the same class as them. She was looking a little peeved, was Joan, seeing Marie as a rival who was stirring up a lot of interest. Still, she comforted herself, it was only because she was new. And Bobby didn't seem that interested anyway. He was being friendly, but his eyes weren't popping out of his head like her brother's. Silly nit, he hadn't a clue about girls. If Marie spoke to him he'd probably curl up and die.

When things had calmed down, Bobby took David's arm and led him over to where Andy was sitting. 'I want to tell Mr Porter about me job.'

And because young Joey told himself the boys wouldn't be here but for him, he trooped after them. He wasn't going to be left with a group of giggling girls. Then, in his head, he apologised to his sister, who wasn't a giggler unless it was over something worth giggling about. And Amelia was a very quiet girl, the sort he could put up with. He reserved judgement on Marie even though from what he had seen she was the happy-go-lucky sort. But he didn't need to reserve judgement on Joan – he'd always thought she was a pain in the neck.

The girls sat on the wooden dining chairs around the table, talking about their new jobs and their ambitions. Ginny glossed over hers by leaving out any mention of Frances Landers and concentrating on the good things. Marie's goal in life was to be a shop assistant. Amelia wanted to move to another department where the wages would be better. Joan didn't seem to know what she wanted. She didn't mind Dunlop's, but it was the smell that put her off. Her dad had said she'd get used to it and wouldn't even notice it after a few days, but this had been her third day and she still hated that smell.

Andy sat in his fireside chair, deep in conversation with the boys who squatted on the floor around him. For once Joey was quiet as he listened to the older lads. It wouldn't be that long before he left school and then he could join in with them. It slipped his mind that as he grew older, so would the others and they'd always be those three years ahead of him.

Now and then roars of laughter would come from the group, and the loudest was Andy's. Even Beth, who was sitting on the arm of her husband's chair, had tears of merriment rolling down her cheeks due to the tales Bobby was telling them about the man he'd been put to work with. From the boy's description, the chap was stocky in build, had red curly hair, hazel eyes and a ruddy complexion. Along with these came a brilliant sense of humour and a smile that was always quick to appear. His name was Jeff Walsh, and from the enthusiastic way Bobby spoke and the laughter in his voice, this man was just the person to help him along the road to recovery after losing his father.

'Yer should hear the things he says about the other apprentice he

237

had. It came to the point where he was more relieved when the lad took the day off than when he came in. One time, he was fixing a leaking gas pipe in a house, and he thought the apprentice was watching him as he was supposed to do. Anyway, he just happened to turn around and found the lad about to have a sly smoke. He had a cigarette in his mouth and was just going to strike the match he had in his hand when Jeff threw himself on top of him. If that match had been lit, they would both have been blown to kingdom-come, and the house with them. And after the shock, Jeff said he was shaking like a leaf at how close he'd come to losing his life, while the lad couldn't understand what all the fuss was about and got a real cob on 'cos his ciggie had been broken in two.' Bobby's chuckle was deep. 'The first thing Jeff said to me after we'd been introduced, was, "Ay, mate, I hope yer don't smoke?" '

By this time the girls were more interested in the conversation taking place in the corner of the room than they were in their own. So they each had an ear cocked, listening.

'And the lad didn't learn his lesson, like most people would have. Jeff said he was as thick as two short planks, 'cos he didn't understand the danger involved in gas fitting. Not long after the first incident, Jeff was repairing a gas leak and had the lad standing next to him, talking him through the job. He happened to say he'd need a blow torch later, to solder the pipe. The lad walked off without saying anything, and Jeff said he thought he must have gone to the lavatory. But then he began to feel uneasy, and had a foreboding that something bad was going to happen. So he switched the gas off at the mains and went looking for the missing apprentice. And didn't he meet the silly nit coming towards him with the blow lamp! Now an apprentice has to have a good few years' training under their belt before they can touch a blow lamp, but this lad wasn't only carrying it, he'd lit it! Jeff didn't think it was funny at the time and he could have strangled the lad. But he said afterwards, when his heart and stomach were back in the right place, he could see the funny side because the lad looked like Florence Nightingale carrying her lamp. The only difference was, Florence Nightingale didn't go around blowing people up.'

While the males laughed and the girls giggled nervously, Ginny asked, 'Why don't yer come and sit at the table? We seem to be missing all the fun.'

Bobby wasn't so sure about that. He was at ease in male company, but four young girls were a bit of a challenge. 'I'm only telling them about the bloke I work with, yer wouldn't be interested.'

'We're talking about work, too,' Joan said. 'But we're not laughing our heads off.'

Joey had his own solution, which was abrupt and to the point. 'If yer all shut yer mouths and gave yer tongues a rest, yer'd hear what was being said. Bobby can't repeat things just for your benefit.'

'There's not much more to tell, anyway,' he said. 'But I'm sure there will be, 'cos Jeff never stops laughing, he's great to work with. So in future I'll make a note and remember to tell yer any funny incidents.'

'Well, why don't yer have a game of cards to pass an hour away?' Beth suggested. 'Yer can have a laugh playing cards.'

Marie's rich chuckle filled the room. 'Yer can if I'm playing, I'm hopeless! But I don't mind yer laughing at me, and I don't worry about losing either, as long as it's only the game and not money.' Her head went back and again her laughter filled the air. 'Mind you, I'd have a job to lose any money 'cos I haven't got none.'

'We'll teach yer how to play,' David dared to say. 'Rummy isn't hard, yer'll soon get into the hang of it.'

'We can't play cards, Mam,' Ginny said. 'We've only got one pack and that's no good with six people playing. Seven, if our Joey wants a game.'

'I can borrow a pack off Lizzie, if yer like?' Beth offered. 'I know they've got a few packs 'cos they play a lot. So if you get yerselves sorted out with chairs, I'll nip across the road.'

But Ginny didn't see how seven people could share four chairs, or five if you counted the rickety one in front of the window. 'We haven't got enough chairs, Mam!'

'Oh, for heaven's sake, sunshine, yer'll just have to make do! I'm not going to borrow chairs as well as cards. You and Joan could share one, neither of yer has got a big bottom.' Beth slipped her arms into her coat. 'Just use yer imagination and have yerselves sorted out by the time I get back.'

As she was crossing the cobbles, she was muttering to herself, 'I hope this isn't going to become a regular thing. I don't mind once in a while, but we never seem to have been free of visitors since Christmas. Dot's offered to have them one night, so I'll take her up on that.' As she waited for an answer to her knock, she added, 'Still, it's better than them roaming the streets, at least we know where they are and who they're with.'

Mick O'Leary, at sixteen, was Lizzie's eldest child. Having been brought up in Liverpool, he had no trace of an Irish accent, but he'd spent his life listening to the lilting brogue of his parents and when the mood took him, his accent was pure Irish. And this is the way he greeted Beth. 'Is that yerself, Mrs Porter! Sure it's happy I am to see yer, and it's very welcome yer are, so it is. Bring yerself in to see the family. They'll be delighted to see yer, and that's the truth of it.'

'Less of yer blarney, Mick O'Leary, and let me in, I'm freezing.'

Lizzie looked up from the sock she was darning. 'This is a surprise, me darlin', I wasn't expecting yer this time of night.'

'I'm on the cadge as usual.' Beth smiled at Paddy who had looked up from his paper. 'Every time I see Mick, he gets to look more like you.' The Irishman had black hair, deep brown eyes and a weatherbeaten complexion which came from working outdoors all of his adult life. He was also built like a battleship, with hands as big as shovels. But his size belied his nature, because he was a gentle, caring man who wouldn't hurt a fly. 'Except for his blue eyes, of course, and I've heard it said that black hair and dark blue eyes are the signs of a real Irish beauty.'

'Well, if yer've come to cadge something, me darlin', ye're going the wrong way about it, so yer are,' said Lizzie, whose own auburn hair and green eyes had been inherited from her mother and then passed on to three of her children: Seamus, who was fifteen and working, and her two daughters, Molly who would be fourteen and leaving school in the summer, and Eileen who was almost twelve. 'Yer've just insulted two-thirds of me family.'

Beth lifted her hands in mock horror. 'Well, begosh and begorrah, sure that wasn't me intention at all, at all. And yer mustn't be forgetting I've insulted meself at the same time, so I have.' Beth's wasn't a good imitation, but it was funny and had the kids laughing. Slapping an open palm to her forehead, she looked up at the ceiling and asked, 'How do I get meself out of this?' And then, as though with divine intervention, she smiled. 'Auburn hair and green eyes are well known as the perfect combination for beauty.' With eyelids fluttering and stroking her hair, she added, 'And, of course, it goes without saying that blonde hair and blue eyes are the stuff that sexy film stars are made of.'

'Well, me darlin', seeing as yer've put us at level pegging in the beauty stakes, I think we'll forgive yer. But what was it yer came over to cadge?'

'A packet of cards, if ye're not going to use them. Ginny's got some friends in and they seem to be running short on conversation so I thought a game of cards might put a bit of life into the proceedings. Hannah's two grandchildren are there, and a friend of Ginny's from work, plus Dot's two, so our one pack of cards wouldn't be enough.'

'We won't be having a game tonight so ye're welcome to them, me darlin'. But why not let Mick run over with them, and you stay and visit for a while? It's not often we get the pleasure of yer company.'

That sounded too tempting to refuse. 'I'd be very happy, as long as Mick doesn't mind taking the cards over. Yer could stay for a game yerself if yer like, sunshine, it would be a change for yer. David and Bobby are your age, both working, so yer'd have company. And there are four pretty young ladies.'

Mick's deep blue eyes twinkled as he puckered up his lips and let out a loud whistle. 'Sounds good to me. Are the cards in the sideboard drawer, Mam?'

Beth thought she'd better tell him that it wasn't all milk and honey. 'There's one drawback, though, Mick, I'm afraid. We haven't enough chairs to go round so yer'll just have to muck in and make the best of it.'

He slipped the packet of cards into his pocket before lifting one of the wooden dining chairs. 'I'll take me own chair, then perhaps one of the pretty girls can sit on me knee.' He was only joking because if a girl ever got that close to him, he'd run a mile. 'As yer say, Mam, yer never know yer luck in a big city.'

'Don't take the chair, Mick,' Beth said. 'If the neighbours see yer, they'll think we're really poverty-stricken.'

'The neighbours don't pay yer rent, Beth,' Paddy said. 'Nor do they put the bread on yer table. So I'd not be worrying about what they think.'

'Yeah, ye're right, Paddy, why should I worry about them? Go on, Mick, and enjoy a game of cards. And tell my feller I'll be home in about an hour.'

There were a lot of surprised faces around the table when Mick walked in with a chair in one hand and a pack of cards in the other. 'I'm not as pretty as yer wife, Mr Porter, but she said to tell yer it's only for an hour.'

Andy was laughing as he stood up. 'She's a crafty beggar is my one, I can't keep up with her. Anyway, put yer chair down and make yerself at home. I think yer know everyone except Amelia and Bobby Bailey, and Marie. . . .' He raised his brows at the girl. 'I'm sorry, love, I don't know yer surname.'

'That's me mate for yer, she's got no manners.' Marie stuck her hand out, thinking this young man had to be the most handsome she'd ever seen. 'Marie Whittaker.'

Amelia was more shy, lowering her eyes as she shook hands. But

Bobby got on with Mick from the word go. 'I know David works with his father, and I believe you do, too. What type of work d'yer do?'

'Me dad's a skilled bricklayer, that's all he's ever done. But I'm only just coming out of me second year so I've got a long way to go yet.'

'Yer mean, yer build houses, like?'

Mick grinned. 'We sometimes pull them down, if they become dangerous. And we work on the roads, so it's pretty mixed.'

Ginny knocked on the table. 'Excuse me, but we're supposed to be playing cards, not talking shop. So will yer all settle yerselves down, please? Me and Joan are going to share this chair, and our Joey has offered to stand. Well, perhaps offered wasn't the right word, but he's going to stand. And as he's a cheat, yer'd all do well to keep yer cards close to yer chest.'

Andy wasn't going to play, but he shuffled the cards and dealt the first hand. Then he returned to his *Echo* with the words, 'Yer can look after yerselves now until the missus gets back. Yer'll get a cup of tea then.'

It turned out that, apart from Marie, everyone was pretty good at the game. But she didn't mind being called a slowcoach, and no one could fall out with her when she smiled and said, 'Everyone has to learn, it's just that I'm slow in starting. But I will catch yer up.'

Joan huffed. 'When, like? This time next year?'

Marie was undaunted as she faced her old classmate. 'When I've learned me two times table, clever clogs. I'll let yer know when I find out meself.'

The truth was, Joan was jealous that Marie was getting all the attention from the boys. She wasn't that funny, so why were they laughing at everything she said?

When the game got into its stride, there was lots of chatter, jeering and cheering, and everyone was enjoying themselves, even Joan. In fact she was holding her own with Marie when it came to making them laugh, especially when she was taking her mother off.

Ginny herself was feeling very proud. The first time she'd had friends around and it was going great. Marie had just surprised herself by putting three sixes down, and her antics had them in hysterics. Anyone would think she'd won the pools. And Amelia and Bobby really seemed to be enjoying themselves. Ginny was glad about that because she often lay in bed and wondered how she would feel if she lost her dad or mam. At a time like that you need friends to help you keep your sanity. In fact, everyone needs friends, whether they be girl or boy, and she hoped all those around the table tonight would stay friends and always be there for each other in times of need.

Bobby leaned across the table. 'A penny for them, Ginny? Yer were miles away.'

'They're not worth a penny, Bobby, yer can have them for nothing. I was just wondering how I came to be lumbered with two friends who are tuppence short of a shilling.'

'Well, you cheeky article!' Joan feigned horror. 'It's a pity about you now!'

'It certainly is.' Marie did her Stan Laurel impersonation, making her hair stand on end and putting on a tearful expression. 'If that's the way yer feel, Ollie, then I'm not going to let yer teach me me two times table, so there! Yer can put that in yer pipe and smoke it.'

Beth was crossing the cobbles when she heard a burst of laughter coming from her house, and hugged herself. How lucky she was with her family and friends. No one could have better.

Chapter Twenty

The coldest winter for years moved on to make way for the winds and showers of March and April. Then along came May, bringing sunshine, blue skies with white fluffy clouds, and smiles to the faces of people who'd thought the good weather would never come.

Ginny had been working at Woolworth's for just over four months now, and if it hadn't been for her senior assistant, life would have been blissful. She'd got to know most of the women behind the counters she had to pass on her way to the canteen, and although there wasn't the time or opportunity to become close friends, at least there was always a smile and a wave from them. And at break time she had Marie and Pat to talk to, and Miss Sutherland when she took over for the dinner break. The work was enjoyable, meeting new customers every day and exchanging pleasantries. She was allowed to serve now, but wasn't allowed to give receipts or handle any money. Ginny had been told this when she'd come for the interview, so knew exactly where she stood and was in agreement with the rule. Staff had to prove they were capable before being given responsibility.

For the first few weeks she'd worked there, she'd thought Frances Landers was strange, and frightening in a way. She was a horrible woman, and dreadful to work with. But Ginny had made up her mind to take it all in her stride and not be put off the job she enjoyed. It wasn't easy when working in a restricted area with someone, but she'd managed it by spending more time at the front of the counter filling up so she wouldn't have to witness the bizarre actions of a woman she was secretly convinced was sick in the head.

However, for the last two months Ginny had been carrying around a dark secret, one she was too frightened to confide in anyone. She was almost sure Miss Landers was stealing money and hiding it in her shoes. Too often now Ginny had caught her bending down, several times with her fingers actually in her shoe, and each time the girl had been the victim of a vicious tongue lashing. At first she was too naive to suspect the woman of stealing, but over the weeks she would have had to be stupid not to see what was happening. It terrified her. Who was going to believe her word against a woman who had been a senior assistant for years? It was too terrible to contemplate and Ginny was at her wit's end as to what to do. They'd think she was making it up and sack her. Either that or Frances Landers was clever enough to turn it around and make out Ginny was the thief.

Another thing that kept her awake at night was the stocktaking she'd been told about. It hadn't happened yet, but if it came before she told someone of her fears she could end up in real trouble, branded a thief and sent home in shame. If only she had someone to confide in, it would lift the heavy burden from her shoulders and ease her mind. She had thought of telling Miss Sutherland yesterday, when they were together behind the counter, but was afraid she wouldn't be believed. She'd have to tell someone soon, though, or she'd make herself really ill with the worry.

'Are yer not going out tonight, sunshine?' Beth asked, eyeing her daughter's face which lacked its usual animated smile. 'No Joan or Marie, or card game anywhere?'

Ginny shook her head. 'I felt like a night in for a change.' She glanced at the top of her father's head as he bent forward to read the paper. This would be an ideal time to unburden herself because Joey was out playing with his mates and wouldn't be home until after nine. But how to begin, she just didn't know.

The decision was taken out of her hands when Beth asked, 'What's the matter, sunshine? Yer look sad somehow. In fact, yer haven't looked yer chirpy self for a while now, is there anything bothering yer?'

Andy looked up from his paper. He'd noticed himself that Ginny had been looking pale but had put it down to a woman's complaint. 'If there is, sweetheart, get it off yer chest. Yer know what they say about a trouble shared being a trouble halved. Me and yer mam are very good listeners, that's what we're here for.'

'There is something worrying me,' Ginny admitted, feeling sick in her tummy. What if her parents thought she'd made a mistake and didn't believe her? 'I've been terrified to say anything in case no one believed me.' Then the words came tumbling out. 'That woman I work with, my boss . . . well, she steals money and hides it in her shoes. I didn't believe it meself at first but I've been keeping an eye on her for the last few weeks, just to make sure it wasn't me imagination or me having a bad mind 'cos I really don't like her.'

Beth gasped and sat forward. 'Haven't yer told any of the bosses, sunshine? That's what yer should do to clear yerself.'

'That's another thing that's been frightening me. Suppose she puts the blame on me?' Ginny went on to relate what she'd been told about the stocktaking, and about the implied threats in the words used by her senior. 'Yer don't know what she's like, Mam, she's really wicked.' The tears couldn't be kept back any longer and rolled, unchecked, down her cheeks. 'She's given me a dog's life since I've been there – I hate her! But that's not why I'm saying she steals money. I wouldn't do that, not even to her.'

'Yer've got to report it to someone in authority, sweetheart,' Andy said, trying not to show he was shocked to the core. 'And as soon as possible.'

'I'll come with yer to work tomorrow.' Beth's anger was rising. How dare the woman upset her young daughter like this? It was unforgivable. 'We'll go and see one of the bosses and get it sorted out. I'm not having you working with this woman any longer, she could ruin yer life for yer. No, she's got to be stopped before your name gets dragged through the mud.'

'No, Mam, I don't want yer to come with me. They'll think I'm a baby and can't speak up for meself.' Ginny sniffed. 'This is something I've got to do.'

'Yes, but *what* will yer do, sunshine? This senior of yours is a grown woman and can probably out-talk someone as young as you. It would be far better if I came with yer, at least they'd have to listen to yer then.'

'No, Mam, I've got to do it meself. And I promise I will, honest! I've got to, otherwise I've got a feeling Miss Landers will find some way of hurting me, and getting me into trouble. She's quite capable of lying about me and getting me the sack. And if that happened I'd never be able to get a job in a shop again.'

'Ye're talking sense now, sweetheart,' Andy said. 'So I want yer to show the same sense tomorrow and get it all out in the open. When I come home tomorrow night, I want yer to be able to tell me yer've reported this woman.'

'I will, Dad, I promise.'

'Who will yer go to, sunshine? The woman in the Personnel Office?'

Ginny shook her head. 'I don't think so, Mam, I think I'd be better talking to Miss Sutherland when she comes to relieve Miss Landers tomorrow dinnertime. I get on very well with her, she's really nice and has always treated me like a friend. She isn't that keen on Miss Landers herself, and I think she had an idea she'd be difficult to work with. But she wouldn't run her colleague down and I admire her for that.'

247

Ginny lowered her head for a few seconds, wondering whether to tell the whole story. After deciding her parents deserved to know the truth, she went on to tell them about her senior being jilted at the altar. 'I believe everyone felt sorry for her, and made allowances for her behaviour. But Miss Sutherland knows she isn't easy to get on with, and told me if I ever needed help I could always go to her. And I do trust her. So when she relieves Miss Landers tomorrow, I'll tell her everything and ask her advice on what I should do. And I won't put it off any longer, I promise. Even if I'm shaking in me shoes, which I will be, I'll get it off me chest.'

'Does Marie know, or this Pat yer talk about?' Beth asked. 'Have yer told them about the woman yer work with?'

'They know I don't like her, but that's all. I haven't breathed a word to anyone about what I've just told you and me dad. I was too frightened that if there was any gossip, and it got back to Miss Landers, she would turn the tables on me and I'd be the one in trouble.'

'I'd give her trouble if I could get me hands on her,' Beth said with feeling. 'A grown woman to treat a fourteen year old the way she's treated you . . . she wants putting across someone's knee and teaching a lesson.'

'Don't worry about it, Mam, I'll definitely sort it out tomorrow, one way or the other. Then perhaps I'll be able to enjoy a laugh again, and me headache will go.' The smile Ginny forced was an attempt to ease the worry she could see on the faces of her parents. 'And I'll be able to lay me head down on me pillow at night and drop off to sleep right away, like I used to. So, roll on tomorrow.'

Ginny was a bag of nerves the next morning. Try as she might, she couldn't stop her hands from shaking or her teeth from chattering. Marie noticed it at their morning break and asked, 'What's wrong with yer? Yer face is as white as a sheet, as though yer've seen a ghost. Or else looked in the mirror and didn't like what yer saw.'

'I think I've got a cold coming on,' Ginny lied. 'I can't stop shaking.'

'Blimey! Yer go all through that cold weather we've had without even getting a runny nose, and then catch a cold when the sun's shining! Ye're not made right, kid!'

Pat was a little more sympathetic. 'It might be just a chill yer've got,' she said, munching on her meat paste butty, 'yer'll probably be all right tomorrow. But yer could go and see the nurse, she'd give yer something for it.'

'No, I won't bother. As yer say, I'll probably be all right tomorrow. I hope so, anyway.' Ginny was glad when the break was over. She had to keep going for two more hours, and then she could unburden herself to Miss Sutherland. It was going to be an ordeal, and she was dreading it. But she'd promised her parents and she wasn't going to let them down. So there was no backing out.

She'd only been back a few minutes when the lady who worked in Henderson's walked up to the counter. Alicia Meadows called at least once a week, even if she didn't purchase anything, and she was always very friendly and seemed really interested in Ginny's well-being. Frances Landers had told her junior assistant that she shouldn't waste time talking to someone who wasn't going to buy anything, but while she would give the girl down the banks over it, she didn't dare say anything to Alicia. For the woman had an air of authority about her that suggested she was used to giving orders and having those orders obeyed. She wasn't hard, or bossy, it was just that she gave the impression of being able to run her life exactly as she wanted it to be run. And over the months Ginny had grown fond of the woman and was always glad to see her.

'You're looking very peaky this morning, Miss Porter, are you not well?' Alicia fastened her eyes on Miss Landers, as if to say she hoped the older woman wasn't responsible for the young girl's pale face. 'Or has something happened to upset you?'

'No, I'm all right, Miss Meadows, really. I think I might have a bit of a chill, that's all. I'll be fine tomorrow.'

'I hope so, dear, it's not like you to look out of sorts. You have a nurse here, I believe, so why not pay her a visit? She could perhaps give you something to ease what ails you.'

'No, I'll work it off, thank you, Miss Meadows. I'll be fine tomorrow, you'll see.'

'I shall pop in, my dear, to make sure. In the meanwhile, why not take a couple of aspirin? They usually do the trick for me. Anyway, I'll see you tomorrow.'

Frances Landers was seething. 'If you waste time on that woman once more, I'll report you to Miss Halliday.'

Ginny turned her head, refusing to be drawn into an argument. She had more on her mind than squabbling with a woman she'd never heard say a kind word about anyone.

Dorothy Sutherland was in a really good mood when she left her counter in Helen's charge while she did her daily stint on haberdashery. Looking down the aisle into Church Street, she could see the sun shining down on people going about their business and it lifted her spirits. Sunshine to her was like a tonic, guaranteed to cheer her up. She nodded to Frances Landers and waited until the assistant had stepped out from behind the counter before standing next to Ginny.

'Good afternoon, Miss Porter, and what a beautiful afternoon it is, too! Isn't it a pity we have to work for a living? If we were rich, we could take a picnic basket and spend the day in the country. Or if that wasn't to our liking, we could lounge on the beach somewhere, or even have a game of tennis. But, alas, we were destined to work for a living.'

A customer came to the counter at that moment, and it was then Dorothy noticed Ginny's hands were shaking. A closer look showed a face devoid of colour and lips that were quivering. 'I'll serve this customer, Miss Porter, you tidy under the counter if you will, please.'

When the customer had been served with a card of hair clips and a hair net, Dorothy bent down and put a hand on each of Ginny's arms. 'Come on, pet, stand up.' She gasped when she saw fear in eyes that were moist with unshed tears. 'What is it, Ginny?' The rule on not using Christian names during working hours was often broken when there were no senior staff around. But such was Dorothy's concern, she didn't even give it a thought. 'Are you not feeling well?'

In a shaking voice, Ginny said, 'It's not that I'm sick, Miss Sutherland, it's just that I know something so terrible, I don't know how to tell yer. But it's been on me mind for weeks now and I haven't been able to sleep for worry. I told me mam and dad last night and they said I had to tell someone before I got the blame and lost me job. I promised them faithfully I would report it today, and you're the only one I can think of that might believe me.'

'Of course I'll believe you, pet, but try and calm yourself down while I serve this customer. And stop worrying, nothing is bad enough to make yourself ill over.'

Ginny didn't say it aloud but it was a bad thing, and she couldn't help but make herself ill worrying about it. All she needed was someone like Miss Sutherland to say they believed her, and then she wouldn't feel so alone.

'We don't have a lot of time now, Ginny, so would you rather wait until the shop closes and I can meet you outside?'

She shook her head. 'No, I want to get it over and done with, I can't stand it any longer. My head will burst if I don't tell someone.'

'Go ahead, I'm listening.' Dorothy Sutherland didn't know what to expect, but she certainly wasn't prepared for what a tearful Ginny told her. She kept shaking her head as though in disbelief, but never once

250

was there any doubt in her mind that the girl was telling the truth. But she had to ask, 'Are you sure about this, Ginny, because it's a very serious complaint against a senior assistant?'

'I am sure, Miss Sutherland. It's been going on since the day I started, but I didn't know then what she was doing. I mean, you don't expect people like Miss Landers to steal money from their bosses, do yer?' Ginny then went on to tell of the stocktaking and the veiled threat on who would get the blame for any discrepancies. 'If she hadn't told me that, I would probably never have noticed what she was doing. But I started to take more notice, and I have seen her putting money in her shoes. I don't know how much, but I do know that on the day I started, the customer she served had given her a silver sixpence. When she bent down I thought she'd dropped it and offered to help. Then she got really angry with me and told me to keep away from her and not to spy.'

'I've got to say I am really surprised.' In fact, Dorothy was almost speechless. 'And now you have told me, I will have to report it to Miss Halliday. But don't you worry, pet, you won't get into trouble. It's taken guts to tell it like you have.'

'Miss Halliday won't come and ask her in front of me, will she? Because I know she'll lay the blame at my door. She could even say I was making it up because I don't like her. Well, that would be true, I don't like her. But I would never tell lies, 'cos that would be a sin.'

'Well, we'll leave it for now because there's nothing I can do at the moment as I can't leave you on your own to look after the counter. However, Helen is quite capable of managing on her own, so when your senior returns I will make some excuse and absent myself for a while to seek advice. But I must warn you that no one must know what you've told me. Once I've started the ball rolling, it will be out of our hands and up to senior management how the situation is handled. I think you have the advantage at the moment, in as much as you haven't breathed a word to anyone, not even your best friend. Management will take that into consideration because the last thing they would want is a whispering campaign. I don't think you have anything to worry about, so try and stay calm and behave normally.'

Two customers approached the counter and Ginny served one while Dorothy attended to the other. It was while the girl was waiting for the change of a shilling to be handed back to her customer that Dorothy whispered, 'There's no time for any more discussion on the subject as the break is over. Carry on as usual, but don't let yourself be drawn into conversation of any kind. And please don't approach me in the cloakroom this evening, we can't afford even a hint or a whisper of scandal.'

It wasn't hard for Ginny to keep her promise because there was never any attempt at conversation from her senior. She watched Miss Sutherland go back to her own counter, saw her talking to Helen, and then she was hurrying past the haberdashery counter without a glance at either of the assistants. And when she hadn't returned half an hour later, Ginny's nerves were at breaking point. Perhaps it would have been better if she hadn't said anything. She could have just given her notice in and looked for a job elsewhere. But even as she was thinking this, she knew it wouldn't have been the answer. If the stock sold didn't match the money taken over the counter, then her leaving would look as though she'd been the guilty one.

It was three-quarters of an hour before Dorothy Sutherland passed on her way to her own counter. She didn't slow down or stop, but a slightly raised brow told Ginny that she'd done what she'd set out to do. The outcome of it the girl couldn't even guess at.

Ginny had been so wrapped up in her thoughts she didn't see the figure approaching until she noticed a hand resting on the counter. And when she looked up, she nearly jumped out of her skin. 'Miss Halliday!'

But it was on the senior assistant that the supervisor's eyes rested. 'I'm taking your assistant away for a short while, Miss Landers, but I'm sure you can manage without her.'

The answering smile and voice were sickly sweet. 'Of course I can, Miss Halliday! But Miss Porter hasn't done anything wrong, has she?'

'Good grief, what makes you ask that? As far as I'm aware, she hasn't done anything wrong. But as her senior, you should be the one to know that.' She turned, saying over her shoulder, 'Follow me, Miss Porter.'

The supervisor strode purposefully to a door at the back of the store, with Ginny hurrying to keep up with her. She pushed open the door and held it for Ginny to pass through. 'We're going up to Miss Ormsby's office, and Miss Harper will be there.'

'I'm sorry, Miss Halliday, I didn't want to cause you any trouble. But I told me mam and dad last night, and I promised them faithfully that I'd tell someone in authority today. They're very worried about me, yer see.'

They began to climb the steps up to the first floor. 'Of course they're bound to be worried, they're good parents, and it was right for you to tell Miss Sutherland your fears. But we must be very sure there hasn't been a mistake before accusing anyone.' She lifted her hand when

252

Ginny went to speak. 'No, we mustn't discuss it now, wait until we're in Miss Ormsby's office. I've already spoken to her so she knows you're coming, and why.'

The office was as she remembered it, and Miss Ormsby's smile was just as friendly. 'Hello, Virginia, please sit down. You will remember Miss Harper, of course. She and Miss Halliday are going to stay and hear what you have to say. And please don't be afraid, we just want you to tell us, in your own words and time, exactly what relations have been like between yourself and Miss Landers, and why you have cause to suspect her of being dishonest. Now begin at the beginning, please, Virginia.'

Ginny's mouth was dry with fear, and her voice was thick at first. But when she got into her stride, and was describing how she'd been humiliated and belittled by the woman who was supposed to be training her, her speech became clearer. She left nothing out from the first day she'd started, even down to the supposed snagging of a stocking and the ensuing telling off she got for trying to be helpful. The stocktaking, the threats, it all came tumbling out. And telling of the injustices she'd suffered brought tears she could no longer hold back. 'I'm sorry,' she sobbed, 'for causing yer so much trouble. I'll give me notice in if yer want and look for another job.'

'There'll be no necessity for that, Virginia, you have done nothing wrong.' Miss Ormsby glanced over to where Miss Harper was sitting, looking quite flabbergasted. 'Will you ring the canteen and ask them to send a pot of tea up, please? And I think a plate of biscuits would be much appreciated. You may ring from here.'

After the call to the canteen had been made, Miss Ormsby sat back in her chair. 'Now that ordeal is over, Virginia, I would like to ask you some questions. I do not doubt your word on what you believe has been happening, but it would be very difficult for us to charge a woman without proof. So I want you to think carefully before answering my questions. Now, do you think Miss Landers has a system?'

Ginny looked mystified. 'A system? I don't know what yer mean.'

'A pattern, then. Have you noticed if this alleged pilfering happens on certain days, or any particular times of the day?'

'In the morning, mostly, before she goes for her dinner break. I have never seen it happen of an afternoon.'

Miss Ormsby sighed inwardly. After listening to Virginia, she was convinced that what they were hearing was the truth. The young girl answered each question without hesitation and never once averted her eyes. She was clearly incapable of lying, and certainly would never fabricate such a story. 'Every day, Virginia?'

Ginny shook her head. 'No, Miss, I don't see her do it every day. Perhaps twice a week. But I can't speak for the times I'm on me break.'

'I believe you hadn't been working here more than a day or so when a customer complained to Miss Landers about the rude way she addressed you and has since asked that the complaint be recorded. Is that true?'

'Yes, Miss, the customer comes in a couple of times a week. Her name's Miss Meadows and she works in Henderson's.'

The three women exchanged glances before Miss Ormsby asked, 'Why didn't you complain yourself about the way you were being treated, Virginia?'

'I was only new here, Miss, and I didn't want to cause no trouble. Besides, who would believe me against her?'

A member of the canteen staff arrived then with a tray set with four cups and saucers, sugar, milk and a plate of biscuits. 'Miss Halliday, will you do the honours, please?'

'Hadn't I better be getting back to work, Miss Ormsby? I'm sure Miss Landers will be wondering what's going on. And she's bound to ask me what yer wanted me for.'

'You won't be going back on the haberdashery counter, Virginia, we're moving you elsewhere. No one will think that unusual. It is our policy to move junior staff around from time to time so they get used to working on every counter in the shop. We will be putting another assistant on with Miss Landers to monitor the situation. But I must ask that once you leave this room, you will not utter one word to anyone, except your parents, about what has been said. Not even your best friend.' Sarah Ormsby tilted her head. 'Are you still friends with Marie Whittaker?'

'Oh, yes, Miss, we're good mates. We travel to work together every day.' Ginny's eyes regained their brightness as she spoke of her friend. 'She's been doing homework every night, getting her father to set her some sums, and on the tram coming to work I give her sums to add up in her head. She can add up as good as me now, but she still keeps at it. Yer see, she's determined to be a counter assistant one of these days, like me.'

Miss Halliday had scarcely spoken since the interview began, but beforehand she had mentioned to Miss Ormsby that she was afraid the junior who'd left after working with Frances Landers a very short time, Joyce Connor, may have experienced a similar situation as Virginia, and had given in her notice rather than report the woman. It took guts on the part of a fourteen year old to do what Virginia Porter had, and a lot of integrity. Mary Halliday now smiled across at her. 'Marie is very popular in the stock room. A very pleasant, happy girl who is not afraid of work.'

'And you say her ambition is to work behind a counter, then, Virginia?' Miss Ormsby swivelled her chair from side to side. 'Does she not like working in the stock room?'

'Oh, she never said that, Miss, she gets on well with all of them. But everyone has a dream of something we'd like to happen in our lives, and Marie's is to serve behind the counter.'

'That is something we will look into at a later date. Right now we have to decide where best to put you.'

Mary Halliday tapped the end of her pencil on her teeth and pondered for a short while. Then she said, 'In my opinion the best and easiest solution would be to put Virginia with Miss Sutherland, and Helen Bleasedale on haberdashery. We would gain nothing but a repeat of what we have now if a very young junior is put with Miss Landers. It would certainly be unfair to the junior. In Helen Bleasedale you have the perfect person. She is still regarded as a junior because of her age, but she is as capable as any senior in the store. She is also very reliable, honest and trustworthy.'

'And how do you explain the move to her?' Sarah Ormsby asked. 'She's bound to be curious, and even a little put out if she's happy where she is.'

'Somewhere along the line we have to trust someone. We can't sort the problem out ourselves unless a thorough stocktaking is done, and then if it is found that there are discrepancies, we would have to involve the police. I'm sure that is not something we would be happy about. My suggestion would be to confide in Helen and ask her to be watchful for any wrongdoing. Virginia kept it a secret, and I'm sure we could trust Helen to do the same.'

'I agree!' Sarah Ormsby decided quickly. The last thing she wanted was bad publicity for the store because she was the one who would have to explain to the Managing Director. 'Let's do it now. Miss Halliday, I would like you to take Virginia down to Miss Sutherland's counter, stopping on the way to explain to Miss Landers that juniors are being moved around. Then ask Helen to accompany you back here.'

Ginny saw this as a sign of dismissal and got to her feet. 'I'm sorry for causing yer any trouble, I didn't mean to. But it was that or packing the job in and I wouldn't want to do that because I like working here.'

'I think you have behaved in a very responsible manner, Virginia, and you can tell your parents I said they have raised a daughter they can be proud of. Now, please go with Miss Halliday, but remember it is important you do not discuss this meeting with anyone.'

Ginny followed close on Miss Halliday's heels as she walked down the aisle looking neither left nor right. Out of the corner of her eye she saw Frances Landers raise her hand as though to stop them to ask why her junior wasn't coming back behind the counter. But Ginny found that even though her tummy was churning over, her mind was clearing with relief that she had been believed and she wasn't going to lose her job. She didn't have to worry what Miss Landers thought, because the woman couldn't hurt her any more.

Dorothy Sutherland welcomed Ginny with a wide smile and a pat of encouragement. But when Helen was asked to accompany the supervisor, she looked perplexed. For once she forgot and broke the rule regarding the use of first names. 'Ginny won't be staying here for good, will she?'

'Come with me, Miss Bleasedale, and everything will be explained to you. There is absolutely no need to feel apprehensive.' Without allowing time for any further questions, the supervisor nodded to indicate that Helen should follow her. And after a quick surprised look at the woman she'd worked with for over three years, the girl did as she was bidden.

Chapter Twenty-One

Four weeks passed, and what happy weeks they were for Ginny! Instead of criticism there was praise; instead of sharp words and dark looks there was laughter. Dorothy Sutherland was a dream to work for, and coming through the doors of Woolworth's each day was a pleasure. Ginny hadn't spoken one word to Frances Landers since the day she'd been taken off haberdashery, and although she met Helen in the canteen on most days, not a word was mentioned about her former senior. Of course Ginny was curious about whether Helen had noticed anything untoward happening on haberdashery, but she never asked. She did wonder, though, if Miss Landers had been forced to mend her ways with the arrival of an older assistant who wasn't likely to be intimidated by her.

It was on the Tuesday of Ginny's fifth week on purses and wallets that the bubble burst, but it was done so quietly and efficiently no one in the shop sensed anything amiss. Only the supervisor, Miss Halliday, and the senior management were aware of what had been happening, and how they were going to deal with the matter. Oh, and Helen knew, of course, because she was part of it. It turned out she'd had cause to suspect Miss Landers of being a thief in her first week on the counter, but although she passed on her suspicions to Miss Halliday, she had no proof. So she became more vigilant and watchful. Soon a pattern began to present itself. It was every Tuesday and Thursday, and always in the morning, just before dinner break. If a customer bought goods which amounted to sixpence, the senior assistant would press the silver coin into her left palm while opening the till with her right hand. Then, almost in one movement, she would pretend to throw the coin into the till while quickly closing the drawer. She would wait until Helen was serving, therefore not watching what she was doing, and then the coin would be slipped into Miss Landers' shoe. It was done so brazenly, Helen felt like confronting her there and then, but she'd had strict instructions she must not do that.

Miss Ormsby decided after four weeks, with a record of times and dates, it was time to act. They still had no proof, but Helen had been so eagle-eyed she would swear that when the senior left the counter to go for her lunch she would first visit the cloakroom for her handbag and purse. The sixpences would be put with the rest of her money and no one could prove she had stolen them. But Helen was so angry that someone she was working with would steal from their bosses, she'd thought of a way to catch her. This was passed on to Miss Halliday, who advised Miss Ormsby and Miss Harper. And so the scene was set.

So while Ginny was humming to herself as she helped a customer to choose a navy blue purse which was nearest in colour to the handbag she was carrying, a drama was taking place near by. The beginning of the end for the woman who had made her life a misery.

Mary Halliday stood in the aisle, her eyes focused on Helen Bleasedale as she waited for the signal. When she saw the assistant put a hand to the crown of her head, the supervisor hurried to the cloakroom door, passed on the signal then waited. Inside, near to where Frances Landers hung her bag and coat, stood Miss Ormsby and Miss Harper.

Miss Halliday inclined her head in acknowledgement of Frances Landers' smile, then waited a few seconds before following her. The senior counter assistant had been making an extra shilling a week by thieving for such a long time, and getting away with it, she'd become complacent. She didn't think there was anything afoot when she saw the two women from Personnel. But when Mary Halliday caught up with her and took her by the arm, alarm bells started to ring. They were just three or four pegs away from where her coat and bag were hanging, and she would have walked on if the grip on her arm hadn't tightened and brought her to a standstill.

Sarah Ormsby, her face expressionless, stood in front of her. 'Miss Landers, would you accompany us to the office, please?'

Her bag and safety so near, this wasn't to the woman's liking. 'Will it not wait until after I've had my lunch, Miss Ormsby? I'm feeling quite hungry.'

'No, it will not wait. I have asked you to accompany us, now I am ordering you to. Follow me if you will.'

'I would like a handkerchief from my handbag, can I bring it with me?'

'No, you cannot!' Sarah Ormsby's voice was abrupt. If any doubt had been lingering in her head about whether the senior assistant was guilty of pilfering, it had now gone. 'I want this matter dealt with as quickly as possible.'

As soon as the four women were in the office, and Miss Harper had closed the door, the Head of Personnel asked, 'Miss Landers, would you kindly remove your shoes, please? Both of them.'

A consummate actress, the senior assistant feigned surprise. She realised she could be in serious trouble, but she wasn't going to let them see. After all, they couldn't be sure she had money in her shoe, so if she bluffed it out she might just get away with it. Without proof, they didn't have a leg to stand on. Nobody could have seen her slipping the sixpence into her shoe because she was always very careful. 'Why do you want me to take my shoes off? I'd be very embarrassed if I did, because I've got holes in the toes of my stockings.'

Sarah Ormsby was losing patience. This certainly wasn't a job she enjoyed doing, but it had to be done. 'If you don't take them off, Miss Landers, I'll have no alternative but to bring in the police. Surely you don't want that?'

'But I don't understand why? It seems ridiculous to me when I haven't done anything and you haven't given me a reason.'

'Then you have nothing to fear by removing your shoes. By doing so, you will save yourself the humiliation of being searched by the police.'

Frances Landers didn't show any sign of fear or remorse, but she did show her rising temper. She didn't see herself as being in the wrong. In her twisted mind, she was the victim and these women were the persecutors. She lifted her right foot and kicked the shoe off with such force it sailed through the air and landed on the far side of the office. She waggled her foot, saying with a sneer, 'There you are, a hole in my stocking as I said there was. Now are you satisfied?'

'We will stop this nonsense right now, and you will act your age or suffer the consequences. I'll have your other shoe, without the temper.'

The quick change in Frances Landers' mood brought raised eyebrows from the two Personnel Officers, but to Mary Halliday it brought concern because over the years she'd had more dealings with the counter assistant as she worked on the shop floor every day. There'd always been a little voice nagging at the back of her head that told her there was something strange about the woman, but she didn't mention it to her superiors because there was no proof, and she didn't want to be the cause of anyone losing their job. Now she was wishing she'd given a hint over the years so Miss Ormsby was fully aware of the nature of the person she was dealing with and could handle the situation with care. So while Mary listened and watched, she kept herself alert, ready to act quickly should it become necessary.

'You can take my word for it, Miss Ormsby, there is nothing in my shoe. If some mischief-maker has been spreading malicious rumours about me, then I can assure you they are untrue. I would never steal from anyone, I am a very honest person. Bring the culprit here now and get them to repeat what they said to my face. I bet they wouldn't dare, 'cos they know it's not true. So can I go for my lunch now?'

There came a deep sigh from the Personnel Officer. If the woman had been showing signs of fear, or of being upset, she would know how to deal with her and even feel pity for her. But on the bold face before her there was no sign of fear, just a hardness that prompted the question, where do we go from here? 'No one has been spreading lies about you, no one knows you are in this office or why. You must have realised you would be caught out one day. The takings on your counter do not tally with the amount of stock you have, and although we have allowed for some thieving by customers, it couldn't possibly account for the shortfall. You would have been brought to book long before this, if we had had the proof.'

Miss Landers pursed her lips and nodded her head knowingly. 'It'll be that Miss Porter. I knew from the minute I set eyes on her that she couldn't be trusted. It's her you should be talking to so send for her and let me go and get my lunch.' She started to cross the room to where her shoe had landed, but spun around when she heard what Miss Ormsby was saying.

'Miss Porter cannot be blamed for this, there were discrepancies long before she came to work with you. I would say you have been stealing from the till consistently for the last few years and I am quite sure that in your left shoe you have secreted a sixpence. So, you either take your shoe off and settle this matter with as little fuss as possible or I'll have no alternative but to send for the police. And if I have to resort to that, you will find yourself being escorted from the premises by a constable, with everyone in the shop looking on.'

With her eyes almost popping out of her head, her nostrils flaring and a roar of rage coming from deep within her, Frances Landers stretched out her arms to grab hold of the Personnel Officer. But Mary Halliday stepped in between the two women. 'Now, Frances,' she said, soothingly, 'this is no way to behave. Come and sit down and let's talk about this sensibly.' Her eyes sent a message to Sarah Ormsby asking for co-operation. 'Perhaps Miss Harper could have a cup of tea sent up from the canteen? Would you like that to calm your nerves, Frances?'

The answer came in the form of a grunt, so while they waited for the tea to arrive, Mary Halliday kept talking calmly to the woman whose eyes were darting around like a wild animal's looking for a way of escape. But finally the supervisor's coaxing voice seemed to be getting through and Sarah Ormsby walked around the desk to sit down. She didn't interrupt or interfere as Mary seemed to be getting closer to the woman than she ever could.

'Can I put my shoe on now, and go for my lunch? I'm very hungry.'

'Why are you pretending to be stupid, Frances, when we both know you are far from it?'

'How d'you mean? Of course I'm not stupid.'

'Then why are you acting as though you are? You know, and I know, that there is a silver sixpence in your shoe, so why pretend? The truth is, Frances, you've been found out and there's no point in denying it.' The door opened then and Miss Harper came through with a cup of tea and a plate of biscuits. 'Ah, here's the tea. Now drink it up while we're talking, and you'll feel a lot better.'

The cup was meekly lifted from the saucer and a quiet voice asked, 'Can I eat these biscuits, 'cos I'm starving?'

Mary Halliday nodded. Whether she was going to be able to pull this off, she had no idea. But if she didn't, it would mean bringing the police in and she wouldn't wish that humiliation on her worst enemy. 'Slip your shoe off, Frances, please. You know it's going to happen eventually so why prolong the agony? Once you've done that, Miss Ormsby will explain to you what your position is.'

'I'll get the push, won't I?'

Mary glanced at the Personnel Officer and waited for her nod before saying, 'Yes, you will be dismissed, Frances, but I think you knew that the minute you were brought into this office. If you co-operate, at least you'll be able to walk through the shop without a police officer holding your arm.'

The cup was returned to the saucer and Frances bent down to remove her shoe. She placed it on the desk then picked up the cup again. All resistance seemed to have gone from her but there was still no word of apology or sign of remorse so it was difficult for the watching women to feel any sympathy. 'What will happen now?'

'I will have your cards ready this afternoon,' Sarah Ormsby said, 'and your wage packet will include this week's wages and your week in hand. That will save you from ever having to return to the shop. None of the staff will be told the reason for your leaving, but if you wish to save face, you can tell one of the counter staff on your way out that you've been offered the chance of a job nearer home. That, however, is entirely up to you.'

'If I go after another job, they'll want to know why I left here. What

261

am I supposed to tell them? I need a job because I live on my own. And what about a reference? I'll need one to go to the Labour Exchange.'

'I'm afraid I couldn't give you a reference for work in another shop. Or anywhere where you would be handling money. Any possible future employer could give me a ring here, and I will discuss the matter with them over the telephone. I will not give you a written reference because I am not prepared to lie about your character, that wouldn't be fair to any employer. But if a job comes along that doesn't involve you working with money, then I will give a decent reference with regard to your punctuality and reliability as a worker. More than that I cannot do for you. And that is more than you deserve because you have only yourself to blame for this whole sorry mess. It is to be hoped you have learned your lesson. Stealing and telling lies will not bring you many friends. Once you lose a person's trust, you never get it back again.' Sarah Ormsby pushed her chair back and got to her feet. 'I think you will be too late for your lunch now, so I suggest you either use our cafe on the top floor or go to the Kardomah. I'll have your cards and wages ready for you by two o'clock.'

Frances Landers didn't ask any questions, it was as though she hadn't heard a word that had been said to her. 'I'll go and get some lunch, then. And I'll stop by the counter on the way out, to tell that Helen Bleasedale I'm leaving and won't be coming back. And after I've had my lunch, I will come up the side stairs to this office, I won't go near the shop.'

The three women couldn't get over how calm and matter-of-fact she was. No one would believe she'd been dismissed for stealing, which was gross misconduct. The seriousness of the situation didn't seem to have sunk in. Or, if it had, she really couldn't care less. There'd be no tears shed for the loss of a good job that had kept her in moderate comfort for so many years, or shame for betraying the trust put in her.

'I'll walk down with you, Frances.' Mary Halliday followed her to the door. There were things needed to be said that would not be welcome, and she didn't want any fuss made in front of the two Personnel Officers who were clearly out of their depth with a woman whose mind was unstable. 'I won't be long, Miss Ormsby.'

All the way down the stairs, Frances was muttering about the two toffee-nosed snobs and how they hadn't frightened her. Mary let her carry on until they reached the bottom of the stairs and the doorway into Church Street. Then she said, 'You do realise you will never be allowed into the shop again, even as a customer?'

262

'Why not? I can come in to buy something if I like, they can't stop me.'

'Oh, yes, they can. You have been discharged for gross misconduct and, as far as I'm concerned, you've been let off lightly. But if you are seen in the shop again, for whatever reason, the police will be called and then everyone will learn the truth. So take my advice, Frances, and forget Woolworth's. You are a good worker, very efficient, and with a bit of luck you won't be long out of work. But heed the lesson you've been taught today.'

Mary took to the stairs again and never looked back. She'd been afraid of the woman coming into the shop one day and kicking up a stink. Hopefully, that wouldn't happen now.

'Has she left the premises?' Sarah asked when Mary pushed the door open. 'I was quite concerned at times because the woman is clearly not normal.'

'She'll be back for her wages, but after that you will never see Frances Landers again. And, yes, you're right, the poor soul is far from normal. I just hope this episode has taught her a lesson and she mends her ways. She's got off very lightly, and I told her so.'

'I think you handled the situation very well, Mary,' Miss Harper said. 'She would never have responded to Sarah or myself as she did to you. Very well done!'

Sarah Ormsby sighed with relief. 'I've had the unpleasant task of sacking quite a few members of staff in the years I've beeen here. I've encountered tears, shame, and often pleas for another chance. But never have I seen a reaction like the one we've just witnessed. There was no sign of tears, or shame, or even sadness at having to leave the job she's held for many years. She doesn't seem to have normal feelings at all. In fact, there was a moment I was actually afraid of her.'

'Well, she's gone now so the worst is over. But we are going to be a senior assistant short, and this will play havoc with filling in at breaks.'

'You go and have your lunch, Mary, you deserve it.' Sarah felt as though a weight had been lifted from her shoulders. 'I'll go along to the Managing Director's office now, and inform Mr Sanderson of what has gone on. Then I need to make sure the wages are ready for Miss Landers to pick up. But if you could spare half-an-hour this afternoon, we'll discuss what to do about staffing problems.'

Mary Halliday wouldn't tell anyone for the world, but although he was well out of her reach she had a soft spot for the Managing Director. He was in his late-forties, tall and slim, with thinning sandy hair and hazel eyes. It was his gentlemanly manner and old-world charm she'd

263

fallen for, but, as she frequently reminded herself, he was out of her reach. 'Does Mr Sanderson know anything about Frances Landers?'

'Only of our suspicions. He doesn't know we were confronting her today because I wasn't sure how things would work out. Thanks to you, I can tell him the situation has been resolved. Anyway, you run along and have your lunch. I'll see you later.'

When Mary went up to the Personnel Office at four o'clock that afternoon her heart flipped when she saw Clive Sanderson there. She told herself that at thirty-nine years of age it was ridiculous to be blushing, but she couldn't help it. She had never married, although there had been plenty of offers when she was in her early teens. But her father had died when she was only eighteen, and her mother couldn't come to terms with his loss and frequently took to her bed, which meant that when Mary got home from work every night there was no time for the pictures or dancing. There was cooking and washing to do, and her mother to attend to. She never complained, though, because her parents had always been wonderful and she'd loved them dearly. But she had missed out on the social life her friends were having. And at twenty-seven, when her mother died, she was too old to go to dances on her own, and all her friends were married with children. So she now lived alone in the house where she was born. She still had friends, of course, particularly amongst the neighbours she'd known all her life. 'Good afternoon, Mr Sanderson,' she said to her boss.

'Good afternoon to you, Mary.' His smile was slow and gentle. 'I've been listening to your praises being sung. Apparently you put in some sterling work with a difficult employee. Or should I say former employee?' He rose and offered her his chair. 'And I've also been hearing that we have some very loyal counter assistants, which makes up for the odd bad one.'

'You could stake your life on most of the staff we have, Mr Sanderson, even the very young ones.'

'That is precisely what we've just been saying.' Sarah Ormsby, who seemed to be very pleased with herself over something, pointed to a chair in the corner. 'Bring the chair over, Clive, we can't have you standing. Miss Harper, who is aware of what I have in mind, will be along soon as she wants to know what you think of our plans. If you don't think they'll work then we'll go back to the drawing board and begin again.'

They didn't have to wait long for Miss Harper, who looked a lot more cheerful than she had a couple of hours earlier. She perched on the end of the desk to listen closely and watch for Mary Halliday's reaction.

Sarah Ormsby sat forward in her chair and leaned her elbows on the desk. 'I don't want you to think we've arranged anything behind your back, Mary, because we haven't. It's just that Clive remarked on the part played by the two junior assistants, Virginia Porter for being honest enough to risk losing her job by reporting a thief, and Helen Bleasedale for helping us to catch her. Clive thought such loyalty should be rewarded. So I'll tell you what we have in mind and see if you agree because you have far more knowledge of the assistants than we do. I'd like you to tell me if you think Helen Bleasedale would make a good senior assistant? I know she's only eighteen, and wouldn't go on full senior wages for a year or so, but there would be half-a-crown increase on her present wage. What are your thoughts on that?'

Mary's face broke into a smile. 'Oh, she would be over the moon, and I can assure you she is as capable as any senior assistant in the shop. She's an excellent worker and I would have no hesitation in recommending her for promotion. But that would mean taking on another junior.'

'We have one in mind who I hope will meet with your approval.'

Mary showed her surprise. 'You've got one in mind?'

'Well, actually, it was you who put her in our minds. You will, of course, remember Marie Whittaker, from the stock room?'

The astonishment on Mary's face brought a chuckle from Clive Sanderson. 'I would say you have taken her by surprise, Sarah.' This was the first time he had sat next to Mary Halliday; in fact there was seldom reason for them to meet. He realised now he'd never noticed how pretty she was. Whenever he had glimpsed her, he'd always thought her very businesslike and efficient. He knew that like himself she had never married, but that was all he knew about her private life. 'Have you lost your voice, Mary?'

She looked at him and shook her head. 'It's just that I was expecting today to be a day for nasty things to happen – I really wasn't looking forward to it when I got out of bed this morning. But I have to say that Helen Bleasedale, Virginia Porter and Marie Whittaker are three people I have come to like very much. In fact, Mr Sanderson, I think you should meet them and form your own opinion. I think that would be very interesting.'

Sarah Ormsby smiled, remembering how lively and full of laughter Virginia and Marie were when they came for their interview. Both had

265

pretty, open faces and smiled a lot. 'Yes, I think that would cheer you up no end, Clive. Three pretty, lively young girls whose smiles would warm the cockles of your heart.'

Miss Harper was enjoying this. It wasn't very often they had such excitement in the office, and although she could do without the treachery of Frances Landers, she welcomed a little light relief. 'Shall I bring Helen up first?'

Mary held up a hand. 'You can't leave the counter without an assistant, so would you ask Miss Sutherland if she would try and run the two counters for half-an-hour with the help of Miss Porter?'

Helen was mystified when told she was wanted by Miss Ormsby, and even more mystified when Ginny was put on the haberdashery counter for the time she'd be away. Under the watchful eye of Miss Sutherland, of course. But Helen wasn't even given the chance to ask questions, only time to shrug her shoulders at Ginny to show she hadn't a clue what was going on, and then she was stepping smartly after Miss Harper.

Across the aisle from Dorothy Sutherland's leather goods counter was the jewellery counter which Ginny thought was wonderful, a real Aladdin's Cave. There were rings, ear-rings, brooches and bangles, all shining with coloured glass stones. The rings went from a penny each to sixpence, and they were real bobby dazzlers. The senior assistant there was Margaret Sullivan – a proper live wire and always on the go. Even when she wasn't doing anything, she looked busy. She had been watching the goings on with mounting excitement, and as soon as Miss Harper was out of sight crossed the aisle like a bullet from a gun. 'It rather looks as though the rumour is true. I pooh-poohed the idea at first, but it seems I could be wrong.'

'What rumour is this, then?' Dorothy asked. 'I haven't a clue what you're talking about.'

'Oh, haven't you heard? The shop's been buzzing with it! Apparently, Frances Landers told one of the girls she'd been offered a job with more money and she was taking it, leaving right away. As I said, most people didn't believe it, but there must be something going on or why would they be taking Helen up to the office?'

'I haven't got a clue, Margaret, but we'll find out as soon as she gets back. As for the queer one, I won't miss her if she has left. I couldn't stand the woman.' Dorothy didn't want to get too involved, so she cut the conversation short. 'You've got two customers, Margaret, and I've got to keep my eye on Ginny.'

It was twenty minutes before Helen came back, accompanied by

Miss Harper. She looked as though she was walking in a dream, but with a broad grin on her face and her eyes shining, it was a very happy dream. 'Can I tell Miss Sutherland, please? It won't take me a minute. I've got to tell someone or I'll burst.'

Miss Harper didn't have the heart to refuse. 'You've got one minute, Miss Bleasedale, because, as you know, I have to take Miss Porter upstairs.' She tried to keep the smile from her face when she heard the shrieks of delight from the next counter. As a senior staff member she wasn't encouraged to get too friendly with the staff on the shop floor, but right now she envied the closeness of the two women who were hugging each other.

'Why does Miss Ormsby want to see me?' Ginny asked, giving a few skips to keep her feet in line with Miss Harper's. 'I'm not in trouble, am I?'

'I'm not in a position to tell you, Virginia, but I can't believe you would do anything to get yourself into trouble.'

When Ginny saw a man sitting in the office, she told herself she must be in for a lecture of some description if one of the big bosses was involved. But before she had time to worry, the door opened and Miss Halliday came through, followed by Marie. The two girls stared at each other in surprise, but because of the company they were in, they were too shy to acknowledge each other.

'Don't look so afraid, girls, there's no cause for alarm. Quite the opposite, in fact.' Oh, how Sarah Ormsby was going to enjoy this. It would more than compensate her for what had happened earlier. 'This is Mr Sanderson, our Managing Director. Mr Sanderson, may I introduce Miss Virginia Porter and Miss Marie Whittaker?'

Clive jumped to his feet and solemnly held out his hand. 'How do you do, Miss Porter? I am very pleased to meet you.'

His gentle voice and kindly eyes calmed Ginny's racing heart. She smiled. 'And I'm very pleased to meet you, Sir.'

Marie followed her friend, smiling and repeating what she'd said. But while Ginny might have had an inkling that she was here because of Miss Landers, poor Marie didn't have a clue and was expecting the worst.

'I won't ask you to sit down because this isn't going to take long. Come and stand either end of my desk, please, Miss Halliday has something to say to you.'

Mary Halliday was grateful to Sarah Ormsby for giving her this privilege, and with Clive Sanderson and Miss Harper also looking on, said, 'I have some news that I think will please you very much. Firstly,

Virginia, you will be staying on leather goods with Miss Sutherland. Would you be happy with that?'

'Oh, I'll be made up, Miss Halliday.' Ginny laced her fingers together and held her hands to her chest. With a beaming smile, she told them, 'Me and Miss Sutherland get on well together, she's really nice to work with.'

'Good,' Sarah Ormsby said, 'we thought you would be happy with those arrangements.' She glanced sideways to where Marie was standing, her eyes showing she didn't know whether being here was a good thing or a bad. 'And now we come to you, Marie. Your good friend Virginia told me recently about how you have been brushing up on your arithmetic as you want very much to become a counter assistant.'

That didn't sound like trouble so Marie giggled. 'Did she tell yer me dad set me sums every night and she had to check them the next morning 'cos he seldom got them right? And coming to work on the tram, she gives me sums to do in me head. And I am getting better, Miss, I really am.'

'I'm sure you are, Marie, I'm sure you are.' Mary Halliday's smile told how pleased she was. 'Now, Miss Ormsby has something to tell you.'

'Because of Virginia's recommendation, Marie, and Miss Halliday's, we would like to offer you the position of junior counter assistant.'

It took a few seconds to sink in, then that wonderful smile covered Marie's face as she rushed around the desk to hug Ginny. 'Ooh, ye're a good pal, Ginny, I won't ever forget yer for this. I'll mug yer to a bar of chocolate when I get me wages at the weekend.' Her laughter came from her heart. 'Only a penny bar, mind, so don't be expecting a tuppenny one.'

The office had never known such laughter as the two friends clung together. Their joy rubbed off on those watching. If the truth were known, the three women all had lumps in their throats and if it weren't for the Managing Director sitting there, they would have shed tears of joy. Little did they know that Clive Sanderson too was very moved by the scene. Up in his office he saw little of what went on, hardly ever met any members of the shop staff, and he lived a lonely quiet life when he got home. Seeing these two young girls being made so happy by such a small change in their lives made him consider his own.

'Marie, you will not be going back into the stock room. We have promoted Miss Bleasedale to senior counter assistant and you will go on haberdashery as her junior. Miss Harper will take you down and introduce you to her, before informing the stock room of the change. Any problems, please discuss them with Miss Halliday. And now you may go and start your new job as junior counter assistant. I am sure you'll do very well.'

The two girls stopped at the office door and turned around. Ginny spoke for both of them. 'We haven't really thanked you, but we both want yer to know how grateful we are. And we won't ever let yer down.'

After they'd left, Mary Halliday stood up. 'I'd better get down and see how things are but I have thoroughly enjoyed the last part of this afternoon. I hope my sleep won't be interrupted tonight with nightmares over Frances Landers as it was last night.'

Clive pushed himself off his chair. 'I'll come out with you, Mary. And I second what you said. It has been an enjoyable experience for me, too.' When he grinned he looked a lot younger than his years. 'I've got a feeling those two young ladies will go on to be senior assistants, and then who knows how far they'll climb after that?'

Out in the corridor, he walked with Mary towards his office. 'I rather think I would enjoy spending more time on the shop floor, I really should know more about the staff and the work they do. I bet there's not one person working down there who has ever seen me or even knows I exist. Perhaps you would take me around one day, when you have time to spare? We could do it on a regular basis, say once every month or so. Then I could get to know the staff, and they could get to know me. Do you think that's a good idea, Mary?'

Her heart was pounding in her chest. A good idea? She thought it would be a marvellous idea to see this man more often. She wouldn't start getting her hopes up or be childish about it. Just seeing him and being in his company would suit her fine.

'I think the staff would appreciate it, Mr Sanderson. Yes, I believe it's a jolly good idea.'

Chapter Twenty-Two

It was a quarter to four and Beth was in the kitchen peeling potatoes when she heard the knocker. Wiping her hands down the front of her pinny, she hurried through the living room, muttering, 'Who the heck can this be? They're not getting in, anyway, no matter who they are, or I'll never get the dinner on.'

When she opened the door to find Flo standing on the pavement, she sighed in exasperation. 'Oh, not you again! This is the third time today, anyone would think yer had no home of yer own to go to!'

Flo was wearing a floral cotton dress which was stretched tight across her mountainous bosom and tummy. The short sleeves were straining at the seams and digging into her flesh. The little woman shook her head and put on her sad clown's face. 'D'yer know what, girl? Yer other friends mightn't like telling yer this, but I will. The older yer get, the less neighbourly yer are. Years ago, yer would have opened the door to me with a welcoming smile on yer face as though yer were really glad to see me. Now look at the clock on yer, it's enough to turn the milk sour.'

'I had a welcoming smile on me face this morning, sunshine, when yer came for yer usual cup of tea. And I had a welcoming smile on me face when yer called for me to go to the shops! In fact, Florence Henderson, the ruddy muscles in me face are sore with all the flaming smiling I'm doing! Now will yer just tell me what yer want this time, then I can get on with peeling the spuds?'

'D'yer mean ye're not even going to ask me in? That yer'd treat a bleedin' dog better than what yer would me?'

Beth frowned. 'In the name of God, where does a dog fit into all this?'

'Ah, yer've got a bad memory when it suits yer, girl, but I haven't. And I remember a few years back, yer said yer wouldn't even leave a dog standing on yer step in bad weather.'

Beth looked at the bright blue sky and the golden sun shining down. 'I don't think yer'd call this bad weather. And besides, that was the

271

middle of winter, when the snow was thick on the ground and Mrs Harcourt wouldn't open the door to her husband because he'd come back from the pub rotten drunk. It was just a figure of speech, yer daft nit, I didn't mean it!' Beth threw up her hands and stepped aside. 'Oh, I give in, what's the use! Otherwise yer'll keep me talking until Andy comes home from work to no dinner on the table.'

Flo was in like a shot. 'The girls are out playing, I've got me pan of hotpot simmering on the stove, and I felt like a bit of company.'

'Well, yer can stand in the kitchen and watch me peel the spuds so I can get the dinner on the go. The mushy peas are done, they only need warming up, and the sausages don't take that long to fry.'

'I thought yer got stewing meat for a hotpot, same as me and Dot?'

'Yeah, I did get stew, sunshine, but we're having it tomorrow. I just fancied sausages and mash with mushy peas.'

Leaning back against the sink, her arms folded and lost to sight under her bosom, Flo watched her friend pick up the potato knife. 'It's only about another six weeks before our Amy leaves school. That'll mean a few extra bob a week, I won't know I'm born. Mind you, I'll have to fork out for new clothes for her, she can't go after a job in her gymslip.'

'Try Mary Ann at the market, her and Sadie will fix yer up. I could do with getting a few things meself, for Ginny and Joey, but I never seem to have any spare cash.' Beth turned the tap on over the pan and swirled the potatoes around to clean them. 'The worst thing I ever did was borrow that pound off Ma Maloney. I've paid her sixteen shillings in interest, and only ten bob off the loan! She must be coining it in, and off people who can't even make ends meet.' She lifted the pan on to the gas ring before wiping her hands on the piece of towelling on the drainboard. 'I'm having a struggle to pay her back, but at least we're not on the poverty line. Not like some poor buggers I've seen with her. I know a couple of them have got a gang of kids, three or four at least, and only their husband's wages coming in. They'll be in debt to that witch for the rest of their lives, and most of them are so thin they look haggard and half-starved. And they look twice their age! I don't know how that woman has the heart to steal money off people like that because the interest she charges is stealing, and she shouldn't be allowed to get away with it. I don't know how she can go to bed at night and sleep, I know I couldn't.'

'Ah, yes, girl, but the difference between you and Ma is that you've got a heart and she hasn't. I told yer in the beginning that she was as tough as an old boot. I still owe as much as you, but I think Dot and

Lizzie are just about out of her clutches. But then, they've both got three wages coming in.'

'Hannah did the right thing by telling Claire early on about the loan. A few weeks after she started that job in Sayers, Claire paid it off in full. It spared Hannah having the worry of it, and it saved them quite a lot of money in interest.'

Flo's chins agreed with her nodding head. 'And it saved you the worry, too, girl! Knowing you, I bet yer'd have worried yerself sick over Hannah. That's your trouble, yer know, girl, yer take everyone's troubles on yer shoulders.'

'I can't help the way I'm made, sunshine, and I'd rather be like that than like Ma Maloney. Who the hell gave her that name, anyway? If yer didn't know her, and someone said Ma Maloney, yer'd expect to see a motherly woman who was kind and gentle, not someone who'd take yer last ha'penny and see yer starve.' Beth popped her head around the kitchen door to see the time on the clock on the mantelpiece. 'Now I don't want to seem un-neighbourly, and please note that I have a smile on me face, but it's not a smile of welcome, it's a smile of goodbye. I would very much like yer to make yerself scarce, sunshine, so I can get on with the dinner.'

Flo moved slowly towards the door. 'Ah, well, it's passed half-an-hour away, so I suppose I can't moan even if it hasn't exactly been half-an-hour of fun.' She held on to the door frame while she stepped down on to the pavement. 'I'll see yer in the morning, girl, unless something happens that yer think will liven me up. In the event of that happening give me a knock on the wall.'

'Don't hold yer breath, sunshine, 'cos the likelihood of any excite-ment is pretty remote. In fact, I don't think me heart would stand the strain.' Beth began to close the door. 'See yer in the morning, but not before ten, please. Give me a chance to wake up.'

After leaving Marie, Ginny couldn't get home fast enough. She ran like the wind, and by the time she reached her door she had a pain in her side and was gasping for breath. When Beth opened the door, it was to find her daughter doubled up. At first she thought there was something wrong and she was filled with concern. 'Oh, what is it, sunshine, are yer not feeling well?'

'I've been running, Mam, that's all, there's nothing wrong with me.' Ginny pressed at the stitch in her side. 'In fact it's been a wonderful day, one of the best I've ever had. That's why I was rushing home – to tell yer about it.'

Beth smiled, thinking how good it was to be young, when nice things happened to make you feel on top of the world. 'Come in and sit down, sunshine, and when yer've got yer breath back, yer can tell me all about it.'

Ginny put a clenched fist on the table and took a few deep breaths before saying, 'Oh, Mam, yer'll never in a million years guess what's happened!'

'Wouldn't yer like to wait until yer dad gets in? He'll be here any minute and it would save yer going over it again.'

'Ah, no!' Joey said with disgust. 'She doesn't have to wait for me dad, she can tell us now, save us being on pins.'

'There's no need, yer dad's here now, I've just heard his key in the lock.'

Andy walked in to find three pairs of eyes on him. His deep brown eyes twinkled. 'I am in the right house, aren't I? Only yer've all got funny faces on yer.'

'We can't help having funny faces, can we, love?' Beth said, sending him that special look that told him she loved him, while ruffling her son's hair. 'Especially as this young man is the spitting image of yer. If he's got a funny face then it doesn't say much for you, does it?'

Ginny was moving impatiently from one foot to the other. 'Come and sit down, Dad, I'm dying to tell yer all what went on in work today.'

'Just hang on until I lower the gas under the frying pan otherwise yer'll be getting burnt offerings for yer dinner.' Beth hurried through to the kitchen and was back in a flash. 'Don't bother washing yer hands yet, Andy, do it later. Otherwise our Ginny will burst a blood vessel if she doesn't get it off her chest soon.'

When they were all seated and agog with interest, Ginny felt very important. 'Before I start, I've got to say that what I tell yer mustn't go any further than this room.' She eyed her brother. 'D'yer think yer can keep a secret, Joey?'

'Of course I can!' He tutted in disgust. 'I'm not a flippin' girl, I know when to keep me trap shut.'

Ginny eyed each of them in turn, then said in a very dramatic voice, 'Miss Landers got the sack today.'

She got the response she was hoping for. Beth's hand flew to her mouth as she gasped, 'Go 'way, sunshine, how did that happen?'

'Not before time,' Andy said. 'She's had it coming long enough.' He snorted, 'I can't abide liars or thieves.'

Joey had never met Miss Landers, he only knew she'd made his sister very unhappy and for that reason he didn't like her. 'I'm glad she

274

got what was coming to her. She was wicked, she was.'

Ginny didn't know any of the details of what had transpired in the Personnel Office, and never would. Only the senior members of staff were privy to that information, and that's how it would stay. 'A rumour went around the shop that she'd told one of the assistants she'd been offered a better job, with more money, and she was taking it. She was being allowed to leave straight away without having to serve her two weeks' notice. Everyone was talking about it, and they all believed her because no one knew anything about her stealing, only Miss Sutherland, Helen and me. And we wouldn't say anything, and we never will. I haven't even told Marie! She doesn't know she only got her transfer 'cos Miss Landers got the sack. I didn't like the woman, she was horrid, but she did Marie a good turn.'

'Yer've lost me now, sunshine,' Beth said. 'What's Marie got to do with all this when she works in the stock room?'

'Oh, well, Mam, a lot of things happened quickly once Miss Landers had gone. Helen Bleasedale was sent for by Miss Ormsby, and when she got to the office she was told she was being made up to senior assistant on haberdashery, even though she's only eighteen. All the other seniors are much older, but Helen is a really good worker. When she came back after being told the good news, I was sent for. It was only to tell me I would be staying on leather goods with Miss Sutherland, but Miss Ormsby told me that because I had told them once that Marie was doing homework every night to get her sums up to scratch so she could apply for a job behind the counter, they were going to take her out of the stock room and make her junior assistant to Helen. And they let me stay in the office when they told her.'

This news was greeted with smiles all round because Marie had become a great favourite with the family and with all their friends. 'Oh, I bet she was over the moon,' Beth said. 'And I'm really glad 'cos she's a smashing girl.'

'Ooh, I nearly forgot to tell yer, there was one of the big bosses in the office as well. He stood up to shake hands with us. I think his name was Mr Sanderson, but I was so shy and me hands were shaking so much, I could have got it wrong.'

Andy was delighted for his daughter. 'So, mixing with the big wigs, eh?' He laughed. 'It's been quite a day for yer, love, and yer deserve it for being honest and having the guts to let everyone know.'

Ginny giggled. 'Marie's gone home wagging her tail. She said she couldn't feel her feet on the ground 'cos she was walking on air. And she's promised to buy me a slab of Cadbury's for recommending her for the job. But it'll only be a penny bar, mind, so I'm not to expect a tuppenny one.'

Beth was chuckling as she got to her feet. 'I can just see her face as she said that. I bet her smile was a mile wide. Anyway, I'll have to see to the sausages or they'll be burnt to a cinder. But I'm glad it's all come right for yer, sunshine, 'cos I know yer've been worried. And I'm glad for Marie, too, she's a really nice girl.'

Ginny followed her into the kitchen. 'She's coming round tonight, Mam, so yer'll get to hear it all over again. And there'll have to be a meeting of the gang, 'cos she's dying to tell Amelia and Joan.'

'She's got every right to be proud, sunshine, so let her enjoy it.'

Ginny's laugh was loud. 'Mam, you try and stop her!'

The four friends were leaning against the wall which ran between the Porters' house and the Flynns'. It was a lovely evening, too nice to be indoors, and all the girls were wearing floral cotton dresses. Amelia showed her pleasure at Marie's news, just as they had a few weeks ago when she'd told them she'd been taken off washing the jam jars at Hartley's and put in the department where the jars were filled with jam. It was a much better job, the extra shilling a week very welcome.

Joan was trying to be enthusiastic because her brother had told her she was becoming a right pain in the neck the way she was always putting people down and being sarcastic. Deep down she really liked Marie, but she was jealous of the growing friendship between her and Ginny. They saw a lot of each other, travelling to work together and sharing their break times, and with Marie coming round every night now, Joan was beginning to feel pushed aside. But conscious of her brother's remarks, she put a smile on her face. 'I'll have to get a job at Woolworth's meself, then we can be like the girls we saw in that picture, "The Three Smart Girls".'

'I thought yer were quite happy with yer job at Dunlop's?' Ginny said. 'Ye're always saying what a good laugh yer have, and the lads there are very good-looking.'

'Yeah, they're all right.' Joan's face became animated. 'Ay, one of them asked me for a date. And he kept giving me the eye until me dad told him I was only fourteen. The lad hasn't looked at me since, me dad must have frightened the life out of him.'

'Yer are a bit young to go dating,' Marie said. 'My mam would kill me if she thought I even looked sideways at a lad. How old was the one yer were talking about anyhow?'

Joan shrugged her shoulders. 'About seventeen or eighteen, I guess.'

Amelia pulled a face. 'That's far too old for you, Joan! Would yer have gone out with him if yer dad hadn't said anything?'

'Chance would be a fine thing!' she said, tossing her head. 'Our David said if I kept flirting with the lads, I'd get a name like a mad dog. I only have a laugh and joke with them, and I don't call that flirting. But yer know what me brother's like, he's a proper stick-in-the-mud.'

'No, he's not!' Ginny wasn't going to let Joan criticise David behind his back. 'He's a nice lad is David, and he's right. If yer do play up to the fellers in work, yer will get a bad name. You might think it's just being friendly and having a laugh, but the fellers might not see it that way. And it would be embarrasing for yer dad and David.'

'Oh, blimey, I'm getting a lecture off you now! Ye're not me mother, Ginny, and yer can't tell me what to do.'

'I can't tell yer what to do, but I can give yer my opinion. It's a free country and I'm allowed to speak me mind.'

Oh, dear, Amelia thought, there's going to be a right argument here. And all over nothing really, only Joan being big-mouthed as usual. Then she saw a welcome sight. 'Here's our Bobby coming up the street. He's going out with the two O'Leary boys and David.'

Just a mention of boys and Joan was interested. 'Oh, aye, where are they off to?'

Amelia shook her head. 'I dunno, I didn't ask. Probably to the flicks or just for a walk. Ask them yerself.'

Bobby smiled across and waved before knocking on the O'Learys' door. Mick and Seamus must have been watching for him, the door was opened right away. 'Joan, will yer go and tell your David?' he called. 'Save us waiting.'

When the three lads crossed the cobbles, they stood by the girls. 'Is this a mothers' meeting or are young men invited?' Mick's Irish eyes were full of mischief. 'Women always seem to have more to talk about than men, I wonder how that is?'

His younger brother Seamus gave him a dig in the ribs. 'Yer know why, 'cos me mam's told yer often enough. All girls are born talking, and they don't know how to stop.'

Ginny pulled a face at them. 'We had something nice to talk about tonight, so there! And you can do yer share of talking, Seamus O'Leary.'

'Aren't yer going to tell us what it was?' Bobby looked from one to the other. 'Take no notice of Seamus, 'cos us lads are only jealous that girls have far more to talk about than us. Work and football, that's as far as we go.'

'And the pictures,' Mick reminded him. 'We talk plenty when we've seen a good murder mystery or a Tarzan film.'

David and Joan came out to join the group. 'Our Joan said yer've had some good news today, Marie, but she wouldn't tell me what it was. So out with it.'

For all her wide smile and dancing eyes, Marie blushed. David had that effect on her. If any of the other boys had asked she wouldn't have turned a hair, but where David was concerned she thought he was that little bit special. 'I've been promoted to junior counter assistant, I don't work in the stock room after today.'

'That's what yer've been after, isn't it?' Mick asked. 'Well, I'm very pleased for yer, and I think it calls for a celebration. What d'yer say?'

'Blimey, anyone would think she'd got a supervisor's job or some-thing!' The second the words left her mouth, Joan regretted them, and she could tell by the faces around her that they thought her remark was uncalled for. 'I didn't mean it to sound the way it came out. I'm made up for Marie, really.'

Mick rubbed his hands together. Although there was a smile on his face, his words were serious. 'Then I think yer'd be doing yerself a favour, Joan, if yer got yer brain in motion before yer mouth. Then yer wouldn't upset people.'

'That's my sister for yer,' David said. 'If ever there was a big mouth, it's her.'

Ginny thought her friend had been out of order, but Joan looked so miserable she had to help her out. 'Ay, don't all be picking on me best mate, I won't have it.'

'Me neither,' Marie said, also feeling sorry for the girl who she knew was jealous of her friendship with Ginny. 'We girls have all got to stick together in times like this. So instead of wasting time pulling our mate to pieces, what was this yer said about a celebration?'

Mick grinned. 'Well, I wasn't thinking about a party. And we can't go to a pub 'cos we're too young, and haven't got that sort of money anyway. But me and the lads are going for a walk to the park, seeing as it's such a grand night. And on the way we intend calling into that shop on Stanley Road, the herbal shop, for a drink of dandelion and burdock. Ye're all more than welcome to come with us.'

'I haven't got no money,' Joan said. 'And me mam won't lend me any 'cos I already owe her tuppence.'

Mick bit on his bottom lip before saying, 'I'll pay for your drink, it'll be worth it to stop yer from talking.'

'Ay, you!' Joan clenched her fist and was about to shake it in his face when she saw the gleam in his eyes. 'Right, I'll let yer pay for me drink for being so cheeky.'

'I haven't brought me purse with me.' Marie was red-faced with embarrassment. 'But that doesn't mean the others can't go.'

'I'll pay for yours,' David offered, even though he'd have to borrow the tram fare to work the next morning off his dad. 'It's only a penny a glass.'

'I'll pay yer back tomorrow night, then.'

David shook his head. 'Yer will heckerslike.'

Amelia felt in her pocket to make sure the two pennies were still there. 'I'm all right, I've got coppers on me.'

Seamus was a quiet lad, not as outgoing as his brother. But then Mick had had a year's start on him. Like David's, his voice was in the process of breaking, and when he spoke now it was deep and gruff. 'I'll pay for yours. Me mam would go mad if she knew we'd let a girl pay for herself.'

Bobby smiled at Ginny. 'That just leaves you and me, babe. Would yer do me the honour of allowing me to buy yer a glass of dandelion and burdock? Or, if you wish, you can have a glass of cream soda instead.'

'That would be nice.' Ginny returned his smile. 'But I'll have to tell me mam in case she wonders what's happened to me.'

'I'll tell me mam as well,' Joan said. 'I won't be a minute.'

And so it happened that when the four couples began to walk up the street, Beth and Dot were there to wave them off, and they were quickly joined by Lizzie, who had been watching the scene through her window. 'Well, will yer look at that now!' The Irish lilt was ever present. 'Sure, it's a sight for sore eyes, so it is.'

'That's the first time any one of them has been out on a date,' Beth said. 'I know they're only kids, and it's not a proper date, but I bet they feel all grown-up.'

'I wonder if any of them will pair off when they get a bit older?' Dot mused. 'It should be very interesting.'

Beth wagged her head from side to side. 'Oh, they'll probably be in and out of love dozens of times before they settle down with anyone. Especially when they start going to dances. But I hope they'll always be friends, and I think they will.'

'Sure, I'd be happy enough to have your Ginny for a daughter-in-law, so I would.' Lizzie quickly realised Dot wouldn't be very happy with that remark, so she added, 'Or Joan for that matter. And I'm sure Marie or Amelia would meet with our approval 'cos they're both nice girls.'

'Anyone who takes our Joan on will need nerves of steel. He'd have to be really tough with her 'cos she's a determined little faggot. She'll have her own way if it kills her.' Dot was grinning as she spoke. 'I was exactly the same at her age, always thought I was right. But I grew out of that when I started courting Bill. I know he doesn't look the strong masterful type, but he tamed me all right.'

Beth thought of Andy's handsome face and those gorgeous brown eyes, and said, 'That's what love does to yer.'

The herbalist's shop on Stanley Road didn't have chairs for sitting down. You could buy a glass of whatever concoction you fancied, and drink it standing up or leaning against the wall outside. There was a wonderful smell when you walked in, coming from the huge glass containers that stood on the counter and on the strong shelves that went halfway around the room. All the drinks were made from herbs and wild flowers by the dapper little man who owned the shop, and they tasted much better than the bottles of pop you could buy from the sweetshops. If you brought your own empty jug or bottle, you could have them filled with any flavour you liked, all for threepence.

The girls had never been in the shop before, but rather than show their ignorance they opted for dandelion and burdock, the same as the boys. On the walk to the park they all agreed that it was a very tasty drink, nice and cool, and they'd be going there again without a shadow of doubt.

Walking through the park gates, they could hear and see children playing on the grass while their parents sat on blankets, keeping a watchful eye on them.

'Ooh, doesn't it smell lovely?' Ginny said, sniffing the scent of early-summer flowers which were coming into full bloom, and the newly cut grass. She gazed with appreciation at the trees and bushes which were neatly trimmed. 'They keep the park looking nice, don't they? It's a shame we don't come more often.'

'Let's walk through to where the swings and see-saw are,' Mick said. 'Then we can walk around the lake.'

'When we're on our holidays at the end of July, we'll take yer in a rowing boat on the lake,' Bobby said to no girl in particular. In his head he meant Ginny, but he'd get his leg pulled soft if he said so. After all, she was only fourteen. No, she was fourteen and a half now. When Christmas came, she'd be fifteen, and perhaps by then she would have noticed him.

'Me and Marie don't get any holidays this year,' Ginny told him.

280

'Because we haven't been there long enough. So while you're all out enjoying yerselves, just think of us sweating away at work.'

'I get holidays 'cos the factory closes down for two weeks, but I won't get paid for them.' Joan clicked her tongue in disgust. 'Fancy giving yer two weeks off without pay! I'll be on holiday without a bean to me name.'

'Same here,' Amelia said. 'All the factories close down for those two weeks, otherwise I'd offer to go into work.'

'Me and the lads are going over to New Brighton one day.' David spoke to the group, but his eyes lingered longer on Marie. 'We won't forget yer, though, we'll bring yer a stick of rock back.'

'Ooh, yer kindness is killing me!' Joan wagged her head. 'Seeing as yer'll all be getting two weeks' wages, it wouldn't hurt yer to pay for us girls to go with yer.'

'Don't be so hard-faced, Joan!' Ginny was fuming. 'We can pay for ourselves if we want to go.'

'It's a good way off yet,' Marie said, 'we've got time to save up a few coppers each week if we want to go, and we don't want to tack ourselves on to the lads, we'd spoil their chances. They'd never get a click if we were with them.'

But Mick was chuckling as he led the group over to where the big swings were. Joan's tongue would get her into trouble one of these days. But at least you knew where you stood with her, she wasn't two-faced. 'Come on, girls, who wants a push on the swings?'

'Not me,' Amelia said, 'I don't trust yer and I don't fancy going over those top bars.'

'Yer can trust me,' Seamus told her. 'I won't push yer high.'

Amelia went first, and Ginny followed, to be pushed by Bobby. There were only three swings, and David took hold of the chains of the end one and held it steady for Marie. 'Come on, girl, ye're safe with me.'

There was a lot of laughing, Joan being the noisiest as she waited for her turn. 'Blimey, Ginny, can't yer go higher than that?' And, 'Marie, use yer legs and push! Honest, kids of five could do better than you.'

The three girls on the swings all had the same idea in mind, had they but known it. Just wait until it was Joan's turn and they'd rib her soft!

But they didn't get the chance because Joan was a real daredevil. Using her legs to push herself higher, she was coaxing Mick to push harder. With her long hair dancing in the breeze, she was loving every minute of it. When the swing came up to the level of the bar on top, those watching had their hearts in their mouth. Even Mick was

281

beginning to worry that she'd go over the top. But the girl herself was laughing with exhilaration, feeling as free as a bird. And when Mick decided enough was enough, and the swing slowed down, she was still laughing, and her eyes were shining with pleasure. 'Ooh, that was great! I felt like a bird flying through the air. Ooh, I could stay on all night.'

'Not with me pushing yer couldn't,' Mick told her. 'I had visions of yer really flying through the air, and I was thinking up excuses to tell yer mam and dad how we'd come to lose yer.'

'Let's go down to the lake now,' Bobby said. 'But will someone keep a tight hold on Joan in case she feels like being a fish and dives in?'

'Nah, yer don't have to worry on that score,' she assured them. 'I'm not partial to fish, unless it's battered and lying on a bed of chips. Anyway, I wouldn't want to get me next to best dress all wet.'

'Tell them the truth, Joan,' Ginny said, laughter gurgling in her throat. 'Yer look a sight when yer hair's wet, and there's no curling tongs down here.'

Joan pressed her nose close. 'Ay, ye're supposed to be me best mate. And best mates don't tell tales.'

Chapter Twenty-Three

It had been an idyllic summer for Ginny and her friends. On many a fine sunny evening they'd gone to the park with the boys or taken a tram to the Pier Head to watch the ferries coming and going. They'd been to the sea shore at Hall Road on a couple of Sundays, and it had been so much fun. None of the girls wore bathing costumes, they were too shy, but the boys all had swimming trunks and spent hours in the water showing off and playing tricks on each other. And when one of the lads was being pulled under, to come up spluttering, the girls would nod their heads at each other, as if to say they were glad they didn't have bathing costumes on 'cos sure as eggs Mick and the others would put them through the same torture. It was fun to laugh at another's misfortune, but they'd scream blue murder if it happened to them.

As summer had passed into autumn the gang still met together once a week, even if it was only to stand on the street corner talking about work and having a laugh. Then the boys had plucked up the courage to go to a dance in a local church hall, and they were full of it. Many a tale they had to tell of their prowess on the dance floor. They did invite the girls to go with them, but the four mothers decided they were too young. Perhaps they'd think about it again after Christmas when they'd be fifteen. Joan kicked up a stink about this, saying if she was old enough to go to work, she was old enough to go dancing. But Dot put her foot down in no uncertain terms. So when the boys went jazzing, the girls went swimming or to the pictures.

Then, as winter approached and the nights started to draw in, the gang went back to their once-a-week card nights. Not that they were so keen on cards, they spent more time laughing and pulling each other's legs. They were all good mates and good company. They took turns as to whose house to use, and the parents looked forward to the card nights and the laughs that went with them. Having youngsters in the house made them feel young again.

And now it was winter, with Ginny's birthday just a few weeks away, followed closely by Christmas. She'd worked at Woolworth's for eleven months now, and apart from the first few weeks, she'd loved every minute of it. Happy with her home life, her friends and her work, she was well content with life.

Dorothy Sutherland made Ginny start when she touched her arm. 'I don't know where your thoughts were, pet, but wherever it was it must have been nice because you had a smile on your face.'

'I was thinking I'd been here eleven months now, and the time has flown over. It's getting exciting with all the Christmas decorations going up. The shop looks really bright and cheerful. I missed all this last year because it was over by the time I started.'

'You'll be more tired than excited when we start to get really busy. I think next week should see the rush begin, with paper chains, tinsel and silver balls the main buys.' Dorothy let her eyes slide sideways, and there was a smile of affection on her face. She really was very fond of her junior assistant. 'You'll be too tired even to celebrate your birthday.'

'Oh, no, I will not!' Ginny sounded very definite. 'Yer see, we're going to celebrate three birthdays in one. Me, Marie and Joan, we're all fifteen within days of each other, so we're having one big party. Me mam said I can have it in ours, and the other mothers are going to chip in with food and things. 'Course, the trouble with having a birthday so near Christmas is yer lose out on a decent present.'

Two customers approached the counter and both assistants moved forward with a smile. Dorothy's customer wanted a man's comb in a leather case while Ginny's wanted a purse that had two compartments in. Both were for Christmas presents, the customers said, so the assistants patiently displayed the different coloured combs and purses they had in stock. Ginny was a good saleswoman. Handing the woman a black purse that had a pattern in cross stitching on the front, she said, 'I'm buying me mam one of these for her Christmas present. She likes to have two compartments, as well, and of course black goes with any coloured handbag.'

A woman came up behind the two others and poked her head between them. 'Only sixpence? That's dirt cheap, that is. I've just been over the road and purses exactly the same as that are four times the price.' She squashed herself nearer the counter. 'I'll have one of those, girl, for me mother. That'll be one present sorted out.'

'Would you hang on a moment, please, while I see if this lady is going to take the purse or not?'

'Of course I want it, I didn't need her to tell me how cheap they are.' The customer handed the purse back while her eyes threw daggers at the stranger. 'Wrap it up for me please, while I get the money out.'

284

Dorothy's customer had been listening with interest. 'I'll take the black comb set, dear, it's the best colour for men. And I think I'll take one of those purses, too, it'll make a good present for a lady friend. Would you please take the price tag off? There's no point in giving the game away. My friend is a bit of a snob so I'll tell her I bought it over the road.'

Ginny couldn't help but giggle. 'That's a fib.'

The woman actually smiled. 'I'm only doing the same as she does. Every time I go to the house she tells me how she always buys expensive things. Won't entertain cheap muck at any price. According to her, everything in her house has come from over the road, so the purse should feel quite at home.'

Left alone, Dorothy rubbed her hands. 'Three purses and one comb set, that's not bad going.' Then she whispered, 'Here come Miss Halliday and Mr Sanderson doing their usual weekly rounds. It's a pity they didn't come a few minutes earlier.'

'That's all right,' Ginny whispered back, 'we've got another two customers.'

'D'you think you can work a miracle and sell them three purses?'

Ginny was smiling broadly when the two bosses approached the side of their counter. She used to be afraid of them, but over the months she'd lost her fear and actually enjoyed talking to them. 'Good morning, Mr Sanderson, Miss Halliday. Would you mind if I help Miss Sutherland with one of the customers?'

Dorothy smiled in acknowledgement. 'I can manage, Miss Porter, you are free to talk.'

Over the last few months, Clive Sanderson's life had changed completely. He now spent a lot of time with Mary Halliday, which brightened his days, and he enjoyed coming into the shop and talking to the assistants. When he got home each night he was still alone, but now he had something and someone to think about. He could put names to nearly all the counter assistants, and knew the names of the people in the stock room.

'Miss Halliday and I have been watching you from a distance, Miss Porter.' Clive often thought that if it hadn't been for the honesty of this young girl, he would still be stuck in his office each day, with hardly any human contact. 'You did very well selling three purses when originally only one was asked for.'

Ginny giggled. 'Be careful, Mr Sanderson, or I'll be selling you one. Would you like a black one with two compartments, or a brown with a single compartment?'

285

'Alas, my dear, I have no one to buy a purse for. But if I did, I would most certainly buy one from you.'

Dorothy was free then, and came to join them. She never ceased to be amazed at the lighthearted way Ginny spoke to two of the most senior people in the store. She was never cheeky with them, though, she knew just how far to go, and they seemed to enjoy talking to her. 'Everything's fine, Miss Halliday, we've had quite a busy few hours. I think we will need more stock, though, especially purses.'

Much to Dorothy's surprise, Mr Sanderson asked, tongue in cheek, 'Would that be black with two compartments, Miss Sutherland, or the brown with one compartment?'

'Both, I think,' Dorothy told him, while thinking Ginny was right, he was a lovely man. And from the look on Miss Halliday's face, she thought so, too! 'Although the black do sell better. And I think perhaps we should have more comb sets in stock.'

Mary Halliday made a note on the paper on her clip-board before saying, 'We've been talking to Miss Bleasedale and apparently you and Miss Whittaker will be celebrating your birthday soon. Fifteen is a lovely age to be. I hope you both make the most of your youth while you can. Time has a habit of passing by very quickly.'

'Oh, we do make the most of it, Miss Halliday. Me and Marie have got loads of friends and we do enjoy ourselves.' Ginny's face became animated. 'We'll be going dancing after Christmas. It's only to a church hall, but that's fine by us because we've been told that everyone that goes is a beginner so we won't feel daft.'

'Somehow I can't see you or Marie ever feeling daft, you are both more likely to make a joke of it.' Mary Halliday looked up at Clive. 'I think we'd better be on our way, Mr Sanderson, it's almost break time.'

While Dorothy and Ginny were serving an ever-growing stream of customers, the head supervisor and the Managing Director were making their way up the stairs to the offices. They had reached the top corridor when Clive asked, 'Do you always have your break in Miss Ormsby's office or do you use the canteen?'

'It depends how busy I am. If I've time to relax, I will have it with Miss Ormsby and we discuss staff and sales. If I'm rushed off my feet I'll manage a quick cup of tea in the canteen.'

'And where do you stand today? Are you rushed off your feet?'

She did have lots to do, but something in his voice made her think twice about saying so. 'Let's say I'm not rushed off my feet, but I do have to get these orders to the stock room. As you know, most of the counters are running low.'

'How about sharing a pot of tea with me in my office?' There was a shyness about him when he asked, as though saying what he had had taken some willpower. 'I would be delighted if you would, it would be a change to have someone to talk to.' Then he looked down at the floor as though embarrassed. 'Of course you may not want to, Mary, and I would understand because I know your job keeps you very busy.'

If the shop had been running out of stock and there was a panic, or if it was on fire, nothing would have stopped Mary from saying, 'Oh, I can spare time to share a pot of tea with you, Mr Sanderson, but I do need to get these absentee figures to the wages office first. So while you order the tea, I'll nip along there.' And when she left him outside his office, she carried on down the corridor with a spring in her step.

'Will yer be going to the market one day, girl?' Flo asked, swinging her legs under the chair. 'We should be getting a bit in each week for Christmas.'

Beth nodded. 'Yes, but I can't go until Saturday afternoon when I get Andy's wages. Then again, it'll be packed on Saturday, so perhaps we'd be better waiting until a week day. What d'yer think, sunshine?'

'I think ye're probably right, girl, we'd get trampled underfoot on Saturday. Anyway, we'll ask Dot and Lizzie this afternoon when we go to the shops. Have yer got any money saved up, or are yer skint?'

'I've got a few bob saved, sunshine, which is better than I was last year. At least I don't have to go crawling to the Maloney woman.' Beth shivered. 'Even just thinking about her gives me the creeps.'

'Then I better hadn't tell yer what I heard this morning, girl, or yer'll blow yer top.'

Beth shook her head in disbelief. 'What d'yer mean, this morning? It's morning now!'

'I mean early morning, before the streets are aired.' Flo's chins quivered. 'Anyway, yer know our Wendy goes out the back way in the morning when she goes to school, 'cos it cuts a corner off? Well, I had some stuff to put in the bin so I went down the yard with her. And as I was waving her off, the woman what lives at the back of us, Mrs Graham, her yard door opened. And we got talking, like yer do, and she was calling Ma Maloney for everything under the sun. Yer think my language is bad, girl. Well, it's mild to what she came out with.'

'Don't tell me Aggie Graham borrowed off her? I thought she had more sense.'

'No, girl, she hasn't, but her neighbour has. Yer know the one with the four young children, Vera Duffy? Well, she lives every week hand to mouth, 'cos as yer can imagine it must be hard going keeping a husband and four kids on the money a bleedin' labourer earns.' Flo's bosom left the table when she took a deep breath, then when she blew out, it settled itself down again. 'Aggie was saying Vera borrowed a pound off Ma Maloney a few months ago, but couldn't pay it back. So what did the old faggot do? She gave her another pound loan on top. And now the poor woman is out of her mind because she doesn't stand a snowball's chance in hell of paying it back. She's up to her neck, and with the interest mounting up each week, she can't see any way out.'

'I've said all along that woman shouldn't be allowed to charge so much interest. Vera Duffy will owe her four pound now, not two. Someone should have Ma hung, drawn and quartered.'

'Aggie's quite worried about Vera. Said the woman was so frightened of her husband finding out, she was thinking of putting her head in the gas oven.'

Beth tutted while shaking her head. 'I think we should get a group of women together who've been stung by this she-devil, and frighten the life out of her. I'd be quite prepared to face her and say I'm going to report her to the police, but I would expect some back-up.'

'You can count on me, girl, I'd be delighted to see her get her comeuppance. And Dot and Lizzie will be right behind yer.' Flo had a sudden thought and banged one fist on the table. 'Aggie was saying there were a dozen women in her street who would willingly choke the moneylender, so I think between us we could get a small army together.'

Beth's eyes narrowed. 'This is what we'll do.' She told Flo of her plan and ended by saying, 'Don't forget, no one is to say a word to Vera Duffy. We don't want her any more worried than she is already.'

'And where do yer want us to meet tomorrow, and what time?'

'Outside here, at ten in the morning. And for heaven's sake, sunshine, don't tell your feller in case it gets back to Andy. He wouldn't be very happy if he knew what was going on.'

'My lips are sealed, girl, yer can rely on me.' The chair creaked ominously as Flo's bust and tummy began to shake. 'Haven't yer overlooked something? If I snitched on you, I'd be giving the bleedin' game away on meself! Now I might look daft, and I might act daft, but I'm not that flippin' daft in the head.'

'Don't I know it! Ye're as cute as a box load of monkeys, you are, sunshine!' Then Beth remembered something. 'Ay, your Amy's starting young, isn't she? I saw her talking to Seamus O'Leary in the street last night, and her mouth was going fifteen to the dozen. She takes after you for talking.'

'She's a damn sight worse than me! She can talk me under the table any day. She used to be so quiet until she left school, now we can't shut her up. It's going to work what's done it, it's brought her out of herself. Fourteen going on forty, that's her.' Flo jerked her head back and sent her layers of chins rippling. 'My Dennis says that if our Wendy turns out to be the same when she leaves school next summer, him and me won't be able to get a word in edgeways with the two of them at it. He's threatening to spend every night in the pub getting drunk, or packing a case and going to live in the Seamen's Mission.'

Beth chuckled. 'Yer've got to be a sailor before they let yer in the Seamen's Mission, sunshine, so he'd never get in.'

'I told him that, girl, but like everything else, he had an answer to it. He said it's easy enough to buy one of the peaked caps the merchant seamen wear, so he could mug himself to one of those and a navy blue reefer jacket.' This time the chair gave some very serious creaking and Flo's bosom and tummy lifted the table from the floor. 'I told him it would be cheaper to sell the girls off in marriage. You know, like they do in those foreign countries. Two camels and yer daughter's off yer hands.'

'Oh, yer might have a problem there, sunshine, 'cos I haven't seen no camels down Walton Road or County Road.' Beth was straightfaced. 'Mind you, that's not to say there isn't any, 'cos my eyesight's not what it used to be.'

'Oh, I thought of all that, girl, and I told him. But he said there's always a couple of stray cats in the entry, and if the men were foreign and didn't speak English, they wouldn't know the difference.'

Beth's head went back and she roared with laughter. 'Yer know, sunshine, you and your feller have some really intelligent conversations. Me and Andy couldn't keep up with yer, yer'd leave us standing.'

'That's only what we get up to in the living room, girl,' Flo said. 'Yer'd never guess what we get up to in the bedroom.'

Beth pushed her chair back with some speed. 'No, sunshine, and I don't want to know. That is strictly between you and Dennis. Now, will yer go and get yer coat because Dot and Lizzie will be here any minute.'

Flo's shoulders were shaking as she made her way to the door. 'I hope ye're not as shy in the bedroom as yer are downstairs, girl, or poor Andy must be a very frustrated man.'

'Out, woman, before I throw yer out!' When Beth closed the door on her friend she was chuckling inside.

'Shall I pour, Mary, or would you like to be mother?'

'I'll pour, Mr Sanderson, I'm not used to being waited on. Besides it's a woman's job, really, so you can sit and watch.'

'If I can call you Mary, why can't you call me Clive? I would like that very much.'

Mary Halliday cursed the blush she could feel covering her face. 'I don't think that would be right. You are my boss, and it would sound disrespectful.'

'Outside we can behave in a businesslike manner, Mary. But this is my private office, surely we can be friends while we're in here?'

'Of course we can be friends, inside your office and out. But I don't want to appear to be getting too familiar. What if I should slip up and one of the staff heard me?'

'Oh, would that be so terrible? I'm just an ordinary bloke, Mary, who would like to be your friend. It gets very lonely sitting here alone day after day, studying books and figures. The only time I have company is at the board meeting once a month. I meet Sarah, of course, and yourself, but usually the meetings are brief and we only discuss business. At least that's how it was for years until you suggested I took an interest in the shop and the staff. That has made such a difference to my life, and I am grateful to you. And now I am asking for one more favour from you. While we are in my office, please call me Clive.'

How could she refuse a man she had admired so much, for so long, from afar? 'If that is what you wish, Clive, then so be it.' Mary placed a cup of tea in front of him. 'I believe that is how you like it, not too strong and with milk and two sugars.' When he smiled and nodded she sat down and straightened her skirt over her legs before picking up her own cup. 'I'm going to enjoy this, I feel quite parched.'

'I'm not surprised, you have a very demanding workload. I had no idea the amount of work you put in until you were kind enough to introduce me to the workings of the shop and the stock room. On top of making sure the two departments run smoothly, you also have to keep a tab on absenteeism and breakages, etc. That is a lot of responsibility for one person, and I really feel we should take on another supervisor to take some of the weight from your shoulders.'

'Oh, no, that won't be necessary, Clive, I like to keep busy. A full day's work then when I get home in the evening, after making myself a meal, I'm ready to put up my feet and relax, listening to the wireless.' Mary, who wore her dark hair combed back into a businesslike bun in the nape of her neck, tilted her head. 'I don't want to sound inquisitive, but I know that like myself you live alone. Who caters for your needs, Clive, like keeping the house in order and cooking meals for you?'

'I have a housekeeper who's been with me for years. She doesn't live in, she comes to the house after I've left for work and keeps the place spotless. She attends to the washing, ironing and shopping. There's a hot meal ready for me every night, and after washing up, she goes to her own home. I really don't know what I'd do without her.'

'You live in a big house, do you?'

'Yes, a huge sprawling place, as big as a barn.' Clive placed his cup and saucer on the tray. 'You see, my father was a doctor and he needed a big house to have two rooms to use as his surgery and waiting room. Then, after he died, Mother refused to move, she wanted to stay there because it held so many memories.' He leaned forward and there was a boyish smile on his face. 'I really shouldn't be boring you with tales of my family, you must be finding it very dull.'

'Not at all, I find it interesting.' Mary felt light-headed to be actually sitting so close. This was something she would not have thought possible. And if it never went any further than sitting having a cup of tea in his office, she would be satisfied. 'What happened to your mother, did she die?'

'Good heavens, no! Mother is very much alive and living in a hotel for gentlewomen in Bournemouth. She decided to retire there after visiting a friend. I speak to her twice a week on the telephone, and I visit whenever possible. It is quite a distance to travel, and Mother understands why my visits are infrequent. But I don't really believe it worries her because she has made many friends down there and is very happy.'

'You do surprise me. I took it for granted that, like myself, you had lost both parents. But my home isn't a big sprawling place, it's very modest and easy to manage.'

Clive wasn't to know it, but his mind was running along the same lines as Mary's. It was such a pleasant change to be talking in a friendly manner with a member of the opposite sex. Particularly one as pretty as Mary. She wasn't in the full bloom of life, but neither was he, and he could never feel so comfortable with someone younger. 'Perhaps you would like to see my house? I could ask my housekeeper to make tea for us one day, perhaps on a Wednesday afternoon when we're both free? I would very much like that, but perhaps I am putting you in a difficult position where you would find it hard to refuse under the circumstances? Please don't be afraid to put me in my place, Mary, I would quite understand.'

There were many thoughts running through her head. What would the staff think if they found out? Then she steeled herself. Why couldn't she do what she really wanted to do without worrying about what other people thought? She had reached a stage in life when she must grasp what happiness came her way with both hands. And this was more happiness than she could ever have imagined in her wildest dreams. 'I would like that very much, Clive, thank you for asking me.'

The gentle smile that crossed his face sent her heart lurching.

There were fourteen women outside Beth's house the next morning at ten o'clock, and they were being very loud and vocal. A couple of them were known big mouths, and were talking black eyes, etc. Beth thought it best to put things straight before they started. 'Just listen for a minute, if yer will. We're doing this for Vera Duffy, who is terrified of her husband finding out about Ma Maloney. But she'd be even more terrified if she knew we'd caused trouble with the moneylender and fists were flying. She certainly wouldn't thank us for that. So I propose we approach the woman quietly and with dignity. Have I got your promise on that?'

Flo hitched up her bosom and nodded vigorously. 'Yes, yer have, girl, I've told everyone we don't want no trouble, or Vera *will* stick her head in the bleedin' gas oven. So we'll go along with whatever yer say.'

'D'yer know what ye're going to say?' Dot asked. 'Have yer got it planned in yer head?'

'Pretty much, but it all depends on what Ma Maloney says when she knows why we're there. She might tell us to sod off, or she might be understanding.'

'There's not much hope of that, lass,' one woman shouted. 'All that old devil understands is money.'

'We'll see how it goes and take it from there.' Beth took hold of Flo's arm, Dot took Lizzie's, and they led the way down the street and through two entries to the back yard of the moneylender.

Ma Maloney was standing by her door as usual, waiting for her customers. She was surprised when she saw the large group of women coming down the entry, but it didn't worry her, she thought they were taking a short cut to the shops. Even when they came to a halt and gathered around her door, she didn't think anything was amiss. Nothing to worry about, anyway. 'What the bleedin' hell are yer standing there for? Go on, sod off, the lot of yer, I'm waiting for someone.'

Beth lifted her hand to stem the growls she could hear behind her. 'We're here to talk about one of your customers and issue an ultimatum to yer. Vera Duffy – yer know her, don't yer? First yer lent her a pound, then when she couldn't pay it back yer lent her another one to get her even deeper in debt.'

'What's that got to do with you lot? That's between me and Mrs Duffy. Now bugger off, the lot of yer, and go about yer own business instead of sticking yer nose in mine.'

Beth's voice was deceptively quiet when she asked, 'Oh, yer haven't heard the news, then? I'm surprised someone hasn't told yer.'

'I don't listen to gossip. Now will yer bleedin' well get yerselves away from my door. Go on, scram.'

'The news I was talking about wasn't gossip.' Even if I have to lie, I'll take you down a peg or two, Beth thought. 'Yer see, Vera Duffy was so frightened of her husband finding out she'd borrowed money she couldn't possibly pay back that she tried to commit suicide by putting her head in the gas oven.'

Ma Maloney fell back a step and they heard her breath catch in her throat. It took her several seconds to recover, then she snarled, 'That's nowt to do with me. Now move while I close the door.'

Aggie Graham, who lived next door to Vera Duffy, shouted, 'Nowt to do with you! A poor woman with four young kids tries to kill herself and it's nowt to do with you? I'd like to get me hands around yer bleedin' throat, yer hard-hearted cow!'

'There'll be no fighting,' Beth said, but she had a strong urge to slap the woman across the face for the misery she'd brought to so many people. 'Yer lent her two pound but she owes yer four. Now I'm sure the police would be very interested to know the rates of interest yer charge, and also the threats yer make. In fact, ye're supposed to have a licence to lend money, and I have it on good authority that you don't have one. So, you have two options and I'm not threatening yer, I'm telling yer the truth. Yer can come to the police station with us, and every woman here can testify to the interest yer charge, or we can get them to come here. The second option is that yer forget about Vera Duffy's loan altogether. She won't owe yer a penny. But there are strings attached to that. You are not to tell her you were forced into action by us – she must never know we've spoken to yer or she'd be ashamed to lift her head in the street. Yer can make up some cock-and-bull story about yer feeling guilty about getting her into debt, with her having four young children.' Beth put her face close to Ma Maloney's, even though she found the woman repugnant. 'Or yer can say yer've had a win on the gee-gees, it's up to you. But yer'd better make it convincing, and yer'd better do it today. Otherwise, we'll all be back here tomorrow with a policeman. Suit yerself.'

Aggie Graham had to have the last word. 'I live next door to Vera, and I'll be watching out for yer. In fact, just to make sure, I might even go and sit with her until yer've been. She wouldn't think anything because I often go in for a cuppa or to mind the kids for her. Be there before twelve so she can enjoy the rest of the day without worrying about how she's going to pay yer back.'

The fourteen women didn't wait for a response. They knew Beth's words about Vera trying to commit suicide and the threat of the police were enough to put the fear of God into the moneylender. They turned as one, and marched back down the entry. No one spoke until they were out in the street.

Flo slapped Beth on the back with such force she nearly sent her flying. 'I'm proud of yer, girl, yer were brilliant.'

'Sure, yer never spoke a truer word,' Lizzie said. 'Yer did well, me darlin', and I'll bet money on Vera having a visitor within the next hour.'

Aggie Graham gave her a hug. 'Yer did great, girl, and I think it did the trick. I am so grateful to yer, 'cos I've been worried sick about Vera. I've been dashing in and out of her house by the minute, trying to keep an eye on her, and I haven't had a good night's sleep for weeks. But I'll get round there now, and as soon as the queer one comes I'll let yer know.'

When the women from the next street had left, Dot said, 'Come on in mine for a cuppa, girl, yer deserve one.'

Flo got on her high horse. 'Ay, I hope me and Lizzie are invited!'

Dot chuckled at the expression on the little woman's face. 'If I said yer couldn't come in, Florence, would yer take any notice of me?'

'Would I heck! I'd just push yer out of the way and be in the house before yer.'

Dot slid the key into the lock. 'I thought as much. So I might as well be gracious and invite yer in. But it's one custard cream for you and Lizzie, and meself, and two for the hero of the hour. That's as far as they'll stretch.'

The conversation around Dot's table centred on whether they thought Ma Maloney had been scared enough to do as they asked, or if she would force them to go to the police as they'd threatened. As Flo said, 'She's a funny bugger, that one, yer wouldn't know what she was going to do.'

'Oh, I think she'll see the light of day right enough,' Lizzie said. 'Lending money without a licence could see her going to jail, and she'll not be wanting that, not at all, at all.'

'Well, let's get to the shops and be back as soon as we can in case Aggie comes.' Beth began to stack the empty cups and saucers. 'I'll give yer a hand with these, sunshine.'

Dot shook her head. 'Leave them in the sink, I'll do them when I get back.'

But a rat-tat on the knocker had her racing to the front door. 'Come in, Aggie, the others are here.'

Her face was flushed, and she was so excited she couldn't get her words out quick enough. 'She's been! I was sitting in Vera's when she came, and heard every word she said. I couldn't believe me ears when she told Vera, like you said, Beth, that she'd had a win on the gee-gees and wanted to surprise one of her customers by giving them a present. And the two-faced cow said she'd decided that Vera was a worthy case, with her having four young children, so Vera needn't pay her the loans back, she could treat them as a present.'

Dot was pulling a cynical face. 'And Vera believed that?'

Aggie nodded. 'I know what yer mean, 'cos I wouldn't have fallen for it. But Vera did, and while she felt like being sick at first, with the shock, she was looking ten years younger when I left to come round here.'

'It doesn't matter that we wouldn't have fallen for the lies, as long as Vera did! That's the important part. And I hope no one will be daft enough to say there's something fishy about the whole thing. If they do, then they can take responsibility for Vera being ill again.'

'Beth, if anyone looks sideways at Vera I'll throttle them. I've watched that girl struggle to keep those kids clean, put clothes of some description on their backs and feed them to the best of her ability. She goes without herself to give to them, and she's like a ruddy skeleton. I've seen her walking round in the winter with big holes in the soles of her shoes and her hands and face blue with the cold.' Aggie wasn't talking for talking's sake, she meant every word of it. 'No one will hurt Vera Duffy if I've got anything to do with it, she's too nice a person.'

The four friends were quite moved by what Aggie had said, and they exchanged glances which said they'd help if they could. They didn't have much themselves, but they were living a life of luxury compared to that young woman with her husband and four young children to feed and clothe. Beth acted as their spokeswoman. 'We'll see what we can come up with to help the little ones out at Christmas, Aggie, even if it's only second-hand clothes. But we'll see yer before then, and thanks for coming to tell us the news, it's cheered us all up.'

'The thanks are all down to you, girl, the women in our street

295

thought yer were as good as a solicitor. Not that any of us has ever had a solicitor, but that's the way we'd expect him to act if we had one. And God will pay yer back for what yer did today, girl, you'll see.'

After Dot had seen Aggie out, the four friends looked at each other. It was Lizzie who said, 'Threepence a week from each of us for the next couple of weeks – that should buy a few things for the children for Christmas.'

Her three friends nodded. Then Beth said, 'We could have a word with Mary Ann and Sadie at the market, they might help us out.'

Flo threw out her chest. 'Well, not a bad day's work, even if I say it meself.'

Dot gaped. 'You haven't done nothing, it was Beth!'

'Ah, yeah, but she wouldn't have known nothing about it if I wasn't such a nosy bugger. It was me what started her on her way to becoming a saint, so I hope she doesn't forget that when she meets Saint Peter at the pearly gates. I'm going to need a very good reference if I'm to get into heaven, and my mate is the only person I know what can write a good letter and get the spelling right.'

Chapter Twenty-Four

'Mam, I've got a favour to ask of yer.' Ginny was facing her mother across the breakfast table. Her dad had left for work and Joey could be heard getting dressed for school. 'Yer've heard me and Marie talking about Pat, the girl who started work the same day as us? You know, she works on the cosmetics counter.'

Beth nodded. 'I've heard yer talk of her often enough, and I know you and Marie have made friends with her. Why do you mention her now?'

'We were wondering if we could ask her to the birthday party? She knows about it, 'cos we've been talking about nothing else for weeks, and we feel mean not inviting her.'

'Oh, sunshine, the place will be stretching at the seams if yer ask any more! Yer won't be able to move as it is. If ye're going to invite anyone else, I think it should be Amy from next door. Yer've known her all yer life, she's working now, and Auntie Flo will be really hurt and upset if yer leave her out. Flo hasn't said anything, but if I was in her position, and they were having a party next door and you weren't invited, I'd take it as an insult and be really hurt.'

Ginny took a deep breath and sighed. 'Ooh, I'd never thought of Amy, but ye're right, Mam, I should invite her. I'll give her a knock tonight when I get home from work.' Her eyes were pleading as she looked across the table. 'But can I ask Pat as well? Go on, Mam, say I can, please?'

Beth started to tick off the names on her fingers. 'By my reckoning, that's six girls and five boys. I'll have to borrow a couple of chairs from Dot and Flo.' Resting her chin on a clenched fist, she narrowed her eyes. 'Me and yer dad were talking about the party last night, after yer'd gone to bed, and we decided that if we put the couch under the front window and the table on the wall that would leave the centre of the room free.' She chuckled. 'That's just in case the boys ask yer to dance.'

Ginny was reckoning up in her head and frowning. 'Yer said five boys, Mam, but there's only four. David, Bobby and the two O'Learys.'

'Oh, aye, and what about yer brother? Have yer forgot about him?' Beth put her hand back on the table. 'And before yer say he's just a kid, remember that this time last year you were only a month older than he is now. He's fourteen a few weeks after Christmas, and with a bit of luck he'll be able to leave school before the Easter break. He will if he can get fixed up with a job, and yer dad's working on that now.'

Ginny was looking shamefaced. 'Oh, Mam, me own brother and I never gave him a thought. But that's because I live with him, and without really thinking about it, I must have taken it for granted that he'd be here because this is his home.'

'Well, mention it to him when he comes down. I don't mean give him an official invite, just a casual mention, like.'

'Yeah, I'll ask if he's looking forward to it.'

'Oh, he's looking forward to it, all right, sunshine, he can't wait!' Beth lowered her voice. 'Yer see, he's been putting tuppence of his pocket money away for the last three weeks so he can buy yer a pressie.'

'Go 'way!' Ginny was very much moved, and tears stung the back of her eyes. 'But he only gets threepence a week including the penny me Dad gives him.'

Beth cocked an ear to make sure the object of their discussion wasn't coming down the stairs. 'I'm not going to pretend he's been unselfish, denying himself for the sake of his sister. Me and yer dad have had many a laugh over it. He's only been able to buy one comic, so he's been cadging a loan of the other one off his mate so he can keep up with the daredevil antics of his heroes.'

'Ah, I'll make it up to him, Mam, honest. I'll buy him something really nice for Christmas, and his birthday.' Ginny leaned across the table, her bright blue eyes gleaming. 'What's he buying me, Mam, d'yer know?'

'If I did I wouldn't tell yer, sunshine, no matter how much yer coaxed. This is a big thing for him, he's gone without to achieve it, and I want to see his face when yer open it up. Oh, yeah, it's going to be wrapped up, he's not just going to hand it to yer. This will be done in a proper manner if it kills him.'

'Ooh, I feel terrible now, Mam. But I do love him, yer know, and when his birthday comes around I'll buy him something grown-up instead of comics or sweets.'

'Yer'd better buy him a decent present, sunshine, or yer won't get an invite to *his* party. He reckons if you can have a party, so can he.'

Ginny hunched her shoulders and giggled. 'And who is he going to invite to his party?'

'That is something I couldn't tell yer, sunshine. But I can tell yer who he most definitely *isn't* inviting – that's Amy from next door 'cos she never stops talking, and your mate Joan for the same reason. Then there's poor Jimmy, his mate. He's not setting foot over this door because he wouldn't lend Joey his comic when he'd finished with it.' A floorboard on the landing creaked and Beth put a finger to her lips. 'Here he is now, so not a word.'

'Just three quick ones, Mam. Can Pat come?'

'As long as she knows it's standing room only.'

Joey came down full of the joys of spring. 'What's this yer saying about standing room only, Mam?'

It was Ginny who answered. She'd have to be leaving for work in five minutes, and she didn't want to leave without letting her brother know she was thinking of him. 'Me mam reckons there'll be no room for everyone to sit at me party, but we'll manage. Are you looking forward to it, Joey?'

'Yeah, it'll be all right.' He wasn't going to get excited about it, only girls did that. 'But it's not just your party, what about gabby Joan and Marie?'

'Oh, I haven't forgot them, 'cos their mams are helping out with the food and things. But with it being here, in my house, I keep forgetting and saying it's my party. I can hardly say the three names every time I mention it.' Ginny drained her teacup before pushing her chair back. 'I'd better get cracking, I don't want to keep Marie waiting in this cold weather.' She gave Beth a kiss before putting an arm across her brother's shoulders and hugging him. 'It won't be long before ye're going out to work yerself, our Joey.'

His smile was so bright, it was as if the sun had come out. 'Yeah, that'll be the day, that will. I hope I can go to work with me dad, same as David and Mick work with theirs. I'll be wearing long kecks then, just imagine!'

'And very handsome yer'll look, too.' Ginny dropped a light kiss on his forehead. 'I'll be off. See yer tonight.'

When Beth had seen her off at the door, she came back into the room to find her son had helped himself to a slice of toast and was being very liberal with the raspberry jam. 'She's not bad, our Ginny, is she, Mam? She doesn't talk a load of rubbish like some I could mention.'

'Well, don't mention them now, sunshine, not with yer mouth full. I'll make us a nice pot of fresh tea to warm yer up before yer go out.'

'D'yer think me dad will ask his boss about me today, Mam?'

'He said he'd try, but don't get yer hopes up. It might be after

Christmas before any firm thinks about taking apprentices on.' Beth stood at the kitchen door with a hand on her hip. 'Anyway, sunshine, even if yer dad couldn't get yer taken on with his firm, a handsome, fine-built lad like you will have no trouble finding a job.'

Joey smiled as he bit into his toast. A compliment like that would keep him in a good mood for the rest of the day.

Ginny had just turned the corner into County Road when she heard her name being called. She looked towards the tram stop to see Marie jumping up and down and waving her hands, urging her forward as a tram trundled towards the stop. Ginny took to her heels and flew like the wind, jumping on the platform just as the conductor pressed the bell to tell the driver all was clear.

'I just made that by the skin of me teeth.' She took a second to get her breath back. 'It's full downstairs, let's go on top.'

The long seat at the back of the tram was their favourite spot, and they made their way to it, holding on to the backs of seats to keep their balance. 'I thought yer were going to miss it,' Marie said, plonking herself down by the window. 'What made yer late?'

'I waited for our Joey to come downstairs 'cos I don't want him to feel left out over the party. Being me brother, and living in the same house, I never gave a thought to talking to him about it. But me mam said I should, so I did. And I also had a word with her about Pat, which didn't take that long, but it was enough to make me a bit late.'

Marie had never before been to a party which was for girls and boys in their teens. The last she'd been to was years ago and there were only young kids there so she was getting very excited about Saturday when three of them would be celebrating their fifteenth birthday. 'What did yer mam say about Pat?'

'Yes, she can come,' Ginny was happy to say. 'As long as she knows it's a two-up-two-down we live in and it'll be rather cramped because the living room wasn't built to house parties of eleven people.'

Marie's eyes widened. 'Who are the eleven?'

So Ginny went through the list. Then she said, 'I wish I had a new dress for it, I've worn the ones I've got loads of times.'

'I'm getting a new dress for Christmas, but me mam won't let me have it before. So I'll be in one of me old ones, as well.' But Marie could never be downhearted for long. 'Anyway, it's not a posh do we're going to, is it? And if we did have a new dress on, we wouldn't enjoy ourselves 'cos we'd be frightened to move in it.'

'Yeah, when yer come to think of it, all the lads have only got the one suit and I bet they're not worried that we've seen them dozens of times.' Ginny fingered her long blonde hair which was fanned out on her shoulders. 'I'd like to do something with me hair, though. I might put some pipe cleaners in, see if I can get it to curl.'

Marie, whose mousy-coloured hair was thick and naturally curly, eyed her friend. 'If yer wet it with sugar and water before yer put them in, that will make it curly.' Then she had a thought. 'Have yer got any curling tongs?'

'I haven't, no. But one of the neighbours uses tongs so perhaps she'd let me borrow them. And if you came a bit early, yer could curl it for me.'

Marie's wide grin appeared. 'Ay, if yer think I'm going to help make yer look better than me, yer've got another think coming. Yer've got a head start as it is, 'cos they say that boys prefer blondes.'

They had the tram fare ready in their hands when the conductor came around, and after he'd clicked their tickets, they went back to the subject of the party which had been their main topic of conversation for weeks now. What shoes would they wear? Did they have a pair of stockings that didn't have a ladder in? Oh, there were so many things to discuss they forgot to keep watch on the places they were passing.

It was pure chance that Marie happened to take her eyes off Ginny's face for a second and noticed they were passing St George's Hall. She gasped and jumped to her feet. 'Come on, quick, the next stop is ours.' Lucky for them, there were a lot of people getting off in Church Street so they weren't taken past their stop. 'Thank goodness for that,' Marie said. 'If I hadn't turned me head when I did, we'd have ended up down by the Pier Head.'

'And here's me wanting to be early so we could have a few words with Pat. She's probably left the cloakroom by now.'

'There's no panic, is there?' Marie seldom got ruffled unless it was something really serious. 'We'll be seeing her at break time, yer can tell her then.'

'Yer know me, I want everything to happen right away.' Ginny linked her friend's arm as they walked through the store to the cloakroom. 'Have you said anything to yer mam about us going to a dance with the boys? She did say when yer were fifteen she'd think about it.'

'I haven't asked her. Why, have you asked yours?'

'No, I was waiting to hear what yours said.' Ginny undid the buttons on her coat and slid her arms out of the sleeves. 'If your mam said it was okay, then I think my mam would be more likely to agree.'

'How soft you are, letting me do all the dirty work! No, you can ask your mam first, then I'll butter mine up.' Marie glanced along the rail of coats. 'I can't see Pat's coat, it doesn't look as if she's in yet.'

'Who's taking my name in vain?' Pat came up behind Marie and laughed when the girl jumped. 'It just goes to show yer should be careful when ye're talking about anyone 'cos yer never know whether they're standing behind yer or not.'

'Oh, I'm glad ye're here,' Ginny said. 'Me and Marie want to invite yer to our birthday party on Saturday. Will yer come?'

'Oh, yeah, I'd be made up! That's lovely, that, thanks for asking me.' Pat hung her coat on one of the hooks, and when she turned there was a question on her lips. 'It's not a posh do, is it, 'cos I don't possess an evening dress?'

Ginny chuckled at the thought of anyone coming to their house in a long dress. It wouldn't half give the neighbours something to talk about. 'Me mam said to tell yer we live in a two-up-two-down, so there won't be enough chairs to sit on and it'll be standing room only.'

'Now I know I'm going to like your mam, she sounds really down to earth. So if none of the girls is wearing a tiara, I'd love to come.'

Miss Halliday's voice had them moving quickly. 'Come on now, ladies, it's time you were behind your counter, the doors will be opening in five minutes. Make haste, but do not run.'

When Ginny got to her counter it was to find Miss Sutherland busy filling up and making the counter look attractive. She smiled at her junior. 'I've got a feeling we're going to be very busy today so I hope you've got comfortable shoes on?'

'The shoes I've got on are the only pair I have, but they're comfortable enough.' Ginny dropped down on her haunches to pass items up as her senior asked for them. 'After Christmas me and Marie are going to save up and buy some decent clothes and shoes. Especially dancing shoes if our mothers say we can go to a dance.' Ginny's pretty face lit up when she said, 'I fancy silver ones meself, with high heels.'

'I have silver ones, but I don't wear them with a very high heel because I find them too uncomfortable to dance in.'

'Me and me mates won't be going to proper dances, like you, we'll be starting off at a small church hall where beginners go.' She handed up four tortoiseshell combs used by women who wore their hair in a bun or swept upwards in the modern fashion. 'Where's your favourite dance hall?'

'I like the Tower at New Brighton best, it's big and it's got a sprung floor. But my boyfriend is not keen on the travelling to get there, so we mostly go to the Grafton or the Locarno.'

Ginny straightened up to find two customers at the counter examining the purses. She smiled at one, leaving the other to Dorothy. 'Can I help you, Madam?'

After that there was a steady stream of customers and they were rushed off their feet. But Ginny enjoyed it because the customers all seemed to be in a happy frame of mind as they chose presents for family and friends. As Dorothy whispered: 'There's nothing makes a woman happier than spending money.'

Not all of the customers spent money; some of them were just browsers who'd come into town to while away a few hours. They'd pick up almost every item on the counter and examine it while the assistant looked on, hoping for a sale. Then, after wasting time, the woman would finally walk away without making a purchase.

Ginny found this very frustrating. 'I could have served six customers, the time I've spent with her.' She spoke softly out of the corner of her mouth. 'Every purse she asked me to open, then said she couldn't make up her mind and she'd come back tomorrow.'

Dorothy, with years of experience dealing with the public, took it all in her stride. 'There's nowt so queer as folk, pet, you'll find that out. Just keep a smile on your face and don't take it too much to heart.'

When the time came for Ginny's break, she offered to stay behind and help. 'It won't hurt me to do without a cup of tea. I can't leave yer on yer own, it's too busy.'

'Go and have your drink, I'll manage.' As she was talking, Dorothy was taking purses that were being handed to her to wrap, and working the till as well. She still kept the smile on her face. 'Not that I won't be glad to see you back, so don't be too long.'

When Ginny stopped at the next counter for Marie, it was to find they too were very busy and her friend said, 'I'm not coming today, Ginny. I don't like leaving Helen on her own with all these customers to serve, I'd feel mean. I'll see yer at dinner time.'

Ginny went back to leather goods. 'Me mate's staying, and so am I. It's only an hour and a half to lunch break, it won't kill me to wait until then.'

It was fifteen minutes to the lunch break when Miss Halliday stopped by the counter. 'I believe you and Miss Whittaker worked through the tea break, Miss Porter?'

Ginny glanced quickly at Dorothy Sutherland. She hoped her senior wouldn't get into trouble for this. But she couldn't tell a lie. 'We were so busy, Miss Halliday, we've been rushed off our feet. But I wanted to stay, even though Miss Sutherland said I should go for me break. I've enjoyed it, 'cos I like to be busy.'

'Well, things will be a little easier for the dinner break. I'm bringing a couple of women out of the stock room to help, even though they've never been behind a counter before. They will not be allowed to use the till, but they will be quite capable of serving and wrapping. It's very unfortunate that on such a busy day we have several staff off work with colds, but there is little we can do about it.' With a glance at the clip-board she was seldom seen without, she said, 'I'll be back in ten minutes with a temporary assistant.'

'Here, there's two front seats, let's grab them.' Beth took Flo's elbow and steadied her as the tram began to move. 'You get in by the window, sunshine, and try and squeeze up to make room so I can get at least half of me bottom on the seat.' She turned her head to smile at Dot and Lizzie who were seated behind. 'Let's all pay our own fare, save messing.'

'I hope Paddy's Market is not too busy,' Dot said, leaning forward. 'It would be nice if we could take our time looking at what Mary Ann has to offer.'

'Oh, yer'll not be able to do that today, me darlin', or any other day for that matter. From now until the shops shut on Christmas Eve, no matter where yer go, it's going to be packed, so it is.' Lizzie's nodding head confirmed that her mind was in agreement with her mouth. 'But I've got to say, I like the hustle and bustle at Mary Ann's stall, and that's a fact. She's quite a character, so she is, with the things she comes out with. Sure, her and Sadie make a good team the way they laugh and joke with the customers.'

Flo, pressed tight against the side of the tram, was terrified to move in case she sent Beth flying off the seat. So she kept perfectly still and raised her voice so Dot and Lizzie could hear what she had to say. 'I've got twelve shillings with me, and I'm hoping it stretches far enough to get everything I want.'

'I think we've all got about the same,' Dot said. 'And with a bit of luck and help from Sadie, we should be four happy bunnies on our way home.'

Flo's eyes slid sideways. 'Ye're very quiet, aren't yer, girl? Are yer going to tell us how much yer've got with yer, or is it a secret?'

Beth chuckled. 'About the same as yerself, sunshine, and there'd be no point in trying to keep it to meself when I'm going shopping with

304

yer, would there? Yer've got eyes like a flippin' hawk, they don't miss a thing. I bet that when we get home yer'll be able to tell me to the penny how much I've spent.'

'I'm leaving nothing to chance, girl, I've brought a piece of paper and a pencil with me, so I can write it all down.' Flo's whole body began to shake, causing Beth to grab hold of the bar in front. 'That's just to make sure yer don't get nothing cheaper than me. I know Sadie's got a soft spot for yer so I'm keeping me eyes open.'

The conductor came around then, dinging his ticket machine. 'I'm only paying yer a penny fare,' Beth said, ''cos I've only got a quarter of a seat. The queer one sitting next to me should be charged double on account of the size of her posterior.'

Flo took great exception to anyone making free with the size of her bottom, and she fairly bristled. 'Well, the flaming cheek of you! Anyone would think I was fat, and I'm really only a slip of a thing.'

Bill, the conductor, knew Flo of old, and was aware she was always game for a laugh. 'Yeah, my wife's clothes prop has got more flesh on it than you have, sweetheart.' He punched her ticket and handed it to her. 'And it's nicer looking.'

'You cheeky swine, Bill Stanton! Anyone would think yer were the spit of Ronald Colman to hear you talk. But yer look more like Frankenstein after he's had the operation!'

Dot held out her fare. 'I'm not saying a dickie bird, lad, in case yer wife's got a mop and I put yer in mind of it.'

He let out a loud guffaw. 'If my wife's mop looked like you, sweetheart, I wouldn't be coming out to work. The wife could get a job and I'd stay home and keep the mop company.'

'Take my money, lad,' Lizzie said, 'before yer think of something in your house that I resemble. I'm out for a day's pleasure, so I am, and I don't fancy being insulted.' She took her ticket then tapped Beth on the back. 'Next stop is ours, me darlin'.'

'Well, you two get off first, sunshine, and yer can help Flo down the high step. I'll carry her bags till she's off.'

When they reached the market it was to find it buzzing. The crowds around each stall selling new goods were three or four deep, and Beth sighed. 'Let's make for Mary Ann's first and come back here later. I'm hoping to get a decent dress for meself and one for Ginny. And I could do with a cardi to wear around the house when I let the fire die down. Standing in our back kitchen peeling spuds in this weather is like being in one of those countries yer see on the Pathé News where the people live in houses made of snow.'

'Ooh, I know what yer mean, girl, 'cos mine's the same.' Flo's hip knocked against Beth's as she swayed along. 'I know everyone thinks me fat should keep me warm, but the ruddy draught that comes under our kitchen door is enough to freeze a monkey's you know whats. It's that bad sometimes I have to hold on to the sink or I'd be blown over.'

'I know something worse than that, girl,' Dot said. 'And that's going down the yard to the lavvy. Honest to God, I keep crossing me legs, 'cos the thought of sitting down there puts me off. Mind you, I've got to go in the end, but I bet no one has ever spent a quicker penny than I do on a winter's day.'

They pushed their way through the heaving crowd, with Flo and Beth in the lead. As they neared the stalls they were heading for, they heard a loud burst of laughter. So loud, it could have come from the Kop at Anfield football ground when Liverpool had scored a goal. 'Just listen to that,' Beth said. 'I'm laughing meself and I don't even know what the joke is.'

They walked to the trestle table at the far end, where they always stood because it was less crowded. Then they saw the cause of the laughter – Mary Ann and Sadie were doing an Irish jig in the clearing in the middle of the stalls, and as her legs were moving with some speed, the stallholder was shouting, 'Yer can all hold yer bleedin' horses while we get some circulation back in our feet. But don't think me mind is frozen like me toes, 'cos I can still see what's going on.' After a nifty twist, with Sadie's pretty face lit up, Mary Ann shouted, 'Ay, Aggie Mac, put that bleedin' jumper down before yer dirty it. I was going to charge yer threepence, but I'm adding a penny now for wear and tear.'

'Yer can sod off, Mary Ann,' Aggie shouted back, really enjoying the exchange. 'It's got a bleedin' big hole in it, big enough to get me fist through.'

'That means the hole must be nearly as big as yer mouth, Aggie.' Mary Ann was puffing and blowing, and now and again her face would crease with pain as the circulation began again in feet that had been freezing since she'd set the stalls up at eight o'clock. She just knew her chilblains would give her gyp tonight when she went to bed. 'If it had been as big as the foot ye're always putting in yer mouth, Aggie, I might have knocked tuppence off the price.'

Another voice piped up, 'How much is this blue blouse, Mary Ann? It can't be much 'cos it's got a button missing.'

She grinned. 'Yer might have got away with that, Sarah, if I hadn't seen yer pulling the bleedin' button off.'

Sadie brought the stallholder to a halt. 'Ay, Sarah, that blouse belongs on my superior quality stall, and everything on there is sixpence. And if you've pulled a button off, then yer'll have to buy it at the right price of sixpence.'

Sarah was looking red-faced and guilty by this time. She had pulled a button off the pretty, pale blue blouse which she'd had visions of wearing on Christmas Day, but she didn't think anyone had seen her. 'Yer've got eyes in the back of yer head, Mary Ann, yer miserable bugger.'

Mary Ann turned her back on the woman, and as she bent down and swished her long black skirt up, said, 'I've got eyes in me backside, as well, Sarah. And I know that little pearl button is clutched in yer left hand.'

A voice called, 'Ay, Mary Ann, if yer were trying to do the can-can, yer were doing it the wrong way round. Ye're supposed to kick yer bleedin' legs in the air and give everyone a treat.'

'If I kicked me legs in the air, Lizzie, the sight would be such that I'd charge yer a penny more than I'm going to charge yer for that cardi yer've got wrapped around yer hands to keep them warm.' The stallholder squared her shoulders, grinned at the pretty young girl who had brought a lot of joy into her life, and told the crowd, 'Now, me and me young assistant are ready to do business. So make sure yer have the right money ready, if yer can, to save time.'

As she walked towards the middle trestle table, Mary Ann said, 'Lizzie, will yer take yer bosom off the clothes, please?'

'I'm only leaning on the bleedin' clothes, Mary Ann, I'm not doing no harm.'

'Lizzie, your bosom weighs heavier than my whole body! Of course ye're doing harm, yer silly nit! Those clothes on top of the pile are getting more wear and tear out of your bosom than they've had since they were hanging up in the Bon Marché shop.'

There were guffaws and titters from the crowd. 'The Bon Marché, Mary Ann! Yer must think we were born yesterday,' Lizzie said, quite put out that her breasts were now the centre of attention. 'If this dress I'm leaning on has ever seen the Bon Marché, then I'll eat me bleedin' hat.'

'Which hat is that, Lizzie? I've never seen yer in no hat.'

'It's the hat I'll buy the day yer can prove this bleedin' dress ever saw the inside of the Bon Marché.'

While all this was going on, Mary Ann and Sadie were taking money for the blouses, skirts and cardis that were being shoved into bags. But still the stallholder kept the conversation going. 'I can prove it to yer, Lizzie. In fact if yer look at the label sewn into the back of the dress, yer'll see I'm right. And as it happens I've got a few hats for sale as well so yer can look at them at the same time. But pick one what won't play havoc with yer digestion when ye're eating it.'

Lizzie began busily looking for a label on the dress. When she found it, she waved it in the air triumphantly. 'There yer are, clever clogs! This label doesn't say Bon Marché, it says Phillips of London.'

The stallholder pushed a lock of her red hair back under the scarf she was wearing, then, shaking her head with a sad expression on her face, said, 'Lizzie, ye're as thick as two short planks. Of course Bon Marché don't make their own clothes, they buy them in. And in that case they bought the dress from Phillips of London, what makes clothes for the toffs. And while it was hanging in their shop with a five-guinea price tag on, along came a wealthy lady and bought it. After a while she got tired of it, as rich people do, and it eventually ended up on my stall. But I'm not going to charge yer five guineas for it, I'm not even going to charge yer one. Seeing as ye're one of me regulars, I'll let yer have it for a shilling, and I'll throw a hat in for nothing.'

Lizzie bristled, or pretended to. 'Yer can stuff yer dress, and yer hat, where Paddy stuck his nuts, Mary Ann. I'm not giving yer no shilling for no bleedin' second-hand dress, even if it was made for a toff.'

'How much are yer willing to pay for the dress then, Lizzie?'

'A tanner, and not a penny more.' Lizzie's lips formed a straight line of determination and her bosom took on a life of its own.

'Okay, that's fine by me.' Mary Ann took the sixpenny piece before saying, 'If yer'd used yer eyes, Lizzie, yer would have seen that everything on this table is fourpence. What a pity, eh? Still, I'm sure you and the dress will get on well together, if yer ever get it over those two mountains that stick out in front of yer.' Mary Ann saw the corners of Lizzie's mouth turn down, and although she knew the woman was putting on an act, like herself, she felt a moment's tenderness for her. It was people like Lizzie, Aggie and Sarah who put the bread on her table. 'Here's yer tanner back, so hang on to it while I look for something more suitable for yer.'

Lizzie kept her smile back because it wouldn't do to let everyone see that Mary Ann was going to give her special treatment, 'cos then they'd all want it.

Sadie had spotted the four friends and waved. 'I'll be with yer as soon as I can. We've had a bit of a rush on since half-past eight.'

When she finally had time to go to them, Beth said, 'Yer don't look as though yer've been at it all day, yer look very pretty and healthy.'

'That's because I'm very happy.' Sadie's bright blue eyes shone. 'I got engaged to me boyfriend Harry last week. I haven't got the ring on so I can't show it to yer. I won't wear it for work in case it comes off and I lose it.'

There were sincere congratulations from the four friends who had grown fond of the blonde-haired girl with the film-star looks who always went out of her way to help them. 'And when's the wedding to be, then, girl?' Flo asked. 'Soon?'

'I wish it was tomorrow, I can't wait to marry him. But we have to save up for the wedding first so it'll be next year some time.' Sadie saw Mary Ann struggling to keep up with the hands reaching out to her to be served. 'I'll have to leave yer for ten minutes, but I'll be back. In the meantime yer could try looking through that rack over there, there's some nice things on it.'

'How come there's not crowds around it, like the stalls?' Beth asked.

'Because everything on it is dearer than the clothes on the stalls. With it being a weekday, there's not much money around. But come the weekend that rack will be busy. The clothes are worth the difference in price, they're good quality.' Sadie raised her brows at Beth. 'Remember yer son's overcoat? That was worth the money, wasn't it?'

'It certainly was, sunshine, he's had plenty of wear out of it. Anyway, you go and help yer boss and we'll see yer a bit later when ye're not so busy.' Beth jerked her head. 'Come on, gang, let's see if there's anything on the rack that takes our fancy.'

Chapter Twenty-Five

The four friends walked down their street with bags and baskets full. Their trip to Paddy's Market had been fruitful and enjoyable, but also very tiring.

They reached Beth's house and she put her basket down to get the front door key out of her pocket. 'I'll be glad to get in and take the weight off me feet and have a nice quiet cuppa. I'll see yer tomorrow.'

'Are yer not going to ask us in?' Flo looked and sounded put out. 'If ye're making a pot of tea it's not going to kill yer to put an extra spoonful of tea in the ruddy pot!'

Beth turned on the step. 'Have none of yer got homes to go to?'

'I'm all right for another hour,' Dot said. 'I prepared the dinner this morning before I left the house, so I'm in no rush.'

'And I've nothing to worry about until four o'clock when the girls come home from school.' Lizzie couldn't look Beth in the face because she knew she'd burst out laughing. 'And, sure, I'm dying for a decent cup of tea, and that's the truth of it.'

Beth shook her head as though in disbelief. 'Well, why can't we go in one of your houses? Why does it always have to be mine?'

Flo tutted. 'Because, soft girl, you're the one making the pot of tea, that's why! And what a waste it would be to make it just for one. Not only a waste, but flamin' selfish as well when yer know yer best mates are dying of thirst. Now hurry and get that bleedin' door open, the string handles on this bag are digging into me hands.'

With a resigned sigh, Beth opened the door and they all trooped in after her. 'One of these days I'm going to put me foot down with you lot. Anyone would think I was running a ruddy cafe!'

'Just go and put the kettle on, girl, and stop yer moaning. I'm going to empty me basket and have a proper look at what I bought today. Yer can't always tell when ye're at the market, there's always too many people want serving.'

Beth filled the kettle and put a light to the gas ring. Then she set the cups and saucers out ready, and stood the milk jug near. While she was waiting for the kettle to boil, she told herself she may as well go and look through the clothes she'd bought. But first she'd better look to see if she had enough biscuits to go round. If she remembered correctly, there'd be just enough for one each.

When she walked into the living room, Beth's mouth opened wide with horror. The room looked like a second-hand clothes shop! There were clothes draped everywhere: on the backs of chairs, on the couch, the table, and there were mounds of them on the floor where they'd been tipped from bags. 'In the name of God, will yer just look at the place! I hope yer intend to clear it up before my husband comes home from work, 'cos he'd have a fit if he saw it in this state.'

Flo sidled up to her holding out a green woollen dress. It had long sleeves and a plain round neck with a lace-trimmed collar. 'Ay, look at this, girl, wasn't it a bargain for one and six? I'll be all dolled up for Christmas Day, yer won't know me.'

Dot was busy holding a deep mauve dress up to herself. It had a shaped waist which would suit Dot with her being so slim, three-quarter sleeves and a square neck. 'Look at this for two bob! I mean, yer wouldn't be without for that price, would yer?'

Not to be outdone, Lizzie lifted up a dark brown woollen dress. It was very plain, with long sleeves, a high round neck and a belt covered in the same material. 'I think we hopped in lucky, so we did. Each of us has got at least one bargain. I'm going to put this away until Christmas Day and give me darlin' Paddy a surprise. I bet he'll fall for me all over again, so he will.'

'Aren't yer going to get yours out, girl?' Flo asked. 'Let's have a proper look at it. All I can remember is that it's blue.'

'No, that one's not mine, sunshine, that's the one I got for Ginny. The one I got for meself is beige, trimmed with brown. I'll show them to yer some other time. But what I'm really thrilled about is getting a pair of long trousers for our Joey! There's not a break in them, they've hardly been worn. And for two bob, I'd have been daft not to get them.'

'Yeah, but as Sadie said, in the posh houses they get their best stuff from, those folk have money to burn and can buy new. They don't wear things out like we do, they go out and buy new when they're fed up with or grow out of something.'

'It's no good telling us what the things are like, girl,' Flo said, 'we want to see them!'

'Well, yer can't, can yer, 'cos there's the kettle whistling. And while I'm making the tea, I want you three to pack all those clothes back in yer bags and make me room look a bit more presentable.' Beth stood with her hand on the kitchen door. 'I'll show yer my things some other time, but for now they're going straight upstairs, out of the way of prying eyes.'

'What about this bag of children's clothes that we got for Vera Duffy?' Dot asked. 'They'll need washing before we give them to her.'

'Wait until I pour the tea out, then we can sit comfortably and discuss how to go about that. Right now, all I want is a nice cup of tea.'

'Hear, hear,' said Lizzie, pushing the clothes back into a large bag. 'Me mouth and throat are as dry as sandpaper.'

By the time the tea was brewed and poured out, Beth's living room was back to normal. All the bags had been put in the tiny hall out of the way, except Beth's, which had been put on the bottom stair. 'That's more like it, I can see what I'm saying now.'

Dot took the cup she was handed, sat back and crossed her slim legs. 'Now, what are we going to do about the things for Vera's kids?'

Beth sipped on her tea before answering. 'I don't think we should be the ones to give them to her. She'd be really embarrassed if we knocked on her door to say we had some clothes for her kids. I mean, it's not as though we know the woman very well. She might think we're giving her them 'cos we don't believe she looks after her children properly.'

Lizzie nodded. 'I think Beth is right, so I do! I'd not be happy if someone knocked on my door, right out of the blue, and handed me some clothes. Especially if I hardly knew them. I'd be insulted, and that's the truth. Me pride would be hurt, I know that.'

'Then what did we get them for, if we're not going to give her the bleedin' things?' Flo asked, as her chins went the way of her shaking head. 'Surely we're not going to waste them?'

'No, of course not, not when the kids really need them! I just wondered if we could get them to her some way that wouldn't make her feel bad. We could do it through Aggie, that might be the best solution 'cos they're good mates. Aggie could say a friend of hers had some stuff that her children had grown out of, and she was going to give it to the ragman until Aggie stopped her and said they were too good to throw away and she knew someone who would be glad of them. They'll probably all want altering, but Vera Duffy can do that, it's easy to turn hems up. And I'm sure she'll be glad of them.'

Dot thought this was a very good idea. 'We'll wash and iron them first, to make them look nice and fresh.'

Beth glanced at Flo. 'You know Aggie better than any of us, sunshine, so yer could have a word with her on the quiet. Just explain that we wanted to help Vera, but didn't want to be seen pushing our noses in. See what she thinks.'

According to Flo's reckoning, this put her a little bit ahead of her friends. So she sat up straight, as did her bosom and tummy. 'I'll give her a knock later, girl, and let yer know what she has to say.'

Beth shook her head. 'Don't bother telling me tonight, leave it until tomorrow. I'm feeling whacked now, and I want an easy night with me feet up.'

The creaking chair warned them that Flo was up to something. 'Oh, aye, girl, are yer having an early night in bed? Is your feller on a promise?'

For all Beth had been neighbours with Flo for nearly twenty years, and should be used to her by now, the little woman still had the power to make her blush. 'Yer'll get me hung one of these days, you will. Yer mind is never long out of the bedroom, it's no wonder Dennis always looks worn out.'

Flo and the chair chuckled. 'Ah, but have yer never noticed my feller always has a smile on his face? That's 'cos he enjoys himself so much making himself tired.'

'I think we'll leave that subject, if yer don't mind, sunshine, we've more important things to talk about than your love life.' Beth bit on the inside of her cheek to stop herself from laughing when she saw the devilment in her neighbour's eyes. But it wouldn't do to encourage her 'cos if yer gave her an inch she'd take a yard. 'Now, I want a volunteer to wash the children's clothes. I've got enough on me plate with seeing to things for the party on Saturday. I can make the jellies tomorrow, they'll be all right for a few days in the pantry and will be one thing off me mind. But there's so much to think of, and I really want everything to go off just right, 'cos it's the first grown-up party for any of the kids.'

'I'm going to make a large sponge cake, girl, and I'll ice the top and put the three girls' names on,' Dot said. 'And I'll make a dozen fairy cakes as well, to help out.'

'I'm buying a dozen sausage rolls, me darlin',' Lizzie said. 'They can be cut in two and they'll go further.'

Beth was wondering how the sausage rolls would go further if they were cut in half. All the kids would do would be to take two halves. But her train of thought was interrupted by Flo, who had no intention of being left out. 'I'm giving yer a hand with the sandwiches, girl, so that'll be a big help. I'll get a quarter of the best boiled ham, a quarter of corned beef and a jar of meat paste. That should be plenty, but just in case, I'll make it a large jar of meat paste.'

314

Beth smiled. 'That sounds great, sunshine, the table should look nice. Our Ginny is really looking forward to having a party with all her friends here. She knows it's not just her party, that Joan and Marie are celebrating their birthdays as well, and she's not going to hog the limelight. But she's never had a party before, and at fifteen years of age it's a big thing.' She kept glancing at the clock to make sure she was leaving herself enough time to get the dinner on the go. 'I think me and Andy will make ourselves scarce once the kids have settled down. They'll enjoy it better without two grown-ups watching their every move.'

'Well, why don't the men go to the pub and us girls go to the pictures?' Dot thought she'd had a brainwave. 'We never go anywhere, it would do us good.'

Beth could see Flo and Lizzie nodding their heads in agreement, and although she would have liked to stay near to keep an eye on the party and see it didn't get out of hand, she knew as she was thinking it that it wasn't necessary. Mick, David and Bobby were turned sixteen years of age, very capable and sensible. She'd trust them with her life. 'Okay, but it'll have to be second house.' She pushed herself to her feet and picked up her cup and saucer from the table. 'Before I throw yer out, would yer mind rinsing yer cups and saucers under the tap, please? Save me a job.'

Ginny came in from work and flopped on the couch before she even took her coat off. 'Oh, Mam, we haven't half been busy today. Me legs and me feet are so tired, I'm not going to move after I've had me dinner. I'm going to steep me feet in a bucket of warm water and then put them up on the couch.'

Joey held his nose between two fingers and pulled a face. 'Yuk! Yer mean we've got to sit and smell your sweaty feet?'

'Mam!' Ginny's voice was high. 'Tell him I haven't got sweaty feet! He'll go out and tell everyone in the street if yer don't stop him. He's a little horror!'

Her brother was grinning from ear to ear. 'Little horror? I'm taller than you are! And I won't be telling everyone in the street 'cos I wouldn't want them to know me sister's feet smell.'

'If I wasn't so tired, I'd get up and clock you one.' This was an empty threat as sister and brother may fight verbally but they had never raised a hand to each other, even when they were little. 'Ay, Mam, guess what?' Ginny could hear her mother pottering around getting the dinner plates ready, but she couldn't keep this piece of news to herself until after they'd had their meal. 'Yer'll never guess in a million years.'

'Well, I haven't got that long, sunshine, 'cos yer dad will be home any minute.' Beth came to lean against the door jamb. 'What is it?'

'D'yer know that Miss Meadows I've told yer about? She works in Henderson's and comes in to see me at least twice a week. She's very posh, but very nice. You remember, she's the one who told Miss Landers off for the way she spoke to me.'

'I do know who ye're talking about, sunshine, so will yer get on with whatever it is yer want to tell me? Yer dad will be here any minute.'

Ginny's expression was dramatic. 'Well, she came in today and asked me if I'd like to go to her house for tea on me birthday. She said she'd be delighted if I'd say I would.'

'Go 'way! What did yer say?'

'I told her I was having a party here, with me friends, so she said that perhaps I'd go another day. I didn't know what to say, 'cos she's really posh and speaks frightfully far back. Not that there's anything wrong with that, 'cos she's been really friendly with me. But I don't have the right clothes to go somewhere posh, and I'd feel awkward and embarrassed.'

'Has she got a family of her own? It's unusual for a woman yer don't really know to ask yer to tea. I mean, she's only ever seen yer in the shop.'

'She said her name was Miss Alicia Meadows the first time she came in the shop, so she can't be married. Dorothy Sutherland said perhaps she hasn't any family of her own and is lonely. She couldn't understand why I didn't jump at the chance of going to Miss Meadows' house for tea. But I thought I'd better ask you first, see what yer think.'

'Ooh, I don't know, sunshine, I'd have to give it some thought. The woman is probably very nice and very respectable, but we don't know that for sure. Do yer even know where she lives?'

'I didn't like asking her, but she did say to tell yer that she'd see I got home safely. She's really nice, Mam, and I'd be thrilled to go to her house for tea, but my main worry is that I haven't got anything really decent to wear.'

Beth thought of the blue dress, bought that day and now lying at the bottom of her wardrobe. 'Clothes are the least of yer worries, sunshine, we can always find something to make yer look presentable. But I'd feel happier if we knew more about the woman. Just because she's posh doesn't mean she's a good person. The best thing is to wait and see what yer dad has to say, then we'll take it from there.'

Andy was inclined to take the opposite view to Beth. He thought that being posh didn't necessarily mean Miss Meadows was a bad person. 'She stuck up for our Ginny when she heard her being put on, and she's made a friend of her ever since. I'd say she's taken a liking to Ginny, and there's no harm in that. The only misgiving I've got is that she might live miles away, and with the nights being so dark, it's not safe for a young girl to be coming home on her own. I wouldn't like that, I'd be worrying meself sick the whole time she was out. But if Ginny wants to go, I wouldn't mind going to pick her up.'

'Miss Meadows said to tell yer she'd make sure I got home safely so yer wouldn't have to worry. And I would like to go, but I haven't got anything decent to wear. Not to go somewhere posh, anyway. So I'll ask her to leave it for a bit, shall I, and I can save up and buy meself a nice dress?'

Beth held her daughter's eyes for a second before looking across the table to where Joey sat eating his dinner, apparently not the least bit interested in the conversation. Then Beth glanced again at her daughter, and there was a message in her eyes which told Ginny not to ask any more questions. 'A nice dress is the least of yer worries, sunshine, we can always sort yer out with one. But I'd like to know a bit more about Miss Meadows. Like where she lives, and who with. And how is she going to make sure yer get home safely? I've nothing against yer going, sunshine, because the experience will do yer good. And I'm sure if yer told the woman about my concern, she'd understand.'

'I could tell her I'll go on Sunday, 'cos that's me real birthday. But are yer sure about me having something to wear, Mam?'

Beth winked. 'Oh, I think so, sunshine. In fact I'm certain of it. I can't help yer with a coat, though, so we'll have to do our best with the one yer've got. A sponge down and pressing, it'll come up like new.'

'Ask the woman if I can come to tea with yer,' Joey said. 'I've never been in a posh house.'

'And ye're not going in one now, either!' Ginny raised her eyes to the ceiling. 'I can just imagine you in a posh house. Yer'd be wiping yer nose with the back of yer hand and asking where the lavvy was.'

Joey wasn't put out 'cos he knew his sister was pulling his leg. So he pulled tongues at her. 'The toffs don't say lavvy, they say toilet, so that's how much you know. And I wouldn't wipe me nose on the back of me hand, I'd pretend I'd dropped a spoon, and when I was bent down, I'd wipe me nose on your underskirt.'

'That's enough now, get on with yer dinner, both of yer,' Beth said. 'You can find yer own posh friend, Joey, if yer want to see how the other half live. But let me know when yer do, so I can make sure yer have a clean handkerchief with yer.'

'The table looks really nice, Mam, yer've worked very hard.'

'Oh, I had help from me mates, sunshine, I didn't do it all meself so I can't take the credit.' Beth looked at her daughter with pride. 'That dress looks lovely on yer. The colour highlights yer blonde hair and blue eyes.'

'I can thank you for that, Mam, I got them from you.'

Joey tutted in disgust. 'Did yer hear that, Dad? It's enough to make yer want to be sick.'

'Ay, smarty pants,' Beth said, laughing. 'If you hadn't inherited yer dad's looks, yer wouldn't have been so handsome.'

Now that was a compliment if ever he'd heard one, and Joey felt quite chuffed. If he grew up as handsome as his dad, he'd be more than happy. So happy was he, he decided to pay his sister a compliment. 'Those pearls yer bought, they look nice with the dress.' Then being an inquisitive young lad, he couldn't help asking, 'How much did yer pay for them?'

'I paid sixpence for them. Pat had put them away for me, and I paid her when the shop closed and we got our wage packets.' Ginny fingered the imitation pearls. 'No one could tell they weren't real, could they, Mam?'

'I certainly couldn't, but then I couldn't tell a real diamond if I saw one.'

'Oh, I could,' Andy said. 'As soon as I clapped eyes on you, love, I knew yer were a very precious stone.'

'Well, we are full of blarney tonight, aren't we?' Beth undid the tie at the back of her pinny and took it off. 'They'll all be here any minute now, I don't want them to think I'm the maid.' When the knocker sounded she threw the pinny into a cupboard in the sideboard. 'Here's the first of them so open the door to your guests, Ginny.'

Flo's daughter Amy and Joan were the first to arrive, followed closely by Amelia and Bobby. Playing the dutiful hostess, Ginny took their coats and placed them on the bed in her bedroom. She was coming back down the stairs when she heard a rat-tat, and then her mother saying, 'Come in Mick, Seamus – Ginny won't be a minute.'

Mick winked at Joan. 'Ye're looking very nice in that dress, Miss Flynn. Or should I say birthday girl?'

It wasn't often that Joan blushed, but she did now. 'Me mam bought me the dress for Christmas, but she let me wear it tonight because Ginny's got a new one and I didn't want to be left out.'

'Yer do look nice, Joan,' Bobby agreed. 'And I think Ginny looks very fetching in her new dress. The colour suits her blonde hair.'

'Who's to come now, sunshine?' Beth asked. 'Is it only Marie and yer other friend, Pat?'

'And David.' Ginny cocked her head at Joan. 'Where's your David, why didn't he come with you?'

'He was taking ages getting ready, so I wasn't going to wait any longer for him. He spends more time on his hair than I do! Every hair has to be in place before he's satisfied.'

'Well, it shows for it, 'cos he always looks neat,' Mick said, his blue eyes holding laughter. 'Me, now,' he patted his thick mop of dark hair, 'I put the comb through this about four times a day, and that's it. Takes ten seconds each time.'

His brother Seamus huffed, 'Don't tell so many lies! Yer spend half yer life looking at yerself in the mirror.'

'I might do if I got the chance. And if I spend half me life looking in the mirror, then I spend the other half watching you standing in front of it, asking, "Mirror, mirror, on the wall, who is the fairest of them all?" And I don't know why yer won't believe it when it tells yer that *I* am the fairest of them all.'

Seamus held out his hands to Beth. 'Mrs Porter, that's not a thick mop of hair he's got, yer know. He's really only got a bit of hair on a big head.'

Ginny was laughing went she went to answer the next knock on the door. She was surprised to see her three late guests had arrived together. 'I met Marie at the top of the street,' Pat said, 'and she's introduced me to David so at least I'll know someone here.'

There was a lot of chatter as introductions were made, and Beth gave her husband a sign to say it was time they left because her mates would be waiting for her to go to the pictures. She'd had strict instructions from Flo that she better hadn't be late 'cos she wanted to see the short comedy before the big picture. 'Listen, can I ask yer to be quiet for a minute? Me and Mr Porter are going out to let you have your party without us watching over yer, but we're expecting yer to behave yerselves. There's three sixteen-year-old lads here, and I'm putting them in charge to make sure the neighbours are not given anything to complain about, and me home isn't wrecked.'

'Before yer go, Mrs Porter, can we give the three birthday girls their cards and presents?' Amelia produced a card and small package from her bag and other parcels began to appear from bags and Mick's jacket pocket. The three giggling girls lined up and were presented with a card from each of their guests and shared presents from the O'Leary house and the Baileys. When Bobby saw Mick giving Joan a kiss as he held out her present, he quickly took the parcel Amelia was holding and whispered, 'You give them the card, I'll give Ginny her present.' And Ginny got a kiss, as did the other two girls. This caused great hilarity as the girls blushed with embarrassment, but were secretly thrilled. They received ten cards each, and five presents, more than they'd ever received in their lives. The presents were the same for each girl, so there could be no jealousy. Bracelets made up of coloured stones, necklaces to match, woollen gloves, underskirts and stockings. And the happy faces on the girls showed how delighted and thrilled they were.

'Yer've done well, sunshine, I'm very happy for yer.' Beth gave her daughter a hug. 'Me and yer dad are going to leave yer in peace now.' She took her husband's hand and led him to the door. 'Have a nice time, kids, and don't be afraid to eat the food when yer get hungry. We'll be home about a quarter to eleven.'

Beth was about to close the door behind her when Andy asked, 'How are Marie and Pat going to get home at that time of night? I wouldn't like a daughter of mine walking the streets in the dark.'

Beth bustled back inside. 'I won't keep popping up like a jack-in-the-box, but we've just thought on about how Marie and Pat will get home?'

'Don't worry, Mrs Porter,' David said. 'The lads will make sure they get home safely. After all, there's no work to worry about tomorrow, so it won't matter if we're late getting to bed.'

'That's one worry off our minds.' Beth included everyone in her smile. 'I promise I won't be popping back again, so enjoy yerselves.'

Joey had watched all this with interest. After all, it wasn't long before his birthday, and it seemed the more people you asked, the more presents you got. It was worth bearing that in mind.

There was an embarrassing silence for a while as the girls sat on one side of the room and the boys the other. Then Bobby asked, 'Ginny, has yer mam said yer can come to the dance with us yet?'

'Oh, I think she'll let me go. Especially if Joan, Amelia and Marie are going.'

'Have yer asked your mam, Joan?' Mick asked. 'Yer could come with us the week after the holidays.'

'If Ginny goes, I go.' Joan was confident. 'I'm not going to make a fool of meself on me own. I can just see meself falling flat on me face, or on me backside.'

'We can have a little practice now, if yer like?' Mick said. 'We've no music, but yer don't need it to learn how to waltz.'

When the girls shrank back with something akin to horror on their faces, Bobby said, 'We can't dance proper ourselves yet. So really we'd be using you to learn on. Come on, it'll save us sitting here looking at one another, and it'll be a laugh.'

'I'm game for a laugh,' Marie said, with her wide smile. 'I don't mind making a fool of meself if it teaches me how to dance.'

David was on his feet like a shot. 'I'll be yer partner, Marie, as long as some of the others get up and they don't just sit gawping at us.'

Mick grinned across at Joan. 'Are yer game to trip the light fantastic with me? I promise that in half-an-hour yer'll know the basic steps for a waltz.' Then with a cheeky grin, he added, 'Yer won't talk all the time, though, will yer, 'cos it'll put me off.'

'Ay, you, anyone would think I talk too much!'

'Well, yer do!' Joey piped up. 'Yer never stop.'

Mick crossed the room and held out his hand. 'He's only pulling yer leg. Come on, let's see how quickly yer can pick up just three steps.'

When Bobby crossed the room to stand in front of Ginny, she asked, 'Is it really only three steps, or is he having her on?'

'That's all yer need to learn to start with, yes.' He held out his hand. 'Come on, yer've got to learn sometime. Better in yer own home than on a dance floor.'

Amelia could see Seamus hesitating and she took the plunge. 'I'm not going to be a wallflower, so up yer get.'

Apart from Amy and Joey, and nothing on God's earth would get them up, there was only Pat left, and when Ginny saw her, she felt guilty. 'Will yer get Pat up, Bobby, and I'll sit and watch? I feel mean leaving her on her own 'cos she doesn't know anyone, only me and Marie.'

'But it's you I want to dance with.' There was disappointment on the lad's face. 'Can I ask her after?'

'No, her first and then me.' Ginny was determined her workmate wasn't going to be left out. 'Pat, will you let Bobby show yer how to waltz, and I'll watch? I know I'd be hopeless.'

'That's all right, Ginny, I can dance. I've been going dancing for six months now.'

The chattering stopped and all eyes were turned on Pat. 'Yer mean, yer can dance proper, like?' Mick asked. 'Waltz, quickstep and that?'

She nodded. 'Yer see, I've got two sisters older than me, and they taught me how to dance when I was only thirteen, before me mam would allow me to go to a dance with them.'

'Oh, well,' Mick said. 'We'll let the expert show the girls how to do the waltz, then she can help the lads with the quickstep, 'cos none of us can master that.'

'We're not exactly experts at the waltz, either,' David said, his hand holding Marie's in readiness. 'In fact, the girls will knock spots off us after one lesson.'

'I'm not what yer would call a professional,' Pat told them. 'But I think it would be better if the boys taught the girls, rather than me, so they get used to the way yer dance. Otherwise they'll be lost if a stranger asks them up for a dance. Don't worry about me, you all go ahead and I'll watch.'

'Just show us, Pat, so we get some idea,' Joan begged. 'If we see you doing it, it's better than being told what to do.'

'Okay.' Pat jumped to her feet. 'The girls always start off with the left foot in a waltz. So it's back with the left foot, side step with the right, then bring the left foot over to the right.' She repeated it several times, saying 'one, two, three, one, two, three' over and over again. 'There now, that's not hard, is it? Try it with your partners.'

It looked easy when Pat did it, but the girls didn't find it easy at all. At first they were calling themselves stupid when they used the wrong foot or stood on their partner's toes, until Marie saw the funny side and started to laugh at herself for being clumsy. That set everyone off, and the next few hours were filled with merriment and laughter. No one cared if they had two left feet or couldn't manage a spin when they came to turn. A few steps were learned, and Pat did a tango on her own which had not only the gang in stitches but young Amy and Joey too. They laughed till the tears rolled down their faces. It was a time of great pleasure, a group of young friends starting out on the road to adulthood and enjoying the process. The bonds of friendship were strengthened, and hopefully they would remain so.

Chapter Twenty-Six

The family had finished their breakfast when Ginny came down on the Sunday morning. Beth had let her sleep in because she knew she'd be exhausted, more by excitement than anything else. 'Good morning, lazy bones.'

'Good morning.' Ginny rubbed her eyes. 'Ooh, I slept like a log, I don't even remember putting me head down on the pillow.' She pulled a chair from the table and was about to sit down when she saw two cards standing by her plate and two small wrapped parcels. She looked up to see three pairs of eyes on her, and before she could say anything she was being kissed on one cheek by her mother, and on the other by her father.

'Happy birthday, sunshine! We didn't give yer the cards and presents yesterday because we knew yer'd be getting plenty.'

Andy held her tight. 'All the best, love, and may yer have many more happy birthdays.'

Joey couldn't make up his mind. Kisses were for cissies, but on the other hand he was lucky to have Ginny for a sister. So he rounded the table and gave her a quick peck on the cheek. 'Happy birthday, Sis.' And he couldn't resist adding, just in case she took ages to open her present and he couldn't wait that long, 'I hope yer like what I bought for yer.'

'I'm sure I will if you chose it, Joey, 'cos yer know what I like.'

Now he wasn't expecting this reply and had to think quickly. 'Well, I did ask Marie what she thought yer'd like more than anything, and asked her to get it for me.'

Beth and Andy smiled with pride. They were indeed blessed with their children. 'D'yer want yer breakfast first?' Beth asked. 'Or would yer rather open yer pressies?'

Joey was standing beside his sister, and she could almost feel him willing her to say she wanted to open the presents first. He was so pleased with himself for having saved his pocket money to buy Ginny the present that Marie had said she'd love.

'I'll open me presents.' Ginny had lost her sleepiness now, and excitement was building up inside her. 'I wasn't expecting anything 'cos yer did the party for me, Mam, and that was enough.' Her hand reached for the nearest parcel which she could see had Joey's name on it. It was very small and she wondered what it could be. Whatever it was, she was going to make a big fuss over it after him going without his comics to buy it for her. 'Yours first, eh, kid?'

Her parents and brother were hoping for a happy reaction, but they got far more than they'd hoped for when Ginny shrieked and nearly toppled the chair over when she pushed it back. 'Oh, I don't believe it! I don't believe it!' She gazed down at the ring which had a large red square glass stone set in claws. 'Oh, it's lovely, Joey, thank you.' She kissed and hugged him. 'I was going to buy it for meself next payday.' She giggled. 'Well, one just like it anyway.'

Joey was delighted he'd made his sister happy, but one hug and kiss was enough for anyone. 'Marie said yer'd like it,' he told her, while disentangling himself from her arms. 'And she was right, wasn't she?'

'I go over to the jewellery counter nearly every day with Marie, 'cos they have lovely things on it. But this ring took me eye the first day I saw it, and it's been me favourite ever since.' Ginny put the ring on the third finger of her left hand and held it up for all to see. 'Isn't it lovely? I'll wear it this afternoon to go to Miss Meadows, shall I, Mam?'

'That's up to you, sunshine, but if she's posh, I can't see it being the sort of thing she'd go for. She probably wears the real thing.'

'Yeah, ye're right, Mam, perhaps she'd think this was common. I'll wear it when I go dancing, though, 'cos those boys and girls won't know it came from Woolworth's.' She grinned. 'That's if yer'll let me go to the dance next week? Yer did promise I could when I was fifteen. Amelia, Joan and Marie said they're almost sure their mams will say they can go.'

'If the whole gang are going, and yer won't be walking home alone in the dark, me and yer dad don't mind yer going, do we, love?'

'Not at all, as long as we know who she's with,' Andy said. 'And she wouldn't come to any harm with the lads that were here last night. Smashing lads, all of them.'

Joey gave his sister a dig in the ribs. 'Ay, yer've still got a pressie to open.'

'I know, I haven't forgotten. I just wanted to keep meself in suspense a little bit longer.' Ginny picked up the small parcel which had no weight to it at all. 'Mmm! It feels soft, I wonder what it can be?'

'It's from yer dad, sunshine, I had nothing to do with it. I'd already bought yer the dress and the party cost me a few bob.'

Ginny tore the paper off to reveal two fine linen white hankies, with an inset of wide lace in two of the corners. 'Oh, aren't they pretty!' She shook one of the hankies out of its square shape and held it up. 'These are too nice to blow me nose on. Thank you, Dad, they're a lovely present.'

'Yer could take one of them with yer this afternoon,' Beth said. 'I've been thinking, the sleeves on yer new dress taper in at the cuffs, so yer could push one of those up and leave the lace showing. Now that would look very chic.'

Ginny's pretty face was aglow. 'I am one lucky girl, aren't I?'

'I'll say,' said Joey, 'first the party and presents, and now more presents!'

'The party was a success then, was it, love?' Andy asked.

'Oh, Dad, we did nothing but laugh. If yer'd seen the state of us learning how to do the waltz, yer'd have done no more good. It was absolutely hilarious.'

'It was, Mam, honest.' Joey was grinning from ear to ear. 'Me and Amy never stopped laughing, only when it came time to eat. That girl, Pat, she was a scream. Yer should have seen her doing a tango on her own, it was dead funny. She said that's the way George Raft did it in a film, but I don't think he would have been as funny as her.'

'You all seemed to have enjoyed yourselves when we got home,' Beth chuckled. 'I had to laugh when Mick said he'd see Joan home. Her face was a study when she said, "I only live next door, yer daft nit." '

'I wonder what time the boys got home after seeing Marie to her door and then going on with Pat?' Andy said. 'Marie only lives ten minutes' walk away, but Pat said she had to go five stops on the tram.'

'They're young, love, they can stand the pace. We used to be the same at their age.' Beth stretched her arms high above her head, gave a little shiver and then stood up. 'I'll make some toast for yer now, sunshine, and a fresh pot of tea all round. Then I'll have to start on the dinner, although heaven knows, I don't feel like it. I could just do with a really lazy day, with me feet up and doing absolutely nothing.'

'Don't make much dinner for me, Mam, or I won't be able to eat anything at Miss Meadows'. And I don't want to tell her I'm not hungry if she's gone to the trouble of making a spread for me.'

When Beth went to the kitchen, Andy asked, 'She's meeting yer off the bus, isn't she? Did she say where?'

'Yeah, she said if I get the bus opposite Queen's Drive baths, I can ask the conductor to put me off at Childwall Fiveways. She'll be waiting at the stop for me at four o'clock. And yer've no need to worry about me getting home in the dark, Dad, 'cos she's promised I'll be brought right to the door. She said to tell yer she won't keep me late, I'll be home for nine o'clock.'

'She sounds a very caring person, and seems to think a lot of you.'

Ginny nodded. 'She is nice, Dad, you'd like her.'

'If she asks yer back again, tell her yer've got a brother,' Joey said. 'I might get an invite next time if yer do. I don't see why you should have all the fun.'

'Your turn will come, son, and soon,' Andy said. 'Only a few more weeks and yer'll be fourteen. Able to go out to work and make yer own friends.'

Joey thought about this with his brow furrowed. 'Dad, do yer meet any posh people in your job? I mean, if I'm going to work with yer, I'd like to know.'

He couldn't understand why his dad and sister laughed, and his mam could be heard chuckling in the kitchen. Grown-ups could be a bit daft at times.

From the moment Ginny stepped on to the platform of the bus, she started to get the collywobbles in her tummy. She'd spent ages brushing her hair till it shone, her shoes had been polished so you could see your face in them and her nails were clean. But did her coat look as though it had been bought second-hand? And the dress, would it pass inspection?

Ginny gave a start when the conductor called, 'This is your stop, love. Childwall Fiveways.' She pulled herself up by the top of the seat in front, then held on to each seat to steady herself as she made her way down the aisle to the front of the bus. Her hands were shaking and she felt quite sick.

Alicia Meadows came towards her, smiling. 'Hello, Virginia, I am so glad you made it. Happy birthday, my dear.'

Honesty was the best policy, Ginny decided, and said, 'I'm very nervous 'cos I've never been out to tea before. I've been in neighbours' houses, but that's not the same 'cos I see them every day and can't remember a time I didn't know them.'

Alicia cupped her elbow. 'There's nothing to be nervous about,

Virginia. Surely you're not afraid of me?'

'I'm not afraid, Miss Meadows, just shy. I'm not usually, but I am now. It will wear off, though, or so me dad told me.' As they were walking along Queen's Drive, Ginny was noting the big detached houses with their well-kept gardens. Some of them even had a car standing on the drive. They must be rich people who lived along here, and she'd bet they'd never lived in a two-up-two-down.

'We're home now.' Alicia opened the gates to a large house which was all painted white except for the front door which was dark with a bright brass lion's head knocker. 'I'll leave the gates open because my nephew will be coming shortly in his car.'

Ginny's eyes were everywhere when they entered the hall which was almost as big as their living room. There was an umbrella stand just inside, with umbrellas in and a couple of walking sticks. Then there was a table in shiny dark wood with a parade of ornaments which the girl could tell were expensive. The hallstand on the opposite side was intricately carved, like the antlers on a reindeer, and the whole hall floor was covered wall to wall in thick carpet which Ginny's feet sank into. Fancy having carpet in the hall! She'd never known that before. In their house, and all the neighbours', the floors were covered in lino with small rugs here and there. And it was freezing getting out of bed in the winter and putting your feet on cold lino.

'Let me take your coat, Virginia.' Alicia looked for a tag on the neck of the coat to hang it up by but there was none. So as not to make her young visitor embarrassed she just hung it by the collar. 'Come into the drawing room, my dear, and get warm. Sit by the fire while I make a drink. Would you like tea or coffee?'

Ginny had never drunk coffee in her life because her mam said it was too dear. She'd smelt it in the canteen, and thought the aroma was lovely, so now was her chance to find out. 'I'll have coffee, please, Miss Meadows.'

It was hard for Ginny not to cry out when ushered into the drawing room. She had never seen anything like it. Once again the whole floor was covered in thick carpet, but where the hall one was patterned, this carpet was a uniform pale beige. The fireplace was very ornate with a huge mirror above it, and in the magnificent grate a cheery fire burned.

The room was at the back of the house, and Ginny could see a large garden outside with many tall trees. She would have loved to have been nosy and stood up to see everything there was to see, but didn't like to. So she contented herself with sitting back on a large moquette-covered couch which had two matching chairs. The walls were covered in

327

pictures, but although Ginny liked them, she would have been stunned if she'd been told how much they were worth. The same with the Edwardian sideboard – she had no idea of its age or value. She thought it was lovely, and very nicely polished. But then, Miss Meadows had no children. Her mam could keep her furniture nice if she and Joey weren't there, Ginny told herself.

Alicia came in with a small table covered with a snow white, lace-trimmed cloth. She set it down in front of Ginny and went back to the kitchen to fetch a silver tray on which sat a silver coffee pot, milk jug and sugar basin, and cups finer than any the young girl had ever seen. 'I'm not going to offer you biscuits because I've arranged to have tea at five o'clock. My nephew agreed to run you home in his car, so I invited him too.'

Ginny's jaw dropped. 'Yer mean, I'm going home in a car?' When Alicia nodded, the young girl couldn't hide her excitement. 'I've never been in a car before! Oh, I hope the neighbours see me, I'll be proper posh.'

Alicia patted her hand. This was what she so liked about Virginia. There was no side to her, she didn't try to be something she wasn't. She would always be straight and tell you exactly what she thought. But she would always do it in a way that wouldn't hurt you. 'You'll like Charles, he's very easy to get along with.'

Ginny wasn't really listening now, her mind was full of the thrill of being driven home in a car. Oh, she hoped her mam and dad looked out of the window and saw her before the man drove away!. Then she had another thought. Oh, please, don't let their Joey be in the street with his mates, 'cos they'd be all over the car and make a holy show of her. Then she felt a stab of guilt. He was her brother, and like all boys would be interested in cars. She must never be ashamed of someone she loved.

Ginny was brought back to reality by the ringing of a bell and Miss Meadows jumping to her feet. 'This will be Charles now.'

The male voice Ginny heard was deep, and she was expecting a man to walk in. But much to her surprise, the person who followed Miss Meadows into the room was young! He didn't look any older than Mick or Bobby. He couldn't be the one driving her home, he was surely too young to drive?

'Charles, this is Virginia Porter whose birthday it is today. Virginia, this is my nephew, Charles Moore-Latimer.'

Charles saw a very pretty girl with lovely blonde hair and bright blue eyes, wearing a nice blue dress which really suited her. She was also wearing a very shy expression. He held out his hand, saying, 'I won't eat you.'

'I know yer won't, 'cos I won't let yer.' Her handshake was firm and her eyes looked straight into his. 'I thought Miss Meadows said her nephew Charles was driving me home, but that can't be you 'cos ye're not old enough to drive. I must have got the wrong end of the tale.'

'No, I am the nephew, and I will be driving you home!' Charles, like his aunt, was very well-spoken, and very confident for his age. 'I'm seventeen and have been driving for six months now. In fact, Father bought me the car for my birthday in July.'

'Golly, that was some birthday present, wasn't it? I got hankies for mine.'

At first Charles thought he detected sarcasm in her words, until he noticed the laughter in her blue eyes. 'We both received useful presents then. My car enables me to travel to and from college, while your hankies are useful for blowing your nose.'

Ginny's rich, throaty chuckle filled the room. 'Oh, I don't think so, Mr Charles.' She plucked the dainty hankie from her sleeve and held it out. 'One good blow on this and it would fall to pieces. It's only for show, yer see.'

Smiling broadly, he dropped into one of the easy chairs. 'I smell coffee, Aunt Alicia. It seems my timing was perfect.' He crossed his legs, brought his hands together and laced his fingers – a young man very sure of himself and very much at home in his aunt's house. 'Would you like me to pour?' he suggested.

'No, of course not.' Alicia was delighted to be entertaining two of her favourite people. There were times when she regretted not being married. She'd certainly had plenty of offers, and from men of means who would have kept her in luxury for the rest of her life. But she was independent and pig-headed when she was younger, and she loved her job at Henderson's. It had been stimulating and satisfying to work her way up over the years to the position she held today, that of Welfare Officer. She still loved working for the firm that had been so good to her, but lately she had been looking ahead to a future which seemed very bleak. While she was working she had something to occupy her mind, but when she retired her life would be very lonely. She only had the one sister, Bernice, who was Charles' mother. They met quite often for meals or a trip to the theatre. There were also several cousins dotted about the city, but they only met at weddings and funerals. Most women of Alicia's age would be married with children and have a long-term circle of friends.

329

'Aunt Alicia, where have you gone to?' Charles was leaning forward with his elbows resting on his knees. 'Have you forgotten you have visitors?'

Alicia shook herself mentally. 'Most certainly not! My mind strayed for a moment, that's all.' She waved a hand. 'An incident at work, something quite trivial.'

'Work should be forgotten when you have a birthday girl here who is dying of thirst. Not to mention your favourite nephew.'

'I'm not dying of thirst,' Ginny said. 'Anyway, yer can't always tell what yer mind is going to do, it plays tricks on yer sometimes.'

While he watched his aunt pick up the elegant silver coffee pot, Charles chuckled. 'Like yours did when it told you I would be an old man.'

The richness of her surroundings had made Ginny feel out of place at first, but Miss Meadows and her nephew were very friendly and she began to relax. 'It didn't tell me yer'd be an old man, just someone old enough to drive a car. And I still don't think yer look old enough to be allowed to drive. Ye're not that much older than me, and anyone who allowed me behind the wheel of a car would want their bumps feeling.' Again that contagious chuckle, bringing smiles to the faces of the two watching. 'That's if I hadn't run over them before they had time to get their bumps felt.'

The Liverpool accent, the grammar and the jokes were novel to Charles. His family and friends didn't have an accent, nor did they have that easygoing sense of humour. This young girl was very interesting as well as being very good-looking. 'I promise I won't run over anyone while you are a passenger in my car. Does that make you feel any better?'

Alicia had a smile on her face as she poured the coffee. Things seemed to be working out as she had hoped. Bringing Charles and Virginia together had been in her mind for a while, and the girl's birthday had been the ideal excuse. The pair were from very different backgrounds which was obvious, but both were good at heart. And although Virginia was a little rough around the edges, it was nothing that couldn't be put right with time.

It was in the dining room later, when they were enjoying the delicacies being served by Alicia, that she suddenly asked, 'Do you ever go to the theatre, Virginia?'

Ginny shook her head. 'No, I've never been, Miss Meadows. My mam has never had the money to take us to places like that.'

Charles had had a privileged upbringing and never for one moment

330

had he thought about people who couldn't afford the luxuries he took for granted. He was about to ask Ginny why her father didn't give her the money to go to the theatre when his aunt caught his eye and shook her head slightly. 'What a pity,' Alicia said. 'We must take you one night, I'm sure you would thoroughly enjoy the experience.'

'Oh, I say, that would be jolly good fun,' Charles agreed. 'I'll find out what shows are coming to the Playhouse or Royal Court and I'll let you know, Aunt.'

Virginia nodded but didn't say a word. They were being kind to her, she knew that, but they weren't her type of people and she would feel totally out of place in their company. She would love to go to a theatre – what girl wouldn't? – but she'd rather go with someone who spoke as she did, and didn't have loads of money or wear fancy clothes.

In her mind's eye, Ginny could see the living room at home as it was last night. She could see her friends falling about laughing, and really enjoying themselves. None of them had ever been to a theatre because none of them could afford to go. But they didn't mind, they made the most of what they had and enjoyed life.

'What time are your parents expecting you home, Virginia?' Charles asked. 'I don't want to get in their bad books.'

'Miss Meadows said I'd be home by nine o'clock, so that's what I told them. They'd worry if I was much later, 'cos they don't know you.'

'Have no fear, I'll have you home on the dot, safe and sound. After your parents have met me, and seen that I'm not an ogre with two heads, I'm sure they'll have no objection to your accompanying Aunt Alicia and myself to a theatre.'

Ooh, thought Ginny, what if me mam has got pipe cleaners in her hair? She wouldn't like a stranger walking in on her unexpected. Especially one who was dressed like a toff in a fine suit, with snow white starched shirt and perfectly knotted silk tie. And if his shoes weren't real leather she'd eat her hat. He was a handsome lad, with dark hair, hazel eyes and a set of strong white teeth. And he was nice as a person, very friendly, and didn't make her feel out of it or talk down to her. But he would be a bit much for her family if they weren't expecting him. 'I don't think you'll get to meet my parents tonight, they said they would be having an early night in bed after being up till the early hours of this morning 'cos of me party. But some other time, perhaps, eh?'

It was Alicia who answered. 'Yes, of course, we understand it might not be convenient. If your parents agree to your coming out with us one night, we can pick you up from home and meet them then. I would very much like to make their acquaintance.'

After being treated so kindly in this beautiful house, and plied with delicious food made solely for her to celebrate her birthday, what could Ginny do but nod her head in agreement?

'The next street on the right is where I live,' Ginny said as they drove along County Road. 'You can drop me at the bottom and I'll walk up, it's not very far.'

Charles turned in and immediately drew into the kerb. He was surprised at how narrow the cobbled street was, and the terraced houses to either side looked very small. Too small to bring up a family in. He turned off the ignition and faced the girl who was so obviously eager to be off and away. 'Before you go, I just want to say that you made Aunt Alicia very happy today. She often talks about you, and I know she is very fond of you.'

'I like her, too!' Ginny told him. 'She's always been nice and friendly towards me and shown me nothing but kindness. It was really thoughtful of her to invite me to tea and I am very grateful.' Then she quickly added, 'And to you of course for bringing me home.'

'I hope you will stay her friend, Virginia. You see, although I call to see her as often as I can, I know she is sometimes very lonely. Having a young friend really would mean a lot to her.' But Charles was thinking of himself as much as his aunt. As well as being pretty, Virginia was good company and he'd like to see more of her.

'Of course I'll always be her friend. I never forget people who are good to me and treat me proper. And I do see her a couple of times a week when she comes in the shop.'

'I was hoping you could perhaps see her sometimes away from the shop. As a young companion to call for tea now and again, or, as Aunt Alicia suggested, an occasional night at the theatre? I would run you home afterwards so you'd be perfectly safe. Would you ask your parents for permission?'

Ginny nodded. 'Yeah, I'll ask them. And I'll let Miss Meadows know what they say when she comes in the shop. But it won't be in the next few weeks because of Christmas and New Year. I think the family should all be together at times like that.' She felt for the handle on the car door. 'How do I get out?'

Charles guffawed. 'Now if anyone was listening they'd get the impression I was holding you captive, Virginia. The car door is quite easy to open when you know how. Just push the handle up. But please let me drive you to your door because my aunt stipulated that I must see you enter your house safely.'

'Yes, okay.' He'll think I'm a right baby if I insist upon getting out of the car now, she realised. And after him being so good to me. Anyone would think I was doing him a favour, instead of the other way round. 'Our house is halfway up on the opposite side. I'll tell yer when we get there.'

Charles made no effort to get out of the car when he stopped outside Virginia's home. He was of the opinion, and quite rightly, that if he pushed too hard he'd frighten the girl off. 'Sleep well, Virginia, and I hope to see you again very soon.' With a wave of his hand he set the car in motion and drove away.

Ginny waited until the car was out of sight before knocking at the door. Her face was beaming when her dad answered her knock. 'Yer'll never believe it, Dad, but I've just been brought right to our door in a car.' She brushed past him and entered the living room where Beth and Joey were waiting wide-eyed. 'Did yer hear that, Mam? I got brought home in a car by Miss Meadows' nephew. He dropped me right outside the door.' She slipped her coat off and flung it on the couch. 'I was sorry it was dark and nobody saw me. Can yer imagine the state of the neighbours' faces if they'd seen me stepping out of a posh car?'

Beth put down the shirt she was sewing a button on. 'Who did yer say brought yer home, sunshine?'

'Miss Meadows' nephew, and guess what his name is? Charles Moore-Latimer!'

'Ooh, ay, a double-barrelled name!' Beth was suitably impressed. 'I bet he's posh, is he?'

'I'll say! He's only seventeen, and his dad bought him the car for his birthday. But he's very nice, and Miss Meadows did a lovely spread for me.'

'Seventeen and he's got a car!' Joey's voice was high-pitched with surprise. 'The lucky blighter! I'll be lucky if I've got a car by the time I'm seventy, never mind seventeen.'

Ginny went on to describe the house and furniture in detail. 'And there were carpets in every room, right from skirting board to skirting board, and they were so thick me feet sank into them. Honest, Mam, yer wouldn't believe it unless yer saw it.'

'I believe yer, sunshine, and I'm glad yer enjoyed yerself. But don't start getting big ideas 'cos they must be loaded and we're not. But we're happy all the same.' She tilted her head. 'This lad Charles, did yer take a fancy to him?'

Ginny blushed. 'Ah, ay, Mam, of course I didn't! I thought he was a nice lad, but that's about all.' Shall I mention it now or leave it? she asked herself. Then decided it was best to get it over with. 'Miss Meadows asked me to ask yer if yer'd let me go to the theatre with her one night?'

It was Andy who voiced what was on his and his wife's mind. 'Why would an older woman want to take a young girl to the theatre, love? Hasn't she got any family or friends of her own?'

Ginny shook her head. 'Charles told me she gets very lonely. Yer see, she never got married so she's got no family. She's a nice woman, Mam, honest, yer'd like her. I could always invite her here so yer could see for yerselves. Charles would run her down one night if it would make yer feel better.'

'I don't doubt that she's a lovely lady, sunshine, 'cos that's the impression I got when yer first told us about her. But she is from a different class than us and we could never keep up with her. And I'm frightened that she might show you a life we could never give yer.'

Ginny ran to sit next to Beth on the couch. She put her arm around her mother and hugged her. 'Oh, Mam! No one could ever make me any different from how I am now. I don't want to have pots of money and fancy clothes. I just want to be happy with the mates I've always had. My own kind of people.'

'So yer don't want to go to the theatre with Miss Meadows?' Beth asked. 'And don't be afraid to say what yer really think.'

'I would go to the theatre with Miss Meadows for her sake, if it made her happy. I've never forgotten how she went out of her way to stick up for me. Not many people would have done that, they'd have just walked away rather than put themselves out. But as for me going to the theatre because I really want to, then to be honest I'd have to say it wasn't something I really wanted to do. When I'm older perhaps and can afford to treat meself, well, that would be different, but not now. I'm more interested in going to me first dance next week, with me mates.'

Beth breathed a sigh of relief. She should have known her daughter was too down to earth to want something that was beyond her. 'I'll leave it to you, sunshine. If yer want to please Miss Meadows, then do so by all means. Me and yer dad would have no objection, would we, love?'

'None at all, as long as she doesn't keep you out till all hours,' Andy said. 'There'll be no objection from me.'

Joey grunted, 'I still think she should tell this posh woman that she's got a brother. I've missed out on all that food Ginny told us about, and a ride in a blinking car!'

Beth grinned. 'It's a hard life, isn't it, son?'

'It sure is, Mam, it sure is.'

Chapter Twenty-Seven

Ginny was surprised on the Monday morning when she arrived at the counter to find Miss Sutherland on her haunches sorting the stock out. 'Ye're early, aren't yer? I could have come in earlier if yer'd asked me to.'

'I haven't been here that long, pet, so don't worry your head about it. I wanted to make a list of the stock we'll need, and have it ready for when Miss Halliday comes. I won't have time when we start getting busy.' She grinned at her junior. 'If you think we were busy last week, then all I can say is you haven't seen anything yet. Five shopping days left, including Christmas Eve, and we'll be run off our feet.'

'I know what to expect now, and so do me feet. They didn't half kick up a stink last week, but after a soak in a bucket of water they were quite happy.'

Dorothy Sutherland put a hand on the counter and pulled herself up. 'How did your two parties go? I was thinking of you over the weekend, telling myself you were a lucky blighter.'

'It was only one party, really, and that was on Saturday night. We had a marvellous time, laughing ourselves sick at the state of us trying to learn the steps to a waltz. I don't think we learned anything, but it was dead funny. I enjoyed going to Miss Meadows', too, she'd made a lovely spread for me. Half the cakes she had I'd never seen in me life before, but they were delicious.' Ginny told herself it wouldn't be right for her to tell anyone what a wonderful home Miss Meadows had. It had nothing to do with her or anyone else. 'It was very kind of her and I appreciated it. And, just listen to this, her nephew drove me home in his car. Right to me own door.'

Dorothy managed to look suitably impressed. 'My goodness, you'll never forget your fifteenth birthday, will you! And how old was this nephew, if I might ask?'

'He was only seventeen and a half, but he looked older.' Ginny blushed at the knowing look on Dorothy's face. 'He's a very good driver, I didn't feel a bit frightened.'

'Any chance of a romance there?' Dorothy asked, jokingly. 'I wish I could meet a man who had his own car, I'd grab him with both hands.'

'No, he's way out of my league. He's too posh, I'm too common. But he's a nice bloke and it was good of him to drive me home. It was a thrill for me 'cos I've never been in a car before.'

That was all the time they had for conversation because people were out early, and they were out in force. All of the counters were busy, but those selling Christmas decorations or anything that would pass as a present were literally run off their feet. When Miss Halliday came, with Mr Sanderson, Dorothy had a long list of stock needed. 'It's pretty urgent, Miss Halliday, we're almost out of purses and comb sets.'

Mary, usually so calm and composed, looked flustered. 'All the counters are running low, but I'll get them down as soon as I can. As you can imagine, the stock room is busy too.'

As she bustled away, Clive followed her for a few yards, then touched her arm. 'Let me go straight to the stock room. You've taught me all about the running of the shop over the last few months, things I wouldn't have a clue about but for you. I am quite capable of getting the stock Miss Sutherland has asked for, and getting it down to her.'

'I can't allow you to do that, Mr Sanderson, what would the staff think?'

'I imagine they'll be only too glad to get the necessary stock before they have to start refusing customers. Now give me the lists from Miss Bleasedale's haberdashery and Miss Sutherland's leather goods. That will be two less for you to worry about.' He saw she was about to protest, and lifted a hand. 'I have two orders for you, Miss Halliday, and I want them carried out to the letter. First, give me the two lists I've asked for.' They were handed over without a word. 'And now, my other order is that you bring yourself to my office at eleven-thirty prompt where there will be a well-deserved pot of tea waiting. Is that understood, Miss Halliday?'

Mary nodded. 'Yes, Mr Sanderson.' She watched him turn in the direction of the stock room before looking at her watch. And after that, she glanced at it every five minutes until eleven-thirty-one, when she was knocking on his office door.

'Ah, Mary, sit yourself down for that well-earned rest. The tea is being brought up now.' Clive sat down and looked across his desk at the woman who had brought meaning into his life. He wished he wasn't as shy as he was for there were things he would like to say to her, to ask her. 'I have mentioned once before that you need an assistant. You were against the idea then, and I foolishly gave in to your wishes. But after the last few hours, I can see it is essential that you have help before you make yourself ill.' There was a knock on the door before it was opened by one of the waitresses from the cafe on the top floor. 'Thank you, please set it down and leave us to pour.'

'I'll do that.' Mary was glad of something to do other than looking into his face, which lately she found unnerving. 'I think we are going to have a bumper Christmas. Sales are well up on the last two years.'

'Mary, can we set work aside for just twenty minutes? You, above anyone, need a break from it. Tell me what you're doing on Christmas Day?'

'Spending it at home, as I usually do. I have several good friends who invite me each year without fail. But they are married with children and I always feel as though I don't belong there on that particular day. Other days, yes, but not Christmas Day.'

'I would invite you to my house and we could be two lonely people together, but unfortunately my housekeeper doesn't work Christmas Day. If I had the slightest idea of how to cook I would ask her to prepare the food the day before, then I would only need to put it on the stove and warm it. But I am quite helpless and hopeless.'

'You can come to mine if you wish.' There, it was out! Mary felt weak in the knees. 'I always make a roast dinner even though I eat it alone.' She made herself look busy putting milk and sugar in the cups so she wouldn't have to see the expression on his face. 'My house is a very modest one, but it is big enough for me. You are welcome to share my Christmas dinner if you wish.'

Clive didn't answer until she was handing him his cup and was forced to look him in the face. And what she saw there filled her with relief. She was afraid she'd made a fool of herself, but his expression told her otherwise. 'Mary, I would be delighted and am looking forward to it already. But I will only come if you will let me repay you by taking you for a meal on New Year's Day. Perhaps at the Adelphi or the State?'

Her head was in a whirl, wondering if she had the right clothes for those places. Then she thought, Blow it, I'll worry about that later. There's nothing to stop me looking for something suitable in my dinner hour. She could try Blackler's or Owen Owen's. Oh, what did it matter? She could dip into her savings and buy something really attractive. She wanted him to be proud of her. 'That would be lovely, Clive.' And his slow, gentle smile almost had her swooning like a young girl.

* * *

When Beth heard the knock on her door, she thought it would be Flo ready to go to the shops. And it was Flo, but she wasn't alone – Dot was with her. Without waiting to be asked in, the little woman pushed Beth aside and bounced into the living room. She looked at each of the wooden dining chairs, trying to remember which one she could expect the least objection from. 'Blow it, they're all the bleedin' same,' she said aloud, before plonking herself on one that wasn't prepared for her eighteen stone and groaned like mad. 'You can just shut up while we find out what shenanigans our so-called friend's been up to.'

Beth shrugged her shoulders at Dot. 'What's she on about?'

'Well, I've got to admit to being as curious as her,' Dot said, sitting on the arm of the couch. 'I mean, it's not often yer see a car in this street, and certainly not one that stops outside anyone's door.'

The light dawned, and Beth tutted. 'Oh, my God, have yer both got nothing better to worry about? And how come anyone saw it, because I didn't.'

'It's just as well we did see it 'cos you wouldn't have told us!' Flo started plucking at the chenille tablecloth. 'If I hadn't been looking out for our Amy, who'd been told to be home by nine o'clock, then I'd have been none the wiser.'

'I heard it stopping,' Dot said, 'and peeped through the curtain.'

'Well, I'll put yer out of yer misery quickly, 'cos I want to get to the shops as soon as I can. I've promised meself to go and see me mam and dad this afternoon in case I don't get another chance. And Hannah's coming with me 'cos she hasn't seen them for years.' Beth pulled out a chair facing Flo. 'Yer know our Ginny was going to tea with a woman who often comes in the shop, that she's got friendly with? Well, this woman's nephew offered to drive Ginny home so she wouldn't have to travel on her own in the dark. And that's all there is to it.'

'Ye're coming up in the world, aren't yer, girl?' Flo said, plucking away at the tablecloth. 'Yer'll be too big-headed to speak to us common people, what yer used to call yer best mates.'

'I don't know why ye're making a big thing out of my daughter getting a lift home in a car.' Beth was privately asking herself why her two neighbours had seen the car and she hadn't. Not that a car was anything to get excited about, but she'd have liked to have seen it all the same. 'And will yer stop pulling at those tufts in me tablecloth, sunshine, before yer have them all out? It's the only chenille cloth I've got to me name.' She was beginning to see the funny side, but she wasn't going to let her two mates know. 'Just out of curiosity, why didn't you two knock for Lizzie? She won't think much of yer when she finds yer've left her out.'

Dot had the grace to blush as she moved from the couch to one of the dining chairs. 'We did knock for her, girl, but she was busy filling the dolly tub. She said she'd be over as soon as she could.'

Beth was the first to see the humour in the situation, followed by Dot who howled with laughter. And the poor chair Flo was sitting on got a real hammering as her enormous body shook with mirth. 'Ye're a nosy pair of beggars,' Beth said. Then she asked, 'By the way, what colour was the car?'

'I couldn't tell yer, girl, 'cos I didn't see much of it.' Flo was doing her best to keep her body still. It always gave the game away. 'I could ask Dennis for yer tonight, he'll know 'cos he saw more of it than I did.'

Beth's voice was shrill. 'Dennis saw it!'

'Yeah, I called him over, and I was sorry afterwards 'cos he pushed me out of the way. By the time I'd pushed him back, the bleedin' car had gone.'

'Well, that takes the cake, that does. I was probably the only one in the street who didn't see me daughter coming home in style. Just wait till I tell Andy.'

But Beth was to tell Hannah before her husband. She called for the old lady after she'd finished shopping with her mates, and it was while they were sitting on the bus to Huyton that she told the tale. They had a darn good laugh about it because Beth liked nothing better than to impersonate Flo. 'I can just see her jumping up and down, waving Dennis over. And I can see her getting her dander up when he wouldn't budge and she missed seeing the car drive away. I bet he got a right earful off her then.'

'And who was the person who owned the car?' Hannah asked. 'Not many people we know could afford one.'

'Yer've heard Ginny talking about Miss Meadows? Well, it was her nephew's car. Ginny said he's only seventeen, and his dad bought it for him for his birthday.'

'Seventeen and owning a car?' Hannah looked as though she didn't approve. 'They must have more money than sense.' She folded her arms and looked out of the window at the passing fields. Then she asked, 'Is Ginny seeing him again?'

'Oh, I couldn't tell yer that, sunshine, but I shouldn't think so. Anyway, she's got her head screwed on the right way, has Ginny.'

'I know that, sweetheart, but a car is a big attraction. None of the boys round our way could offer her anything so glamorous. And I know one boy who would be upset if he thought Ginny had got herself a boyfriend.'

'Oh, aye, who's that, sunshine?'

'Our Bobby. He's never said anything, and he'd go mad if he knew I was telling yer this. But I've got eyes in me head, sweetheart, and I've seen the way his face lights up when she's around.'

'She's only fifteen, Hannah, too young to be thinking of boys.'

'Bobby's two years older and on the threshold of becoming a man. My husband was two years older than me, it didn't make any difference.'

'Andy's two years older than me, as well, sunshine, but I can't live Ginny's life for her, she has to do that herself.' Beth stuck her arm through the old lady's and grinned. 'I'd be over the moon if she picked someone as good as your Bobby.'

Hannah patted her hand. 'Yer know how fond of her I am, sweetheart, and I'd love her to be a member of my family. So while Ginny does her growing up, I'll do my praying.'

It was on the Wednesday that Alicia Meadows came into Woolworth's. She had to talk to Ginny over the heads of customers. 'I won't keep you, Virginia, I can see how busy you are. But did you ask your parents about the theatre?'

'I did, and they said they had no objection as long as I wasn't coming home alone in the dark. But can we leave it until after the holidays, Miss Meadows, when me head's a bit clearer and me feet aren't so tired?'

'Yes, of course, my dear. Have a lovely Christmas with your family.'

'And you have a nice Christmas, too,' Ginny said, feeling a bit mean knowing the woman had no family of her own. It must be awful to be alone at the time of the year when every family in the country would be together, rejoicing. 'I'll look forward to the theatre.'

It was Thursday morning and Ginny and Marie were on the tram heading for the city centre. Tonight was the big night, when they went to their first dance with the boys. Eight of them were going, four girls and four boys. But while Joan and Amelia had their dance shoes, Ginny and Marie hadn't bought any yet. 'Have yer got enough money on yer, Marie,' Ginny asked, 'so we can dash out in our lunch break?'

She nodded. 'I've got five bob on me, they shouldn't cost any more than that.'

'I've got the same. Miss Sutherland said there's a shoe shop in

Whitechapel and they're quite cheap. And she said there's loads to choose from.'

'Ooh, er, I'm getting all excited.' Marie gave a little shiver as her smile widened. 'I'm not going to worry about making a fool of meself, 'cos me mam said everyone's got to learn sometime. And we'll only be dancing with our friends, won't we?'

'I certainly hope so, 'cos I'll tell yer something for nothing – if I saw a stranger coming towards me I'd make a bee-line for the door.' Then she chuckled. 'Chance would be a fine thing, wouldn't it?'

Marie's eyes slid sideways. 'Would yer ever ask this Charles to come to the dance?'

Ginny doubled up. 'Marie, yer don't know how funny that is! We're going to a tuppenny hop at a church hall, and yer can take it from me he wouldn't be seen dead in such a place. Not that he's not a nice bloke, 'cos he is, but he's been brought up with money and doesn't know any different.'

'Joan was a bit sarcastic about it, wasn't she? There was no need for what she said.'

'That's Joan all over. I'm used to her, Marie, and I don't take no notice of her.'

'Well, if yer ask me, I think she was green with envy.'

'No, yer don't know her as well as I do. The only thing wrong with Joan is that she doesn't think before she opens her mouth. I've told her her tongue will get her hung one of these days, but she'll never change. I hope when she gets a boyfriend, he'll be someone who can keep her in check, 'cos that's what she needs.'

Marie jumped to her feet. 'Next stop ours, kiddo. Another hectic day of being rushed off our feet and trying to keep a smile on our faces to make the customers happy.'

Ginny followed her down the aisle of the swaying tram. 'Never mind, we've got something to look forward to. And don't forget we're going for our dancing shoes, so get away on the dot.'

When the lunchtime break came, it was a rush for the two friends. They had to get their coats and bags from the cloakroom, then dash like mad along to Whitechapel. They found the shoe shop easily enough, and there was a wide selection of dance shoes in silver, gold and black, but as both had their hearts set on silver, they didn't bother trying any of the others on. They decided that the very high heels wouldn't be suitable for learners, so they opted for cuban heels instead. And so they wouldn't get mixed up, they chose different styles.

Outside the shop, the friends looked at each other and burst out

343

laughing. 'We did very well, I think,' Ginny said. 'Yer couldn't fall out with them for two and eleven.'

'I'll say! I wasn't expecting to get change out of me five bob.' Marie gazed up at a huge clock over one of the shop fronts, and grabbed Ginny's arm. 'We'd better put a move on, kid, or we won't have time to eat our sandwiches in the cloakroom.'

'Let's run, then.' Ginny tucked the shoe bag under her arm and took to her heels. 'I'll have to have something to eat or me tummy will be rumbling all afternoon. But I feel pleased with meself over the shoes, we got a bargain.'

The gang had arranged to meet at eight o'clock outside the Baileys' house as it was on the way down to the main road. It wasn't far to the church hall, only a five-minute walk, and the four girls walked ahead, chattering away, while the boys were behind, discussing either their work or their workmates. They were completely unaware that they had an audience. Beth had come to the door to watch her daughter going to her first dance, and Dot, who had the same idea, soon joined her. They'd been seen through the window by Lizzie, who reckoned that with two of her sons involved, she had a perfect right to join them.

'It doesn't seem that long since I was taking Ginny to school on her first day,' Beth said. 'The years have just flown over.'

'I can remember that day as though it was yesterday.' Dot let out a deep sigh. 'I can even remember what the girls were wearing.'

'Life is a journey, so it is,' Lizzie said. 'And the road the children are on now, we were on some eighteen to twenty years ago. Let's pray to God that they enjoy what we enjoyed, and when the time comes for the darlin's to settle down, may they have the good fortune to choose decent, upstanding young men as their parents did.'

'Whoever Ginny chooses will have to go through me first,' Beth said. 'If I don't think he's good enough for her, I'll be showing him the door.'

'Ooh, I think I'll be giving our Joan to the first one what comes along,' Dot said, pulling a face. 'She's one holy terror who thinks she knows it all. I feel sorry for any boyfriend she has 'cos he'll have his hands full with her.'

'If she falls hard enough for a lad, then she'll be putty in his hands,' Beth said. 'Me mam was only saying on Monday that I was a handful at Ginny's age. She said I used to give her cheek and would never do as I was told. But from the day I met Andy, apparently I changed so much me mam and dad thought I was sick.'

'But your Ginny doesn't give yer cheek,' Lizzie said. 'Sure, she's a very well-behaved young lady, so she is.'

'I know, she's an angel.' Beth began to chuckle. 'That's why I'm not going to tell her what me mam said about me. It might give her ideas.' She turned when there was a rap on her window, and there was Andy beckoning to her in no uncertain terms. 'Oh, lord, he'll think I do nothing all day but gossip. Yer know what men are like – he said I was a nosy beggar for coming out to watch the kids. Anyway, I'd better get in 'cos there's a play on the wireless he wants to listen to. It's a murder mystery, so me and Joey will have to breathe quietly in case he misses finding out who the murderer is. So while my dear husband sits with his ear glued to the wireless, and Joey gets his nose stuck in a comic, I'll be sitting quietly darning socks. And they have the nerve to say men have a hard life! I'll tell yer what, I'd swap places with them any day.'

The dim light from the street lamp cast a glow over Beth's blonde hair and anyone would be forgiven for thinking it was Ginny standing there. The girl was the same height as her mother now, and had the same slim figure though as yet hers hadn't blossomed into womanhood. 'My feller wouldn't know what hit him if he had to do the shopping, the cooking, washing, ironing and all the other things, including darning socks. I'd give him a week and he'd be begging for mercy.'

'A week!' Dot huffed. 'I'd give my feller two days at the most. Anyway, yer'd better go in, your Andy's going red in the face. We'll see each other in the morning.'

'Yeah, we can swap tales about what our kids tell us, without a man with a red face shaking his hand at us.'

'Ah, sure, the man isn't doing no such thing, so he isn't.' Lizzie smiled and nodded her head at Andy. 'He's got a grin on his face as wide as the River Mersey.' She started to cross the cobbles to her own house. 'I'll see yer tomorrow.'

'D'yer know where the hall is?' Marie asked. 'Because we could run ahead and pay for ourselves, save embarrassing the boys. Me mam said they won't be earning much money and it wouldn't be fair to expect them to pay for us.'

'There's the church,' Amelia said, nodding her head. 'And I believe the hall is next to it. Come on, we'll find it.'

The boys saw the girls take flight and looked at each other in surprise. 'What's got into them?' Mick said, scratching his head. Then he suddenly put a spurt on. 'I know why they want to be there first – so they can pay for themselves.'

Three of the lads, Bobby, Mick and David, were all nearing their seventeenth birthday, and by their reckoning that made them old enough to pay for any girl they took out. It made no difference that the girls were neighbours and mates, they'd been invited to come to the dance.

The girls were huddled together in the entrance hall, their tickets clutched in their hands, eyes wide with apprehension. This was their first grown-up adventure and they were filled with a mixture of excitement and fear.

David marched straight up to his sister. 'That wasn't very clever of yer. We asked yer to come, and we were going to pay for yer.'

'Don't be shouting at me, it wasn't my doing.' Joan's eyes flashed. 'If yer want to blame anyone, blame Marie's mam, she said we should pay for ourselves.'

'There's no harm done,' Mick said, thinking it was a good start to the night. 'And don't be so quick to flare up, Joan Flynn. It's never your fault, yer've always got to blame someone else.'

Seamus, the quietest of the lot, bought his ticket from the man sitting at a small card table near the entrance. Then without a word he took Amelia's elbow and led her through the main door into the dance hall. 'Come on, leave them to it.'

'Well, I like that!' Joan said. 'Cheeky beggar!'

Mick strode to the man selling the tickets, bought three and handed one each to David and Bobby. Then, he didn't just take Joan's elbow, he grabbed it. 'And will yer keep quiet for a change? We came to dance, so let's do it.'

Ginny giggled. 'That's put her in her place.'

'And shut her up.' David jerked his head. 'Shall we follow them in?' He took Marie's arm. 'Don't expect anywhere posh, 'cos it's only a church hall, but we like it.'

When Bobby reached for Ginny's hand, she thought nothing of it. After all, they were mates, were't they?

There was no band there, just a gramophone playing records. But the music was good enough to dance to and the floor was crowded. There were no experienced dancers or show-offs. In fact most of the couples on the floor were raw beginners. But that wasn't sufficient to entice the girls on to the floor. The first dance was a quickstep which had them shaking their heads vigorously. The second, a tango, looked even more complicated. But when they announced a waltz, Mick said, 'Joan, are yer going to try this?'

346

'Huh! Wild horses wouldn't be able to drag me on to that floor to make a fool of meself.'

'In case yer hadn't noticed, I'm not a wild horse so that lets me out.' With that he literally dragged her on to the floor while the others looked on with interest. 'Now behave yerself, Joan Flynn, or I'll be forced to put yer across me knee and spank yer.'

Joan, a sharp retort ready on her lips, looked into his dancing Irish eyes and forgot what she was going to say. 'As long as they don't laugh at me. If they do, I'm off.'

'My kid brother's having a go with Amelia so ye're not on yer own.' He took one of her hands in his, lifted it into the position for dancing, and said, 'Now put yer other hand on me shoulder. And when I say "go", step back with yer left foot, like we showed yer the other night.'

Bobby took his courage in his hands. 'Come on, Ginny, don't be frightened. Yer'll never hear the last of it off yer mate if yer don't try.'

His heart went thump when she smiled. 'It's not what me mate might say that would worry me, Bobby, it's buying a new pair of dance shoes and not even going on the floor in them. I'd kick meself tomorrow if I did that.'

He looked down, and although it was dark and he couldn't really tell, said, 'The shoes look nice on yer, so does yer dress.' And when she took his hand and he led her on to the dance floor, he added, 'But then, yer always look nice, Ginny.'

It was David's turn now. 'How about it, Marie? We'll never learn standing here.'

'I thought yer'd never ask.' She allowed herself to be led on to the floor. 'I thought I was going to be a wallflower, all on me own.'

While David manoeuvred them both into position, he was thinking she would never be a wallflower. Not with that wonderful smile and happy nature.

When the waltz was over and the group met up again, it was the general opinion that they'd all done very well. Not brilliantly, but that was asking too much. At least no toes were broken and no one had ended up on their backside in the middle of the floor. So congratulations were the order of the day until the next dance was announced: a slow foxtrot. The girls didn't wait to be asked but shook their heads and said they'd watch from the sidelines. The boys didn't try to coax them because they weren't very good at the slow foxtrot themselves and they'd look stupid trying to teach something they hadn't mastered yet.

The four couples took to the floor when the next waltz was announced, and it was as they were doing their best to keep to the three steps that Bobby remarked casually, 'What's this I hear about yer having a boyfriend with a car?'

Ginny's concentration was interrupted and she stood on his toe. 'That's yer own fault for saying daft things, Bobby Bailey. And, if yer want to know, I haven't got a boyfriend with a car, nor have I a boyfriend without one.'

Bobby knew his toe was hurt, but he ignored it. What Ginny had said more than made up for any pain he may feel. 'I'm glad yer haven't got a boyfriend, Ginny, 'cos I was going to ask yer to come to the pictures with me one night. That's if yer mam says it's all right, of course.'

Ginny could feel herself blushing. 'Ooh, I don't know. I think me mam will say I'm too young to be going out with boys. Perhaps it would be better to leave it for a while.'

'If I leave it, yer might find yerself another boyfriend and forget about me.'

'Don't be daft, I'm not going to find a boyfriend. And anyway, how could I forget about you when I see yer nearly every night?' Ginny's face broke into a smile. 'Ay, just look at Mick and Joan, they're going round the floor really well. She's doing better than me, so can we stop talking and let me concentrate on learning this flippin' waltz? At this rate, I'll be twenty before I get as far as the tango.'

The night was voted a great success as the gang made their way home. The pavement wasn't wide enough to take the eight of them in a line, so they split into fours. Seamus, Amelia, Mick and Joan walked in front, while Ginny, Bobby, Marie and David followed behind. They had their arms around each other and they laughed and joked the whole way home. 'Next week I'm definitely going to try the quickstep,' Joan said. 'And the week after I should be ready for the slow foxtrot.'

'I think yer'd be better sticking to the waltz for a few weeks,' Mick said, looking down into her laughing face. 'Me feet are black and blue now, after a waltz. Just think of the damage yer could inflict doing a quickstep.'

'I only stood on David's toes twice,' Marie said. 'So I didn't do so bad.'

'I can go one better than that,' Ginny said. 'Bobby's only got one broken toe.'

Seamus winked down at Amelia. 'Me and Amelia have got yer all licked. We didn't tread on each other's toes once. In fact, I think Fred

348

Astaire and Ginger Rogers had better pull their socks up or we'll be taking over from them.'

And so the night ended in laughter.

Chapter Twenty-Eight

Beth's three neighbours had called for her to go to the shops, but she wasn't quite ready and had asked them in. 'I've only got to comb me hair and put me coat on, I won't be two shakes of a lamb's tail.'

'I thought yer'd be ready, girl, knowing how busy the shops are going to be,' Flo said. 'They'll be packed solid today, what with the Tontines being paid out, and people drawing on their Christmas clubs.'

'I'm ready now, so stop yer moaning.' Beth was reaching for her key out of the glass dish on the sideboard when there was a knock on the door. 'Oh, lord, who can this be?'

'I'll get it,' Dot said, and within seconds she was ushering Aggie Graham in. 'Aggie wants a word with us.'

'It's just to tell yer how happy Vera was with the clothes.' Their neighbour from the next street could see they were ready to go out so she didn't waste any time. 'I told her they were from a friend whose kids had grown out of them. And d'yer know what? I nearly burst out crying 'cos she was that grateful, anyone would think I'd given her a pound note.'

The four friends were glad they'd stumped up a few coppers each to pay for the clothes. Hearing of Vera's pleasure was payment enough. 'We're going to mug the kids to some sweets, Aggie,' Beth told her. 'Not much, but they'll help out. So Flo will pass them over to yer when we get back from the shops and yer can tell Vera they're from you. Don't mention us, 'cos I'd hate her to think we feel sorry for her.'

'I'm buying them a pair of socks each,' Aggie said. 'It's not much, but I can't afford any more with me own gang to see to. Besides, they'll be made up 'cos half the time they've no socks on their feet.'

'We don't know we're born,' Lizzie said. 'The poor soul must be out of her mind with four children to feed and clothe. And like every mother in the land, sure, she'll want to give them something for Christmas. There's nothing more joyful than a child's face on Christmas morning when he comes down to see Santa hasn't forgotten him. We'll

351

do what we can, Aggie, and little as it may be, it will be better than nothing.'

She thanked them again, then said a quick 'ta-ra' so she could nip to the shops to get her own shopping in.

'That's cheered me up,' Beth said, putting the handle of the basket in the crook of her arm. 'It does yer good to know yer've helped someone who's worse off than yerself.'

The four friends walked down the street towards County Road. 'If we give threepence each that should get the kids an apple, an orange, some nuts and sweets,' Dot said. 'And if we can sweet talk Bill in the butcher's, he might give a few sausages for a deserving cause.'

'It's worth a try,' Beth said. And looking down at Flo, who was linking her arm, she said, laughingly, 'We could tell him Flo was the deserving cause.'

Flo didn't answer because she didn't hear. She was too busy watching the familiar figure standing on the street corner. 'Ay out, what's Ma Maloney standing there for? She usually keeps to the side streets or entries.'

'Well, she won't be looking for us, that's a dead cert,' Beth said. 'Some poor beggar must be in her bad books.' But what a surprise the women had when the moneylender, who always looked like a tramp, stood in front of them, stopping their progress.

'Can I have a word with yer?'

'I can't imagine what yer would want a word with us for,' Beth answered as the woman was looking directly at her. 'None of us has any dealing with yer now.'

'It's nothing to do with any of you, it's Vera Duffy I want to talk about.' Now the women weren't to know that when they'd told the moneylender Vera Duffy was contemplating suicide because she couldn't pay her loan back, it would have a profound effect on Ma. She was well aware she was disliked by everyone, even the women who borrowed from her, and if she'd been the cause of a young mother taking her own life, leaving four young children behind, then Ma Maloney knew she would have been hounded out of the area. Because of the scare she'd had, she was now more lenient with those who borrowed from her, and had dropped her interest charges to sixpence a week. 'I wondered how she was getting on, like?'

The four women exchanged glances, wondering what the old witch was up to. But to find that out, they'd have to talk to her. If they pushed her out of the way and walked on they'd always wonder what she'd wanted. It was Beth who spoke up. 'Struggling, I suppose, same as yer'd expect a woman with four children to be doing when her husband works all week for buttons. But I'm sure ye're not interested in that, so what d'yer really want to know?'

A wrinkled hand was pushed into a pocket of Ma's scruffy coat, and when it came out again, it reached out to Beth. 'I was thinking of the kids, yer know, like, having nothing for Christmas, so I wondered if yer'd get them something with this two bob? It'll buy them a few bits and pieces.'

Beth looked at the outstretched palm, and the two-shilling piece in the middle of it. Her first reaction was to tell the moneylender to keep her blood money, but wisely she kept her true feelings to herself. After all, while it wouldn't do her any harm to refuse the money, there were four young children to be thought of. 'Me and me mates,' Beth waved her hand to her neighbours, who were watching in disbelief, 'we've clubbed together to buy the kids something, but this two bob will make a big difference.' She picked the coin from the open palm. 'D'yer want us to tell Vera it was you what gave it to us?'

'No, let her think it came from you. I'd rather no one knew about it.' The woman, who looked as though she hadn't a penny to her name but was probably very well off through her moneylending, nodded before shuffling away.

'Well, I declare!' Lizzie said. 'Who'd have thought of that now? Sure, if we told anyone they'd think we were pulling their leg.'

'Ours is not to reason why, Lizzie. If it hadn't been for Vera and the kids, I'd have thrown the money back in her face. But two bob will buy a lot for those kids if we play our cards right. By the time we've finished shopping we'll have enough to fill four stockings. And when we get back, we'll take them to Aggie's so Vera will know her kids have something to come down to on Christmas morning.'

Flo was scratching her head. 'Ay, they say a leopard never changes its spots, so what's up with Ma Maloney? I wonder if she's found religion or what?'

'I don't care what she's found, sunshine, as long as she doesn't come and ask for her money back. And I think we should keep this to ourselves. I won't even tell Aggie, 'cos I'd hate it to get back to Vera.' Beth slipped the coin into her pocket. 'That was the last thing I was expecting, but I'll tell yer what, it's not half cheered me up.'

'Are yer still going to ask the butcher for six sausages?' Flo asked, as the friends turned into County Road. 'If yer send sausages round to Vera's, as well as the fruit and sweets, not to mention the clothes, she'll twig there's something fishy going on.'

'I was just thinking the same thing, sunshine.' Beth squeezed the little woman's arm. 'They say great minds think alike, and there's no one with greater minds than ours, Florence Henderson. Anyway, to answer yer question, no, I'm not going to cadge six sausages off Bill. As yer say, it would be too much. But we'll try and work our charms on Greg for some cheap apples and oranges. And I want us all to stand together on this, 'cos he's not likely to turn down four good customers, is he?'

'Ye're a crafty bugger, Beth Porter.' Flo was chuckling inside at the prospect of having fun with the man in the greengrocer's. 'But seeing as it's in a good cause, we'll stand foursquare behind yer, won't we, girls? If Greg can't find it in his heart to listen to a sad story then he'll get his just deserts.'

It turned out that he didn't have time to listen to the sad story, he was rushed off his feet. When Beth and Dot fluttered their eyelashes, and asked him if he could possibly find it in his heart to help out a poor family, he didn't argue the toss but threw four extra oranges and apples in Beth's basket and thought it well worthwhile when he got a kiss off both of them. Mind you, his face paled when Flo came towards him with her lips puckered. 'Ah, no, Florrie, I don't deserve that after being so generous with yer.'

He pushed his flat cap to the back of his head, remembering what she'd done to him last year. Her lips had been puckered, just as they were now, and he'd bent down to give her a kiss on the cheek. But before he knew it Flo had her arms around his waist and had picked him up as though he was a rag doll. No amount of pleading with her to put him down helped; in fact it had the shop full of customers in hysterics. She'd done no worse than carry him outside and sit him in a wooden crate which was half full of oranges, but he'd had a hell of a time getting out of the orange box because he had no leverage, and people passing by stopped and joined in the laughter of his customers. Well, he wasn't falling for that again! 'I'll tell yer what, Flo, to show there's no ill feeling, and I love the bones of yer, I'll give an extra orange if yer don't kiss me.'

A woman standing close by heard the offer. 'Ooh, I'd thought of giving yer a kiss, Greg, seeing as it's Christmas.'

'Stay out of it, Nellie, yer've never wanted to kiss me before, Christmas or no Christmas.'

'I know that, lad, but I didn't know yer were giving oranges out to customers what didn't kiss yer.'

What could Greg do but laugh his head off? I mean, it might be

Christmas, and he might have a shop full of customers, but his sense of humour was still intact.

The last stop for the four friends was the sweet shop, and by the time they came out of there, bags and baskets were full and very heavy. They stood on the pavement outside the shop and Beth placed her basket on the ground to give her arm a rest. Their street was only a short walk away, but as a joke she said, 'I wish there was a bus stop near so we could get a bus right to our doors.'

Flo appeared not to be quick on the uptake, which led the women to think she didn't realise that her neighbour and best mate was joking. 'There's a tram stop right here, girl, we could get a tram.'

'I know!' Beth's face was deadpan, while Dot and Lizzie turned away. 'But isn't it a pity we've got no tram lines in our street?'

'Oh, yeah, I forgot.' Flo Henderson must be the best actress since Ethel Barrymore. She glanced down at the pavement, as though deep in thought, then looked up with a smile on her face. 'I know what we can do, girl! The coalman is due along here any minute, he'd be dead chuffed to give us a lift.' Then, seeing the expression on the faces of her three friends, she added for good measure, 'It wouldn't cost us nothing either!'

Beth had been biting on the inside of her mouth. Now she said, 'I'm going to roar with laughter any minute, sunshine, are yer ready?'

'I'm ready, girl.' But as Flo's body began to shake, she said, 'You three would fall for the bleedin' cat, yer would.' And when everyone standing in the sweet shop, the butcher's and the greengrocer's, heard the laughter it brought a smile to their faces even though they didn't know what the joke was.

It brought a lot of pleasure to Greg, 'cos as he was weighing out carrots and spuds, he was thinking some other sucker had fallen for one of Flo Henderson's tricks, and hoped it was the man in the sweet shop who was a miserable bugger at the best of times. His wife was all right, but how she put up with her husband God only knows.

'We need another stocking.' Beth looked at each of her friends in turn. They'd split the oranges, apples, nuts, sweets, painting books and colouring pencils into four piles, and there was only Flo not busy filling a stocking. 'Flo, you haven't brought one, so will yer cough up, please, so we can get these filled and round to Aggie's?'

'I haven't got no bleedin' stocking to spare! I've got one good pair which I'm keeping for the holidays, no matter what.' Flo's face was set in determination. 'All me old ones which I use for round the house are full of bleedin' ladders.'

'The one I brought had ladders in,' Dot said, 'we don't expect yer to give a decent one to fill with fruit and toys, it would be a waste.'

'Mine was falling to pieces, as well.' Lizzie flicked through the painting book she was about to put in the stocking she was holding. 'A few ladders are neither here nor there.'

'Look at this one, sunshine.' Beth held out the one she was filling. 'It's got enough ladders to start a window cleaning round.'

Flo stopped swinging her legs under the chair. 'Ay, that was good that was, girl. I'll have to remember to tell my feller tonight.'

'Well, yer set yer legs in motion again, sunshine, and get to your house and root out an old stocking from under the cushion on the couch.'

Flo pressed her chubby hands down on the table and pushed herself up. Then she put her face close to Beth's and pulled tongues. 'I don't keep them under the cushion, smart arse, I shove them down the side.' With a toss of her head she left the room.

'She's a bloody hero, that one,' Dot said. 'No one could be miserable for long with her around.'

'Ay, did yer see the look of fear on Greg's face?' Lizzie asked. 'Sure, didn't me heart go out to the poor man? Him with a shop full of customers too!'

'I wouldn't worry about Greg, or Bill at the butcher's. They'll both tell yer they love to see her coming into their shops 'cos she always gives them a laugh. Some of their customers are real misery guts so Flo brightens up their day for them.' Beth's hearty chuckle filled the room. 'Christmas Eve is different, like, with them being so busy. But yer can't tell me mate to be funny for three hundred and sixty-four days of the year, and then quiet and ladylike for the other one.'

When Flo came back she threw a lisle stocking on to the table. 'That's the only clean one I've got, so I'm afraid it's a case of like it or lump it. Anyway, it hasn't got ladders big enough for the oranges to fall out.'

'Start filling it then, sunshine, so we can get them round to Aggie's.' Beth wagged her shoulders with delight. 'I'm so happy we're able to do this for Vera's kids. I mean, we've been skint many a time, but we've never been poverty-stricken. Years ago our husbands' wages weren't great, but we scraped through by helping each other out. But with four young children, and her husband on a low wage, Vera must be really pushed to manage.'

'Well, we've done our best to help, girl,' Flo said, 'we can't do no more.'

356

'I think we've done very well.' Dot lifted the stocking she had filled and it looked quite heavy and healthy, with bumps where the oranges and apples were sticking out. 'The kids will be over the moon.'

Lizzie was more thoughtful. 'The two bob we got off the moneylender was a big help. And I never thought I'd say it about Ma Maloney, but God bless the woman.'

After being together at Midnight Mass, the four families were joined outside the church by the Bailey family. Seasonal greetings were exchanged, and as they wouldn't be seeing each other on Christmas Day, they wished each other a happy and peaceful one. But they'd be getting together on Boxing Day, when Beth was opening her house to all the parents, including Hannah and Claire, and Lizzie's was the venue for the youngsters. Food and drinks for both houses was being paid for out of a kitty they'd all contributed to.

When Beth woke up on Christmas morning, she stretched her body and told herself it was a lovely feeling that the whole day belonged to her, Andy and the kids. The dinner had been prepared the night before, so there was little to do but relax. She didn't care if the dust was an inch thick and met her at the door, she wasn't going to touch a duster. All she intended doing was to spoil herself for just the one day.

Andy stirred, felt Beth moving and slipped an arm across her waist. 'Happy Christmas, my beautiful, dearest wife.'

Beth turned her head for a kiss. 'Happy Christmas, sunshine.' She cuddled into him. 'Ooh, I don't half love you. I love the bones of yer.'

'And I love you.' Andy was nuzzling her neck when she said, 'I wouldn't be getting too loving, 'cos our Joey's been awake for about half-an-hour.'

Andy whispered, 'How d'yer know? I can't hear anything.'

'I've been listening to the springs on his bed. He's been tossing and turning, waiting for us to get up. He's still only a kid, remember, and Christmas Day is a big day for him, or have yer forgotten what it was like at his age?'

'D'yer think I could bribe him to go to sleep again for half-an-hour?'

There came a tapping on the wall that was paper thin and wouldn't allow secrets to be kept. 'I know ye're awake, Mam, so can I get up?'

'How about staying in bed for another half-hour, sunshine, so I can have a lie in? Besides, our Ginny won't want to get up yet. She was rushed off her feet yesterday and was half dead when she got home from work.'

Then they heard a sleepy voice call, 'I've been awake for ages, Mam. Our Joey woke me up to ask me what the time was, and I couldn't get back to sleep again.'

Beth lifted Andy's arm from her waist and slipped her legs over the side of the bed. 'No rest for the wicked.' She shivered and rubbed her arms. 'I'll go down and warm the room up first, so stay where yer are, Joey. I left the fire banked up, so all I need to do is rake it out and put a few pieces of coal on. There'll be a fire up the chimney in no time.'

'I don't feel the cold, Mam, so can I come down with yer?'

'No, yer can't! Yer'd be like a cat on hot bricks wanting to open yer presents, and yer know we open them together. So hold yer horses for just ten minutes and I'll give yer a shout when the fire's on the go.'

As she stood up and slipped a cardigan over her shoulders, Andy said softly, 'I'll be a good boy and do as I'm told, as long as yer promise me I can have an extra Christmas present?'

'Oh, aye, sunshine, and what's that, then?'

'That we have an early night tonight.'

She bent down and kissed his cheek. 'Yer don't ask for much, sunshine, so yer have my promise on that.'

Twenty minutes later Beth was calling up the stairs, 'Come on, lazy bones. The fire is up the chimney and the tea's in the pot. What more can yer ask?' She stepped back quickly as Joey came bounding down the stairs. As she was to say later, he'd got himself so wound up he would have walked through her. 'Ay, watch it, sunshine, I don't want to end up in hospital with a broken leg on Christmas Day.'

He looked penitent at first, then when he realised he hadn't hurt his beloved mother, a cheeky grin spread across his face. 'I would have come and visited yer in hospital, Mam, even though I'd have to walk 'cos there's no transport on a Christmas Day. As soon as I'd opened me presents I'd have started walking.'

She ruffled his hair. 'Cheeky article! I've a good mind not to give yer any presents now.'

Ginny came down then, rubbing the sleep out of her eyes. 'Ooh, I could have slept through the day, I'm dead beat.'

'Well, we've got a lazy day, sunshine, yer can put yer feet up on the couch and relax. And we'll all have an early night so we're refreshed for the parties.' She looked up to see Andy on the landing. 'Here's yer dad now, so yer can start giving the presents out, Joey.'

Tiredness was forgotten for the next hour as paper was ripped from presents. Andy was pleased with his shirt and socks, Beth showed her appreciation of a pink underskirt and stockings while Ginny was over the moon with the dress Beth had bought her from Sadie at Paddy's Market. But the person who brought them all the most pleasure was Joey when he saw his first pair of long trousers. He was so excited anyone would think he'd won the pools. 'Mam, can I put them on now?'

'Of course yer can, sunshine, and Ginny can try her dress on while I make us some toast. Yer dad will clear the mess off the floor for me.'

It was a day of family closeness and contentment. When the dinner was over, they all helped with clearing the table and washing the dishes. Joey wanted to go to their two neighbours' houses to show off his first pair of long trousers, but his mother very neatly put him off without him being disappointed. She said wouldn't it be better if no one saw them until he turned up wearing them at the party next door? What a surprise they'd all get! And after careful consideration Joey agreed and contented himself with walking the living-room floor with his hands deep in the trouser pockets and his chest sticking out a mile.

While the grown-ups were comfortably settled in Beth's, with glasses in their hands and gossip, jokes and laughter on their lips, in the house opposite the youngsters were having a wonderful time. Mick and Seamus had turned out to be ideal hosts, keeping their guests highly amused with their long list of Irish jokes, then singing a duet in voices that everyone agreed were as good as Bing Crosby's. After they'd bowed to the applause, whistles and cat calls, they suggested someone else should now take to the floor. But no one had the nerve so there were no takers.

'Well, let's have a game of pass the parcel,' Mick said. 'We can all play that.'

'Oh, yeah!' Joan was all for it. 'That's good that is. If ye're left holding the parcel when the music stops, yer have to pay a forfeit.'

'What kind of forfeit?' Ginny asked, looking doubtful. 'Don't ask me to sing 'cos I can't.'

'Yer'll be all right, Ginny,' Bobby told her. 'Yer can recite a piece of poetry, anything.'

So the furniture was pushed back to leave the middle of the room clear for the circle of chairs which the boys set out. Only then did they remember there was no music. So it was agreed that Joey would stand with his back to the circle and shout 'Stop' at intervals. Amelia was the first one to be caught out, and although the boys tried, no amount of coaxing would get her to sing. The most she would do was recite 'Old Mother Hubbard', and that was with her face as red as a beetroot. The next one to be caught out was Marie, and this brought a complaint from the girls that the boys were cheating. So for spite Marie also recited a nursery rhyme. This didn't go down very well at all, so Mick suggested they each write a forfeit on a piece of paper and the person caught out would have to do what it said on the paper which would be folded four times and, with eyes closed, picked out of Mr O'Leary's best hat.

There was much laughter amongst the boys as they wrote out their forfeits, and Ginny knew they were up to some tricks. So when she was the next one to be left holding the parcel, she was filled with apprehension as she dipped her fingers into the hat and pulled out a piece of paper. She opened it and gasped. 'It says, do a tap dance! I can't tap dance to save me life!'

Bobby would have rushed to her rescue by offering to do the forfeit for her, but Mick's face was set. 'Yer'll have to do the best yer can, Ginny, like we'd have had to do if we'd picked that piece of paper. So, in the middle of the floor with yer and do yer best.'

Ginny was glad she had her dance shoes on, at least her feet looked all right even if they were only stamping up and down. And it was the shortest tap dance in history.

The girls squealed with delight when Seamus was left holding the parcel next. His forfeit was to do an Irish jig, which to the annoyance of the girls he did very well. Marie was most impressed and asked, 'How did yer learn to do that?'

Seamus grinned. 'Me mam taught me and our Mick when we were little. I thought it was daft meself, but it came in handy tonight.'

Joan wasn't laughing when she picked her forfeit. 'It says I've got to kiss one of the lads! Some hope they've got!' She folded the piece of paper and threw it back into the hat.

Ginny clamped her mouth tight on a chuckle and beckoned to Joan to bend down while she whispered in her ear. When Joan straightened up she was giggling. 'Okay, I'll do it. I'll kiss one of the boys.' She put a finger on her bottom lip and tilted her head. 'Now, let's see, who shall I kiss?' Playfully she stood in front of Mick who rubbed his hands in glee, until she spun around and caught poor unsuspecting Joey.

'Ay, geroff!' His face flaming, he rubbed hard on his cheek where the kiss had landed. 'I'm going to tell me mam on you, yer daft nit.'

There was loud laughter at the boy's embarrassment, then they sat down and carried on passing the parcel. The loser was Seamus again, and his forfeit said he had to kiss a girl. He didn't hesitate, and Amelia didn't protest. But all the girls said it was a fiddle when one after the other, Mick, David and Bobby came out with the same forfeit. However, they lifted their cheeks for a kiss because they didn't want to be thought spoilsports. And although Joey complained that he was fed up standing with his back to them, the game went on. It was a definite fiddle, though, because now all the slips of paper said kiss a girl or kiss a boy. But although the young girls were embarrassed getting a kiss, even though it was on the cheek, they got used to it and really found it quite exciting. Safe to say the youngsters had far more fun at their party than their parents did at the one taking place opposite.

Although, if you'd stood in the middle of the street, you would have found it hard to say from which house the loudest laughter came. For with the beer and milk stout flowing freely, and Flo's non-stop entertainment, well, perhaps when it came to enjoying themselves, the older generation were able to hold their own.

Chapter Twenty-Nine

The winter months after Christmas were happy ones for Ginny. She loved her job and the people she worked with, and enjoyed the nights she spent out with her friends. Her dancing had improved and she wouldn't be embarrassed to dance with anyone now. Not that dancing with a stranger was likely to happen as the gang still stuck together. There'd only been one incident to mar her happiness, and that had been telling a lie to her mates. For Miss Meadows had booked tickets for a play at the Playhouse, which really hadn't been to Ginny's liking as she found the actors all spoke with posh voices and were a bit wooden. Not that all her attention was on the stage: she was very impressed with the theatre itself which was an eye opener for her, as were the clothes the women were wearing – long fur coats, short fur jackets and beautiful capes over dresses which must have cost the earth. And the amount of jewellery adorning their necks, wrists and fingers . . . well, if that was real, they must all be millionaires.

Once again Charles had accompanied them and insisted upon driving her home. She'd made him stop at the top of the street, though, so no one would see her, and no amount of coaxing on his part would make her agree to his driving her to her door and meeting her parents. When she still refused, he asked if she would come out with him one night, without his Aunt Alicia acting as chaperon.

By this time Ginny was getting agitated in case she was seen by any of the neighbours and her friends found out. Not that she should worry about them pulling her leg, it was only in fun. Except for Bobby. She didn't think he'd find anything to laugh about. He seemed to be very possessive when they were together, and although Ginny really didn't understand why, she found she enjoyed being in his company. So to leave the car before she was seen, she said she would have to ask her parents' permission to go out on a date because she was, after all, just turned fifteen. That night she'd scrambled out of the car, flown hell for leather down the street, and told her mam and dad what had happened. But she made them promise not to tell the neighbours because her friends would only pull her leg. It seemed harmless enough, so they agreed, but Ginny couldn't help feeling that by not telling her friends, she'd lied to them.

All this was going through her head while she was filling up the counter on a day in March. Bobby and Mick had had their seventeenth birthdays, and the joint party they'd held was marvellous. And now David's seventeenth was coming up, with the prospect of yet another celebration. The only niggle in Ginny's head was would the boys feel they were too grown-up now for the church hall dances, and staying in one night a week to play cards? Would they be ready to spread their wings and go further afield for their pleasure?

Ginny jumped when Dorothy Sutherland touched her arm and said, 'In the last few minutes I've watched your face light up in a smile, and then the corners of your mouth turn down as though you're thinking of something sad.'

'I was thinking about me friends,' Ginny told her, with a smile. 'Three of the boys are now seventeen and I was wondering if they'd be moving on to pastures new. They probably won't want to bother with fifteen-year-old girls.'

'Time moves on, Ginny, and each phase of your life is different. Two years from now you will look back and wonder how you ever enjoyed the things you're enjoying today. As for the boys, well, only time will tell whether they like what they have now, or, as you say, think it's time to move on to pastures new.'

'That's why I was looking sad,' Ginny told her. 'I don't want things to change.'

'They're bound to, pet, nothing can stay the same forever.' Dorothy took a box from under the counter. 'Make yourself busy, here come Miss Halliday and Mr Sanderson.'

Ginny's smile was wide. She had grown very fond of these two people, but wouldn't for the world tell anyone because they'd think she was crazy. 'Good morning.'

Miss Halliday was looking very well these days. Her face wasn't so drawn and she was wearing more modern clothes. She did have a deputy now who was a good worker and had taken some of the strain from her, but she insisted on doing the morning round herself with Mr Sanderson. 'Good morning. I hope everything is running smoothly, Miss Sutherland?'

'No problems, Miss Halliday.'

Clive Sanderson smiled. 'I think we can safely say that leather goods and haberdashery are run like clockwork.'

364

Ginny was always polite, but she never had a problem talking to either of these bosses as an equal. 'Have yer told Miss Bleasedale and Miss Whittaker that, Mr Sanderson?'

'No, my dear, I haven't. But I will do if you think I should.'

'It's nice to be praised, Mr Sanderson, and I'd hate to sit in the canteen having me cup of tea and bragging to Marie about what yer said. Wouldn't be fair, would it?'

He chuckled. 'No, you are quite right, Miss Porter, and Miss Halliday and I will act on it immediately.'

As the couple walked away, Ginny said, softly, 'I think they go really well together. Two very nice people.'

Ginny would have been very happy if she'd been in Mr Sanderson's office half-an-hour later and heard what he was saying to a blushing Mary Halliday. 'Mary, I think we get on very well together, don't you?'

'Yes, of course we do, Clive, very well.'

'Can I ask how deep your feelings go for me? Do you see me as a nice chap and easy to get on with, or do you think of me with real fondness?'

'Really, Clive, I don't know what to say.' Mary dropped her eyes for a second. Then she met his eyes and asked, 'What are your questions leading up to?'

'If you are feeling embarrassed, my dear, then imagine how I feel. But I've put this day off for too long, and I made up my mind in bed last night that today would be the day I found the courage to say what I've wanted to say for some time. If you return my feelings of respect and affection, Mary, would you allow me to court you?'

Her heart was singing, but she didn't want to get her hopes up to have them dashed down. 'Clive, when you court someone, it is with a view to marriage, and I can't believe that is what you have in mind?'

'Oh, but it is, my dear! I have grown to be very fond of you and my life would be complete if you agreed to be my wife. But I am old-fashioned enough to want the joy of courting you, in the hope I can eventually win you over.'

'Clive, you won me over years ago.' Mary felt she owed him the truth. 'I have admired you from afar, never dreaming that one day we would become close friends. So the last few months have been heavenly for me.'

A lock of his fine hair dropped over his forehead. As he pushed it back, his slow smile was spreading across his face. 'Does that mean you will agree to be my wife?'

Mary closed her eyes and let out a sigh of happiness. 'Clive, that would be a dream come true for me. But there is so much to think about first. There's my job here . . .'

That was as far as she got before he was holding her hand and shaking his head. 'I will not listen to any reasons why you think we shouldn't be married in the not-too-distant future. There is nothing to stand in our way, Mary, you have a perfectly capable deputy to take over when you leave. Why do you think I insisted on you getting an assistant? It wasn't in the certainty that you would accept my proposal, but in the hope. Those few days we spent together over the Christmas period were the happiest of my life, and I knew then I wanted you there permanently.' He gently squeezed her hand. 'Are you going to give me an answer, Mary, or must I go home tonight to my lonely house without anything to look forward to?'

'Of course I will marry you, Clive! You've made me feel like a young girl again, and I thank you for that, and for the honour you have bestowed upon me by asking me to be your wife.' She lifted his hand and kissed it. 'My feelings go far beyond affection and fondness.'

He pulled her to her feet. 'Oh, I say, what a wonderful day this is turning out to be! Shall we be daring and seal our engagement with a kiss?'

It was a tender kiss, soft as a butterfly, but it proved to both of them that they really were made for each other. Mary was a little embarrassed as she pulled away. 'I should go now, Clive, I've gone well over the break time.'

'I don't want you to leave, but I know you must. I will drive around to your house tonight so we can have a good talk.' His boyish grin reappeared. 'I'm so happy, I have to tell someone. Would you mind very much if I tell Sarah Ormsby? I know she will be discreet.'

'Very well, Clive, and I'll see you this evening about eight.' Mary knew she was walking along the corridor but she couldn't feel her feet. And her head wasn't on her shoulders, it was on cloud nine.

Ginny saw Miss Meadows walking towards her and greeted her with a warm smile. The woman was always nice and friendly, and Ginny genuinely liked her. 'Hello, Miss Meadows. Are yer on yer dinner break?'

'Yes, dear.' Alicia wasn't going to say she could take her lunch break any time she liked, and for as long as she liked. 'How are you, Virginia?'

'I'm fine! And how are you?'

'Looking forward to your coming to tea one day. How would this Sunday suit you?'

Ginny didn't do much on a Sunday because everywhere was closed, and she did feel sorry for Miss Meadows having no family. 'Yes, I'd like that.'

Alicia's face lit up. 'Wonderful! I'll look forward to it. Shall we say I'll meet you off the bus at four o'clock?'

Ginny nodded. 'But I could find my own way, I know where your house is. Save you coming out in the cold.'

'No, dear, I'll meet you.' Alicia nodded to Dorothy who couldn't pretend she wasn't listening. 'Goodbye, Miss Sutherland.' Then, with a big smile for Ginny: 'I shall look forward to seeing you on Sunday, my dear.'

'You're certainly a blue eye with her,' Dorothy said. 'It's funny how she made friends with you simply through shopping on your counter.'

'That's the only good thing Miss Landers ever did for me. If she hadn't been rude to me Miss Meadows would probably never even have noticed I was there.'

Going home from work on Thursday, conversation between Ginny and Marie was animated. It was dance night, and if they'd been going to a dinner dance at the Adelphi, they couldn't have been more excited. 'I'm going to put me pink dress on,' Marie said. 'I haven't worn it for a few weeks now.'

'I'm going to have to wear the blue because I've only got one other decent dress and I wore it last week.'

Marie giggled. 'We go through this every week, and I bet the boys don't even notice what we've got on. Although David always says I look nice.'

Ginny glanced sideways at her friend. 'I'm really beginning to think yer've got a soft spot for David.'

'I have, yeah!' Marie would always be truthful, it wasn't in her to be any different. 'I don't want yer to tell anyone, Ginny, but last Thursday he asked me if I'd be his girfriend.'

'Go 'way!' Ginny's jaw dropped in surprise. 'What did you say?'

'That I'll have to ask me mam.'

'Yer mean, yer want to be?' Ginny sounded even more surprised.

'Oh, yes, I do! I've liked him from the first time I saw him. And me mam said it's all right as long as I take him along to meet her and me dad. She said if they don't like the look of him they'll soon tell me.'

'Yer'll still be coming to the dances though, won't yer? And the card games? Yer won't be breaking the gang up?'

'No, we wouldn't do that, we enjoy being with the gang. It won't make any difference, except we might go to the flicks on one of the other nights.'

It was time for them to get off the tram then, and as they stood on the pavement they agreed to meet at eight outside the Baileys' house, as usual.

Ginny was thoughtful as she combed her hair in front of the mirror in her bedroom. She knew Amelia and Seamus were sweet on each other, it stuck out a mile. Ever since the Christmas party whenever you saw them they were holding hands and laughing at their own private jokes. But Marie and David, now that was a surprise.

Beth was in the kitchen when she heard her daughter coming down the stairs. 'Let's have a look at yer before yer go out, sunshine.' She eyed Ginny up and down. 'I see yer've changed the parting in yer hair.'

'Yeah, I felt like a change. I've parted it down the middle since I started school so it's about time I did something different. Don't yer like it, Mam?'

Beth rested her chin in her hand. 'I can't make up me mind. That's because I'm so used to yer having a centre parting, but I'll get used to it. It'll grow on me with time.'

'I'll see what the girls have to say. If they don't like it, I'll comb it back.'

It wasn't one of the girls who passed comment, though, it was Bobby when he asked her up for the first dance. 'Yer've done yer hair different, Ginny, and it suits yer.'

Now that they were more experienced dancers, they no longer needed to leave a space between them and he was holding her close. Ginny looked up into his face, intending to ask if he liked the new style, but when their eyes met, she felt a strange tingling running down her spine and the words were left unspoken. She felt him pulling her closer until his breath fanned her cheek. All sorts of emotions were running through her body and she didn't know what to make of them. Then she felt a soft kiss on her cheek and the tingling down her spine made her shiver. She pulled back to face him. 'What did yer do that for?'

'Well, yer see, it's like this, Ginny. Yer cheek looked so pretty and attractive, just like a peach. Now if it had been a peach, I would have taken a bite out of it. But I didn't think yer'd take kindly to me biting yer, so I kissed yer instead.'

'In the middle of the dance floor, with everybody watching?' But Ginny wasn't really annoyed. In fact, she was quite enjoying herself. 'If this gets back to me mam, what's she going to think?'

Bobby's eyes were sparkling with laughter. 'Well, if yer tell her about the peach, and how I couldn't take a bite out of it, I'm sure she'll understand.'

'Oh, yeah, she's very understanding is my mam.' Ginny kept her face straight but she might as well not have bothered because her eyes gave her away. 'She'll probably send me to bed at six o'clock every night for a week with no dinner.'

The dance came to an end and Bobby took her hand and led her back to where their friends were standing. They soon found that the brief kiss hadn't gone unnoticed. 'Did yer have jam on yer cheek, Ginny?'

She didn't twig at first, and when she faced Mick her face was blank. 'I didn't have any jam on me face. What made yer ask that?'

Of course she'd walked right into it, hadn't she? Mick's eyes were full of devilment. 'Oh, I saw Bobby licking it off.'

Ginny's face went the colour of beetroot and she was lost for words. But aid came from a very unlikely source. 'Take no notice of him, Ginny,' Joan said. 'He's a fine one to talk when he's always pinching kisses.'

Mick was unabashed. 'It's yer own fault, droopy drawers, for having a face that looks so kissable. Now if yer'd been ugly, I wouldn't want to kiss yer.'

Joan's hands went to her hips and she wagged her head at him. 'And what about me, Michael O'Leary? Am I not supposed to mind being kissed by an ugly feller?'

As Ginny watched, she couldn't help thinking that Joan and Mick, both friends since childhood, were ideally suited to each other. Same as Amelia and Seamus, they made the perfect couple. Funny how she'd never noticed this before. But then she'd never noticed anything between Marie and David until her friend told her today. Now, of course, she could see how David's eyes never left Marie, and he looked so happy to be with her.

Bobby pulled on Ginny's hand. 'Stop daydreaming and have this slow foxtrot with me. And I promise the thought of peaches will never cross my mind.'

They were halfway through the dance when the evening was spoilt for her. 'How about coming to have a game of cards on Sunday night, Ginny?' Bobby asked. 'Me grandma, me mam and me. And we only play for matchsticks.'

Ginny's heart sank. He looked so happy and hopeful, she was wishing the ground would open and swallow her up. 'I'm sorry, Bobby, but I promised to go to Miss Meadows' for tea on Sunday. I didn't know yer were going to ask me to yours for a game of cards, otherwise I wouldn't have agreed to go.' She could feel his body stiffen. 'I'm sorry, Bobby, but I can come next week.'

'I suppose her nephew will be driving yer home in his fancy car, will he? Well, that sure beats a game of cards, Ginny, so good luck to yer.' Bobby was disappointed and hurt, and he wanted to hit out at someone. He knew he was being childish, but he felt a strong dislike for a seventeen-year-old boy he didn't know, just because that boy had a car. And for the rest of the night, although he still danced with Ginny so the others didn't notice anything unusual, he was very off-hand with her.

Ginny felt terrible. She'd do anything to put the smile back on Bobby's face, but the only way she could do that was to say she wouldn't go to Miss Meadows' for tea on Sunday, and she couldn't bring herself to do that. She would never let anyone down, particularly someone who had befriended her and was so kind.

Ginny was relieved when the dance was over because the tension between her and Bobby made her want to cry. She only managed to keep the tears back until her mother opened the front door to her and then the floodgates opened.

Beth held her daughter close and rocked her gently from side to side with her. 'What on earth is the matter, sunshine?' She looked over Ginny's head to where Andy was sitting on the edge of the couch, ready to sympathise, and shook her head to tell him not to get involved. 'Come on, tell me all about it?'

Between gulps and sobs the whole sorry tale came out, leaving Beth more amused than worried. 'But that's nothing to get yerself in such a state over, sunshine! It's a storm in a teacup. Bobby will have forgotten about it by next week.'

'It's not that, Mam, it's just that I felt I was being a snob, saying I'd rather go out to tea at a posh house than have a game of cards with the Baileys. Bobby was upset by it all, I could tell. He said being driven home in a posh car beat a game of cards any day.'

Beth couldn't help but smile. It seemed there was a bit of jealousy here. 'Yer like Bobby, don't yer, sunshine?'

'Yes, of course I do! And I don't want to fall out with him! But I can't let Miss Meadows down, either!'

'Oh, I think we can find a solution to this problem.' Beth put a finger under her daughter's chin and raised her face. 'Go and swill yer eyes with cold water, sunshine, and then we'll sit down and find some way where Miss Meadows doesn't get hurt, and neither does Bobby.'

And by the time Ginny went to bed she was feeling a bit better. If she did as her mother suggested, if she had the nerve, then everything should turn out fine.

Miss Meadows was waiting by the bus stop and greeted Ginny with a smile. 'I timed it nicely and haven't been waiting long.' She linked the young girl's arm and pulled her close. 'There's a nice big fire ready to warm you up.'

She was so kind, and looked so pleased to see her, that Ginny wondered whether she could do as her mother said. She didn't want to hurt her, or make her think she didn't want to be her friend, but every time she conjured up a picture of Bobby's face, looking so dejected, she was torn between them.

'Hang up your coat, Virginia,' Alicia said, 'and then sit by the fire while I make us a nice hot drink.'

Ginny's tummy was churning. On the bus coming along the Drive she'd rehearsed what she would say, but when it came down to it, it wasn't so easy. But it was something that had to be done. So, after giving a nervous cough, she said, 'Miss Meadows, would yer mind if I leave about a quarter to seven?' And then she found herself pouring her heart out and telling the woman the whole story. 'Yer see, I don't want to hurt either of yer.'

'Oh, if only I'd known, Virginia, you could have brought Bobby with you! I'd have been delighted to meet him.'

Ginny's brows shot up. 'You would? Really?'

'Oh, yes, I love to have young company. And I'd like to meet your boyfriend.'

'Well, he's not exactly me boyfriend, not yet anyway. I do like him, though, and I know he likes me.'

'Then you must bring him with you next time you come. And I think I'd better set the table now if you want to be away early.'

'You are very kind, Miss Meadows, and you've been really good to me. I was worried on me way here, in case yer thought I didn't want to be friends with yer, but I really do.'

'Then I am a very lucky woman, and I hope you will always look on me as a friend you can come to if you ever need help.'

There was something else Ginny had to get off her chest. 'Miss Meadows, I don't know if Charles is coming, but if he is, would he mind if I got the bus home?'

'Of course not. I will ring him now and ask him to leave his visit until another day. You are not to worry your pretty little head about anything.'

On impulse, Ginny left her chair to plant a kiss on Alicia's cheek. 'Thank you for being so good to me.'

Alicia was very moved and felt quite emotional. 'It is I who should be thanking you. It is not very often I get a kiss.'

Relieved now of her worries, Ginny grinned. 'Then I shall kiss you every time I come.'

Hannah opened the door to find Ginny standing on the pavement outside. 'Hello, sweetheart, come on in out of the cold.'

Ginny shook her head. 'Is Bobby in, please, Mrs Bailey?'

Ah, thought Hannah, I wonder if this call has anything to do with my grandson being down in the dumps for the last few days? He'd been like a bear with a sore head. 'I'll get him for yer, sweetheart.'

The old lady opened the living-room door and tried to look and sound casual. 'Ginny's outside, Bobby, she won't come in but she wants a word with yer.'

His chair was pushed back with such force it toppled over, causing Claire to say, 'Ay, just watch what ye're doing, it's yer grandma's furniture, not ours.' But she was talking to herself because he was out of the door like a shot and didn't hear a word she said.

For three days Bobby had sworn to himself that he'd never give in first with Ginny. If she preferred her fancy friends, then let her have them, he didn't care. It was easy thinking these things, but not so easy when the girl he'd fallen for nearly a year ago was standing in front of him looking so pretty and so shy. He just wished she'd say something and that his heart would stop thumping. 'Did yer want me for anything, Ginny?'

She nodded. 'I've come to see if yer still want me to have a game of cards with yer? But before yer say anything, I want yer to know I came home from Miss Meadows' on the bus, and the next time I go I'm to take yer with me 'cos she wants to meet yer.'

His eyes widened. 'Did she say that or are yer making it up?'

'I am not making it up, Bobby Bailey! She said the next time I went for tea she'd be delighted if I took me boyfriend with me.'

Bobby's heart was thumping faster than ever. 'And are yer me girlfriend, Ginny?'

She nodded. 'If yer'll have me.'

'Oh, I'll have yer right enough, Ginny Porter.' Bobby stepped down on to the pavement and cupped her face between his hands. And Ginny's first ever kiss on the lips had her feeling giddy with happiness. But she still managed to stutter, 'Me mam will kill yer if she finds out yer've kissed me.'

'I'll walk yer home after we've finished playing cards and I'll tell her.' He took her hand and pulled her up the two steps. 'Come on in.' Once inside the living room, he said, 'Ginny's going to have a game with us.' He lifted his hand to show Ginny's was clasped tight within it. 'Oh, and she's me girlfriend now.'

Claire looked pleased, if a little bewildered, but Hannah was over the moon. This was what she'd secretly hoped for because she loved Ginny and knew her grandson would be getting a good, decent girl. 'Yer've made an old woman very happy.'

Bobby grinned. 'Well then, yer may as well have all the news, Grandma. I've just given me girlfriend her first kiss and she told me her mam will kill me when she knows. So as Mrs Porter's a friend of yours, I'd like yer to put in a good word for me.'

One Saturday in August, Miss Mary Halliday married Mr Clive Sanderson. It was a quiet wedding as Mary thought she was too old for a white dress and veil. She wore a lovely beige silk dress with a wide-brimmed hat of the same colour. She looked so happy, Clive never took his eyes off her during the short service. As the bride and groom had no families of their own, Miss Ormsby was Mary's matron of honour, and Clive's best man was a member of Woolworth's Board of Directors.

The small congregation consisted of colleagues who had been given the day off to attend the wedding. And sitting in the two front pews on either side of the aisle were Miss Harper, Dorothy Sutherland, Helen Bleasedale, Virginia Porter and Marie Whittaker – all the people who had been in some way instrumental in bringing the happy couple together. With the two junior assistants were their boyfriends, Bobby and David, both feeling very proud of themselves in their new suits, bought off the peg from the thirty-shilling tailor. The girls looked very pretty in floral summer dresses and straw hats.

And sitting in a pew further back were four women who didn't know the bride and groom, but had heard so much about them they just had to come to see them married. And what were Beth, Flo, Dot and Lizzie doing? They were crying, of course, 'cos what else do women do at weddings? And between sniffs, Flo could be heard saying, 'She looks bleedin' lovely.'